INTO THE BLACK

A NICK KISMET ADVENTURE

SEAN ELLIS

Gryphonwood

Into the Black

Cover Design © 2011 by J. Kent Holloway

ISBN-13: 978-1-940095-25-7
ISBN-10: 1940095255

Published by Gryphonwood Press
PO Box 28910
Santa Fe, NM 87592
www.gryphonwoodpress.com

Printed in the United States of America

PRAISE FOR INTO THE BLACK

"*Sean Ellis is an author to watch closely. Into the Black is one of the top ten thrillers of the year! An adventure story that will stay with you long after the read is finished. You can count this reader as a huge fan of Nick Kismet!*" – David L. Golemon, New York Times bestselling author of EVENT, LEGEND, ANCIENTS, LEVIATHAN, PRIMEVAL, and in 2011, LEGACY!

"*INTO THE BLACK is a rollicking adventure that races through your hands like a hydrofoil flying across the sea. Filled with masterful action scenes and a great new hero in Nick Kismet – a lucky soul who knows only one way to live: full speed ahead –* Sean Ellis has mixed a perfect cocktail of adventure and intrigue and this one is definitely shaken and not stirred."—Graham Brown, author of the thrillers BLACK RAIN and BLACK SUN.

"*Sean Ellis is a thriller reader's dream come true.*" – Jeremy Robinson, author of PULSE and INSTINCT

"*Sean Ellis brings another high-energy adventure to his fascinating action-hero, Nick Kismet. INTO THE BLACK offers a brilliant blend of science and mythology to each heart-pounding twist and turn that every thrill-seeker craves.*" – Theresa Danley, author of EFFIGY.

"*Sean Ellis is quickly becoming one of my favorite authors. Between his high-flying adventures of Dodge Dalton or the relic hunting exploits of Nick Kismet, Ellis is just plain fun to read. This up-and-comer is someone everyone needs to watch out for!*" – J. Kent Holloway, author of PRIMAL THIRST and SIRENS' SONG.

BOOKS BY SEAN ELLIS

Mira Raiden Adventures
Ascendant
Descendant (forthcoming)

The Nick Kismet Thrillers
The Shroud of Heaven
Into the Black
Fortune Favors
The Devil You Know (novella)

The Adventures of Dodge Dalton
In the Shadow of Falcon's Wings
At the Outpost of Fate
On the High Road to Oblivion

Chess Team/Jack Sigler Thrillers
(with Jeremy Robinson)
Callsign: King
Underworld
Blackout
Prime
Savage

The Jade Ihara Adventures
Oracle (with David Wood)
Changeling (with David Wood-forthcoming)

Other Works
Dark Trinity - Ascendant
Magic Mirror
WarGod (with Steven Savile)
Hell Ship (with David Wood)
Flood Rising (with Jeremy Robinson)

To my brothers in 3rd Platoon, B Company SECFOR, 41st Brigade Combat Team
Afghanistan 2006-2007

ACKNOWLEDGMENTS

I am indebted to author, historian, marine archaeologist, and real-life adventure hero Tim Severin. His 1986 book The Jason Voyage: The Quest for the Golden Fleece, planted the seed that would eventually become this story.

I would also like to thank my editor, Kent Holloway; my friend Robert Charest, for being the first person to really believe in this story, all those years ago; Steve Chown and Mike Belshaw, for encouragement and suggestions along the way; Rich Steeves, Candace Bowen Early, and Nilda Zepeda for proofreading; Ian Kharitonov, for keeping me from embarrassing myself too much with all things Russian (and apologies to him as well for once or twice ignoring his sage advice); Graham Brown, Thomas Greanias, David Lynn, Golemon, Theresa Danley, and Jeremy Robinson for saying nice things about this book and being willing to let me put their names on the cover; and always, always, I want to thank my sons Connor and Campbell for cheering me on.

~ Sean Ellis

PROLOGUE

AFTER THE WARS

Once upon a time, a fairy tale came true. The princess met her prince, and for a brief shining moment, believed that happily ever after just might happen. Then the war came and the prince went away and everything changed....

Her finger hovered over the number pad of the satellite phone. Although she had been planning this moment for days now, she had never really thought about just what she would say, or how this message might tear open some old wounds; wounds that, she realized only now, were still not quite healed.

Dearest Nick, You can't imagine how I've missed you…

"God, that's awful," she murmured and quickly deleted the text. He deserved better than that; deserved better than what she was about to do. Still, she had moved on, and he probably had too. Whatever had existed between them had died a long time ago.…

September 1991

She slammed the door forcefully, angry but not really sure why, and immediately started running. He hadn't asked where she was going. He didn't ask about much of anything anymore.

They had met two years before when she, Lysette Lyon, was a college freshman and he, Nick Kismet, was a sophomore. It had been lust at first sight, a casual but very intimate relationship, yet beyond the physical excitement of their time together, a deeper affection had taken root. After a couple weeks, they were exclusive and she was sneaking out of her dorm every night in order to be with him. They seldom fought, and even when they did, they made up quickly and passionately. They were both counting the days until they could officially move in together, and she had a feeling that he might be planning to ask for something even more permanent. He was a romantic and that was just the sort of thing he might do.

But then Saddam Hussein invaded Kuwait, America marshalled her volunteer armies, and he—a Second Lieutenant in the Army Reserve—was whisked away to another world.

She had been faithful to a fault, writing letters and sending care packages, dutifully watching reports from the desert on CNN, and crying herself to sleep at night because he wasn't there. For a while, he had reciprocated, sending her emotional letters from his training station and then from the front line in Saudi Arabia, but shortly after the beginning of the Hundred Hour War, the letters—all written before the start of the ground offensive—had ceased coming. She had begun watching the news reports with dread, fearing the moment when the anchorperson would speak his name. She had even called his father—his only living relative—to see if there had been any word. No news, as frustrating as it was, was better than bad news.

Three agonizing months had passed before his next letter arrived, a terse missive explaining that he had been wounded in action and was now recuperating in a hospital in Germany. From that moment on, nothing had been the same.

She ran down the walk and hit the pavement at a pace that matched the level of her anger. "Damn him," she muttered under her breath, unconsciously accelerating into a near sprint. The park was only a few blocks away and she knew that as soon as she reached the open manicured green space, her ire would fade. Nevertheless, the root cause of that emotion still remained, like a noxious weed determined to grow back swiftly when plucked. Things were not good between them and hadn't been in several weeks.

Deep down, below the hurt, she knew that it wasn't his fault. Something terrible had happened to him during that war—something he either could not bring himself to talk about, or was compelled by orders to keep secret. His physical wounds had healed but the injury to his soul was still bleeding.

He had spoken of resigning his commission but she knew that alone would not give him the healing he needed.

And then tonight's bombshell. "I think I need to go away for awhile."

"Okay." Her answer had been, of necessity, guarded. She was just three weeks into the term and a vacation was out of the question. Nonetheless, wheels had begun turning in her head; she would make it work somehow. "That's probably a good idea. Where should we go?"

"Not 'we,' Lyse. It's something I need to do alone. I need to find something…"

"*Find something*? What the hell is that supposed to mean?"

"I wish I knew." He had offered a grim smile. "I can't even explain it to you, because if I did, you'd probably want to have me committed."

She had taken a deep breath, trying to buffer the acid of what she'd really wanted to say. "Okay. Maybe a couple weeks on your own will help you get your head in order." She had regretted that immediately; she hadn't meant to imply that he was crazy.

"It might take more than a couple weeks. I'm not even really sure where I'll be looking."

"You're so damn cryptic sometimes." She'd tried to pass her comment off as a joke, but there was no humor in her laughter. He hadn't picked up on it of course, and after listening to a few more halting attempts at an explanation, she'd realized that she had better leave before things exploded. She had left the room, changed into running clothes and headed out without another word.

As she hit the park trail, her thoughts wandered as she had expected, but they didn't stray far. Not for the first time, she wondered what exactly had happened to her lover during that brief conflict. He bore none of the signs of post-traumatic stress disorder; he didn't wake up screaming in the night, reliving a battle or the death of a comrade. Rather, his affliction seemed to be something on the order of a religious experience; it was as if he had received some kind of supernatural visitation and was now struggling to understand his calling. The idea of Nick Kismet as a reluctant prophet brought a smile to her lips but it didn't last long.

She stopped dead in her tracks as she realized where she was—an isolated stand of trees along the trail where the park's lights did not quite cast their rays. It was nearly dusk and the long shadows added to the eerie malevolence of the dark woods. She ran the trail often and was always wary in this section, gripping her pepper spray as she sprinted through, but this time her distracted thoughts had led to a collapse of her innate caution. She fumbled in her waist pack for the defensive aerosol canister but realized with growing dread that she had left it behind, along with her ring of keys. She looked up, peering into the darkness both ahead and behind, and took a deep breath. The wooded section was only about fifty yards long; she could sprint that in a few seconds. Turning back just wasn't in her nature.

She started off slowly, tentatively peering into the shadows, but as she moved deeper into the black, she felt a growing fear—a premonition of danger—that was all too quickly manifest. Something moved from the cover of the tree line to block her path. She skidded to a stop and whirled around but it was already too late. Another figure burst from the woods behind her and without words or hesitation, threw his arms around her.

Adrenaline hit her bloodstream like a sledgehammer, but it also distorted her perception of time. Although the attackers converged on her like feral dogs, from her perspective, they seemed to move in slow motion.

She deftly avoided the attempted tackle. Standing barely five feet tall, she had little difficulty slipping under the arms of the large man, but she was not content to simply evade and escape. As the man's arms closed on empty air, she threw an elbow into his solar plexus and despite his overwhelming advantage of size, he went down gasping for air.

The other man moved in quickly to assist his partner, but Lyse's small victory had emboldened her to stand her ground. The attacker pulled up just out of reach, striking a threatening pose, and she responded by dropping into a ready stance ingrained from more than three years of Tae Kwon Do training. The man threw a punch, which Lyse deflected with an overhead block and followed through with a strike at the man's chin. This time however, her aim was not as good. Her fist glanced off his jaw and left her open for reprisal. There was a flash of light across her vision and a piercing ringing in her ears as she stumbled sideways, but what hurt the most was the realization that she had badly misjudged the situation; she had passed up a perfect opportunity to escape, and now she was about to pay the price.

She scrambled back to her feet, trying to remember what to do next, and narrowly avoided another blow from her assailant by throwing herself onto the ground. The man misinterpreted this as victory and with a lascivious laugh advanced again.

"Wrong move, sucker." Lyse lashed out with both feet, jamming them into his knee with such force that she was propelled backwards toward the tree line. The man's leg bent sideways with a sickening crack and he went down screaming. She scrambled erect, her head still reeling from the earlier punch, and this time she did not let her pride keep her from winning the battle by retreating. Despite the fact that the streetlight down the trail seemed to have split into divergent halves, she set off at a sprint.

Suddenly another figure was standing between her and freedom; a single individual, divided in her double-vision, standing confidently, yet strangely without menace, directly in her path.

"Well done, Miss Lyon."

The speaker had platinum blonde hair and a lean, hungry expression that reminded her of the big bad wolf from the Brothers Grimm. He was too well dressed for a garden-variety rapist—his dark designer label trench coat was unmistakably a mark of affluence—but Lyse had the feeling that this man represented a threat of an entirely different order. She drew up short and took a fighting stance. "Who the hell are you? How did you know my name?"

The man smiled, revealing perfect teeth that nevertheless seemed ready to devour her. "My apologies for this bit of theatre. It was a test of sorts, and you've every right to be outraged, but I assure you, I would not have let you come to any harm."

She threw a glance over one shoulder. If her attackers were still there, they had chosen to nurse their wounds in the darkness. "A test?"

"I'm a recruiter of sorts, Lyse…may I call you Lyse? I've been observing you for some time. Your academic record is outstanding; by itself, that would qualify you for further consideration, but your unique capabilities extend far beyond that. You are a rare blend of intelligence, strength and beauty; traits which would make you a great asset in my line of work."

"Cut the pillow talk. You haven't answered any of my questions and I'm not really job-hunting right now, so if you don't want to join your friends, I suggest you end this little 'interview' and let me be on my way."

The man's smile never wavered; in fact, it seemed to grow, his lips curling back like something from a cartoon. "You are a remarkable woman, Lyse. And I think this is a job you might be interested in taking. You see, I know what you want most."

"Get out of my way. Now." She started forward, brandishing her fists but giving him a wide berth.

He did not move to restrain her physically; his words were enough. "I can help you get him back."

She stopped. Safety was only a few steps away, but that short statement was enough to freeze her in her tracks.

"I know you love him, Lyse, and I know that you think you've lost him. But it doesn't have to be like that."

She turned slowly on a heel and gazed into his azure eyes. "I'm listening."

The Present, Somewhere over the Mediterranean Sea

They were out there somewhere, following her. Even if they had not yet realized what she had done, her sudden departure had surely raised an alarm. She had little doubt that they were actively tracking the plane's transponder; you didn't keep secrets from these people.

Off to her left, the lights of the coastline blinked into view, and she knew she could delay no longer. She picked up the satellite phone again and this time did not hesitate. She tapped out a brief and of necessity vague message, completely dissociating from her emotional link to the recipient, and without a second thought, hit the send button. She then stowed the phone in a small backpack, along with the other item—the object that now imperilled her very life—and activated the autopilot.

Two hours later, the small airplane drank the last of its fuel and dropped unceremoniously into the sea, not far from Gibraltar. The plane shattered on impact, and although some lighter pieces of debris would later wash ashore on the beaches of the Spanish coast, no trace of the unknown pilot was ever found.

PART ONE
AULD ACQUAINTANCE

1

Wispy clouds tugged at the lofty peaks of the distant Atlas Mountains as they arched across North Africa. Shadows played upon their slopes, darkening as the sun sank into the west. Framed by the arched window opening, this view was the first thing that Nick Kismet saw as he peered through the veil of beads that separated the room from the corridor in which he stood. A young servant tugged at his elbow, encouraging him to enter the chamber beyond, but he ignored the boy, choosing instead to continue his reconnaissance. Old habits were hard to break.

In many ways, he was still the same young soldier that had been blooded in the Arabian Desert so many years before. His appearance had hardly changed at all. He still kept his dark brown hair clipped short, now for the sake of utility rather than regulations; he had of late noticed a sprinkling of gray whenever it got a little too long. While he was still physically fit, this had more to do with regular visits to a health club than any regimen of military calisthenics. His shoulders were broader and his face was a little more weathered; he'd been told that he was handsome in a rough way, but no one would ever describe him as boyishly good-looking.

He moved with an abrupt economy of motion, striding deliberately, without swaggering, from one destination to the next, and always remained observant, aware of the potential for hidden dangers that might lurk around the next corner. He was all the more cautious here in the heart of old Marrakech, preparing to take audience with a notorious racketeer.

Just to the right of the window, an enormous Caucasian man lounged on a divan that sagged beneath his bulk, noisily slurping some unidentifiable delicacy. Known locally as 'The Fat Man,' he was a Swiss expatriate who had done quite well for himself in the North African desert. He certainly hadn't missed any meals; the Fat Man's bulk filled to the point of bursting his stained robes. Wavy blond curls strayed from beneath the red fez perched comically atop his porcine head. Kismet felt suddenly as if he was staring at an attraction in a freak show: the world's only four hundred pound infant.

He shook his head to clear the image and looked to the left of the window, where a considerably smaller figure stood facing away from the doorway speaking in a low voice to the Fat Man. Although he could not see the person's face or hear the exchange between the two, he instantly knew who the second person was. Making no attempt to hide his chagrin, he stepped forward through the beaded strings.

"Howdy, stranger."

Every head in the room turned toward Kismet, including two that he had not previously noticed. The latter—big men with swarthy Moorish features—reflexively reached toward the weapons hidden beneath the breast pockets of their oversized suit jackets. Kismet was taken aback by the sudden reaction but managed to keep his composure. The smaller figure jumped in front of them, a woman he had not seen in more years than he could remember: Lysette Lyon.

"Nick!" She smiled. Kismet hadn't forgotten that smile. It was the kind of smile that could easily get a guy in trouble. She turned to the Fat Man. "It's all right. This is my friend."

"Shame on you Monsieur Kismet," clucked the Fat Man in a deeply accented singsong tone. "Sneaking up on people isn't nice." With a shooing gesture he dismissed the boy who had been escorting Kismet, his gaze lingering on the departing figure with unabashed lasciviousness, and then he nodded to his bodyguards. The larger of the two men, marked with a permanent scowl and a long scar that ran the length of his jaw, eased his hand away from the concealed weapon and moved to frisk the new arrival.

Kismet grunted as the search got a little too personal, but kept his eyes fixed on the only thing in the room worth looking at. She was as lovely as ever. Tiny—the top of her head rose barely to the center of his chest—she had always carried herself with an easy grace. Her natural blonde hair was pulled back in a ponytail and she didn't have any make-up on, but she wore her blue jeans and a pastel T-shirt as if they were the latest Paris fashions.

Still a knockout, thought Kismet. *Too bad that it takes more than looks to make it work.*

Indeed, if physical attraction was the element critical to success in a relationship, he and Lysette Lyon would have long ago become a happily married suburban couple. Of course he was as much to blame for that failure as she.

Thinking back, he found he could not recall the details of their parting. Had it been amicable? He couldn't actually remember when they had ceased to be in love. He had gone off in search of answers to a mystery begun during a hellish mission into Iraq during Operation Desert Shield and somehow everything else had gotten lost along the way. Had he even tried to look her up upon returning to the United States, several months later? His memory was especially hazy on that point; he'd had so many other things on his mind back then. He had no idea what vocation she had followed after finishing college, but had difficulty believing that the intelligent and motivated young woman from those days had somehow gotten involved in international intrigue and fallen in with the likes of the Fat Man. Nor could he fathom why, in her hour of need, she had summoned him with a cryptic text message that hinted of peril and promised great reward if he hastened to a rendezvous in Morocco. There had to be more to the situation than what appeared at first glance. He decided to play his cards close to the vest.

"You picked a hell of a place for a reunion, Lyse, but it's good to see you again." He decided not to let her know how good; no sense in giving her that much leverage. "So, I'm here. What's this all about?"

Before she could answer, the Fat Man spoke. "Your lady friend owes me money, monsieur. A great deal of money."

The search turned up nothing; no weapons were concealed in the deep cargo pockets of his olive drab military surplus trousers or beneath the roomy fabric of his Ex Oficio photojournalist-style work shirt. Kismet fixed Lyse with an accusing stare. "Want to tell me about it?"

"I had some bad luck," she replied evasively. She tried to evince anxiety with her facial expression but her body language was confident. She was far more in control of the situation than she wanted Kismet to believe.

"Your friend begged for me to allow her to send for you, Monsieur Kismet. I would have been content to simply sell her to some friends of mine who provide—ah, shall we say special entertainment services?—in order to recoup my losses, but she insists you can help." The Fat Man smiled and wiped his fingers on the front of his robe. "I trust you can?"

Kismet did not break eye contact with her. "What do you have in mind?"

Lyse was still grimacing from the Fat Man's threat, but she looked back hopefully at Kismet. "I've got something you'll want."

She motioned for him to follow her to a table against one wall. The Fat Man struggled to his feet and joined them. Lyse pulled back a covering piece of fabric to reveal a small statue, about a foot long and a hand's breadth high. Kismet reached for it and examined it more closely.

"Know what it is?"

"Golden calf," Kismet muttered, mostly to himself. "Agricultural deity. Designed along the lines of an Egyptian Apis bull. Disk of Amon Ra, the sun god, between the horns."

He rubbed a finger along the surface of the disk, feeling a faint indentation, then held the statuette up to the light and peered intently at the inscription on the disk. Four characters of Semitic script were engraved on the soft metal, the four consonants which represented the name of God. Kismet frowned, then turned the statue over and examined its underside.

"On a hunch, I'd say this is a replica of the golden calf, described in the Bible account of the exodus from Egypt. Possibly used by the Hebrews in calf worship ceremonies in Samaria, circa—oh, say 800 BCE." He hefted it, trying to judge the content of gold. "Not very heavy, probably acacia wood, overlaid with gold. Where did you pick it up?"

"That is unimportant," interjected the Fat Man. "It belongs to your friend; it is her only remaining possession. My sources tell me I can get twenty thousand Euro on the open market. Mademoiselle Lyon's debt to me is more than twice that amount. She says that she can convince you to pay fifty thousand Euro. If you do not, I will sell it to a private collector for whatever I can get—" He glanced over at Lyse, a gleeful look of mayhem dancing in his squinty eyes— "and deal with the mademoiselle accordingly."

Lyse swallowed, a touch too dramatically. "Come on, Nick. You know this thing is priceless. Help me out here."

Kismet turned the statue over once more. "Fifty thousand?" In his head, he juggled the current rate of exchange, converting the figure into an approximate value in American dollars. It remained a large sum in any denomination.

It was not Nick Kismet's job to roam the world purchasing art treasures in order to rescue damsels in distress. In fact, for more than a decade he had been dedicated to the prospect of stamping out the black market trade of cultural art, as part of the UNESCO Global Heritage Commission. Men like the Fat Man, and evidently women like his former college flame Lysette Lyon, were the enemy in that struggle. The idea of paying the Fat Man-- negotiating a ransom price--for something that belonged in a national museum was repugnant.

He did however, have the money.

"This thing is right out of the Bible," continued Lyse, as if the assertion would somehow lend gravity to her plea. "It proves that they really did worship calves."

"It would really help if I knew where you got it," Kismet countered as he continued his examination. He carefully pressed a thumbnail against the soft yellow metal. It was gold all right, and too pure to be an electroplated fake. Nevertheless, something about the statue nagged at him; something about it was not right.

"Enough discussion," roared the Fat Man, his bulk jiggling as he gestured emphatically. "Will you pay, monsieur? Is fifty thousand too much? How about thirty thousand, and I let Tariq have some fun with Mme. Lyon for our viewing pleasure."

Kismet ignored the man's tirade, but one of the bodyguards—the man with the scar—moved closer, as if eager to indulge the proposition. Lyse continued pleading for him to buy the statue, but he tuned her out, focusing on the sun disk. He stared at the inscription for several seconds before realizing what it was about the statue that had been bothering him. He kicked himself for having failed to note the discrepancy in his initial inspection, then lowered the calf and turned to Lyse.

"We need to talk," he said in a low voice.

"No talk," declared the Fat Man. "Buy the statue now or she dies. That is a promise, Kismet. And might I add that it would also be to your own advantage to act quickly."

Kismet glanced from Lyse to the Fat Man, then back again, trying to read the intent on their faces. Someone was trying to con him, but who was the mastermind: the Fat Man or Lyse? There had been times during the course of their relationship when she had delighted in pranks, twisting him around her little finger, but nothing like this.

He was sure of one thing. The Fat Man was not going to let them just walk away. It was time to take the initiative. Hefting the statue casually, he faced their corpulent host. "Well, I don't actually have that much cash with me. Do you take American Express?"

The Fat Man gazed back, incredulous. Kismet grinned, and then burst into motion. Turning on his heel, he swung the statue like a club, catching the bodyguard Tariq in the jaw. The big Moor collapsed backward, dazed but not unconscious.

"Nick, what are you doing?" shrieked Lyse.

As the remaining guard reached for his gun, Kismet hurled the statue at him. The artifact caught the man in the elbow, and his pistol tumbled from his grasp. Kismet leapt across the room, laying the stunned man out with a haymaker punch. Now nothing stood between him and the exit.

Lyse seemed to be frozen to the spot where she stood. Her eyes flashed around the room, glancing rapidly at the Fat Man and the bodyguards, but then her gaze settled upon the golden statue where it lay.

"Are you coming?" growled Kismet.

The Fat Man suddenly began crying out for help, but did not move to hinder either of them. Lyse overcame her shock and dashed across the room, pausing only to scoop up the fallen relic.

"Lyse, that statue—" He was unable to finish the sentence as Tariq got to his feet and charged. Lyse's small form darted through the beaded curtain, leaving him to face the wrath of the bodyguards alone. Rather than attempt to match the big man in hand-to-hand combat, he simply stepped aside at the last minute, sweeping out with his foot out to hook Tariq's ankle. The big man plunged headlong into the wall, and Kismet vaulted over him in pursuit of his old flame.

He caught up to her at the front entrance where she was panting to catch her breath. A dark shape rested on a table beside the door; his waist pack waiting right where he had left it after entering the Fat Man's lair. He looped the buckled strap over his head so that it hung from his shoulder like a satchel, then took hold of Lyse's arm and dragged her out into the street.

"Which way?" she asked, her breathing almost normal again.

Kismet shrugged then chose to follow the street to the right, toward the fading glow of the sunset. The main *suuq*, the *Djemaa el-Fna*, lay in that direction. The crowded marketplace would provide ample opportunity to blend in and escape spying eyes. A moment later Tariq and his companion burst from the house and gave chase.

The streets were narrow, the two and three story buildings seeming to fold over on top of them like a subterranean passageway. He knew that these streets, like some of the forgotten places he had explored in his search for answers about the strange mystery of his life, formed a daunting maze full of dead ends and unpleasant surprises.

As they rounded a corner, Kismet saw that the street ahead was partially blocked; a forest-green Range Rover was parked at an angle to effectively limit access to the avenue. A Caucasian man leaned against the front fender of the vehicle, idly smoking a cigarette and shooing off beggars and children as thought they were flies, with a dismissive smoky wave. When he caught sight of Kismet and Lyse running toward him the half-finished butt fell from his fingers.

A commotion erupted behind them as Tariq, his companion and several other men—undoubtedly the Fat Man's domestic staff—burst out onto the street, shouting angrily and scanning in all directions to locate the fleeing duo. Kismet glanced at them then returned his gaze forward, focused on darting past the parked vehicle. He almost failed to notice the bystander withdrawing a handgun from a concealed holster.

"Jesus," he gasped, whirling in mid-step and all but tackling Lyse in his haste to seek cover. He knew the gesture was futile. At less than ten paces, the man with the pistol could cut them to ribbons. As Lyse went down, barely aware of the new threat, the golden statue tumbled from her grasp. The relic clanked loudly on the brick surface of the street and rolled a few feet away. In his peripheral vision, Kismet saw her struggling to retrieve it.

"Lyse, that thing is—"

The gun spoke. Loud explosions echoed in the narrow confines of the street as the forty-five-caliber pistol discharged several times into the air over their heads. The man continued to pump bullets, not at the hapless pair on the ground, but into the crowd of men pursuing them. Several of the shots found their mark; Kismet heard cries of pain and cursing as the mob scattered, seeking the cover of doorways and debris. He knew it would not be long before Tariq and his cohorts returned fire, with himself and Lyse caught in the middle.

Why the motorist had come to their assistance, Kismet could not fathom, but when he looked up, he found the man gesturing for them to get in the Range Rover. Kismet nodded, and tried to crawl toward the vehicle, but his left ankle seemed rooted in place. He looked back and found Lyse clutching his foot.

"No, Nick. This way." She jumped up, the golden calf tucked under her arm, and began running back the way they had come.

"Lyse! What the hell--?" Kismet gaped in amazement as she threaded the gauntlet seemingly unnoticed by the Fat Man's mob, which apparently had more pressing concerns. He turned back to the pistol-wielding motorist, and found that the man's expression was no longer that of an eager rescuer. A muscle in the gunman's face had begun to twitch with rising ire, leading Kismet to believe that perhaps Lyse had made the correct decision after all. "Oh," he muttered, then took off running.

As he darted through the huddled group of men that had now given up pursuit, he heard the motorist barking orders in German. He risked a rearward glance and found that the fellow had not come to the street alone. Several men wearing casual Western attire materialized from the rear of the vehicle and took up the chase. Kismet swung his eyes forward, straining to catch a glimpse of Lyse, and poured on a burst of speed. Behind him the concussions of pistol fire resumed, but now the shooting was from both parties; a small war had begun in the street outside the Fat Man's house. Sparks danced on the walls to either side telling Kismet that although he was no longer the primary target, he was still in grave danger of catching a stray bullet. Lysette was nowhere to be seen.

"Ni-i-ick!"

The cry for help came from up ahead and to the left. Kismet spied an intersecting street and darted down it, leaving the firefight behind. When he turned the corner, he skidded to a halt.

An old beggar, eyes staring blankly in apparent blindness, sat with his back to one wall, oblivious to the violence a block away. He held a long rod in his fingers, and a straw basket lay before him, its lid resting against his knee.

Lyse was not looking at the beggar, but at his pet, an Egyptian Cobra which hovered in the center of the street, swaying dangerously from left to right, signaling its clear intent that no one would pass unmolested. The toothless mendicant cackled beside them, mocking their fear as he waved the oblong rod toward them. It was a flute, a snake charmer's horn. If they were to pass by, they would have to give alms and wait for him to play his tune.

"Lyse," muttered Kismet from the corner of his mouth. "Pay the nice man."

"Me? I don't have any money. You pay him."

"Oh, for crying out loud." He fumbled for his waist pack, but the intensity of the cobra's stare was hypnotic, depriving him of volition.

On the avenue they had left behind, an ominous silence settled. The shooting had ceased; the battle was over. The victorious party, whichever it was, would soon remember the original purpose for venturing into the streets of the old city. Kismet knew that time was running out. Biting his lip, he tried to force his eyelids down in order to break visual contact with the viper, but they conspired against him; his fear of what the cobra might do if he looked away nearly overpowered his will to even blink. At last succeeding, he turned his head toward Lyse.

She too was transfixed by the cobra's stare. Kismet kept his gaze focused, refusing to believe the hysterical delusions and visual tricks that were being played in the corner of his eye. His rational mind knew that the cobra was not slithering closer even though every nerve in his body screamed that it was.

With a slow, deliberate motion, he reached out for Lyse's arm and plucked the golden statue from her grasp. Before she could protest, Kismet whirled and tossed the relic into the beggar's basket. The old fellow nodded his head appreciatively and raised the flute to his lips.

"Nick, no!" Lyse leaped into motion. She crossed in front of him and reached for the basket.

"Lyse, it's a—" Kismet fell silent as he saw the snake move. He knew that this time what he saw was no hallucination.

The cobra knew its responsibility to its master. Once something went into the basket, it became the old man's property. Theft was to be punished. With the swiftness of a lightning strike, its fangs bared and oozing venom, the snake darted for her outstretched arm.

Kismet was faster. He instinctively stabbed out his right hand and plucked the animal out of the air, arresting its deadly strike, and suddenly found himself gripping the business end of a six foot length of squirming reptile.

He squeezed the serpent just behind the curl of its jaw, clenching his teeth in frustration as the snake writhed and coiled about him, hissing angrily. When the viper finally succumbed to captivity, Kismet turned slowly toward the old man and with a weak pitch tossed the cobra away.

Lyse was stunned by the sequence of events, all of which had transpired in the space of a heartbeat. With a more subdued manner, she retrieved the statue. "Let's get out of here."

Armed men appeared in the vacant space behind them, communicating with each other in Teutonic barks. Lyse grabbed his arm, breaking the spell, and they took off running. If the cobra had any sort of ego to bruise, it recovered quickly and slithered back into the street to waylay the next group of passers-by.

At the end of the street, Lyse ran to the right with Kismet on her heels. She continued to chart a haphazard course through the labyrinth, leading them into a more heavily populated area—one of the many *suuqs*, or covered marketplaces that dotted the city. Kismet was completely turned around now and the growing darkness added to his anxiety. He knew they needed to slow down, get their bearings, but the unknown pursuers were relentless. By fair means or foul, they had quickly dealt with the snake charmer and remained never more than half a block away. One wrong turn into a cul-de-sac might prove fatal. There would be no second chances.

Lyse dashed into a narrow recess, and when Kismet followed, he found himself in near total darkness. He heard strange noises in the pitch black ahead, and sensed that something disastrous had befallen his companion.

"Lyse?"

"Nick." The response was weak, sounding almost distant. It seemed to come from ground level, only a few steps away, but was muffled, as though from a tomb. Kismet advanced cautiously.

His right foot came down on nothing and without warning he plunged forward. His shoulders struck rotted wood as he plummeted into an unseen abyss, and an instant later he was laying face down in something hot and moist. He sat up, shaking his head to clear the sense of dislocation. Then the stench hit him.

"Ohhhh...shit." Fighting back the urge to inhale, he began wiping the streaks of offending matter away from his mouth and nose.

"Nick, is that you? I think we fell into a sewer tunnel."

"You noticed that?" he replied irritably. His only pleasure was in the secret knowledge that if he found the situation—euphemistically speaking—unpleasant, then Lyse, whom he had known to refuse to even enter public restrooms, must have thought she'd died and gone to hell.

Somewhere high above them an opening had been made in the street, guarded only by a simple wooden barricade, affording access to one of the sewer tunnels, which, despite being a relic of another age, still serviced the city above. In any other circumstances he might have found this turn of events amusing, but sitting in rotting human waste soured his sense of humor.

Kismet opened his pack and began sorting through its contents with his fingertips. He could feel the broad outline of his *kukri* knife, sheathed in a traditional scabbard of wood and leather that was integrated into the custom-made bag. He then encountered the solid composite frame of his Glock 17 automatic pistol, but pushed past it as well. His fingers settled momentarily on an envelope, thick with a bundle of paper—nearly one hundred thousand dollars in American Express travelers checques, which he had brought along in the event that Lyse's artifact had proved worth purchasing. At last he found the object of his search, the long black metal tube of a MagLite LED flashlight. He took it out and pressed the sealed rubber button that protected the switch.

A beam of light pierced the steamy atmosphere, picking out a random spot on the curved sewer walls. Kismet swung the beam around until he located his companion. She seemed less beautiful in that moment, up to her elbows in the muck, searching for something.

"For God's sake, Lyse. That statue is a—"

Another shaft of illumination stabbed down into the shadows between them. Kismet swung his own light up and found the hole through which he and Lyse had fallen, fifteen feet overhead, now ringed by hard looking faces. Two of the men held high-intensity flashlights similar to his own. Another, the motorist with the pistol, pointed down at Kismet and barked a command in German. The men looked back hesitantly, but Kismet knew that eventually he and Lyse would have the pleasure of their company in the reeking passage.

Lyse did not relent in her search. "Just help me find it, will you?"

Growling, Kismet plunged his right hand into the slurry and stirred around until he encountered something hard and heavy. He closed his fist around the object, silently praying that it was the statue, and drew it out. Dark matter fell away to reveal gleaming gold. She snatched it from his hand and jumped erect. The sewage came up to her knees, hampering her steps, but she nevertheless started splashing through the tunnel.

Kismet frowned and shined the light across the surface of the effluent. He detected a faint movement, a gradual flow of the sewage in the direction opposite that she had chosen. "Lyse! Wrong way. Get back here." He flashed the light down the passage and located her; she had turned around and was returning to the spot where they had entered.

One of the armed men dropped between them, losing his balance as he landed. Kismet swung the MagLite like a cudgel, connecting solidly with the side of the man's head. Dazed, the stranger fell back into the sewage with a splash.

The heavy-duty light did not even flicker with the impact, but Kismet berated himself for having used their only source of illumination as a weapon. He glanced up and saw another man dangling into the hole, about to drop, and knew that it was time to be moving on. He and Lyse charged into the depths of the tunnel as their foes dropped down to pursue.

If the streets of the city had been a cunning maze, then the underworld below was doubly so. New branches appeared at irregular intervals. Sloping conduits dripping with fecal matter and wastewater increased the volume of the muck though which they struggled. Occasional movements, barely captured in the beam of the flashlight, revealed that other creatures called this dark place home.

Kismet led them true, following the gradual decline of the city's sewers to its eventual destination. After several minutes of desperate wading and running, he and his companion burst out of their underground prison and into the open night. The sewer pipe exited from a steep embankment with the city walls high above. Below the opening however, a drop of several yards, ended in a vast cesspool. Lyse gazed warily down at the murk, then looked to him.

"Now what?"

Kismet was already beginning to climb along the face of the cliff. Lyse attempted to follow, but discovered that the statue she had risked life and limb to safeguard now encumbered her movements.

"Just leave it!" shouted Kismet.

She shook her head, then grasped the front of her T-shirt and untucked it from her jeans. She placed the statue in the makeshift sling of fabric and pulled the hem of the garment up until she could hold it between clenched teeth. Only then did she begin looking around the edge of the tunnel in search of a handhold. Her delay was costly. She had only reached the perimeter of the cesspool when their pursuers appeared at the opening of the sewer pipe. Sliding down the steep face, she dropped at Kismet's side. The weight of golden statue had stretched her shirt so that it almost covered her otherwise bare midriff. Kismet shook his head in mock despair then silently led their flight out across the desert sands.

The beams of their pursuers' lights danced like glowing bats in the darkness behind them. He was amazed at the relentless effort put forth to run them down, but why they were being chased by these foreigners, he could not imagine.

He chose to stay within sight of the old city's walls. Even at the dawn of a new millennium, people resided in the wilderness outside the city as they had for thousands of years before, living in tents and joining together in small ad hoc communities. A column of smoke rising against the twilit sky revealed some manner of civilization directly ahead. Kismet switched the MagLite off, hoping camouflage among the shadows would conceal them, and guided Lyse forward.

A chaotic barrier of wind-sculpted boulders blocked the way to the source of the smoke. As he threaded through he spied a cluster of tents, arranged around a large fire in a clearing not far ahead. A score of camels were tethered to a stake driven into the ground near the edge of the camp. Kismet grinned triumphantly; this was their ticket out of trouble. He grabbed hold of Lyse's elbow and dragged her into the clearing.

The camp belonged to nomadic Tuaregs, a tribe of Berber wanderers who for thousands of years had roamed the ancient caravan routes in robes dyed with indigo. Kismet knew that they were formidable adversaries when threatened and proceeded with due caution.

A few dark figures moved between the tents, but none seemed to take note of the foul smelling pair that crept toward the camp. Although he and Lyse were upwind, Kismet figured that the nomads had already grown accustomed to the stink of the nearby cesspool, and thus would not detect the stench they emitted.

A sentinel had been stationed near the camels; a young man Kismet presumed, though his *alasho*, the traditional swath of indigo fabric that served as both a turban and a veil for male Tuaregs, concealed anything that might have given his age away. The unsuspecting youth was huddled against the cold of the desert night.

Reasoning that the scarf limited the sentinel's field of view, Kismet gestured for Lyse to stay hidden then set out to flank the watch-post. The camels began snorting as he approached, and he immediately dropped flat on the sand. The young man noted the behavior of the herd, but could not comprehend the reason for their agitation. He nervously glanced around, fearful of an intruder, but was unable to distinguish Kismet's dark, earth-colored clothing. Moving slowly and stealthily, Kismet crept behind the guard. He reached out and tapped him on the shoulder, and as the veiled head turned to look, Kismet struck.

The blow stunned the young man for only a moment, but it was enough for Kismet to leap forward and seize hold of his *alasho*. A yank on the fabric loosened the wrap, and before he knew what was happening, the sentinel was hog-tied with his own turban. The young man writhed and moaned on the ground, but the blue cloth between his teeth muffled his cries for help. Kismet rose warily and advanced on the herd.

Lyse stepped from her hiding place and jogged over to join him. "Nick, they cut off body parts when people steal camels around here."

"Have you got a better idea?"

She shrugged.

"I didn't think so," he continued. "But if it will make you feel better, leave that statue behind as payment."

"Absolutely not."

Kismet sighed, then delved into his satchel and extracted a handful of traveler's checques. He wondered if the nomads would understand the value of the currency vouchers, but nevertheless scribbled his signature on several of the documents and stuffed them into the folds of the sentinel's garment. "Better?"

Lyse nodded.

"Then let's get out of here. Can you ride one of these things?"

"Is it anything like a bicycle?"

He shook his head in despair. "Not remotely."

"Good, 'cause I never learned how to ride a bicycle." She kept a straight face for a moment, and then cracked a grin—that winning smile that swept away all resistance. "I'm kidding, okay? Yeah, I can ride a camel. I don't like them, but I can do it."

She walked over to the camels, picked a smaller one out of the group and stroked its nose. After a few seconds it knelt, allowing her to step on its knee that she might ascend to the saddle high above its humps. With unexpected ease, she swung into riding position as the beast rose to full height.

Kismet laughed in spite of himself and went to join her. After selecting a mount for himself he untethered both of their rides and walked his chosen camel away from the campsite. A warm sirocco had picked up since the fall of evening, blowing a haze of dust in its vanguard. "We should rig some kind of safety line so that we don't get separated."

She glanced back hesitantly. "Then what?"

"We ride for the coast. Then we catch a flight back to the States."

Lyse inhaled deeply and let her breath out slowly. "I can't go yet, Nick. I still have things to do here."

"Lyse, if we go back, we're dead. If those guys—Germans, or whatever—don't get us, the Fat Man will."

"I have to go alone. I need you to take the statue back and keep it safe for me. It's important, Nick."

"You're going to have to do better than that if you want my help."

"I'm sorry, but I can't tell you any more than I already have. I'm sworn to secrecy." She winced, as if embarrassed by the declaration. "Look, just take the statue back to the States. Put it somewhere safe until I can catch up with you. I'll pay for all your expenses." She unrolled the relic from her disfigured shirt and tossed it to Kismet.

He caught the statue with his left hand. He knew from experience that if she was intent on returning to the city, further discussion would be futile. He stowed the artifact in his bag, taking something out at the same time.

"Hey Lyse." He held up his Glock. "You might need this."

Her face broke into a smile of sincere gratitude. She slid a hand down the inside of her left thigh, separating the fabric with a rasping noise that could only be the halves of a Velcro closure. A compact automatic pistol--a Glock 26, nearly identical to his only much smaller--appeared in her right hand.

"You had that the whole time?"

"Nick, you know I hate violence. This is for emergencies; a last resort."

Kismet let out a frustrated sigh. "Just be careful, will you?"

"Always." She smiled and turned the camel to ride away.

"Wait a minute. There's something I need to tell you."

She gazed back. "What's that?"

"The statue. There's no way it's an ancient artifact. Whoever made it did an expert job, but the inscription is a style of Hebrew that wasn't used until about three hundred years after the end of calf worship in Samaria. In short, the statue that you refused to leave behind is a fake."

Her reaction left him dumbstruck. Lyse did not protest or question his appraisal, nor did she fly into a rage at having been tricked by a forger. Instead, she simply laughed.

"Nick, I knew that."

She laughed again then urged the camel to a gallop. When the cloud of dust left by her exit had been swept away by the desert winds, Kismet, with a fixed look of disbelief, climbed onto his camel and rode toward the last gleams of sunset.

It was not the blowing sands of the Sahara that tapped lightly against the windowpanes of Nick Kismet's office, but rather a dusting of grainy, New York City snow. Though it was only five o'clock in the evening, the stormy December sky over Manhattan was already dark. The snowflakes were visible only in the glare of street lamps. Kismet gazed absently out the tiny window a moment longer, and then turned away.

The official presence of the UN's Global Heritage Commission was located not in the legendary United Nations building on 44th Street overlooking the East River, but instead several city blocks away in an inconspicuous corner of the American Museum of Natural History. Its extensive collection of anthropological artifacts had made the AMNH one of two locations considered for the dubious privilege of hosting the GHC, the other being the Metropolitan Museum of Art. Natural History had drawn the short straw and grudgingly made room in the lower level of the massive edifice, giving Kismet a converted supply closet just down the corridor from the school lunchroom. It wasn't much of an office, but for Kismet's purposes it was more than adequate.

The Global Heritage Commission had been created in the early 1980's as part of the UN's effort to remodel UNESCO—the United Nations Educational, Scientific, and Cultural Organization. Established in 1946, UNESCO had set forth noble goals for itself—the elimination of illiteracy, the free exchange of scientific ideas, the protection of historical locations and art treasures—but decades of Cold War politics had undermined those lofty intentions. In 1984, the United States of America had withdrawn from membership, removing a cornerstone of financial and political support. Nevertheless, it had taken the United Nations more than fifteen years to address the issues that created the schism in the first place. The Global Heritage Commission had begun as an interim compromise, addressing a narrower band of issues without being subject to the whims of an international governing body. The efforts to repair UNESCO had ultimately paid off, culminating with the official renewal of the United States' membership in 2003.

Despite the reestablishment of its parent organization, the GHC continued to perform a valuable function on the international playing field. Kismet's duties typically involved random inspections of American sponsored archaeological sites, advance negotiations on behalf of pioneering scientists, and acting as a liaison with law enforcement agencies investigating the illicit antiquities trade. In the big picture, it probably wasn't a very important job, and it certainly didn't pay very well, but Kismet found his vocation desirable for one simple reason: answers.

Nick Kismet didn't know a great deal about his own origins. A foundling, he had been raised by Christian Garral, a globetrotting adventurer and a self-made man of means, who had adopted the boy as his own son. His name was itself a relic of his post-natal abandonment—Garral, on one of his adventures, claimed to have encountered a young woman in the throes of child birth and assisted her *in extremis*. Almost immediately following the birth, the mother had slipped away, leaving only a single word, written in the blood of her womb and in a strange alien script. Garral had eventually deciphered it—the Arabic word: *qismat*. To Westerners, it transliterated as "kismet." An ancient and powerful word, its earliest meaning was the portion of land given to the firstborn, but later came to be associated with fate and destiny. Taking this as omen, Garral had elected to adopt the boy and ascribed him that distinctive surname. "Nick" was chosen for more prosaic reasons; Garral's own father was named Nicklaus.

Because he had no memory of his strange nativity, Kismet had over the course of the years, regarded the matter with some suspicion; his father was not above spinning a whopper of a tall tale. His uniquely stimulating childhood had kept him from agonizing overmuch about the matter as Garral's adventures took him to exotic environments in every corner of the globe. When at last it became time for him to formalize his education, his affinity for the many places he had visited in his youth led him to pursue the study of international law. In order to help pay for his studies—a matter of personal pride on his own part, for Garral was certainly wealthy enough to foot the bill—he had joined the Army ROTC, and his grasp of several different languages had led him to choose Military Intelligence as his occupational specialty. It had all been academic up until the events of late 1990, when armies from Iraq had invaded Kuwait and seemed poised to attack Saudi Arabia as well. Although he had always recognized the possibility of a deployment, the activation orders had come with the finality of a guillotine. He had said his good-byes and after a brief train-up, shipped out to Riyadh.

After the initial shock of dislocation had faded, he had come to accept his part in the greater mission to liberate Kuwait, but on one fateful night his world had been turned upside down. Seemingly from out of nowhere, he had been given orders for an over the border operation—the rescue of a defector with important military secrets. Compounding the irregularity of the orders was the fact that he would be accompanied only by a squad of Gurkhas. Britain's answer to the French Foreign Legion, the Gurkhas were a regiment of soldiers named for the fierce warrior tribe of Nepal whose signature weapon was a boomerang-shaped chopping knife called a *kukri*, and like their namesake, the Gurkhas fought heroically wherever they were sent. Half a century after the fact, they were still boasting about the fact the Gurkhas had suffered the highest casualty rates of Allied soldiers during the Second World War. Kismet's escorts had certainly honored the memories of their predecessors that night with a sacrifice of their own blood, but not before Kismet made contact with the defector, a man who identified himself as Samir Al-Azir, an engineer for the Iraqi regime who had, in the course of rebuilding the ancient city of Babylon, discovered a strange and extraordinar-

ily valuable relic dating back to the destruction of Jerusalem by the Babyloni-
an Emperor Nebuchadnezzar. Fearing that the United States might capture
the relic and return it to Israel, Saddam Hussein had ordered Samir to
destroy it, but the engineer had demurred choosing instead to use the artifact
as a bargaining token to secure safe passage for himself and his family.

And that was where it really got strange, for when Samir Al-Azir had
contacted a British government official, requesting asylum, he had specifically asked to be met in Tall al Muqayyar—the ruins of ancient Ur, near the
modern city of Nasyriah—by an American named Nick Kismet. All of this
was revealed to a young and disbelieving Second Lieutenant Kismet in the
half-buried remains of a long forgotten nobleman's dwelling, but before
Kismet could fully comprehend what he was being told, a group of commandos had stormed the location, and slaughtered Samir and his family.
Stranger still, the leader of the assault force, a man who identified himself as
Ulrich Hauser, indicated that Kismet's life was to be spared out of deference
to his mother. Hauser had then disappeared with the captured relic, leaving
only a cryptic reference to Prometheus, a figure from Greek mythology, to
explain his actions.

It might have ended right there. Stranded behind enemy lines as the air
war commenced, Kismet and the contingent of Gurkhas were hunted
relentlessly by Republican Guard forces, and ultimately captured. In the end,
only Kismet and one other soldier, a Gurkha from New Zealand named Alex
Higgins, made it back.

Scar tissue eventually covered the battle wounds, but the events of that
night continued to hemorrhage his soul's essence. Who was Hauser, and
what was his connection to Kismet's mother? How had Samir known to
request him specifically by name, and why? And who or what was Prometheus?

There was of course, one other clue that he could not overlook: the relic.
He had not actually seen it, but had inferred much about it from his brief
conversation with Samir; it was the holiest of holy relics. Hauser had also
hinted that Prometheus' mission was to keep such icons and artifacts safely
locked away, and so Kismet had begun his quest by embarking on a greater

understanding of the world of art and antiquities. If the conspirators he had faced that night in the desert sought ancient relics, then perhaps in the ancient places of the world, he would find their figurative footprints. His quest led to Paris where, despite finding no answers, he cultivated a friendship with the director of the Global Heritage Commission and was ultimately offered a job as GHC liaison to the United States. Reasoning the position would afford him opportunity to investigate the mystery of his life, he had accepted. For years thereafter he had kept his ear to the ground, listening for any whispers that might shed light on what had happened that night in the ruins of Tall al Muqayyar.

He had not even considered what he had lost in his single-minded quests to unmask Prometheus; not until the curious summons had brought him once more in contact with Lysette Lyon. He turned to his desktop where Lyse's latest email continued to shine from the computer monitor:

Nick, thanks so much for bailing me out the other day. I'll be in the city for New Year's Eve. Maybe I can swing by the office. We can settle our business and after that, who knows? I still remember how to say 'thanks' properly. Luv ya, Lyse.

His eagerness to rendezvous with Lyse had nothing to do with her overt promises; things were different now, evidently for both of them, and he was going to exact the price of his favor in information and nothing else. During the days since his escape from Morocco he had mulled over the situation and decided that if Lyse wanted her trinket back—and Kismet knew it was not any sort of rare artifact—she was going to have to make a full confession.

He rose from his desk and paced around the office, then checked his watch again. It was nearly five-thirty and she had yet to show. She was going to have to spring for dinner too, he decided.

The sound of a door opening in the hallway alerted Kismet to the arrival of a guest. He idly ran a hand through his short cropped hair and settled into his chair, then propped his feet up on an open drawer and tried his best to look nonchalant. The figure beyond the frosted pane of the door that bore his name paused then tried the doorknob.

"Mr. Kismet?"

It was not Lyse. He immediately dropped his feet to the floor and sat up. "Yes. Please come in."

The door swung open, revealing a tall man about the same age as Kismet. He was well dressed, bundled against the chill air, and carried himself with the effete manner of a sophisticate. Kismet felt a glimmer of recognition looking at the man's handsome features, wavy blonde hair and thin mustache, but he could not put a name to the face. The man approached his desk, extending a hand, which Kismet accepted, standing to greet the newcomer.

"It's good to see you again," the man offered.

The British accent was maddeningly familiar and his introduction suggested some prior acquaintance, but Kismet once more drew a blank. "What can I do for you?"

The handsome face broke into an odd smile. "You don't remember me?"

"Frankly, I…" All of a sudden, he did remember and the recollection was not pleasant. "Andrew Harcourt."

"Most people call me 'Sir Andrew,' nowadays." Harcourt made no attempt to mask his pride.

"Sir Andrew? Well…congratulations." The pieces continued falling into place, triggering one uncomfortable memory after another, but Kismet nevertheless extended his right hand, accepting Harcourt's quick shake. "Why don't you sit down? You'll be more comfortable."

"Why thank you. I say, were you expecting someone else?"

"I had another appointment, but it seems I've been stood up. No matter though. To what do I owe the pleasure of a visit from Her Majesty's favorite archaeologist? Digging on our side of the pond again?"

Harcourt laughed. "Not exactly, but I am in the planning stages of an endeavor which should prove quite…um, earthshaking. Actually, that's what brings me here today. I wish to prevail upon you to join me."

Kismet stared back at the archaeologist. He rarely made judgments about the academics he frequently encountered, but his one brush with Harcourt had been unpleasant enough that a bad taste lingered. He tried to conceal his surprise. "I'm touched, but why me?"

"Given our history, I think it only makes sense for me to bring someone along from the Commission to avoid the perception of impropriety."

The explanation seemed a little shaky but Kismet decided to play along. "Why don't you tell me what you have in mind?"

"I'd rather show you." Harcourt held up a leather attaché case, which he set down on Kismet's desk and opened. He removed a cloth wrapped parcel and laid it on the desk for Kismet to inspect. In the center of the cloth was a fragment of metal, broken it appeared from an ancient war helmet of Greek design. The piece seemed to have been, at one time, the right forward quarter of the helmet. Kismet took note of the straight edges, which ran along the bottom and leading sides, curving into an eyehole, and then dropped down to shield the bridge of the nose. The breaking points were jagged, as though the helmet had been cut or torn apart, rather than decaying from corrosion. The metal was scored and dented in several places, suggesting that it had seen use in combat, but the minor defects had since been covered by a thin veneer of bright, flawless metal: gold.

Kismet reached for it. "May I?"

"Please do."

The helmet fragment was not solid gold; it was much too lightweight. He felt a faint residue on the surface and noticed a white concentration in some of the cracks, but the artifact had not tarnished at all. A probing finger wiped the substance away, and when he touched it to his lips, there was only a salty flavor, not the expected tang of copper. He flipped it over and looked inside the helmet. A tiny patch of gold had been scraped away, revealing darker metal beneath—tarnished bronze. "You did this?" Kismet asked, pointing to the defect.

Harcourt nodded.

"And the overlay is gold?"

Harcourt pursed his lips. "It's not exactly an overlay. The metallurgists I've showed it to say it's as if the outer surface of the bronze were transmuted."

Kismet raised an eyebrow, but did not pursue the matter; he remembered Harcourt's penchant for blending pseudo-science and mysticism with the facts in order to paint a dramatic, if not entirely authentic picture of the past. He placed the fragment against his face, trying to imagine how it would have looked on the ancient warrior to whom it originally belonged. "What do you think?"

"Very becoming."

The helmet had been fashioned for someone with a smaller head, probably a youth. "Where did you find this?"

"Unfortunately I didn't find it, but rather purchased it. If I knew where it had been found, my quest would be far simpler."

"So it could be from almost any site, anywhere. What makes you think this will lead to an undiscovered site?"

"That piece is like nothing that has ever been uncovered. It is unique in many ways, not the least of which is the gold covering."

"That could have been done later. The Greeks pioneered the technique of electroplating thousands of years ago, but you know as well as I that the ancients didn't waste their gold decorating war helmets. Maybe the person who sold it to you was trying to increase its value."

"Perhaps there is another explanation." Harcourt's Cheshire cat grin suggested he was about to elaborate.

"I'm listening."

Harcourt reached into the case and drew out a large manila envelope, which he casually tossed over to Kismet. The envelope contained five 8"X10" photographs. They were all images of a single piece of white stone viewed from different aspects. Kismet spread them out and began examining from left to right.

The subject of the photos was unquestionably an artifact, a product of some intelligence rather than a random occurrence of nature. Like the helmet, the white stone had been damaged at some point in its long history, destroying its intended symmetry. One of the photographs showed it lying alongside a measuring tape, helping Kismet to understand why Harcourt had not simply brought the piece itself.

The stone was a block, a foot in depth and width, and about two feet to the long point of where it had been broken. The fracture had cleaved a forty-five degree angle through length, more or less leaving the other dimensions unaltered. The fourth picture was a close-up of one facet, and the photographer had adjusted his angle to highlight in shadow a series of carved letters.

"Can you read what it says?"

Kismet shrugged. "Ancient Greek really isn't my field."

"Ah, of course. But you are proficient in its modern equivalent, are you not? There are differences of course, but the letters are similar. Give it a try."

Kismet frowned, but returned his gaze to the photograph. "The first word is partly damaged, but I would imagine that this is an altar stone, so I would infer that it says '*bomos*,' or 'altar of offerings.'"

"I knew you were only being modest. And the second word?"

"'Medea.' Offerings to Medea?"

Harcourt sat back smugly. "What do you think of that?"

Kismet's reply was guarded. "What am I supposed to think?"

"Oh, don't be so coy, Nick. You know as well as I who Medea was; the witch-queen from the legend of Jason and the Argonauts, daughter of the king of Colchis, the land where the Golden Fleece was hidden."

Kismet frowned, recalling the old adage about a little knowledge being dangerous. "Medea was never worshiped by the ancient Greeks. She was merely a character in a story that was a myth even to them."

"I would suggest that the altar stone you see in the photograph proves that someone did worship her."

"Perhaps the stone was a theatrical prop. The legend of the Argonauts was a favorite of Greek dramatists." Kismet knew the argument was weak, but he saw where Harcourt was leading and felt compelled to head him off.

"Then the set designer was rather over-eager, don't you think? That's white marble, a rather expensive choice for use as a decoration."

"Touché." Kismet sighed, staring once more at the words on the photograph. "All right, someone worshiped somebody named Medea. If it was the same person as the one in the legend, what does that prove? There are thousands of altars, temples and shrines to dozens of gods, nymphs and oracles. Those temples in no way prove that such persons or creatures existed."

"You've gotten ahead of me, Nick. I merely present this to you as evidence of an aspect of ancient culture with which we are unfamiliar."

"And you think there's more to be discovered?"

"I am certain of it." Harcourt sat back and pressed his fingers together. "However, let me return to the subject of Medea as an historic figure. Since history does not record the worship of her, and yet we see proof that she was worshiped by someone, what does that suggest?"

"Medea literally means 'a witch' or 'one who is cunning.' There's nothing to indicate that a woman named Medea really existed. If the character in legend was based on an actual person, it is doubtful that her name was Medea, and even less likely that her worshipers would have memorialized her with that derogatory term."

"The word may have been coined because of her."

Kismet found his recall of both his Greek language lessons and Bullfinch's mythology shifting into overdrive. "No. In fact, it is a Greek word, while the Medea of legend was not a Greek. And use of the word certainly pre-dates the theoretical place in history when the journey of the Argo would have occurred."

"Except for that," snapped Harcourt, seeming to lose his cool. He stabbed his finger at the photo. "An altar to Medea."

"Calm down," soothed Kismet. "You're right. This would seem to support what you're suggesting."

Harcourt stared back, unsure of what to make of Kismet's apparent reversal. "I hope you're not patronizing me, Nick." He waited a moment longer, before continuing. "I believe that this altar stone is one end of a thread that will lead us through the labyrinth of legend to the truth about Medea, Jason, the Argonauts and the Golden Fleece itself.

"To begin with, the legend states that Jason and his companions successfully completed their quest, capturing the Golden Fleece. He also took Medea for a bride, and returned to win back the kingdom to which he was the rightful heir. Some versions even speak of him using the Fleece as a talisman to control the weather or heal a blight upon the land. In any event, the Fleece was certainly a great treasure. Yet, following the end of the tale, there is no further mention of it in the mythology of the Greeks.

"What if there really was a Golden Fleece? What if it was a symbol of powerful magic? What if Medea took the Fleece from her husband, and used it to create a cult of her own worshipers? Do you see where this leads? If we can locate the temple of Medea from which this altar stone was taken, we may find also one of the most spectacular artifacts in history: the original quest, the Golden Fleece."

"I counted at least three 'what ifs' Andrew. You are basing your entire investigative process on folk tales."

"And why is that such a crime? Heinrich Schliemann proved that the mythology of Homer was a suitable guide book when he discovered the ruins of ancient Troy."

Kismet dredged up what he knew about the famous German archaeologist who had plundered gold from a site in Turkey near the turn of the twentieth century. Schliemann's wife and partner had reportedly helped him smuggle the artifacts from the site and ultimately back to their homeland by concealing them under her skirt. Those treasures, revered by the German National Socialist party prior to World War II had disappeared following the sack of Berlin, probably taken as booty by Russian soldiers and secreted away in the halls of the Hermitage. It was just the sort of incident the Global Heritage Commission sought to prevent by keeping historical discoveries in their country of origin. Harcourt, like Heinrich Schliemann, was a 'pop' scientist, who liked to make sensational claims that grabbed headlines, and Kismet had no qualms about voicing that accusation.

"Schliemann found a ruin and used the Iliad to fill in the blank spaces. That kind of circular logic might impress royalty and make you famous, but it does little to advance the true cause of science. You of all people should realize that Andrew. Or didn't you learn your lesson with the Beowulf debacle?"

"Schliemann's detractors are now my own, but what does that prove? Merely that the institution of archaeology is governed by narrow-minded men; men without vision. But I assure you I am not doing this to add to my acclaim. The Fleece is a very important, possibly very powerful artifact."

Harcourt's rising passion had already validated Kismet's reticence, but with that last assertion the British archaeologist had crossed a line. "Powerful?"

"Think of the helmet shard. You said yourself that the Greeks would not have wasted gold to overlay a war helmet. But the legend tells how Medea used a magical salve to make Jason invincible, a balm that she spread on both his body and his armor. I contend that the balm she used was derived from the power latent in the Golden Fleece."

Kismet found he was curious in spite of himself. "How do you make that connection?"

"First, the Fleece was in the possession of her father, the king of Colchis. One version of the myth suggests that it was kept in a temple guarded by an enormous serpent, and that Medea herself had access to both the temple and its guardian. The serpent motif is found extensively throughout ruins along the Black Sea coastline."

"And in just about every other culture in the world."

Harcourt conceded the point with a nod, but resumed his argument without missing a beat. "Moreover, she was a witch. She would have believed that the Fleece had magical properties and would have sought to use it."

"Witchcraft and shamanism are also a part of most cultures, both historic and contemporary. That doesn't mean those superstitions are real."

Harcourt smiled cryptically. "A demonstration then." He centered the helmet shard on Kismet's desk, turned so the outward curve faced the ceiling. It looked almost as if a face was pushing through the desktop. "Do you have a letter opener?"

Kismet dug into his pocket and took out an oblong olive-drab colored object: his pocket knife, a Benchmade 53 Marlowe Balisong knife. The Balisong butterfly knife design, which had originated in the Philippines, was different than an ordinary pocket knife where the blade folded into the side of handle. The Balisong handle was split lengthwise, and the blade rotated on two pivot points out of the grooved channels on either side. Kismet squeezed the handle halves together just enough to allow the spring-loaded latch to pop open, then whipped his wrist around. One half of the hinged handle fell away and suddenly three inches of gleaming steel flashed into view. Kismet caught the loose handle half before it could strike the back of his hand, and with the handle halves together once more, the knife was ready for use. He surreptitiously thumbed the latch shut, securing the handle so that the blade would not collapse, then held it out for Harcourt's inspection. "Will this work?"

Harcourt blanched a little. The Balisong was a tricky knife to master-- more than a few first-time users had the scars on their fingers to prove it-- but in skilled hands, the blade and handle halves flashing through the air could prove downright intimidating. Kismet didn't normally like to show-off, but if it meant making Harcourt nervous, he was willing to make an exception.

"I should say so." Harcourt took a step back. "Now, if you please, I want you to stab at the helmet shard. Don't hold back; you can't damage it."

Kismet raised an eyebrow. He wasn't as protective about the relics as some of the bone-diggers, but he drew the line at wanton vandalism. Still, what harm would one more nick or dent matter to a piece of combat gear? He raised the knife over his head, drew a mental crosshair on the helmet piece, and hammered down with his fist.

What happened next was difficult to follow. The blade seemed to skitter along the surface of the helmet shard, redirecting away to the right. The tip gouged a deep furrow in the wood desktop. At the same time, the violence of the blow was reflected in the reaction; the helmet piece shot away, banging against the wall before crashing noisily to the floor. Kismet released his hold on the knife, leaving it upright where it had impaled the desk. "Okay, what did that prove?"

Harcourt raised a forbearing hand as he retrieved the shard and presented it for inspection. The soft gold showed no evidence of having been scored by the hardened steel blade. The relic was undamaged.

"It's not what you think," Harcourt offered in the absence of a comment from Kismet. "Your blade never touched it."

"What do you mean?"

"The metal which you take to be gold on that shard has a rather unusual attribute. From a metallurgical standpoint it is indeed gold, but unlike ordinary gold, this substance can store a transient electrical charge, stealing electrons from the environment. When an oppositely charged item—your knife blade—is directed toward it at high speed, an electrostatic field is created. The helmet shard literally repelled your knife blade, pushing it away as it came close. I had it analyzed by a top European research firm; it is a stable anion of gold—they dubbed it 'ubergold.' It rather reminds me of orichalcum, the divine metal Plato associated with Atlantis. Whether it is a naturally occurring substance is anyone's guess, but they all agree that nothing like it has ever been discovered."

Kismet stared at the British archaeologist, weighing the arguments the other man had presented. The possibility that some kind of magnetic gold might have imbued an object with extraordinary abilities was intriguing, but merely as a curiosity. It would take a lot more for Kismet to want to get on board with Sir Andrew Harcourt. "Well, that is interesting, but I don't see how it supports your broader theory. You still have nothing more to offer than conjecture based primarily on myths and legends."

"I admit that it is a rough beginning, but the goal will be worth the effort if we succeed."

"I still am unclear as to why you want me along. Why not contact England's liaison to the Commission? I imagine he would jump at the chance to accompany the Queen's favorite archaeologist on his latest quest."

"As you might well imagine, celebrity brings with it the jealousy of one's peers. To be honest, I suspect that you are the only one of my colleagues likely to assist me in this endeavor. Oh yes, I do think of you as a colleague; I sense that you are genuinely interested in the pursuit of truth, unlike most of the bureaucrats in UNESCO. And you have a reputation for delivering the goods."

Kismet was unmoved. "I shouldn't have to remind you of your obligation to remain objective, Andrew. We can't let myths and legends affect our perspective. Archaeology is about uncovering the past; reading history in the ruins and bones of ancient civilizations. It's not about proving pet theories, and it certainly isn't about chasing after magical talismans."

Harcourt suddenly broke into a grin, as if he had landed a sucker punch in their verbal sparring match. He stood abruptly, retrieved the helmet shard and returned it to his case. He left photographs on Kismet's desk. "I'm surprised you can say that after having looked upon the Ark of the Covenant."

Kismet felt as though he had been hit broadside. "I think you've got me confused with someone else," he replied slowly, straining to control his expression.

"Oh, really? My mistake." He picked up the case and strolled toward the door. "Consider my offer, Nick. You have a chance to be a part of history. Be seeing you."

Kismet did not move, struggling to keep his balance; the inside of his head was roaring with the sudden rush of adrenaline. He strove to remain imperturbable as Harcourt exited, but the moment he heard the Englishman's footsteps in the hall, he jumped up, retrieved his knife and ran to the door. He opened it a crack and peered after his departing guest.

Harcourt strode purposefully for the exit. A moment later, someone else appeared and headed down the vacant hallway toward him; a shapely feminine figure in a remarkable strapless black cocktail dress that seemed, like Harcourt's helmet shard, to defy the laws of physics.

Kismet groaned; beautiful as she was, at just this moment Lysette Lyon was the last person on earth he wanted to see. As the taller man passed by,

Lyse paused and looked over her shoulder at him. Kismet waited until Harcourt turned the corner leading to the elevator foyer before bursting into the corridor.

"Nick." She flashed her lethal smile. "Sorry I'm late, but this weather has slowed things down and parking was a nightmare."

Kismet pushed past her. He could hear the sound of the elevator in the shaft. If Harcourt was taking it up from the lower level, it stood to reason that he would be leaving through the front entrance facing Central Park.

"Bad timing, Lyse. I'm sorry, but our night on the town will have to wait." As soon as the elevator doors thumped shut, Kismet sprinted past the foyer and down the hallway to a flight of stairs at north end of the building. He could hear Lyse's heels tapping a quick staccato rhythm in his wake.

Rounding the banister, Kismet flashed a wave to the guard posted at the seldom-used 81st Street entrance and pushed through the door. He hastened along the perimeter of the castle-like structure, ducking low alongside the massive stone walls, and paused at the corner where he could surreptitiously observe the stairs that faced the park. Harcourt was descending the stone steps, moving purposefully toward an idling black Lincoln Towne Car. As he approached, the driver of the vehicle got out and opened the back door.

"Care to fill me in?"

Kismet turned to find Lyse peering over his shoulder. She looked somewhat ridiculous as she stretched on her tip-toes in the high-heeled shoes. He noted that she had at least managed to pull a lightweight raincoat over her cocktail dress. A thought occurred to him. "You said you had trouble parking. You drove?"

"Mmhhmm. And what a drive. I'm famished."

"Fine. You go get something to eat. I need to borrow your car."

"What? Not a chance. We may be old friends, but you're too old, and we're not that friendly."

Kismet frowned. "I need to follow that man."

Lyse stared back, her face uncharacteristically serious. "Is it really important?"

"Yeah, I think so."

"Okay. I'll drive you. I owe you one."

"You owe me plenty. But thanks."

The black Towne Car pulled into the moderately light traffic moving along Central Park West, and then signaled for a turn onto 81st Street. Lyse led Kismet back along the north side of the museum, across the lawn toward Columbus Avenue. Traffic was heavier there, but they crossed against the light and jogged down West 81st until Kismet spied an all too familiar shape.

"Oh, God. Not the Bug."

Lyse affected a hurt expression. "Nick, I thought you loved the Bug."

"Jesus, Lyse. That car's older than I am. And it's not exactly inconspicuous."

The last point was difficult to argue. Though he knew from experience that Lyse always kept the candy-apple red 1965 Volkswagen Super Beetle in superb condition, it was nevertheless something of a modern relic.

"Beggars can't be choosers, Nick. Would you'd rather try following him on foot?"

Kismet growled, but conceded her point and squirmed into the cramped interior. With any luck, the scattered snow showers would afford them a degree of concealment as they tailed Harcourt to his next destination. Lyse turned the key and the Volkswagen engine rattled to life. Kismet reconsidered walking, but as Harcourt's Lincoln turned left onto Columbus Avenue only a block away, Kismet knew their window of opportunity would not stay open for long. "Try not to lose them."

"Please Nick," she said, sounding wounded. "It's me."

The Super Beetle slipped easily from its parking space and puttered toward the intersection. Lyse executed a rolling stop, and then darted across two lanes, to the annoyance of a Yellow Cab that had to fan its brakes imperceptibly to let her in. Kismet scanned the road ahead, spying the ornate taillights of Harcourt's car about a hundred yards ahead.

"There he is," observed Lyse, easing back on the accelerator to maintain the distance. "He's staying to the inside. I'd say they're heading downtown. So who is this guy?"

Kismet rubbed his eyes as if he had a headache. Harcourt's bombshell was still ringing in his ears. There seemed but one explanation: the mysterious Prometheus group had resurfaced. But he was not about to trust Lyse with that supposition. Instead, he answered her query with a simple, if incomplete statement of fact. "Sir Andrew Harcourt. He's an archaeologist from London."

"Yeah? From your tone, I take it he didn't get a Christmas card from you this year?"

"We butted heads a couple years back. Harcourt is a sensationalist. Most archaeologists focus on a particular area of study and pretty much devote their career to it. Harcourt is one of those guys who likes to develop flashy theories and make a big production out of his digs; live television coverage and so forth.

"About three years ago, he stumbled onto what looked like a Norse burial mound upstate. He excavated it and evidently found some impressive stuff; it looked good on camera at least. As I recall, he tried to link the burial mound with the legend of Beowulf; an epic poem, written in old English, a fairy tale, about a brave warrior who went on a quest, slew a dragon and got killed for his trouble."

"Saw the movie. Kind of a downer."

Kismet continued with a nod. "Harcourt tried to draw on similarities between the legend and his discovery, suggesting that the poem might have been the story of an ancient warrior who actually traveled to America centuries before Columbus. I don't know if he actually believed that he had found the burial place of the real Beowulf, but when they edited the footage for the Discovery Channel, it sure sounded that way."

"Where's the crime in that?"

"Pop science is great for getting kids interested, but when you try to build on a foundation of mythology—folk tales and superstition—you just cloud the issue."

She threw him a sidelong glance. "Why? I mean, sometimes those legends are based on real events, right?"

"Harcourt's methods tend to blur the distinction. When you try that hard to reconcile fairy tales with established historical facts, you only obscure the truth. Just imagine if I came forward and claimed to have discovered the golden coffin of Snow White. I might get a lot of attention, but the truth of the matter is, Snow White is just a fairy tale. It didn't really happen. So even if I really had found an empty golden coffin, by saying that it belonged to a character from a fairy tale, I would be misdirecting people away from the facts about whose coffin it really was."

Lyse looked unconvinced but Kismet didn't know how to illustrate the problem more simply. "Well anyway, there's more to the story. In addition to the Norse artifacts there were quite a few Native American pieces at the site. Naturally it turned into a pissing contest, and because his theories were so wild, Harcourt ended up getting pushed out. I'm afraid that was mostly my doing."

"Ah, so that's why you two are best pals."

Before he could answer, the black car ahead of them angled left onto Broadway. Lyse peered intently through the drizzle, then downshifted for a surge of power. The Volkswagen shot forward and rapidly closed the gap between the two cars. "They're heading downtown, all right. I'm going to pass them."

"What? I don't want them to see me."

"They're a lot less likely to realize that we are following them if we're ahead of them. Just look away as we go by."

Before he could argue, Lyse swung the Super Beetle into the left lane and drew alongside the Lincoln. Kismet hastily folded himself over, pressing his torso against his knees below the level of the window. He gave her a scorching glance as she looked over to the other driver and smiled mischievously.

"Damn it, Lyse!"

She laughed and floored the accelerator pedal. The rear-mounted engine whined in protest as the smaller car pulled ahead of the considerably more powerful Lincoln. When they had pulled back into the right lane, Kismet sat up and risked a look through the back window. The Towne Car's headlights were twin spots of brilliance, perhaps a hundred yards behind them. "Don't worry. In a few minutes I'll let them pass us again. They'll never figure it out."

Kismet sighed. It was probably a good plan; he was just irked that she hadn't consulted him first. *Typical Lyse.*

"I hate to bring this up," she continued. "But I came to see you for a reason."

"I know, I know. That fake statue. You'll get it tonight. I promise."

She seemed satisfied with his assurance. "Good enough. Now, finish the story. You got him kicked off the dig. Then what?"

Kismet shrugged. "I lost track of him. It's not like it was some kind of grudge match. Anyway, he's got a new pet project: he just walked into my office claiming to have found an historical link to the legendary Golden Fleece."

"Another fairy tale?"

"Exactly. In fact, the legend of Jason and the Argonauts is just about the original fairy tale."

"I've heard of it."

Kismet nodded. "The legend tells of an adventurer named Jason who was sent on a quest to find the hide of a golden ram."

"Real gold? It was worth a lot then?"

"Maybe. Some versions of the legend ascribe various supernatural powers to the Golden Fleece; control over the elements, healing, and so forth. In the legend, Jason got together a crew of heroes, including Hercules, to sail a ship called the Argo to the land of Colchis. They had the usual adventures along the way, monsters and so forth. When they reached Colchis, Jason tried to negotiate for the Fleece, but ended up stealing it with the help of the king's daughter Medea. She was a priestess of the temple where the Fleece was kept and used her witchcraft to help Jason defeat the Fleece's guardians. They left Colchis with the prize and returned to Jason's homeland, Iolcos, where he eventually became king."

"And they all lived happily ever after?"

"Hardly. Jason divorced Medea and married someone else. Medea murdered Jason's new wife, her own children, and just about everyone else he loved. He died a bitter failure. He was resting in the shadow of the Argo when a loose beam collapsed on him and shattered his skull." Kismet sighed thoughtfully, gazing out at the passing buildings. "It's the sort of ironic end that comes to people who spend their whole lives searching for treasure and glory."

"And the Golden Fleece? Harcourt is looking for it, and you want to beat him to it?"

Kismet looked over with a stern expression. "The Golden Fleece is just a fairy tale."

"Then why are we following him?"

"Because he knows something," replied Kismet gravely. "Something that no one is supposed to know."

3

From their vantage half a city block away, Kismet and Lyse watched as the driver of the Towne Car let his passenger out. Harcourt stood on the wet sidewalk, briefly taking in the architecture of the West Village, and then turned to face the imposing edifice before which they were parked—a nineteenth century Catholic Church. He conferred with the driver for a moment, and then ascended the steps.

"What do you make of that?" Lyse whispered, unnecessarily.

Kismet shook his head. "Let's find out."

The procession through downtown had ended here in the West Village. The wet snow had grudgingly given way to sporadic drizzle, but visibility in the dark twilight remained limited. The street on which they now found themselves was quiet, almost unnaturally so for New York City, with only a few pedestrians braving the unpleasant weather. Kismet absently wondered if everyone had already gone off to celebrate the New Year. The only sign of any real activity was a large canister style garbage truck slowly rolling up the street making late pick-ups, evidently extending service on the eve of the holiday so that the following day might be spent with football games and hangover remedies.

Harcourt's driver returned to the black car and drove off, after which Kismet and Lyse approached the front of the church as inconspicuously as possible. Since Harcourt knew his face, Kismet suggested that Lyse take the lead. If the archaeologist happened to be waiting just inside the doors of the church, she could wave him off.

She took a step back, hands on her hips. "I'm not exactly dressed for church here, Nick."

"Come on, you look great. It's New Year's Eve. Everyone is dressed up. Even the nuns."

She shook her head disparagingly, then hopped up the steps to the heavy wooden doors, and peered into the great hall of the church. "No sign of him. In fact, I don't see anyone."

Kismet nudged her inside, closing the enormous door behind them. The nave was gloomy—more like a crypt than a house of worship. A wall of votive candles flickered nearby, but most were on their last breath. Kismet walked by the votary, pausing at the border of the colonnade to see if the Englishman was secreted in the pews.

The church seemed deserted. All but one of the confessionals stood wide open and vacant. The pews were likewise empty, as was the area around the altar. A corridor, situated behind the altar, led away from the main auditorium and appeared to be the only means of egress available to Harcourt. Kismet took a cautious step out from behind the column.

He crossed the distance to the front of the nave quickly, straining to hear some fragment of a voice, or noise of footsteps, alerting him to the approach of trouble. Nothing. The church was as quiet as a tomb.

"We've missed something," he muttered. "Some other way out of here."

Lyse jerked a thumb in the direction of the confessional. "Maybe he's in there."

"I don't think he's Catholic, so confession?" He shook his head dismissively. Nevertheless, he strode toward the stalls and listened for the Englishman's voice just in case. He heard nothing...nothing at all. He moved nearer to the closed door and pressed his ear to the thin panel.

Lyse cleared her throat. "I'm pretty sure you're not supposed to—"

He stepped back and pulled the door open. Lyse squealed involuntarily as Kismet, to all appearances, violated the sanctity of the confessional. The little booth however was empty. He stepped inside, and began probing the screen that separated the penitent from the confessor until it popped loose, swinging on hinges into the emptiness beyond.

"Bless me father for I have sinned," Kismet remarked, observing his handiwork.

"That ain't very damn funny." Then, as if remembering where she was, Lyse grimaced and, looking heavenward, added: "Oops. Sorry."

Beyond the hinged screen the similarity to an ordinary confessional ended. The confessor's bench had been pushed aside to reveal a three foot square opening in the floor, its trapdoor covering carelessly thrown aside. Kismet climbed through the partition and knelt beside the aperture. A fixed wooden ladder descended into the darkness below. Kismet raised a finger to his lips, signaling his companion to keep silent then stuck his head into the opening.

He could hear voices, muted by the distance. No one seemed to be guarding the base of the ladder, but Kismet felt a growing apprehension. After so many fruitless years of searching, had he finally happened upon the sanctuary of the mysterious group that had become the object of his own epic quest? Somehow, secret passages and hidden vaults seemed a little too cliché for the almost faceless enemy he had pursued for almost two decades. Still, there was only one way to find out. Gathering his courage, he lowered his feet onto the first step and began climbing down.

When he had descended to the point where his entire body was below the opening he paused to look around. The floor was further down than he expected. The room into which he was lowering himself was a vast hall, greater in dimension than the church auditorium above. From floor to ceiling there was easily thirty feet of space, the uppermost third given to a framework of exposed wooden rafters. Three long beams ran the length of the hall, a distance that Kismet had yet to determine, while crossbeams and braces spanned every ten or so feet of its width.

The floor was bare stone, devoid of any chairs or fixtures, but the rough wood and stone of the walls were adorned with tapestries and banners, many bearing heraldic crests from various European monarchies, most of which were no longer in existence.

"Well?" prompted Lyse, her voice a stage whisper.

Kismet looked up through the aperture. "I think there's another old church down here. Or maybe a meeting hall, probably for a Hibernian order."

"A who?"

Kismet shook off the inquiry. "Never mind. If you're coming down, try to keep quiet."

She nodded, then slipped out of her pumps and began her descent. Kismet took another step down; his feet were now level with the rafters. The nearest long beam, the one running down the center, was a little more than three feet away. He reached out to it with his foot, then released his grip on the ladder and transferred his weight onto the outstretched extremity.

The beam was wide enough to stand on, but he nearly lost his balance as he stepped across. Though both feet were planted, he had to flail his arms until regaining his balance. He remained there for a moment, arms outstretched like a tightrope walker.

"You've got to be kidding," whispered Lyse.

"It's not that hard," he lied, grinning. "I'll give you a hand."

"I'll give you a hand," she muttered, balling her right into a fist and shaking it at him. She nevertheless reached out and gripped the ladder with her left hand. With the mid-thigh length cocktail dress eased up just a little higher in order to facilitate movement, she extended her right foot toward the beam. Her short legs had more difficulty bridging the expanse, but she succeeded, only to find herself in a situation more precarious than she had first imagined. An instant later, Kismet's steadying hand wrapped around her wrist.

"Slowly," he admonished. "I'll help you over, but if you move too fast, we'll both fall off."

She nodded. "Here I come."

He began exerting a steady pull on her arm. Lyse eased forward, shifting her weight onto her extended right foot while lifting her left from the ladder step. Only his grip held her back from a thirty-foot drop. As Kismet drew her toward him, he turned on the beam, trying to compensate for the change in his center of gravity. Sensing that success was imminent, Lyse brought her feet together too quickly, causing him to teeter over empty space. Realizing her error, she tried to adjust, pulling him closer. For a moment, it was as if they were engaged in a ritualistic dance high above the ground. After what seemed an eternity of wobbling and flailing, their equilibrium stabilized. Lyse spied a crossbeam two steps away and released her grip on Kismet's hand. She hastened toward the upright post and desperately wrapped her arms around the angled braces which ran from the ceiling to the beam.

"That wasn't so bad, was it?"

She threw him a withering glare. "And just how in the hell are we supposed to get off this thing?"

Kismet ignored her question. "Come on."

He eased along the broad rail, exhibiting more confidence about his footing than he actually felt. The sound of the voices below grew louder. After traversing three of the crossbeams, he could make out the conversation at the distant end of the hall, and realized that he was the subject of the discussion.

"How did he react?"

Harcourt tittered obnoxiously. "I could have knocked him over with a feather."

"The question is, will he help us?" Kismet did not recognize the voice, but heard the unmistakable tone of authority it commanded. He was close enough to see the group, which meant he might be visible to them. Hunkering down behind a crosspiece, he eased out just far enough to spy on the discussion below.

There were eight people gathered at the back end of the hall. Four men, dressed and postured like bodyguards, flanked Harcourt and the man to whom he spoke. Three of them wore generic black suits, the conspicuous bulges of shoulder holsters visible beneath their arms. The fourth was too enormous to wear a jacket, but like the others sported a leather holster that wrapped around his shoulder blades. More than six and a half feet tall, with bulging muscles and the battered features of a veteran brawler, his wild eyes were nearly obscured by the mop of curly hair that fell down over his forehead.

The other two figures in the room were seated in a corner. Kismet could see only their feet, close to the legs of the chairs in which they sat. One was clearly female, with shapely calves extending from the folds of a simple wraparound skirt. From his obscured viewpoint, he could see nothing above the knees, but what he could see of the motionless figures was unsettling.

"I don't know," Harcourt answered. "He seemed very upset at the speculative nature of our mission. Perhaps you will succeed in persuading him, where I failed."

The other man sighed and paced around the area, affording Kismet a chance to glimpse him. He was a tall man, perhaps a hand's breadth taller than Kismet himself. A moat of hair encircled a shiny bald pate and continued down the man's cheeks in a bushy, but well-groomed beard. The fellow was on the portly side, but carried himself with a regal posture apropos of his authoritative voice. Kismet noted that his dark suit was of a style that had peaked in popularity near the beginning of the last decade, suggesting that the bald, bearded man had worn his girth proudly for many years.

"A wasted effort," the man declared. Kismet noted also the soft pronunciation of the consonant 'r', and placed the man in an aristocratic New England background. "I should have gone directly to him myself in the first place. But let us focus our attention elsewhere for the moment."

"I see that you have visitors," Harcourt observed.

"Yes. Allow me to introduce Peter Kerns, formerly Petr Chereneyev, a fugitive from Soviet Russia."

"And the girl?"

"His daughter." The man's answer was off-hand, as if the second prisoner was of little interest to him. He did not offer her name.

Harcourt was silent for a long moment. "Is it necessary for them to be tied up like that?"

"Sir Andrew, I don't think you appreciate the urgency of our situation. I require results, and quickly. I cannot invest my resources in the possibility that Mr. Kerns here will cooperate of his own accord. The measures I have taken will insure that he does."

"Nick," whispered Lyse at Kismet's shoulder. "You said that this guy Harcourt knew something he wasn't supposed to know, right?"

Kismet nodded.

"Was it some kind of government secret?"

Kismet's brow furrowed. "I guess you could say that. Why?"

"That guy down there, the fat one. His name is Halverson Grimes; used to be Admiral Halverson Grimes. He was an aviator during Viet Nam; a bona fide war hero."

Kismet looked down at Grimes. As much as he wanted to believe that he had uncovered the hidden lair of the Prometheus group, there was a more plausible explanation for Harcourt's parting shot. If Grimes' background in the military gave him a high enough security clearance, then conceivably he would have had access to the after action review that had followed Kismet's disastrous mission into Iraq, which included his description of the artifact the defector had shown him. It would have been a simple thing to leak that tidbit of information to Harcourt in order to help him recruit Kismet's assistance. But why did the former Admiral Grimes think that he was essential to the recovery effort? For that matter, why was he interested in something as obscure as an ancient Greek legend?

"You look up hawk in the dictionary and you'll find his picture," continued Lyse. "He pushed hard for pre-emptive military action against Iran and North Korea, and advocated a more aggressive posture toward Russia and China. You remember all the controversy about torture of inmates at Gitmo? Well, Grimes was doing stuff that even the former administration didn't approve of. He finally became too much of an embarrassment and they canned him. I'm not sure what he's been up to since then."

"How do you know all this?" Kismet whispered over his shoulder.

Lyse's face went blank. "Gee, Nick, don't you read the newspapers?"

He shook his head in amazement. "I thought I did," he murmured, then focused his attention on the conversation below.

"My investigators," Grimes was saying, "have traced the sale of the arti-facts back to Mr. Kerns. It seems that before he left his homeland, Kerns—or should I say Chereneyev—was a prominent petroleum engineer, and a good communist. Then, without warning, he emigrated to the United States, changed his name, and sold a number of ancient Greek antiquities for a great deal of money."

"You found it, didn't you?" accused Harcourt.

There was a moment of muffled speech, in which Kismet guessed a pris-oner's gag was being removed. Then, a thickly accented voice replied: "Please, don't hurt us. I'll tell you where to look."

"You'll do more than that Comrade Chereneyev." It was Grimes that spoke, filling his last two words with contempt. "You will direct Sir Andrew to the site where you discovered the artifacts. If you attempt to mislead him, I assure you that the consequences to your daughter will be most grave."

"Yes, I will show you. Only please do not hurt—" He was silenced once more by the gag.

"Chereneyev has already given us a starting point," Grimes continued. "I've seen to your travel arrangements."

The burly guards moved toward the seated captives and loosened the bonds of the male hostage. He was helped to his feet and half-dragged to stand beside Harcourt.

Kismet leaned back. "Harcourt is about to leave. Get back to the car and follow him. I want to know where he's going next."

"Nick, I love you, but I didn't come here to be your errand girl. I need that statue back."

Lyse's whisper was growing louder, and Kismet feared she might attract the attention of the men below. He held a finger to his lips, and then took a deep breath. "I think this is important, Lyse. Do this one thing for me, and then we'll be square. I'll text you the name and location of a safe location. You'll get the statue then."

"I'd better," grumbled Lyse. "What about you?"

"I'm going to get the girl."

Lyse flashed a grin. "Don't let little Nick get you in any trouble."

"You're hilarious."

Her smile slipped, replaced by something more sincere. "Good luck, Nick. And be careful."

"You too, Lyse."

She squeezed his shoulder then turned and deftly darted down the length of the beam. Her touch had triggered an unexpected surge of pleasant memories. Kismet's gaze lingered on her for a long, wistful moment. Shaking his head to clear away the nostalgia, he returned his attention to the scene below.

Harcourt and Grimes continued to converse, discussing details about the impending expedition, without ever revealing the ultimate destination. "I have a few matters to attend to before I can join you," Grimes said, "foremost of which is to persuade Nick Kismet to lend his assistance in our project."

"I still fail to understand why you want Kismet along," Harcourt complained. "He's entirely too skeptical."

"Thank you for your opinion, Sir Andrew," was the caustic reply. "In the future, refrain from offering it until you are asked to do so."

The group began moving down the length of the hall, passing directly beneath Kismet. He threw a backward glance at Lyse but she had already vanished through the opening. Moments later, Grimes and Harcourt, along with a submissive Kerns and the retinue of guards, stopped beneath the ladder.

Kismet could no longer hear their conversation, but saw Grimes gesturing to the gigantic man, directing him and another fellow to return to watch over Kerns' daughter. As the two guards wandered back through the hall, Harcourt and the others commenced ascending the ladder. Kismet quickly walked down the long beam until he reached the last of the crosspieces. He tiptoed across the system of braces and perched directly above where Kerns' daughter sat bound and gagged in a chair. Beside her, the slack ropes that had restrained her father lay upon his now vacant seat.

He could not see much of her, only blonde hair cascading over what appeared to be flawless, pale skin. She did not struggle against her bonds, but it was clear to Kismet that she had not surrendered to the idea of captivity. Her eyes darted warily around the hall, following the movements of the giant and the other guard.

The two men paused, waiting until the last of Grimes' party had exited through the opening above. Kismet also waited, weighing his options and formulating a plan of attack.

"Guess what missy," grunted the smaller of the men below Kismet. "As soon as your daddy gets on that plane, me and Rudy get to have some fun with you."

"Fun," echoed the giant, Rudy. Both men laughed hysterically as if they had reached the very zenith of humor.

Kismet fished a coin from his pocket and hurled it the length of the hall. There was a metallic clink twenty yards away, then a pinging ricochet from a second beam. A moment later it clattered on the stone floor.

"What was that?" asked the smaller guard, who being marginally more intelligent, was evidently in charge. "Go check it out, Rudy."

Rudy grunted an affirmative and stalked off to investigate, while the other fellow assumed a defensive stance behind Miss Kerns. Kismet waited until Rudy's footsteps were barely audible, and then cautiously lowered himself from the beam. His grip tightened instinctively as more and more of his body hung out into open space, but he pushed back his primal trepidation, took a deep breath, and let go. A fraction of a second later, he landed directly on the smaller of the woman's tormentors.

His feet struck the man between the shoulder blades, instantly slamming him to the floor, but Kismet lost his balance in the process and went sprawling. His attempt to stay upright succeeded only in his twisting an ankle before he slammed into the stone floor. The guard however had borne the brunt of the impact, and now lay supine alongside Miss Kerns, clutching his chest and unable to catch his breath. Kismet ignored the pain in his foot and pounced, striking the stunned guard at the pressure point behind his ear. Two such blows rendered the man unconscious. The commotion however had not gone unnoticed.

"Frank?" Rudy called, turning around. "Where are you, Frank?"

Kismet ducked behind the bound captive, but could do nothing to hide the slumped form from Rudy's view. He could hear the giant's steps growing louder and as the big man drew near, Kismet crawled around to the other side of the hostage, keeping her between himself and Rudy. In the dim light, the giant never saw him, but Kerns' daughter did, and Kismet got his first good look at her. Her beauty caught him off guard.

Her features were classically Russian: broad cheekbones framing a triangular face, marred only by a strip of silver tape that covered her mouth. Her eyes were liquid black, almost haunting against her delicate white skin. He risked a quick smile before reaching out to take hold of the empty chair beside her.

Rudy was standing over his unmoving companion. "Get up Frank. Quit screwing around."

Kismet quietly stood up, lifting the sturdy chair over his head. Rising onto his toes, he brought the chair down on Rudy's cranium with such force that the wooden seat shattered and drove the big man to his knees. Kismet triumphantly tossed aside the fragments of his makeshift bludgeon, but in the corner of his eye he saw the giant climbing to his feet. Rudy turned slowly, breathing heavily like an enraged bull. Incredulous, Kismet found himself staring, first at Rudy's sternum, which was at eye level, then up into a pair of crimson-rimmed eyes. The giant's fingers were flexing, curling into fists that resembled sledgehammers.

"That could have gone better," muttered Kismet, glancing around for some other weapon to use against the moving mountain that now advanced on him. There was nothing, certainly nothing that could make a dent in such a formidable adversary. With a grim expression Kismet raised his own fists, aware of how pathetic his defense must have seemed to the other man.

Rudy glanced at Kismet's fists, laughing. Nevertheless, the big man appeared wary, refusing to let his own overwhelming size lead him into the trap of overconfidence. If Rudy was in most ways mentally deficient, in matters of combat he excelled. Fortunately for Kismet, he failed to see what his foe was really up to. Following the lead of Kismet's fists, Rudy edged closer.

Kismet feinted, and as Rudy moved to block the punch, Kismet kicked him hard in the crotch.

The giant grunted but shook off the effects of the kick. Kismet on the other hand felt a stab of pain in his injured ankle and hopped back a step, shaking his head. "Why doesn't that surprise me?"

Rudy was in agony, but pain affected him differently than most men; it was like fuel in the engine of his fighting machine. Intent upon dismembering his opponent, he took a step closer but suddenly pitched forward. Surprised, Kismet watched him plummet like a felled tree. As Rudy had passed the bound girl in the chair, ignoring her as she posed no immediate threat, she had stuck her foot out, snaring his ankle to trip him up. Kismet pounced on the giant's back, raining blows with fists and elbows at the base of Rudy's neck.

He knew, even as he struck, that his strength was insufficient to overpower the giant. He could feel Rudy's muscles bunching beneath him, building up like a volcano for a titanic eruption of destructive power. Rudy roared to life, pitching his assailant aside like a rag doll. Kismet rolled away and came to rest against Frank's motionless form.

Rudy rose to his full height a second time, casting a scornful glance at the woman who had felled him. With palpable disdain he lashed a foot against the leg of her chair, causing it to tip. Unable to catch herself, she fell backward, and the chair hit the stone floor with a sickening crack.

Kismet thrust his hand into Frank's jacket, and then turned to face Rudy. The giant stopped the instant he found himself staring into the barrel of a Smith & Wesson .44 Special revolver. Kismet thumbed the action back and jammed the weapon into the Rudy's chest.

"Tougher than her, but are you tougher than this?" Kismet snarled, surprised at his own ferocity. The brutal attack on the helpless girl had ignited his fury. "Down on the floor, hands behind your head."

The glowering behemoth grudgingly complied, sinking first to his knees then lying flat on the stone surface. Kismet kept the pistol ready for use, fully intending to shoot upon the slightest sign of aggression.

He transferred the gun to his left hand and slipped the Benchmade from his pocket, flipping it open one-handed. The blade easily sliced through the knots that held the girl fast. She flexed her fingers to restore circulation then ripped the tape strip from her lips with an unrestrained curse. "*Dermo!*"

"Are you hurt?" Kismet asked in Russian, his eyes never leaving Rudy.

"*Nyet*," she replied.

"*Will you take the gun so that I may bind this man?*"

She nodded, extending an open palm.

"*Are you able to shoot to kill if necessary?*" pressed Kismet, not quite ready to surrender the weapon.

"*I might shoot this dog even if it is not necessary,*" she snapped, directing her venom toward the prone giant.

Kismet found her rage reassuring. "*Please do not shoot unless you must. The sound might raise the alarm and bring his companions.*"

"*I would like to shoot them also, but there are not enough bullets. Do not worry. I will not shoot unless he moves.*"

That was good enough for Kismet. He passed the revolver over to the young woman then knelt beside Rudy. He stripped the giant of his sidearm and slid it toward the girl. He then indelicately grabbed Rudy's wrists and shackled them with the ropes that had bound Peter Kerns only minutes before. Kismet pulled the knots hard enough to cause the giant to wince. He resisted an impulse to kick Rudy, choosing instead to properly greet his new companion.

He found himself staring into the muzzle of the gun. He frowned, wondering if this was her idea of a joke. "*That is not a wise thing to do. Please lower the gun.*"

"*I don't know if you are Mafiya or FSB—I do not really care. But I will not permit you to hold me captive any more than I would surrender myself again to these men.*"

"*You don't understand,*" replied Kismet. "*I am not either. My name is Nick Kismet. I am trying to help you.*"

"Kismet?" Comprehension dawned in her eyes and she smiled wryly, switching fluidly into English with only a hint of accent. "An unusual name. Doesn't that mean something?"

Kismet raised an eyebrow then broke into laughter. "Yes, it does. I wish I had known you spoke English."

"You weren't doing so badly in Russian." She lowered the gun and offered it to him. "Irina. But I've always gone by Irene; Irene Kerns."

Kismet took the revolver and eased the action down. "A pleasure to meet you, Irine. Now, I suggest we get out of here while we still can."

He glanced around, noticing for the first time an enormous tapestry that dominated the end of the hall. The tapestry was weighted at the bottom, hanging all the way to the floor, and its ornate center rippled and pulsated, as though the wall was a living creature. The coat of arms emblazoned there— a white shield quartered by a rough black cross—was oddly familiar, and after a brief scrutiny he remembered that he had seen it in a book detailing an incident of Vatican complicity with Nazi Germany; it was the crest of the Teutonic Knights.

"And should I call you Mr. Kismet?" Irene intoned.

He took her hand and led her back toward the ladder. "Nick is fine."

Despite his outward confidence, he felt a sudden sense of foreboding creeping over him, and he unconsciously tightened his grip on the revolver. Everything that had happened from the moment Harcourt walked into his office pointed to a larger conspiracy. The tapestry seemed like yet another link in a diabolical chain. Perhaps he had been too quick to dismiss the possibility that his old nemeses had returned; perhaps the Prometheus reference all those years ago, had been a smokescreen to divert his attention from this, a reportedly defunct feudal brotherhood with ties to Germany. He was beginning to get the feeling that he was in over his head, and wondered for the first time if Lyse had gotten away safely. Approaching the ladder, he peered upwards. The dark aperture above revealed nothing. He jammed the revolver into his belt. "Wait here."

He ascended quickly, realizing only when he was near the top that the trapdoor had been lowered into place. He kept climbing until his shoulders were against the barrier, then levered his legs to lift it out of the way. Before he could raise it however, he felt the ladder tremble faintly; Irine had begun climbing beneath him. He groaned at her impatience and resumed pushing against the trapdoor. It was heavier than he expected, but when he tried again, it abruptly flew open. The solid planks slammed against the floor of the confessional with a bang that made him wince, but there was nothing he could do about it. He advanced another step up the ladder, poking his head out.

Halverson Grimes stood in front of the opening. Behind him, outside the confines of the confessional, were half a dozen men, uniformly dressed in black suits.

"Oh." Kismet didn't know what else to say. He looked down, his own body blocking his view of Irene. "Get off!" he hissed.

"What?" Oblivious to the threat above, she took another step up.

"Unless I'm mistaken," Grimes observed pontifically, "you must be Nick Kismet. A pleasure, sir. We need to talk." Two of Grimes' men pushed past their leader, assuming defensive postures on either side of the hole.

"Indeed, Mr. Kismet. There is great deal to discuss."

Kismet leaned back a few inches and looked down. Irene's face was visible in the space between his legs. She was peering up at him, still unaware that their escape was in jeopardy. His brain went into overdrive. If they could not go out the way they had come in, what options remained? He contemplated using the captured revolver preemptively, but promptly dismissed that idea. Hanging from a ladder thirty feet up, shooting through a narrow hole in the floor was not his idea of a defensible position. Better, he decided, to get both feet on solid ground.

"Irene," he whispered again. "Get off the ladder."

"What?"

He knew that she had heard him. Her question was not a request to repeat himself, but to elucidate. Kismet growled in irritation. He didn't have time to stop and explain every move to her.

"Please come out of that hole, Mr. Kismet," urged Grimes. "I assure you, you have nothing to fear from me." Then, with a smile that was not as benign as he perhaps intended, he added: "If you cooperate."

"As much as I'd love to stay and chat..." Kismet replied disingenuously. He looked down one final time. With cautious, deliberate movements, he slipped his left foot off the rung, bracing the arch of his shoe against the outside of the ladder. Increasing the tenacity of his handhold, he then lifted his right foot and positioned it similarly. "Coming down," he whispered.

Understanding dawned in Irene's eyes. She quickly scampered toward the floor. Kismet returned his gaze to the menacing group of faces that was drawing ever closer, Halverson Grimes chief among them.

"As I was saying," he remarked, "I've already made plans for the evening. Perhaps we could get together for lunch sometime."

In the instant that Grimes registered a puzzled expression, Kismet released his hold, gripping the outside rails of the ladder loosely with both hands and feet.

Gravity seized hold of him and he plummeted. Immediately, he collided with something—Irene Kerns—and his carefully guided descent went askew as they both dropped to the floor in a painful tangle of limbs.

Grimes' voice was audible above them, ordering his cronies to go down and subdue the escapees. Kismet experienced a moment of déjà vu, flashing back to the sewers of Marrakech. The difference this time, aside from the lack of an unpleasant odor, was that the bad guys had a ladder to climb down. He scrambled to his feet determined to remove that liability.

The opening above grew dark as a descending body eclipsed the aperture. Kismet briefly considered shooting the man right there, but quickly realized the flaw in such a strategy; if the confrontation became a shooting match, Grimes' men and their ammunition would certainly hold out longer than he and his. Instead of dealing with the man, Kismet chose to deal with the ladder.

Dropping into a low stance, his shoulder leading, Kismet rammed the ladder like a charging football linebacker. His shoulder hit the sturdy wooden frame and he bounced back, spilling onto the floor. A flash of pain was followed by a numbed paralysis, but he judged the maneuver to be a partial success. The ladder shook violently with the blow, and the man who was climbing down, now clutched desperately to regain a secure handhold. Kismet got up, lowered his other shoulder to the ladder and charged again.

The right rail of the ladder split nearly in two as Kismet struck it. The descending man now gave up any thought of continuing, choosing instead to regain the safety and stability of the floor above.

Kismet did not charge a third time, but instead seized hold of the bottom rung and wrenched it from side to side. The damage he had already caused to the ladder was quickly aggravated and the rails broke apart near the top where they had been bolted into the underside of the floorboards. With a satisfied grin, Kismet stepped back as the elongated structure tilted sideways and fell over, splintering when it crashed on the stone floor.

The noise of an explosion, like a car backfiring, roared in his ears and reverberated in the confines of the underground room. A bullet kicked up a small puff of dust, just behind him and left a tiny pockmark in the stone floor.

"Damn," he exclaimed, darting away from the remains of the ladder. Irene was already up and moving, seeking cover from the gunfire, which was quickly becoming a hailstorm of bullets. Kismet reached her side and seized her hand, then guided her toward the place where she had earlier been held captive.

They quickly passed out of the broad, cone shaped area where they were in the most danger of being wounded, but Kismet knew that the seconds he had gained by destroying the ladder would be lost by any delay on their part. With his free hand he took out and opened his knife.

"How are we going to get out of here?" Irene asked frantically.

"Back door," muttered Kismet, releasing her hand and sprinting ahead. He was dimly aware that she had stopped running, but he did not slow down. Instead he aimed himself at the wall, focusing on the heart of the enormous tapestry mounted there. The center of the woven shield was like a bull's eye on a target and the blade in his hand was an arrow intent upon piercing it. As he got closer, he raised his arm and brought it down, slashing at the fabric of the great tapestry. The knife cut a long gash in the old cloth before entangling in the fibers. Kismet's momentum caused him to fall forward, into the middle of the ornamental weaving, where he hung momentarily like a fly in a web. As he moved to extricate himself, his weight broke apart the remaining threads, and the tapestry tore in two all the way to the floor, dropping him into the darkness beyond.

Irene approached and looked at him in stunned amazement. Kismet's gambit had revealed a secret passageway. "How did you know about that?"

He got up, wincing from pains old and new. "A guess. Earlier I saw that the fabric was moving, almost like it was being rustled by the wind. I assumed that the tapestry was put up to cover an opening."

"If you had been wrong, you would have run into a brick wall."

Kismet knelt and retrieved his Balisong from the twisted remnant of the tapestry and flicked it shut. "Good thing I wasn't."

"And this will lead us out of here?"

The sound of a shot rang suddenly in the underground chamber, impacting the wall that framed their escape route. The shot had been fired from ground level; Grimes' men had found a way down. Kismet didn't look back.

"It had better," he shouted over the din. "Get going."

"You can't be right every time," retorted Irene.

"Can we discuss this later?" He pushed her into the dark tunnel then turned to face the unseen shooters, his revolver drawn. He pumped three shots randomly into the gloom behind them, hoping not so much to find a target as to give the pursuers one more reason to hesitate. Saving the remainder of the ammunition for future encounters, Kismet shoved the smoking gun into the pocket of his suit coat, turned and plunged into the mysterious opening.

The air in the passage was cool and slightly musty, but it did not have the stale quality of a tomb or crypt, leading Kismet to deduce that there was another means of access and that it was used at least once in a while. His greatest fear was that Grimes might also know about this passage and would already be sending his men to cover the exit. There would be no allowance for delays, wrong turns or dead ends. He kept an outstretched hand in contact with the wall, a blind man's guide through the artificial night. The tunnel was short and quickly opened into a much larger room.

Irene spoke from out of the darkness. "I've run into something. It's a box of some kind."

"Probably a coffin," remarked Kismet, trying to estimate where she was in relation to himself. "Old churches like this usually have catacombs where prominent clergymen are interred. Try to follow the sound of my voice. I think I'm just a few steps away from you...right behind you."

"A coffin?" was the distasteful reply. She was moving, getting closer.

He didn't elaborate; he had been half-joking, but it was as good an explanation as any. Reaching out, he began groping in an arc all around until his fingers grazed something soft. "Don't move."

He eased away from the wall long enough to touch her. His fingers barely caressed her hair, but starting from that point he was able to find her shoulder, and then take her hand. "If we follow the wall, we should be able to move around the perimeter of the room and find another passageway."

Their haste to escape led to more than one minor collision; although it took only about a minute for them to grope along the wall and find a way out of the vault, the irregularities of the room and the arrangement of invisible impediments proved to be a precarious obstacle course. Kismet barked his shins twice, and caught the corner of a protruding piece of stonework squarely in his chest. Notwithstanding this, they reached the opposite side of the room and found a recess that led to a flight of worn stone steps. The treads were irregular, forcing them to proceed slowly. At the top of the stairs a thin strip of light was visible, burning through the space between the threshold and the bottom of an unseen door. Kismet explored the door with his fingertips and located an archaic slide latch that could be worked from either side of the door. "Thank goodness for that," he whispered, and worked the bolt. With the revolver poised, he pushed the door open.

The light beyond was by no means brilliant, but even its dim glory was more than their eyes were used to. Squinting and shading his gaze with a cupped hand, Kismet scanned the area for any movement. Seeing none, he took the last step out of the underground chamber.

The room into which they entered was a pantry, lined with several shelves of canned food. A single electric light bulb hung from the ceiling. Kismet pulled Irene out of the dark stairway and closed the door behind them. It was a sure bet that at least some of Grimes' men were pursuing them through the darkened passage, but Kismet saw an opportunity to cut off that pursuit.

After guiding Irene out of the way, he insinuated his fingers into the space between the wall of the pantry and the upright shelves. The shelf unit was heavy, built of sturdy hardwoods, likely a century before by a craftsman who knew his business. Fortunately, the carpenter had not integrated the shelves into the wall, but left them standing free. Sensing his purpose, Irene offered her assistance to Kismet's endeavor.

He felt his muscles growing fatigued before the shelves moved even a millimeter. Yet, as the cabinet began to tilt, its own weight began to work for them. With a loud grunt, he redoubled his efforts and kept pushing until it went over. Jars of preserved fruits and vegetables exploded on the pantry floor, only to be buried by the cabinet as it fell on top of the debris. The shelves fell directly in the path of the door through which they had escaped. Kismet reckoned that it would be impossible to open the door more than a couple inches. "That ought to slow them down," he observed. "But my guess is that some of Grimes' men stayed topside. We have to keep moving."

From beyond the pantry, they heard sounds of shouting. Kismet concluded that their foes had not initially been aware of the alternate exit from the underground chamber, or were at least in the dark as to where it came out. The priests and nuns who resided at the church however, doubtless unaware of the mob's murderous intentions, would almost certainly be able to give them the details. Kismet opened the pantry door and looked out. The hallway beyond was deserted. Two other doors opened off the corridor, and a third doorway was framed at the far end, presumably the exit. Kismet realized intuitively that they were no longer in the main church building, but in a satellite structure.

The door at the end of the hallway opened into a large kitchen facility, already washed for the evening and put in order for the next day. He moved through the cooking area and peered carefully through the windowpane in the exit door. A large, indistinct object obscured the landscape outside, blocking the dim light of the street lamps as well as Kismet's view of the church courtyard. Fortunately, it would also give them cover for their escape. He opened the door and together they ventured outside.

The object eclipsing the street was the sanitation truck Kismet and Lyse had passed during their initial approach. The vehicle stood at idle, the extended lifting forks slotted into the channels on either end of a medium-sized garbage dumpster. The truck's operator, a pot-bellied fellow with an unlit cigar clamped between his teeth, was standing near the rear of the vehicle seemingly oblivious to the smell. The middle-aged priest with whom he was animatedly conversing did not appear to have the same immunity to the stench, but like the driver was captivated by the commotion that was blossoming around them as black suited men poured out of the main church building and spread out across the grounds.

As Kismet watched his mind turned with possibilities. Then it dawned on him what good fortune had provided for them. Grinning, he faced Irene, put a finger to his lips, and then led the way toward the truck's cab. He opened the passenger door, wincing as the hinges creaked, and climbed inside.

Apparently, the noise had not been loud enough to raise an alarm. The driver's shoulder was just visible in the large mirror mounted on the left door, and it seemed he had not heard the sound over the idling engine.

When Irene was seated beside him, Kismet depressed the clutch and shifted the transmission into gear. There was an audible clanking sound in the differential and an instant later, the driver's face appeared in the mirror. The man's expression was one of confusion and disbelief, which gave way to anger as he realized someone was stealing his truck. Kismet hit the lock with his elbow, and then punched the accelerator. The garbage-man jumped onto the running board and made a vain attempt to open the door while shouting rare curses known only to truck drivers and longshoremen. The enormous machine lurched forward and commenced a broad turn under Kismet's guiding hands that spilled the enraged man from his perch.

Unfortunately, the screams of wrath drew the attention of Grimes' men, who raced to intercept the commandeered vehicle. Kismet checked to be sure that the fallen man was clear of the truck's massive tires, then accelerated, working through the gears as he steered the truck toward the open gates of the church compound. Several of their pursuers were visible behind him, but none were in a position to blockade the exit.

The truck shot out into the street, and Kismet whipped the steering wheel hard to the right. Irene slid across the seat, colliding with him as she fought to get a handhold on her own side. The back end of the truck fishtailed and Kismet fought to regain control, slamming into parked cars, and causing two pedestrians to drop their parcels and dive for safety. He wrestled the steering wheel back and bore down on the accelerator once more. The forward movement pulled the truck out of its thrashing and at last, control was restored.

Despite her earlier terror, Irene now seemed almost to be enjoying the wild ride. Kismet flashed her a grin, then saw in the side view mirror Grimes' thugs pouring into the street and crossing over to the cars his exit had damaged.

"I don't think we're in the clear yet."

Irene craned her head around to look, but the mirror on her side had been knocked askew during their escape. She began rolling down her window, but Kismet forestalled her with a restraining hand and a shake of his head. She frowned in mock disappointment. "So what now?"

"I'll try to lose them. Outrun them or something. This truck sticks out like a sore thumb." He glanced in the mirror, noting the caravan of Buick Skylark sedans that was closing the distance between them. "Better keep your head down in case they start shooting."

Though he lived in New York and walked its streets often, Kismet neither owned a car nor had occasion to drive around the city. He knew approximately where he was, but lacked the familiarity needed to elude the ruthless men pursuing them. He was going to have to equalize the situation; it was time to slow them down.

The street they were on eventually began crossing the main avenues, and Kismet swung the behemoth onto the first one that afforded easy access, driving north through the heart of Greenwich Village. Traffic was light, but this advantage did not compensate for the truck's lack of maneuverability.

Rather than dodge in and out of the flow, he picked the center lane and stayed there, shifting the truck into a higher gear and flooring the accelerator. Cars in his lane hastened to flee before the imposing juggernaut that rolled unstoppably through red lights while blasting its horn like a herald of doom.

Even in this, Kismet realized, they were gaining nothing. The traffic that parted grudgingly to allow them past left a wide-open trail for their pursuers to follow. In the mirror he could see the train of lights racing toward them, and several blocks behind them, the flashing beacons of a police car that had joined the chase.

One of the sedans disappeared into Kismet's blind spot, but before he could act on his sudden inspiration to hit the brakes, forcing a collision, the car reappeared in his mirror, sidling alongside the truck's left flank. A dark silhouette leaned out the passenger side, carefully aiming a pistol up at Kismet.

"Fool," Kismet rasped to no one in particular. If the gunman shot him, the truck would veer out of control, probably killing the inhabitants of the sedan as well as countless innocent pedestrians. Either the man with the gun was too dense to realize that, or too callous to care. With a shake of his head, Kismet took a preemptive measure.

Jerking the steering wheel to the left he crossed several feet into the path of the Buick. The other driver reacted without thinking, braking and swerving reflexively away from the truck. His impulsive response proved disastrous. The sedan slammed into a parked car, jackknifing both vehicles, then plowed onto the sidewalk, stopping only when its front end wrapped around a sturdy light pole. The man with the pistol was catapulted from his window perch, and Kismet caught a brief glimpse of his body rolling like a tumbleweed, into the path of the other pursuing vehicles.

In the mirror he saw the aftermath of the encounter. The array of headlights broke apart, losing symmetry as the various cars swerved to avoid the fallen man, or stopped to render assistance. The maneuver had yielded a few seconds of lead-time—no great margin to be sure, but enough to begin formulating his next move.

"Irene, do you drive?"

"Of course..." She looked at his face, then at the elaborate system of controls on the dashboard. "Oh, you're not serious."

"It's easier than it looks," he lied. "Come on. Slide over here and do exactly as I tell you."

She hesitated, then reached out to him and let herself be pulled close. He liked the feeling of her body pressed against his, and had to force himself to shake off the distracting sensation. "It's simple. It drives just like a car. You don't need to crank the wheel very far to get results. It will resist if you aren't going fast enough, but if you're going too fast you'll roll it over."

"I'm going to have to turn this thing?" she groaned.

"Yes, but if everything goes as planned, you'll only have to do it once."

"And where will you be?"

"I'm going to try to slow them down." He quickly described the foot pedals and gave her a rough idea of how to downshift. "Think you can do it?"

"No," she replied in all sincerity.

"Sure you can." Before moving out from behind the wheel, he located the control box for the lift mechanism and experimentally pushed one of the green buttons. The hydraulic lift lurched, sending a vibration through the body of the truck, and the dumpster rose up, briefly blocking their view as it passed in front of the windshield. There was a deep rumble behind them as the contents of the bin emptied into the large holding canister. Kismet released the button, leaving the lift in the fully elevated position.

"That should do the trick. Okay, your turn." He unlocked the door and worked the lever, careful not to let it fly open. With his other hand he kept the steering wheel steady and scooted to the extreme edge of the bench seat. His right foot was stretched as far as he dared to keep the accelerator depressed.

"Grab the wheel," he instructed. "Get ready to put your foot on the pedal. Now!"

He slid out of the way and she did exactly as told, muttering pessimistically in Russian. Kismet retained his hold on the wheel, but was now standing outside the truck, on the running board. He felt an immediate decrease in power. "Push down a little harder!" he yelled over the sound of road and engine noise. She did, and the speedometer needle registered the acceleration.

"You're doing great!"

"When do I turn?"

"I'll tell you when," he replied. Irene's confidence was already starting to overshadow her inexperience and Kismet felt certain that she was capable of executing his plan. "Okay, you're on your own!"

He eased away from the door, slamming it closed when he was out of the way. Utilizing the door handle and the extended mirror frame like ladder steps, he ascended to the roof of the cab, staying close against the side of the truck in case one of the Grimes' men thought he made a nice target. Once atop the cab, he was blasted by the wind of their passage through the streets. He risked raising his head just high enough to look over the inverted dumpster at the thoroughfare behind them, and saw two sets of headlights racing toward the truck, with a third, the police car, not far behind.

He had been fortunate that the controls for the hydraulic lift were fairly intuitive; the next part of his strategy would require only brute strength. Keeping his arms spread wide for stability, he braced his back against the roof of the cab, extended his feet against the side of the dumpster and began pushing.

The mechanism of the lift was designed to raise the load evenly until, at the last moment, it would be turned almost completely upside down, allowing the refuse inside to fall into the cavernous interior of the garbage truck. Kismet now saw that the lifting forks were not parallel to ground as he had hoped, but angled upward to prevent the dumpster from sliding off—which, unfortunately, was exactly what Kismet wanted it to do.

Nevertheless, the heavy container grudgingly yielded to the insistent pressure from his straining thigh muscles and began to slide. As it crept up the length of the rails the resistance steadily decreased, and at the halfway point, gravity became his ally. The brown dumpster tilted and began to slide independent of his efforts. A moment later, it crashed noisily along the back of the truck before banging down onto the pavement.

Irene was maintaining a good speed and a straight course, using the horn as she entered and crossed intersections under solid red lights. New York drivers answered with angry gestures and blasts from their own horns, but did not attempt to assert their legal right of way. Kismet knew she was going to have to make a turn at one of those intersections, and quickly, so as not to lose any advantage he might have gained with the dumpster maneuver. He cautiously rose to a crouch, peering over the end of the truck to see if his ploy had achieved the intended results. The container had stopped bouncing and now rested on its back, straddling the broken white line in the center of the avenue. The pursuing vehicles had been forced to take evasive action, but were quickly recovering and again closing the gap. It was time to take the next step.

Before he could move from his perch, another intersection flashed by—the perfect opportunity, but already lost. Sliding cautiously toward the right side of the cab, Kismet lowered himself onto the running board. Before he could open his mouth to speak however, something cracked against the outer wall of the refuse canister, pinging away in a flash of sparks. Someone was shooting at him. He pressed himself tight against the door.

"Irene!"

"Now?" Her voice was barely audible.

"No! Take the next right! Got it?"

There was a brief silence and Kismet repeated himself, and then heard her shout an affirmative. He risked a forward glance, marking the distance to the next traffic signal, and then turned his attention to the next part of his plan.

When they had first commandeered the truck, Kismet had spied the mobile control box hanging from a bracket just behind the passenger door. He had suspected its purpose even then, filing the information away without really knowing why. Now he knew. He took a moment to study the switches so there would be no surprises.

The engine revved loudly as Irene depressed the clutch prematurely, her other foot still holding the accelerator. Kismet looked forward again, realizing that she had misunderstood his instructions and was turning down a narrow alley instead of waiting for the next major intersection. The mechanical whine subsided after a moment and Kismet felt the truck slowing as she braked. He mentally commended her for not panicking and more or less getting it right, but his relief turned sour in the next instant.

Irene tried to steer and shift at the same time, and failed to do either very well. The truck angled toward two o'clock, not enough to make the right hand turn, and continued to lose speed. Gears shrieked in metallic agony as the clutch engaged, and then the truck stopped dead. A moment later it lurched forward again, throwing Kismet against its side and nearly dislodging him from his foothold. Only a fierce grip on the frame of the side mirror kept him from spilling into the street.

As the truck began to move again with painful slowness, Irene threw her strength into the labor of turning the steering wheel. The vehicle grudgingly complied and crept into the narrow side street.

Kismet turned back to the avenue behind them. The first of the chasing cars screeched into view. It lost some traction as the driver attempted the turn too fast, but he knew what he was doing and corrected, regaining control without sacrificing any speed. Kismet knew he had to act immediately or his efforts would be for nothing. He pushed the button.

Twin hydraulic cylinders lifted the hatch covering the back end of the refuse canister, exposing its cavernous interior. Kismet's fingers danced toward a different switch, activating a much larger device.

The front end of the enormous tank-like structure began swinging up and immediately the contents of the container were vomited into the alley. A number of plastic garbage bags burst on impact with the street, spewing a foul-smelling mixture of food refuse and other debris into the path of the oncoming vehicle.

The driver of the Buick evidently failed to appreciate what this would mean in terms of road surface. Undaunted, he aimed the car into the heart of the growing obstacle and sped forward. The front bumper plowed into the mound of trash, but then the tires lost traction and the car skidded haphazardly across the narrow street. The sedan's rear end crashed into the wall of a six story apartment building, leaving a trail of sparks as metal scoured brick, before it came to a halt, effectively blocking the street. A second car screeched into the alley, and its driver hit the brakes too late to avoid plowing into the first sedan and disabling both vehicles.

Kismet's triumphant grin lasted only a second. Irene suddenly stomped the brake and the garbage truck's wheels locked. This time he was caught unprepared and was thrown forward, landing on his shoulder and rolling several yards down the street. The fabric of his suit jacket afforded some protection but was nearly shredded by the rough asphalt.

"Damn it, Irene," he rasped, struggling to his feet. "What the hell—?"

As he looked down the alley he saw why she had stopped. Illuminated in the beams of the truck's headlights, behind a fence of blue and white wooden barricades, was a mountain of steaming rubble. A glance to the sidewalk revealed that one of the structures had recently burned and been gutted. Furniture, appliances and other large pieces of debris had been dragged into the street, where they now effectively blocked the way.

Kismet sagged in defeat. Irene's head popped out of the open door of the cab, her face desperate for an answer to the question she framed. "What now?"

Behind them the doors of the wrecked sedans flew open, disgorging seven armed men eager to finish the pursuit on foot. They were less than half a block away.

"Looks like you were right," Kismet muttered, turning to his companion. "I can't be right every time, and I'd say my luck just ran out."

5

The first of Grimes' men to attempt the mountain of garbage found the obstacle more daunting than he had anticipated. After only a few steps, he lost his footing and vanished into the heap. Seeing this, his comrades approached the slippery mass with more caution, but they too had difficulty crossing. Kismet could hear them shouting to one another that the best course lay in trying to go around the perimeter of the spill. Time was running out.

"You've brought us this far," Irene urged. "Don't give up now."

He darted toward the driver's side door of the truck and snared Irene's wrist, pulling her without explanation from behind the wheel. "Right. We're not dead yet."

Despite his assurance, he had not yet settled on his next course of action; he only knew that they had to keep moving. He glanced at the heap of rubble, then at the street around them. Just ahead was the shell of the building that had been ravaged by flames. Its windows were boarded over and smoke stains were visible on the brick of the upper three stories. The skeletal remains of a fire escape hung mockingly above the entrance. Because the edifice shared walls with adjoining buildings, the fire damage had spread out, blackening the exteriors of the neighboring apartments. The damage appeared extensive enough that the structure was almost certainly vacant. As he took stock of his surroundings, the thread of a plan materialized. With Irene's hand locked in his own, he charged toward the steps.

"Where are we going?"

"I wish you hadn't asked that," he muttered. Then, more loudly as if to reassure her, he added: "I've got an idea."

A voice from behind them commanded that they halt. The order was punctuated by the crack of a gunshot. The bullet, perhaps intentionally aimed high as a warning, smacked into the wall overhead, spraying chips of brick and mortar. Kismet steered toward the front porch of the burned out building and bounded onto it in a single leap. Irene slipped as she tried to keep up, landing painfully on her knee, but nothing more than a grunt of discomfort escaped her lips. Through what must have been a monumental display of self-restraint, she did not ply him for the details of his obviously desperate bid for survival.

Four slats of wood blockaded the doorway—a poor substitute for the heavy wooden door that had been hacked apart with a fire-axe and now lay in fragments on the front porch of the building. Kismet did not even slow down as he crossed beneath the lintel, smashing the thin boards apart as if they were strips of paper. The first floor landing was slick with water and debris. He navigated toward the stairs, slowing down just enough to keep Irene half a step behind him.

"Hold on to the rail!" he shouted.

She slipped, landing again on the same knee, but nodded in agreement even as she muttered frustrated curses. The stairs, at least two-dozen steps to the next landing, were structurally sound, but bore the irreversible side effects of the tragedy that had befallen the whole building. The carpet adorning them was swollen and mildewed from the deluge of water that had been used to battle the flames, and the bare wooden banister was coated with slimy, wet ash. As they reached the top of the staircase, their gun-toting adversaries were exactly one flight behind them.

Kismet did not hesitate or look back. He used the railing to launch himself around the turn onto the second floor landing, and held on to it as he ran along the flat balcony to the next flight of stairs. Bullets erupted through the floor, splintering the landing. The shots had no lethal effect, but did trigger a surge of adrenaline in both Kismet and Irene, and subsequently a burst of speed. They gained the third floor before the first of their foes had rounded the bend of the second. Kismet could hear more gunshots, loud in the confines of the stairway, but saw no evidence that the shots had penetrated the walls or steps to endanger them.

The third story appeared to have been the birthplace of the fire that had devastated the building. The walls, which had partitioned several different small residences were gone; only a few blackened and fragile upright posts remained. Beyond those charred timbers was a scene of total destruction; nothing recognizable remained. For the first time since entering the building, Kismet wondered if anyone had perished in the fire. It was a passing thought, and one he did not dwell on as he charged ahead; he was focused intently upon reaching the base of the next staircase. His single-mindedness nearly proved fatal.

Six feet from the end of the landing, his left foot came down, and then went right on through the floor. His weight crumbled the burned wood, and after his leg broke through, the rest of him quickly followed. As his torso went forward, smashing the hole even wider, he flung his hand out to the balustrade. His right leg slipped through the opening, and he found himself dangling over the second story balcony.

Irene knelt at his side, eager to render him whatever assistance she could. The boards beneath seemed soft, almost insubstantial, and suddenly she realized that they had run from one danger, namely the pursuing gunmen, headlong into a potentially greater threat. Now, as Kismet had earlier realized, even a single mistake might prove disastrous.

In his tightening grip, Kismet realized that the fiery kiss of the conflagration had touched the wood of the banister railing to which he clung. Though not completely destroying its integrity, the flames had severely compromised it, and he was certain that it would break apart at any second, delivering him to the waiting arms of the gunmen below. A downward glance revealed that two of the men, realizing that their quarry had run into a dead end, were waiting beneath him. The rest of the gang was doubtless close on their heels.

Irene waved her hand in front of his face. "Take it," she urged.

Kismet pushed it away with his free hand, and winked at her. "Be right back."

He let go of the railing and dropped to the second story landing. The two men standing there had been anticipating his fall, but he landed purposefully, swinging his fist at the nearer of the two. The man was caught totally by surprise, raising neither hand nor sidearm in his own defense. Kismet's blow knocked him back against the wall, stunning him.

The second man tried to aim his pistol, but hesitated for a moment, concerned about accidentally shooting his friend. Kismet moved in quickly, knocking the gun hand aside, and then delivered a quick one-two punch that laid the man out. The first man however had rapidly recovered his breath and wits, and hurled himself at Kismet, wrapping both arms around him from behind. Kismet struggled in the hold, trying alternately to break the man's grip and throw him off balance. The second man, still gasping to catch his breath, rose to his knees, then stood. Kismet noted with satisfaction the trickle of red that leaked from the corner of his foe's mouth. The man wiped at it disdainfully as he balled his fists and stalked toward him.

As the man drew back to strike, Kismet stopped struggling against his captor. He sagged in the man's arms, dropping his full weight against the hold. Even as the man's knees locked to keep his burden upright, Kismet lifted both feet into the air and planted them squarely in the chest of the man in front of him. The force of the kick launched the man backward, his arms windmilling in a futile effort to find a handhold. He slammed into the hip-high railing, and then both he and a long section of the banister went over the side, crashing onto the flight of stairs just below.

The attack worked in the other direction as well. The force of the impact caused the man holding him to stumble backwards and ultimately to fall with Kismet's full weight landing upon his torso. Kismet heard his opponent's wind driven from his lungs in a single wheezing cough. He rolled off of the man just as Irene appeared at the base of the stairs.

"No!" he shouted. "Back up—"

The words were cut off as a pair of hands wrapped around his throat.

Although winded, the man that had held him was not giving up. Kismet drove his right elbow back, striking the man in the sternum, but to no avail. The fingers squeezed tighter. Kismet began to panic. Instead of trying to deal with source of the problem, he found he was able only to focus upon the immediate threat. He reached up to his neck, fumbling to pry loose the choke-hold. Bright spots of light began migrating across his field of view, a warning that his efforts were failing.

There was a muffled crack, like the sound of a hammer striking a tree trunk, and instantly the fingers fell away. Kismet rolled free, coughing and gasping, but ready to fight should the man try again; he would not, for several hours at least. Another figure stood over the sprawled form of the unconscious man, holding a pistol by the barrel.

"I thought you could use some help," remarked Irene, tossing the impromptu cudgel aside. Kismet nodded, unable to thank her because of what felt like a pound of gravel in his throat. He got to his feet and gestured toward the ascending stairs.

"No good," Irene supplied. "The floor up there is a death trap."

"We can't go back down," Kismet wheezed. "Trust—"

"I know, trust you." She grimaced as a fit of coughing overtook him.

Kismet shook off the spasm and mounted the steps once more. At the third floor balcony he slowed, testing each step as he went. Irene's appraisal was correct; the entire floor seemed on the verge of collapse. Floorboards that had held them up moments before now seemed unable to bear their weight. Nevertheless, he trod across the ruined surface, cautiously making his way toward the next staircase.

Irene glanced up and saw that the flight leading to the fourth floor was incomplete. Halfway up, the stairs ended in empty space. Everything above that level had been reduced to cinders. "There's nowhere to go."

"Not the stairs." He pointed past the end of the balcony to a boarded over window frame.

"You're kidding."

Kismet did not answer, but took two more steps and stood before the window. His fingers pried two of the boards loose, creating an opening just big enough for a person to squeeze through. He carefully raised his left foot and stepped out into night, three stories above the street.

"The fire escape," he explained, grinning back at Irene. "Come on, but watch your step."

With some reluctance she crossed the treacherous landing and took the hand he offered. She stuck her head through the opening and gazed out at the night. The fire escape looked nearly as precarious as the burned out edifice to which it was attached. Below them however was a scene that seemed even more threatening. Beyond the truck and the heap of garbage strewn behind, a third sedan had joined the two wrecked vehicles. Its occupants were likely already charging up the stairs behind them. Additionally, two police cars, their lights flashing a multi-hued spectacle up and down the block, were stationed across the end of the alley to prevent anyone from entering or leaving, and in the distance the sirens of reinforcements en route were audible.

"Even if we get down, we'll never get away."

"We're not going down," Kismet replied grimly. "Up. To the roof. From there we can get to another building, and just maybe find somewhere to hide."

Without further explanation he implemented his new plan, carefully ascending the steps of the fire escape. Despite the structural damage, the iron framework was sturdy enough. They quickly made their way up to the platform that ran beneath the sixth story windows. A vertical iron ladder was bolted to the brick face, leading up to the roof. Kismet crossed to it and climbed up.

As he looked over the scorched brick parapet, he saw that the rest of the roof had been burned away. Seven paces to his left was a neighboring building, constructed with a common wall. The fire had partially damaged the apartments along that side, but otherwise, the building appeared to be sound. He pulled himself onto the low half-wall, straddling it so that one of his legs hung down into the ruins. "This could be a little risky."

"What a surprise," Irene grumbled, watching as he leaned forward and began crawling along the narrow brick ledge. "You've done this before, haven't you?"

He paused, looking at her sideways, and then answered with complete sincerity: "I don't know. Probably."

At the end of the parapet, he placed one hand firmly on the ledge of the neighboring building and pulled himself over. There was evidence of some damage here, but for the most part the covering of black tar was intact, as was the structure beneath. He turned back to Irene, assisting her until she was safely beside him.

"What is that smell?" She wrinkled her nose.

"Probably something from the fire."

"No. It smells like..." She looked over the side of the building. "Ugh, garbage."

He followed her gaze. She was right. The trash he had dumped into the street was beginning to release the unmistakable fragrance of rot. Their escape route had brought them back up the block, so that they now stood directly above the slippery mess. Below them, more than a few neighborhood residents were gathering to observe the second plague that had befallen their street in less than one week's time.

"I think we've worn out our welcome," Kismet observed. "Let's head down and find a way out of here."

Irene silently agreed and followed him toward the small rooftop structure that housed a doorframe leading down into the building. He was still a few steps away when the knob rattled and the door swung open.

Kismet immediately extended his arm to block Irene's progress, and began backing away as three figures emerged onto the rooftop. The first was a policeman, his blue uniform jacket bulky over a bulletproof vest, his hand resting but ready on the butt of his holstered sidearm. Kismet's impulse to rush over and beg for protection from the menacing gang that had pursued him across the city evaporated when he saw the second man step out from behind the officer, one of Grimes' stooges. Evidently an alliance had been forged between the black-suited minions working for Grimes and the New

York Police Department. The third man to venture out onto the roof was none other than the panting mastermind himself: Halverson Grimes.

"Great minds think alike, do they not, Mr. Kismet?"

Kismet took another backward step. "Don't flatter yourself Grimes."

"Ah, so you know me also." Clutching his side, Grimes advanced. Beads of perspiration trickled from the top of his balding head and ran down his face and neck. He was clearly unaccustomed to dashing up seven flights of stairs. "Please stay where you are, Mr. Kismet. I have no desire to harm you."

Kismet glanced over his shoulder. One of the men he had battled with in the burned-out stairway was now ascending to the roof of that building, having followed the same route as he and Irene. That avenue of escape was no longer viable. Kismet turned back to Grimes, taking another backward step. Irene, pressed close against his back, moved synchronously.

"Look, Grimes, I really would like to trust you, but you and your men have been chasing me all over the city, shooting at me. That's no way to begin a working relationship." He nudged Irene back another step. The front wall of the building was only a few yards away, perhaps six steps if they turned and ran.

"If he moves again," stated Grimes to his underling, "shoot him where he stands."

"Whoa," the policeman intoned. "Slow down. He's got nowhere to go. Nobody's going to do any shooting."

"That's right Grimes. There's no need for violence. If you wanted my help, you should have just called my office and set up an appointment. I would have preferred that to having to sit through the ridiculous ranting of your lap dog Harcourt."

Grimes' face hardened and Kismet saw that his verbal barb had stuck. He risked another step back, but Grimes' man jumped forward, brandishing a pistol.

"Perhaps you are right," Grimes said with a sigh. "Sir Andrew insisted that he could persuade you. I was wrong to let him try. He has a tendency—"

"To believe in fairy tales?"

"To be overeager. That is why I want you involved in this project. You are a man of action. You get results." He gestured for his man to lower his weapon. "We can make history if we work together, Kismet. I swear to you, this time you will not have your prize snatched away."

"I wish I could believe you. But I don't work for kidnappers and murderers."

The policeman raised an eyebrow, and turned to Grimes. "Murderers? What's he talking about?"

Kismet went into motion, whirling and seizing Irene's hand. He ran straight toward the parapet overlooking the street. The man he had fought in the stairway was jumping down onto the roof, attempting to intercept, but Kismet ignored this threat, peering instead over the side of the building.

As with the neighboring structure, the iron frame of a fire escape zig-zagged across the front of the apartments. An upright ladder accessed the sixth floor deck, but Kismet had no time to find it and execute a correct descent.

"Over the side." He did not wait for Irene's inevitable statements of disbelief, but quickly stepped over the parapet and dropped onto the catwalk below. The steel structure groaned with the sudden impact. A second later Irene landed alongside and clutched his arm for stability. He steadied her, and then hastily located the ladder. Two of Grimes' men were staring down from the edge, shouting and threatening with their guns, but for the moment Kismet was unconcerned; the grill-work of the fire escape would make it nearly impossible for a bullet to find them. The men must have realized this, for they put their guns away and climbed over the side to give chase.

Kismet saw no sign of their enemies on the street below, but knew they were likely running down from wherever they were in order to cut off the escape. The two men on the ladder, only a few steps behind them, were effectively herding them toward the street, where Grimes would either have them shot or arrested. It was time to hasten their descent.

When he reached the third floor deck of the fire escape, he drew to a stop, and waited for Irene to reach him. She stepped down and looked at him for direction.

"Shortcut!" Before she could utter a word, he wrapped one arm around her waist. Irene suddenly realized what he was up to, and Kismet heard the beginning of an oath, spoken in Russian, which had something to do with his mother.

Her foreign curse notwithstanding, Irene seemed to comprehend that what Kismet was about to attempt would require her full cooperation. She synchronized her movements with his own; bending her knees, tensing her muscles as he did, and springing forward when he shouted: "Jump!"

They flew out into the open space above the street, arcing at first, until gravity's pull exceeded the lateral thrust of their leap, and then they plummeted. Irene's skirt filled with air, like an umbrella in a windstorm, and flew up around her head, baring her legs to the world for one and a half heavenly seconds.

Immediately as they jumped, Kismet released his hold, thrusting her away so that they would not collide upon landing. Irene seemed to float an arm's length away, her face eclipsed by the cloth of her dress. An instant later, they hit.

The garbage bags were not as soft as he had hoped for, but sufficiently broke their fall to prevent injury. Upon hitting the pile of trash, Kismet pitched forward, sinking deep into its reeking midst. He righted himself and looked for Irene. She had landed nearby and already freed herself from the mire. As she rolled down to the street, a few fragments of damp paper tumbled from beneath her skirt. Kismet picked his way across to slippery mess to join her.

Suddenly his head snapped sideways. A bright flash scorched his vision, followed by a ringing in his ears. He turned his head back to face Irene, and found her massaging the knuckles of her right hand. A moment later, his jaw started smarting and he raised a hand to gently probe his left cheek. He was almost convinced that he could feel it beginning to swell. Irene regarded him with smoldering rage. "If you ever pull a stunt like that again, I swear I'll do more than just hit you."

He raised a disapproving eyebrow, though he was secretly impressed by how tough she was proving to be. The trials they had faced since escaping the underground church hall were virtually Herculean, certainly more than enough to overwhelm the endurance of most men. Yet this woman that he hardly knew had survived it all and still had the mettle to put him in his place.

Muted popping noises echoed between the buildings, punctuating the impact of bullets on the street all around them. Kismet hastily pointed to the refuse hauler they had earlier abandoned and shouted: "Back in the truck. Move!"

"But the street is blocked!" Irene shouted. He ignored her and was not surprised when she slid into the passenger seat at the same time he pulled his own door shut. He worked the ignition then revved the engine several times.

"We're not going forward," he explained, shifting the gear lever into reverse.

Irene glanced backward. "That way is blocked, too."

"Not for long." Kismet floored the accelerator then slipped his foot off the clutch pedal. The vehicle shot backward with a violent lurch that threw Irene forward onto the floor.

A loud noise rang through the cab as a bullet struck the heavy steel roof of the truck, directly between them. Another shot shattered the windshield, showering fragments of glass upon Kismet and Irene. The truck's huge rear tires, further weighted down by the upraised container, plowed into the mound of trash and either scattered refuse in all directions or simply mashed it flat. Kismet felt his control over the vehicle diminish slightly, but continued to maintain pressure on the accelerator.

The rear end of the truck slammed into the sedan that had crashed sideways across the lane. The Buick spun around and broadsided the truck. The second car, which had crashed into the first, was devastated as the right edge of the holding canister raked along the doorposts, smashing both the front and back windows and obliterating everything on the driver's side.

Although he managed to avoid striking the third car, the driver of which had been foresighted enough to park close to the sidewalk, Kismet was unable to thread his way between the two police cars that had blockaded the way to the intersection. He barely had time to warn Irene before they hit. The truck lurched with the impact but refused to stop. The driver's side wheels climbed up onto one of the cars, crushed its fenders and twisted its frame into scrap metal. Kismet corrected his steering and the wheels dropped back onto the pavement, causing the entire vehicle to bounce violently.

With that final pang they were free, bursting backward into the intersection, where policemen had already stopped traffic. Kismet braked, then shifted into second and steered back onto the avenue. Within moments they had left the scene of the confrontation behind.

"Irene, are you all right?"

She looked up cautiously from where she was huddled down on the floor. "I don't know," she confessed. "Have we escaped?"

"We're not across the finish line yet, but things are finally looking up."

She shook herself, trying to dislodge shards of glass from her hair and clothes. Her seat was similarly littered with sharp splinters, which she cautiously removed before sitting down. Kismet navigated straight ahead, slightly faster than the flow of traffic. Two minutes later he saw the first sign of pursuit: a string of flashing police lights, a few blocks behind and closing fast.

"Uh, oh. That's no good. Where are we?"

Irene scanned a street corner for a signpost. "Madison Avenue. We just passed 34th Street."

Kismet thought for a moment, and then his eyes brightened. "Perfect."

They continued north for several blocks, but as they approached 42nd street, the way became choked with pedestrian traffic. Though midnight was still a few hours away, thousands of native New Yorkers and tourists were braving the inclement weather to ring in the New Year at the Times Square extravaganza. While it would be impossible to fight through the human flood in the stolen truck, Kismet immediately saw an opportunity to gain an advantage on their pursuers, and halted the vehicle.

Irene looked across the cab at him. "Well?"

"What do you say we watch the ball drop?"

She raised a dubious eyebrow, but followed his lead when he opened the door and dropped down onto the pavement. The shouts of annoyance that greeted their abandonment of the sanitation truck were quickly swallowed up by the crowd noise and the swell of music echoing down the rain-slicked streets. After a few steps they could no longer hear the sirens of the approaching police cars in the din of the celebration.

They did not completely blend in with the masses however. People gave a wide berth to the reeking, soot-stained duo, parting like the sea in a Biblical epic. In no time at all they had traversed three blocks and were within sight of the main stage and the legendary lighted ball that would drop at the stroke of midnight. It was impossible to tell if they were still being pursued, but Kismet was sure of one thing; their presence would leave an impression on all those who crossed their path. Simply trying to blend in with the crowd would not suffice.

He pushed through the throng, crossing the wide avenue toward the corner of 42nd and Broadway. Once his feet touched the sidewalk, he spied his next destination: a green globe, like a lamppost, standing above a stairway that descended into the bowels of the city. "There," he said, steering Irene toward the subway entrance.

Pedestrian traffic on the stairs was heavy with people commuting to the celebration, but they managed to force their way through the rising mass into the warmer, more spacious interior of the station. Kismet stripped off his ruined jacket to ease the impact of his appearance and minimize the curious stares of onlookers.

Following the signs on the wall, Kismet guided Irene through the underground maze, down a long escalator to the platform that serviced the numbers one, two and three trains to lower Manhattan and beyond. While traffic out of the station was heavy, there were only a handful of people waiting on the southbound platform.

They hastened down the concrete island, ducking behind one of the enormous supporting columns. After so much frantic action, it was difficult to simply stand still and wait. Irene leaned against the pillar, but the stale air and heat sent a wave of vertigo crashing over her. "I think I'm going to be sick."

Kismet gripped her shoulder reassuringly and eased her to the floor. "It's all right. You've been through a lot today. Just try to breathe deeply, steadily."

She reached up weakly to take his hand in her own. "Thank you, Nick. For everything."

He knelt beside her. "So, do you know what all this is about?"

She pressed her forehead to her knees and breathed in and out slowly several times before answering. When she spoke again, her voice had lost its quaver. "Actually, I'm more confused now than when those men first grabbed me."

"Why is that?"

"I'm feeling better. Help me up." With a measure of her dignity restored, she began self-consciously smoothing out her skirt, ignoring the permanent stains from their earlier misadventure. "When those men took me, I immediately assumed that they were Mafiya—the Russian gangsters that run Brighton Beach."

"You also mentioned FSB—*Federalnaya Sluzhba Bezopasnosti*—back at the church. Why would you have anything to fear from Russian state security?"

"Not so many years ago, FSB was known as KGB; you know this, I am sure. My father escaped from the Soviet Union when I was just a child. We have always lived with the fear that they would one day catch up to us."

"Why? The Soviet Union is ancient history."

"Russians have long memories, Nick. And not all of the people exiled to Siberian gulags were guilty of ideological differences; sometimes it was personal. Nor did all of those KGB agents lose their jobs when the letters changed."

"So it's an old grudge." Kismet maintained a neutral expression. He was still fishing to see how much Irene knew, and what she might reveal. "You said you assumed they were mobsters or FSB; you now believe otherwise?"

She nodded. "They were not Russians at all. I heard only some of their conversations. They must have captured my father sometime earlier in the week. When he saw that they had me also, he immediately agreed to cooperate, so long as my safety was guaranteed."

Kismet held back his questions. He pressed his fingers together, trying to gauge how much he should share with the young woman in an effort to draw her out and win her trust. Before he could reach a decision, a subtle change in air pressure followed by the squeal of metal on metal, signaled the approach of a subway train. He leaned out from behind their place of concealment and checked the platform for any sign of their pursuers. No one appeared to be paying them any special attention.

"Looks like our ride's here. Are you feeling all right?"

"Yes." She stepped in front of him, fixing her dark eyes on his. "Nick, do you know what those men wanted from my father?"

"I have a vague idea." Something about the way she asked the question convinced him of her sincerity, but trust was a different issue altogether. The arrival of the southbound number two train spared him the burden of answering, or worse, deceiving her. The train disgorged another crowd of partygoers, leaving an almost completely empty car. They darted inside just as the doors closed.

Following an unintelligible announcement from the overhead speaker, the subway lurched forward. Kismet stayed low inside the carriage until they passed into the darkened tunnel beyond the station.

"Where to now?"

Kismet sank wearily into the molded plastic seat beside Irene. "My place first, but just long enough to clean up and grab a few things. If Grimes—"

"The big man?"

"Yes. I don't know how he knows me, but he does. Anyway, if he's done his homework, and I'm sure he has, then that's the first place he'll look. Hopefully, we'll be long gone before he comes calling."

She nodded then leaned against him, resting her head on his shoulder. Almost without thinking, he gently brushed a sliver of glass from her hair. There were still more answers he needed from her, but before he could phrase the questions, he realized that she had already left him; Irene Kerns had fallen asleep. With an affectionate chuckle he leaned back, gazed out into the darkness of the subterranean transit system, and fought the urge to join her.

Kismet carefully surveyed the front of his brownstone residence looking for anything out place. They had already made a complete circuit of the surrounding block. If Grimes and his bunch had somehow leapfrogged ahead to the Brooklyn Heights neighborhood where Kismet lived, they would have had to park somewhere, but there were no unfamiliar cars on the surrounding streets. From what he could tell, the coast was clear.

Irene followed him up the brick steps, into the warmth of the interior hallway and up to the second floor. She waited until they were securely inside the apartment before demanding an explanation.

"Keep it down," Kismet urged, ignoring her protest. He left the lights off, motioning for her to stay by the door as he quickly swept the rooms for signs of an intrusion. In the diffused light from the street lamps trickling in through the windows, she got a look at the personal abode of the man who had rescued her. She was strangely pleased at the total absence of feminine influence in the decor of the front sitting room. Kismet reappeared a moment later. "I think we're okay. Come on in."

She followed his lead, passing through the front room with its large window overlooking the street and down a long hallway into a bedroom with a perfectly made queen-sized mattress. Her brow furrowed slightly at this, but when Kismet flipped on the lights, she saw that the room looked almost unused. Remembering her earlier unanswered question, she turned to him.

"All right, it's your turn Nick. There's more to this than you've let on. What's really going on?"

He jerked a thumb toward a door across the hall. "Bathroom's in there. You can clean up, but don't get too comfortable. We won't be here long. As to what's going on...I don't have a clue."

"You do know something. I heard what that man Grimes said to you. Those men weren't just after me. They wanted you too. You're involved in this..." Her eyes widened in sudden comprehension. "You know where they're taking my father, don't you?"

"That's where you're wrong. If anyone knows where your father is going, it's you."

Kismet turned to leave the room, but she raced after him. "Just what is that supposed to mean?" she demanded.

"It means that those men took your father because he knows where to find what they want. I was just supposed to be the hired help."

"But I don't know what it is they want to find."

His expression hardened and he took a step closer, staring into her eyes, as if attempting to discern there the sincerity of her statement. "Grimes and Harcourt are looking for the Golden Fleece."

"Oh."

Irene's monosyllabic answer spoke volumes. Kismet held her gaze even as she attempted to look away. "Then your father does know where it is."

She took a step backwards, looked around then sank slowly onto the bed. "It's not that," she sighed. "If that's really what they are after, then it means that they'll be taking him back to where his enemies are. If they find him there..." She did not complete the sentence, nor did she need to.

Kismet shook his head. "If it exists at all, the Fleece surely wouldn't be in Russia."

"Not Russia. The Republic of Georgia. When I was a girl—when we left—Georgia was simply one more state in the Soviet Union. My father did most of his work in the Caucasus, the mountain range that is the natural border between Russia and Georgia. I didn't understand what that man Grimes wanted from my father, even when he mentioned something about Greek antiquities. But now it makes sense."

"Georgia might as well be in Russia; it certainly tops the list of old Soviet satellites that Moscow wants to return to the fold. Russian troops invaded Georgia recently and there's still a significant military presence in some areas." Kismet rubbed his forehead ruefully. "Why do these ancient treasures always wind up in the middle of war zones?"

"You're not suggesting the Golden Fleece is real?"

"The Black Sea coast of Georgia has always been accepted as the most likely location for Colchis, the legendary home of the Golden Fleece. If he found those artifacts in the mountains, it would provide evidence of an ancient Greek presence in Georgia. From there it would only be a short step to believing that those Greek explorers were searching for the Golden Fleece.

"Still," he continued. "Georgia is a long way from the Kremlin. I wouldn't think the reach of your father's enemies would extend that far."

"We were in Georgia when my father decided to flee."

Kismet couldn't tell how much of her concern was based on real experience and how much was paranoia. Either way, it would do little to alter the situation. "Listen, Irene. I just need to know one thing. If we went over there, to the Caucasus, could you find the place where your father discovered those artifacts?"

"I don't know. Maybe."

"Then we don't have any time to waste. Go get cleaned up; there's time for a quick shower if you want."

"I don't understand. We are going to go over there? We are going to rescue my father?"

"Not if we don't start moving." He stepped away from the doorframe, a reassuring grin breaking across his face. "The shower is in there."

She stood up quickly and moved as if to follow his direction, but when she drew even with where he stood, she stepped close, placing her hand on his arm.

Her sudden action surprised and unsettled him; the former only because he was not expecting it, the latter because he had been secretly hoping for such intimate contact. Her dark eyes looked up into his. "We are going to rescue my father," she repeated, but it was no longer a question.

He nodded, not speaking, and pulled her close. She did not resist, but instead let her arms enfold his torso and tilted her head up to face him, her lips drawn invitingly apart. He lowered his mouth to hers, and a warm sweet euphoria swirled over his tongue like vapors of brandy.

The kiss lasted only a moment, then he heard her whisper: "Thank you,"

He opened his eyes, feasting on her innocent beauty. "No. Thank you."

"Nick," she giggled. "I mean, thank you for deciding to help me find my father."

For some reason he couldn't define, the bloom of passion wilted and he released her with unintended abruptness. "Sure," he replied, gazing past her. "No problem. Better hurry up with your shower."

Irene seemed to sense as well that something had gone awry. She nodded and moved away. Kismet stepped back and watched as she crossed the hall into the bathroom and pulled the door closed. A few seconds later, he heard the sound of the shower spigot running.

He shook his head, stalking from the room into the hallway that led to the dining room and kitchen. He was angry with himself, angry for having kissed her and angrier still at his reaction afterward. Seeing Lyse again after so long had unexpectedly awakened a part of him that cared nothing for the machinations of secret societies and ancient relics.

"Like kissing my sister," he muttered. Although he in fact had no siblings, the approximation was nevertheless accurate. Irene Kerns had come to into his life young and vulnerable. Of course he had offered to help, that was the right thing to do. But to take advantage of her emotional state....

Still, there was nothing wrong with her offering herself to him, nor with his accepting. Intimacy was often based on less substantial foundations. She was an adult. And she certainly was desirable. In frustration he tore off his soiled shirt and tossed it toward the refuse can beside his desk.

Let it go, he admonished himself. There was too much at stake to complicate matters by adding an emotional component. She was just a kid looking for a hero to come and save the day. Maybe he would be her hero, but she would have to wait for someone else with whom to live happily ever after. As soon as she was done bathing....

An image of Irene in his shower sprang unbidden into his mind; her delicate body caressed by the spray, wreathed in veils of steam that could not eclipse the curve of her thighs, but in his mind's eye barely concealed the sculpted contours of her breasts.

He threw a glance over his shoulder toward the hallway leading to the bathroom. He had not actually heard her throw the privacy bolt; did that qualify as an invitation?

"Hell, she's an adult." He started back toward the bathroom then stopped in his tracks.

A man stood in the corner of the dining room, beads of precipitation dripping from his hat and overcoat. The dull metal of his gun however, was bone dry. "Good evening, Mr. Kismet. I hope I am not interrupting anything important."

"Damn," Kismet cursed under his breath. He had underestimated the opposition. He had known from the outset that Grimes would eventually conclude they had escaped Times Square, but had wagered their safety on the belief that their head start was great enough. He had also hoped Grimes would judge him too smart to return to his own home, and thus figured it would be the unlikeliest place for their enemies to be laying in wait. Wrong on both counts, his desire for a brief respite before fleeing the country had led them into a trap.

He turned toward the man, slowly so as not to invite reprisal, and sized him up. The face was familiar, but the images it evoked had little in common with the pursuit they had just so desperately eluded. He searched his memory to place the man.

"Ah, you were hoping to entertain the lady and I spoiled your fun. This is such a nasty business," offered the gunman in mock apology. "Now if you will just give me the parcel, we can avoid further incident."

"Parcel?" Kismet echoed, not really seeking to comprehend the man's request.

The voice, he thought. *Something about the voice, a baritone, faintly accented...* German? One of the Teutonic Knights perhaps?

Suddenly Kismet recognized the intruder. It was the man he had encountered in the street outside the Fat Man's house in Marrakech—the German motorist who had seemingly offered the assistance of his pistol in frightening off the Fat Man's goons, only to turn and pursue Lyse and himself through the length, breadth and bowels of the city.

The gun was not the same. Kismet realized after a moment that something had been added to the barrel of the weapon; a suppressor designed to baffle the noise of firing. It was the sort of modification a spy might use. The pistol was likely a .22 or .25 caliber weapon; quiet, with a subsonic round, but nonetheless lethal at close range.

"Parcel?" he repeated after only a second. Now he wasn't entirely sure what it was the man was after. Was he in collusion with Grimes, demanding that Irene be handed back to his portly conspirator? Or was this visitation entirely coincidental?

"Yes, Kismet. Quickly, or I shall have to use a more persuasive argument; a threat to your life perhaps. Or to the health of your...ah, guest?"

"No," Kismet replied, trying to sound casual. "That won't be necessary. It's just that I'm not sure what it is you want."

"Do not be obtuse, Kismet. You are trying my patience."

He was getting nowhere. It was time to try a different tack. He snapped his fingers as if experiencing a revelation. "Hey, I remember you now. You were in Morocco."

A faint smile tilted the corners of the man's lips. "Yes. And I've come back to finish that business."

Realization dawned. "The calf. You want that statue of the golden calf."

"I do," replied the man. "Please get it for me now."

"You know it's a fake, don't you?"

The man did not reply, not even a flicker of emotion at the statement. Kismet could not for the life of himself understand what was so important about the statue. It had no cultural value and not much artistic importance. Its precious metal content might gain the attention of a petty crook, but would certainly not justify an international retrieval effort, unless there was something else at stake that he had not considered. He understood only one thing: the German wanted the statue badly, therefore he must not be allowed to have it. Kismet needed options. "It's in a safe place," he stated cautiously.

"I would expect so. You will show me." The fellow gestured with his gun for emphasis.

Kismet glanced around his apartment. It was no longer the place where he lived and slept but a battlefield. His eyes roamed every corner, every stick of furniture, as if he were a field marshal organizing a defense against an overwhelming enemy. His gaze settled on the refrigerator, and a plan began to take shape.

"It's in there," he revealed, pointing toward the kitchen. He moved, a little too eagerly, in that direction. "I'll get it."

"Stop," ordered the German. Kismet halted, allowing the German to push past him. "Where?"

Kismet again moved quickly, kneeling before the sink. "I put it down here."

"Do not open that. Back away, slowly."

Kismet did, trying to appear confused. "I thought you wanted me to get the statue."

"Indeed. But will I find the statue down here, or perhaps you have a hidden weapon? I shall be very disappointed if that is what I discover." The German knelt, his pistol trained on Kismet, and opened the cabinet under the sink with his left hand.

Kismet took a careful step backwards. He was now standing in front of the refrigerator. Two more steps in that direction would take him out of that room; closer to his bedroom where the Smith & Wesson revolver he had captured earlier in the evening lay in the pocket of his destroyed suit coat.

A small wastebasket was the first thing the German's searching hand encountered. He risked a brief look then thrust the can aside, spilling some debris on the tile floor. He continued to reach and probe with his left hand, but because he was unwilling to lend his eyes to the search, he was limited to a very small area of movement.

"It's farther back," volunteered Kismet, evincing defeat.

The German grunted, trying one last time to reach into the unseen depths of the cupboard. Finally he eased forward, squatting on his haunches. He switched the gun to his left hand freeing his right for the search. "Let me assure you that I am equally capable shooting with either hand."

Kismet suppressed an urge to laugh. If the man were truly ambidextrous, as he claimed, he would have had no difficulty reaching into the cabinet with his left hand. He added this fact to the body of his overall scheme. Now he had only to wait until his trap was sprung. He gauged his distance to the refrigerator door; he needed to be closer.

"What's the big deal with that statue anyway?" he asked, taking a half step sideways. The German stiffened to an alert pose, waving the pistol to reaffirm his control of the situation. Kismet raised his arms submissively then lowered them when the moment of tension had passed. His left hand came to rest on the handle of the refrigerator door. He wrapped his fingers around it and waited.

"You are better off not knowing," remarked the German. "Some things are better left—"

The German yelped suddenly and snatched his hand back as though it had been burned. Kismet noted with satisfaction that the mousetrap, which he had left set beneath the sink drain, had snapped across the tips of the man's first two fingers.

Kismet pulled on the handle, opening the refrigerator door, and threw himself behind it. The heavy door swung out, shielding him from the view of the frustrated foreign agent. The man nevertheless retained the wherewithal to discharge his weapon. A series of soft coughing noises instantaneously heralded a chaotic pattern of ruptures in the metal skin of the door. Even as a carton of eggs, a plastic jug of milk and a jar of mustard exploded on one side of the barrier, Kismet felt blows slamming into his chest; sharp hits, like a hammer striking against his body but did not let the wounds slow him. Grasping the back of the refrigerator with both hands and bracing one foot against the wall, he pulled the top of the appliance toward himself.

The refrigerator tilted away from the wall, slowly at first, until gravity's downward influence assisted his efforts. The heavy appliance disgorged its contents in a rush upon the unsuspecting German, and then it crashed down on top of him. There was a grunt as the freezer compartment struck him in the head, knocking him senseless, just before the wire shelves pinned him to the floor.

Kismet inspected the mayhem. All that was visible of the man were his feet and his right hand; his swollen fingers were still locked in the jaws of the trap. The intruder did not seem to be moving, but Kismet was nevertheless cautious as he knelt and pushed the refrigerator aside.

He turned the appliance over on its back, so that it resembled a waiting sarcophagus. The cavity inside was now totally vacant, the food and shelves in broken disarray all around the stunned spy. Three holes, each no bigger around than a pencil, perforated the door, and two similar piercings had ventilated the side panel.

Before the German could regain control of his faculties, Kismet kicked the silenced automatic pistol out of reach. He then inserted one arm under the fellow's head, the other under his legs, lifted him up and dumped him unceremoniously into the ruined refrigerator.

The German grunted again, the pain of striking his head a second time rousing him. He started thrashing briefly as his awareness returned, then stopped moving when he realized that his prey now held the upper hand. Kismet picked up the pistol and trained it on a point roughly in the area of the other man's nose. "Now will you tell me why that statue is so important, *mein Herr?*"

There was a flicker of an eyebrow in response to the last two words, but the foreign agent quickly mastered his emotions. He would give nothing away. "You may as well shoot me, Kismet. I have nothing to say to you."

"How unfortunate," mused Kismet, taking a step closer. He slid his foot under the door and leaned over the German. "However, I have no intention of killing you. I'm sure the authorities have more persuasive ways of getting answers from you, and I know they'll be interested in what kind of operations the German intelligence service is running on American soil."

The man did not react at all; his face was an unreadable mask. Kismet frowned as he considered his options, and then decided to play one last wild card. "If you see him, give my regards to Halverson Grimes."

The German jerked suddenly as if suffering an electric shock. "How did—" He silenced himself almost immediately but could not hide his dismay.

Kismet kicked the door of the refrigerator, lifting it high enough with his foot so that it slammed down, entombing the intruder. He hastily grabbed a roll of silver duct tape from the bottom drawer of the kitchen cabinets then leaped onto the door just as the captive inside tried to push it open. The man's cries were muffled by the insulation. Kismet quickly began running strips of the heavy duty adhesive back and forth across the door until even the German's most ferocious efforts failed to crack it open so much as a millimeter. The tiny bullet holes would provide adequate ventilation for the captive, Kismet reasoned. And if they didn't? Well, that was too bad, wasn't it? Spying was a dangerous business after all.

After laying aside the silenced pistol, Kismet stroked his chin thoughtfully. His final comment had been a bluff, based on a whisper of doubt in his mind about Grimes. He hadn't really expected a reaction, but was alarmed by what the German's response suggested. In any event, the entire incident, unexpected as it was, had placed Irene and himself in jeopardy once more. The German might have comrades—reinforcements waiting in the shadows. And eventually, Grimes would send his goons to ransack the residence in search of clues as to where Kismet had gone. They had to get out, and quickly.

Before he could reach the bathroom door, it swung open to reveal Irene. She wore only a towel, wrapped around her torso and tucked in over her left breast. A second towel was twisted turban-like upon her head. Clouds of steam billowed out from behind her. "What was that noise?"

"A big rat in the kitchen. You know how these old buildings can be. Hurry up. There's not much time left."

"Time for what?" Her question became a gasp. "My God, is that blood?"

Kismet looked down, following the direction of her pointing finger. Three crimson spots were visible on the fabric of his undershirt, though the cloth itself was intact. He touched the spots, rekindling the pain in the nerves of his abraded skin. The bullets had given up lethal velocity as they passed through the impromptu shield of the refrigerator door, but had still hit hard enough to cause superficial abrasions.

"It's nothing," he lied, taking her arm and guiding her curious eyes away from the hallway. "You'll have to make do with some of my clothes."

As Irene unfurled her turban, releasing a cascade of damp hair, Kismet felt a pang of regret that their meeting had been so ill-timed and under such desperate circumstances.

Instead of dwelling on the missed opportunity, he opened the closet, pulled a pair of khakis and work shirt from a hanger, and passed these to Irene. As soon as she took them, he abruptly pushed all of the clothes hanging on the dowel out of the way, exposing the wall. He then turned the wooden rod until he heard a click from within the wall itself. Gentle pressure on the panel caused it to swing inward, exposing a small room beyond. Kismet ducked under the low lintel and entered the secret room.

The small chamber was only slightly bigger than the closet through which he had passed. Kismet had built this room himself by creating a false wall in what had originally been a much larger walk-in closet. The space beyond was empty, save for a small worktable against the back wall. The tabletop was piled with various papers, many of which were documents pertaining to his personal quest—more than a decade spent trying to find some trace of the wolf-like Ulrich Hauser and the organization that man had hinted at. Kismet had been discreet, never sure who could be trusted with his knowledge, content to simply listen for certain keywords to pop up in conversation with people who seemed to have a little too much interest in legendary antiquities. Beyond that, the search for answers had begun to resemble a campaign against windmills.

Also occupying the tabletop was his *kukri*, along with a Glock 17 pistol, a cleaning kit, and several boxes of ammunition. He left the .44 Special and the silenced .22 automatic alongside the other weapons; he would think of some way to dispose of them later.

One other item occupied a place on the table. Hidden inside a plastic grocery bag was the object of the German agent's quest. Kismet took it out and held it up to the light. "What are you hiding?" he whispered.

"So exactly what is it that you do, Nick Kismet?" Irene stood just behind him, gazing in awe at the hidden room and its contents. One of his Ex Oficio shirts now clothed her upper body. In spite of the fact that she had left the top three buttons undone, exposing a healthy amount of cleavage, her breasts strained at the fabric beneath the chest pockets. Kismet silently cursed the German once again for his untimely intrusion and tore his gaze from her.

"Believe it or not, I'm a lawyer."

She raised a dubious eyebrow. "This should be interesting."

He laughed. "I work for the United Nations; specifically, for an agency that deals with issues regarding art and antiquities. We basically make sure that art treasures and so forth don't get snatched up illegally by private collectors and black marketeers."

"You make it sound so pedestrian."

Kismet chuckled at the observation. "Well, I do occasionally go into battle in the courtroom, but mostly I inspect digs to make sure that the laws are being observed, and try to shut down illegal art smuggling operations."

Irene pointed to the statue. "Is that something you got to keep?"

"I'm not sure, but it just might be our ace in the hole." He ran his fingers along its length, probing for unnoticed irregularities or incongruous defects. He turned it on its side, and then examined the calf's belly. Finally, he turned his attention to the sun disk between the horns of the idol. The block Hebrew characters--engraved characters of the Aramaic alphabet rather than the more spidery paleo-Hebrew used prior to the third century BCE--looked back at him with all the authority the word inscribed there carried. Some rabbis held that the name itself was a word of great power, but its actual pronunciation was an incomprehensible mystery because the vowels that connected the four consonants were unknown. Did those letters, the anachronism that had revealed the idol's fraudulent nature to him, hold the secret that made the golden calf statue so desirable, both to the German agent and to Lysette Lyon? If it did, the significance escaped him. He turned the artifact once more.

There it was: a faint line as thin as a hair encircling the circumference of the disk. He inserted a fingernail and exerted pressure until the disk popped open like a keepsake locket. A concealed jeweler's hinge held it fast on the bottom edge.

Kismet swiped his finger across the inside of the hollow space and dislodged a tiny reclosable bag, about the size of a postage stamp, which contained a wafer thin piece of blue plastic. Laying the statue aside, he gave closer attention to this new item.

"It's a memory card," he realized aloud. He had completely forgotten his houseguest, and Irene was forced to quickly back out of the hidden enclosure as Kismet raced purposefully back into the bedroom.

Kismet grabbed his notebook computer off the nightstand and slipped the secure digital file storage device into the appropriate port. The file directory opened, but the card evidently had only one executable file, which Kismet double-clicked.

The screen abruptly went black then words started scrolling from bottom to top. German words. He mentally paraphrased a translation, quickly getting the gist of the two paragraph long messages that commenced the program. The first was a security warning, stating that only certain people were authorized to view what followed, and that if one was not a high ranking member of the Bundeswehr, the German ministry of defense or something called Alb-Werk, then continuing to watch constituted espionage and would be dealt with in the most severe way. Kismet glanced at Irene, who was staring once more over his shoulder. "Do you speak German?"

She shook her head.

"Good." The second paragraph was more of a proprietary statement, once more invoking the name of Alb-Werk, followed by a brief introduction stating that what followed was for general presentation purposes only; further technical information would be made available upon request. As the scrolling words left the screen, a logo, stylized from the name of the parent company, flashed in the center, then again went dark. What followed looked incredibly realistic, but Kismet noted a distinctive uniformity in the texture of the images that gave it away as the product of computer-generated animation.

The visual presentation began with a sweeping aerial shot descending down toward a dense forest in the purple of twilight falling. As the perspective leveled out, Kismet saw a generic military compound looming ahead. The point of view switched suddenly to a loose cluster of soldiers standing on the ground and gazing up at the barely visible silhouette of the aircraft as a cylindrical object, presumably a bomb, fell from its undercarriage. The device deployed stubby wings, and adjusted course incrementally as momentum carried it forward in a downward curve. The delivery aircraft then kicked in its afterburners, disappearing from the sky in a blaze of blue flame.

Two seconds later the bomb detonated high above the military base in a burst of brilliance that filled the screen. The light, probably a graphic special effect designed to impress the viewing audience, quickly faded, only to be replaced by what Kismet took to be a more accurate expression of the bomb's capability. The presentation broke from real time in order to relive the bomb blast from different perspectives and at different rates of progress. It was difficult in the first few scenes to understand how the device differed from a nuclear or large conventional explosive, but in the fourth cut scene, Kismet realized what he was witnessing.

The bomb created no shock wave, no blast of kinetic force. Instead, the airburst unleashed a cascade of particles, shown in the presentation as a silvery rain, which destroyed electronic equipment and central nervous systems alike. Living tissue, whether human flesh or vegetation, was vaporized instantly, while radio equipment and missile guidance systems began to spontaneously burst into flames.

The final scene showed a fleet of helicopters moving into the affected area, deploying ground troops across the compound. The men wore traditional combat gear, rather than special protective equipment, as might be used in a nuclear or biological hot zone. It was, Kismet realized, the holy grail of warfare: a bomb that killed the enemy without destroying infrastructure or permanently contaminating the drop site.

The dramatization ended with one soldier stepping forward to proudly raise the black, yellow and red flag of Germany. Immediately, the image on the screen segued into an exploded schematic of the weapon itself. Kismet recognized the basic components of an implosion device, a ball shaped charge surrounded by titanium plates that forced the blast inward, focusing the explosive energy into the fission core. He knew that in a nuclear device, the implosion would drive neutrons through the core material—plutonium or uranium—splitting the atom apart and releasing its latent energy in a tremendous blast, but this bomb was different. The core material was not a radio-isotope. It was identified only by its designation on the periodic table of elements, modified by a minus sign: Au-. The screen continued to show this final piece of information for few more seconds, then blinked out.

On an impulse, Kismet grabbed a battered copy of the New York Library Science Desk Reference from his bookshelf and thumbed through until he found the periodic table of the elements. "Gold?" he murmured. "Negatively charged gold?"

Had German researchers figured out a way to turn one of the most precious of metals on earth, into one of the most lethal, utilizing it in the core of a proposed new electromagnetic bomb? If so, what were those plans doing hidden in a bogus statue? And how had that parcel come into the possession of his old college flame Lysette Lyon?

Slightly annoyed at being ignored, Irene frowned and cleared her throat. "If you don't mind, I'm going to grab a glass of water."

"No!" Kismet looked up suddenly. He saw her jump and instantly regretted the sharpness of his tone. "I'm sorry. The kitchen is a mess right now. Are you hungry?"

"Famished. I could eat a horse."

He snapped the laptop shut without removing the disc. "Actually, I was thinking we could go for Italian."

Despite its reputation as 'the city that never sleeps,' New York does grow quieter as the night deepens. At twelve thirty a.m. however, half an hour into a new year, the streets of Brooklyn were still wide-awake. There had been the requisite bursts of noise, fireworks and car horns at the fall of midnight, followed by the exodus of partygoers trundling home. Kismet kept a solitary vigil, watching the events from the window of Mama Rosa's Italian Ristorante. Irene, drowsy after consuming a helping of leftover eggplant parmesan and a glass of red table wine, had already succumbed to the refuge of sleep. She lay in the darkened dining room, a checkered tablecloth pulled around her shoulders and a bundle of cloth napkins beneath her head, while Kismet nursed the remaining drops of wine, struggling to stay awake until Lyse kept the rendezvous.

He had discovered the Italian eatery shortly after moving into the neighborhood, and had quickly been adopted by Sal, the head chef. Over the years, the relationship had grown close enough that Kismet had been trusted with a key and the alarm code, and was told in no uncertain terms to make himself at home whenever he felt like it, as long as he didn't leave a mess. It was an arrangement that he confidently believed to be a secret from men such as Halverson Grimes.

Lyse arrived half an hour after Irene fell asleep. She entered quietly, nodding in affirmation when Kismet raised a finger to his lips, and followed him to the bar.

"Sorry I'm so late," she whispered, easing onto a stool beside the counter. "I've been everywhere tonight."

"No problem," replied Kismet. "Are you hungry?"

"Oh, yeah. I could eat a horse right now."

He grinned. "That's a popular choice tonight. How about a meatball hero?"

"As long as you do all the work."

"Just like old times." Kismet rose and led her into the kitchen. "So, what's the story? Were you able to follow Harcourt?"

"Yeah. How about you? I see you saved the damsel in distress from the clutches of the evil villain."

"All that and more." He laid a plate in front of her. Upon it was a split loaf of bread, piled with meatballs and dripping with marinara sauce. Lyse rubbed her hands together eagerly as he took a seat at the bar beside her. Given her trim figure, he had always been amazed at her appetite. As she devoured the meal, Kismet recounted the evening's events up to the point where they escaped from Times Square. Lyse nodded often, but offered no opinions. "Now it's your turn," he finished.

She virtually inhaled the remaining bites of her sandwich before answering. "My evening wasn't quite as wild as yours, but at least you were in better company. I spent most of the time driving, by myself."

"How sad for you."

"Spare me the sarcasm. Care to guess where your pal Andy went?"

"He left the country."

Lyse nodded. "He, along with that Russian guy and a couple of the guys in suits that all look alike drove to JFK and got on a flight to Paris. I don't know if that's their last stop."

"It isn't. My guess is he'll make one more stop in Germany to rendezvous with Grimes before leaving for their final destination. Grimes is spying for the Germans."

Lyse's mouth fell open. "That's a pretty serious accusation, Nick. I know he's up to no good, but a spy? And for the Germans? They're our friends."

"I can prove it. The question is: what are you going to do about it?"

There was an almost imperceptible pause between his statement and her rebuttal. "Me? Why should it matter to me?"

Kismet leaned back on his stool and gazed at the ceiling. "Look Lyse, I understand that you probably aren't able to tell me the truth about what you really do. But doing what I do...well, let's just say it's a lot like being a detective, and believe me you've left plenty of clues laying around that point to only one conclusion."

She tried to flash her notorious smile, but couldn't quite pull it off. "What conclusion is that?"

"Do I need to spell it out? It's just three letters: CIA. You don't have to confirm what I say. But if you want to nod or something, that would be helpful."

"I don't have the slightest idea what you are talking about."

"I should have realized it in Morocco," he continued, unmoved by her denial. "The whole situation was just too strange to be taken at face value. What, did you set things up with the Fat Man, so that I would have to help you out? I don't appreciate being used as your mule, Lyse. Especially without knowing what the stakes were. If you'd done your research on that particular piece, you might have actually fooled me, but I spotted the fake and threw a monkey wrench into your plan.

"Even at that, there was nothing to make me suspect that this was about anything besides some elaborate con job you were running. That German who chased us through the streets of Marrakech—there could have been a logical explanation for that—at least until he showed up at my place tonight, waving a silenced twenty-two and demanding I hand over the statue."

Lyse jumped out of her chair and stood bolt upright. "You didn't give it to him, did you?"

Kismet grinned. He drew out the wrapped parcel containing the idol and passed it to her. "If you tell your superiors, or whomever, they might be able to arrest the guy before his buddies come looking for him. He's in my refrigerator."

Lyse paused in her hasty unwrapping of the golden calf long enough to raise an eyebrow at Kismet's last statement. "I take it that this German told you that Grimes is spying for them?"

"Not in so many words. Perhaps your people can persuade him to talk more freely."

"My people?" echoed Lyse. "So you persist in believing that I am some kind of secret agent."

"Your denials are wasting valuable time, my dear. I'm handing you that German and Halverson Grimes on a silver platter. If you don't act quickly, it will be your own loss. I have more important matters to take care of."

Lyse set the idol down on the counter, gazing at it as if it were a trophy she had earned. "Okay, Nick, you're right. I can't tell you anything about what I do, but you've hit pretty close to the mark. And let me just say that Hal Grimes has been the subject of scrutiny for a long time. But he's a very powerful man, with a lot of friends."

"I noticed."

"What doesn't make any sense is his involvement with Harcourt. He's risking exposure without any real gain."

"That's where you're wrong. There's everything to gain if he finds the Golden Fleece."

"That? I thought you said it was a fairy tale."

"I'm revising my opinion. Like you said, it doesn't make sense for him to risk this, unless the Fleece is real. And I suspect that its value may be more than just historic."

"Like what? Magic or something?"

"Maybe." He hadn't worked out all the details, but just now thought better of trusting Lyse—and the people she was worked for—with details about the substance Harcourt had called 'ubergold.' "Whatever the case, Grimes must not find it. I'm going to get it before he does. And hopefully rescue Peter Kerns too."

"Really?" She tried the smile again, and this time pulled it off successfully. "Well, good luck."

"I'm going to need more than just luck, Lyse. I'm going to need your help."

"My help as in my help? Or as in the Company?"

Kismet sighed. "The latter, I'm afraid."

She toyed with her fork for a moment before answering. "I can see where our interests might coincide. What have you got in mind?"

"The first part is easy. I need discreet transportation for Irene and myself to anywhere in southern Europe. Greece would be fine. Or Turkey. Our ultimate destination is the Republic of Georgia."

"Georgia?" Lyse breathed a rare curse. "Things have been pretty volatile there of late. Are the Russians involved in this?"

Kismet shook his head. "I don't think so. But that's why I'm going to need something else from you."

Lyse listened as Kismet briefly outlined his plan, a growing look of incredulity clouding her features. "Absolutely not," she declared when he finished. "Even if I could do that, it's sheer lunacy. With the situation there right now, we could start a war. A real war against a nation with a real military."

"You don't have a choice Lyse."

"Don't have a choice?"

"Grimes must not get the Fleece. That ought to be reason enough for you to help me, but if it isn't, then I'll go one better. I'll trade you for your help."

Lyse stopped fuming long enough to inquire. "Trade what?"

"The final clue that convinced me that you made a radical career change after we went our separate ways all those years ago. The real reason you wanted me to smuggle that golden calf into the United States."

For the second time that evening, Lyse's mouth fell open. She snatched the idol off the counter, felt for the tiny gap in the sun disk, popped it open and looked inside. The hollow space was empty.

"What was that anyway?" Kismet continued innocently. "Plans for some kind of electromagnetic pulse bomb?"

"Give it to me Nick. This goes way beyond our friendship. People have died for those secrets."

"You can have it when—make that if—I get back from Georgia in one piece. It would be a shame if I died over there and took the secret of where I hid it to the grave. Especially if you could have helped me and didn't."

"Nick, this is a matter of national importance."

"So is finding the Fleece. I'm no physicist, but something tells me that Grimes' interest in the Fleece has more to do with your bomb and less a lingering interest in Classical Greek folklore. Trust me, when your superiors find out what's at stake, they'll support the idea."

"Damn you." Lyse leaned back and dropped her hands to the bar. "Fine, I'll tell them about it. I'll do whatever it takes. But you have to give me the information that was in the statue."

"Sorry. That's my insurance policy. Your superiors should be told that as well."

Lyse was silent for several moments. "This isn't my decision. I'll pass it upstairs and see what I can do." She sighed in defeat. "Jesus, Nick. I hope you know what you're doing."

Kismet opened his mouth to reply, and then thought better of it. He gazed across the room, toward the seating area where Irene was soundly sleeping, and realized that his motives were not nearly as straightforward as he had led Lyse to believe. He turned back to her and chose to answer with the truth. "Actually, I haven't the faintest idea what I'm doing."

PART TWO
HIGHER GROUND

Long before man conquered the vast expanses of open ocean that separate the continents, ancient mariners roamed the interior waterways delineated by the coastlines of Europe, Africa and Asia. Ancient tales of maritime explorations recorded by poets and historians of the Classical Age tell of epic journeys by god-like heroes along the coastlines of these lesser bodies of water. Geographers of the day recognized "Seven Seas," a catchall phrase to be sure. For the most part, they are elegantly named. The Mediterranean, once called simply "the Great Sea," literally translates to the Middle of the World. Between Africa and the Arabian desert, there is the Red Sea, best known for being the site of the miraculous exodus from Egypt. Separating Italy from Greece and Macedonia are the Adriatic and Ionian seas. Between Greece and Turkey--and the lands claimed by both--there is the legendary Aegean Sea. And then there is the marine cul de sac, shaped almost like a pair of wings, formed by a recent—recent in geological terms—flood so awesome as to have possibly inspired parts of the Epic of Gilgamesh, which in turn is believed to have been the source of the Biblical story of the Great Flood. Yet, despite its mythic origin and not inconsiderable size, this unusual body of water carries a rather prosaic name: the Black Sea.

Kismet gripped the stern railing and gazed into the distance. The wake churned up by the small chartered boat marked a turbulent pathway on the surface of the water; thick and distinct as it bubbled up from the spinning screw beneath the waterline but quickly spreading out until its message was no longer discernible.

Beyond the point where even the ripples of their passage could no longer be seen, the narrow Strait of Bosporus—the passage from the Aegean Sea into the Black—was still ominously visible. In the legend of Jason and the Argonauts, Kismet recalled, a pair of massive rocks called the Symplegades, had wandered about the sea in pursuit of the swift Argo in an attempt to smash it into timbers. Although Jason's ship had survived the passage, hundreds of other mariners through the centuries had fallen victim to the treacherous narrows of the Bosporus which, although lacking the power of movement, was nevertheless a mighty anvil upon which the stormy seas might hammer unfortunate vessels. Kismet was not overly concerned. The strait was becalmed, with only the merest whisper wind blowing out of the Black Sea.

Irene made her away across the deck and stood beside him. "I don't like that man," she grumbled. "It gives me the creeps when he leers at me like that."

Kismet glanced over at her. They were the only passengers on a small freight hauling vessel owned and captained by a Turk named Achmet. He couldn't fault the boat's skipper for staring. She really looked that good.

Irene had blossomed before his eyes over the past few days. As fierce determination supplanted desperation, she had begun to glow with an inner fire. Of course, replacing the work clothes that he had supplied on the night of their escape from Grimes' clutches, with garments more suitable to her form and gender had accomplished wonders.

Irene may have called it 'leering' and perhaps it was, for Achmet made no effort to temper his lecherous grin, but Kismet preferred to think of it as gazing in admiration. The dress that she now wore, a gown of hand dyed silks, tailored for her in the marketplaces of Istanbul, accentuated her beauty in a way that left him breathless.

"Achmet's all right," he replied, unable to suppress a grin. "He might not win a personality contest, but he won't sell us into slavery either."

"Easy for you to say," she retorted. "He isn't looking at you like you were a piece of meat."

Kismet nodded, ceding the point. He was, in truth, not overly concerned about the operator of their present means of conveyance. Achmet was indeed repulsive, a male chauvinist by the most liberal of standards and every inch the stereotypical sailor. But Kismet had learned over the course of many years to trust his own instincts when judging people, and the Turkish skipper had yet to trigger any intuitive alarm bells. He seemed to be a simple, reliable man who just happened to be, as Irene had so succinctly stated, creepy.

Achmet's boat was only the latest in a series of planes, trains and ships that had taken the two of them across one hundred and five degrees of longitude; from the snowy streets of New York to the somewhat milder climate of the Black Sea, off the Turkish coast. The journey had gone well and speedily, at least to the extent that any globetrotter could hope for, but Kismet was growing anxious. He fidgeted with the zipper of his heavy leather bomber jacket and turned back to his traveling companion.

Irene had focused attention on a single location frequented by her father prior to their flight, a place not far from Poti, the coastal city she and her father had called home for many years. Their goal was on a mountainside in the Caucasus, a remote range straddling the border between Russia and the former Soviet Republic of Georgia. Petr Chereneyev had surveyed this region in search of petroleum for the Soviet Union during the height of the Cold War. While the land where Jason the Argonaut had found the Golden Fleece still had a reputation for yielding up occasional nuggets of yellow gold, it was the quest for black gold that now drove men to comb its remote reaches. However, Chereneyev had found something else in the course of his survey up in those distant mountains; a cache of Greek relics that had financed their escape from KGB assassins.

Peter Kerns had likely returned to that place, now in the role of guide for Sir Andrew Harcourt. When the British archaeologist had dropped in on New Year's Eve, Kismet had not expected to become his rival, much less imagined that the man would become a kidnapping menace. But a menace he was, coercing Kerns into revealing the site where he had unearthed the relics. Kismet's growing anxiety stemmed from the fact that every step closer to their goal was a step closer to what would undoubtedly be a violent confrontation with Harcourt. Moreover, if Halverson Grimes was involved with foreign espionage as he suspected, or perhaps something even more sinister—the same group that had menaced him in the desert years before—then their foes would probably have powerful allies at their beck and call. And as if things couldn't get any more complicated, Poti had been virtually annexed by Russian armed forces following the end of the South Ossetia conflict. At every turn, he and Irene would face dangerous enemies and would almost certainly be outnumbered.

Typical, Kismet thought darkly.

"Why the long face?"

Kismet turned and feigned a smile to conceal his apprehension, and then saw by her silent laughter that she was poking fun at him. He returned his gaze to the sea.

"Just thinking about the Clashing Rocks," he lied. "In the legend of the Argonauts—"

"I know all about the Clashing Rocks, Nick. I can quote you chapter and verse about Jason and the Argonauts. I grew up with it."

"Really?"

"To Americans, Greek myths are just that, fanciful fairy tales from an ancient but ultimately dead civilization. But on the Black coast, they view the legend as true history."

"You're kidding." The shaking of her head was answer enough. "I mean, from an academic standpoint, it's reasonable that the Jason legend might have been inspired by an actual historical figure who traveled along the Black Sea coast, but I had no idea that the people living there today were even aware of it."

"It's a part of their heritage. Why is that so hard to understand?"

Kismet shrugged. "Most Americans are oblivious to the rich heritage of their own native legends. They think American history begins with Columbus. Most don't know, or even care to know, of recent historic events in their own back yard. I guess I just assumed that sort of thinking was universal."

"I suppose it's getting to be that way," Irene conceded. "Everyone is too interested in what's going on right now to worry about the past. As a result, they lose out on valuable lessons that the past can teach them."

The significance of her comments finally clicked into place and he saw a connection that had previously eluded him. "Irene, if you know all about the legend, then wouldn't your father as well?"

"Sure. He explained most of it to me. I was quite young at the time."

"Have the locals ever found any artifacts, besides the ones your father discovered?"

"There are pieces attributed to the serpent temple that show up now and then; nothing of value really."

"And did your father ever indicate that his pieces were linked to the legend?"

"No." It was Irene's turn to appear thoughtful. "But that doesn't mean he didn't make the connection. You have to understand that my father was very secretive about those artifacts. He only mentioned them to me after we were in the United States. Something you learn living in a Communist state is healthy paranoia."

Kismet was silent. Had Peter Kerns had made the connection all those years before? Had he in fact uncovered the very proof that Harcourt was after? More importantly, would he lead the British archaeologist directly to the prize?

The stakes now seemed even greater.

"Clashing Rocks," Irene murmured, mostly to herself.

Kismet shook off his ruminations and returned his attention to her. "What made you say that?"

"Just looking at them...you can almost believe that they are moving."

Although the Bosporus was blurry in the distance, Kismet checked to see if her assessment was correct. It was true that the gentle rocking of wave action caused the eye to constantly refocus, sometimes giving the illusion that stationary objects were in motion, but overall Kismet saw nothing extraordinary.

"That one," exclaimed Irene, pointing in the general area of the strait. "It did move."

"Maybe you should go back to the cabin," he gently suggested. "The sun can be brutal on the open water like this."

"I am not seeing things," she protested. "Look for yourself. One of the rocks is moving—there!"

Kismet looked again. "I'll be damned," he whispered. Between the two large rocks, a smaller lump was indeed moving. "It's got to be a ship."

"Then it's a pretty big one."

"An oil tanker," Kismet theorized aloud. "I'm sure there's no cause for alarm." Then, in spite of his platitude, he left her side, returning a moment later with a pair of battered binoculars. He raised them to his eyes and scanned from left to right until he could make out the mouth of the passage between the seas. His gaze then fell upon the rapidly moving shape that was indeed moving to intercept them. Incredulous, Kismet lowered the binoculars. "Not good."

"What's not good? What did you see?"

He ignored her. "Achmet! Can this tub go any faster?"

The lecherous captain poked his head out of the wheelhouse and barked something unintelligible. Kismet pointed toward the moving 'rock' and handed the binoculars over. Achmet focused in on the shape and spat an oath in his native tongue. He then added in passable English: "I knew you two were trouble."

"Damn it, Nick," Irene persisted. "What is it? Is it the Clashing Rocks for real?"

"No. Much worse."

The shape grew nearer and more distinct in the space of a few minutes. Even from a distance of two nautical miles, there was no mistaking the spiky, irregular outline of a great ship built for war. A large ensign snapped in the breeze from the bowsprit, a white flag with a blue 'X' stretched from each corner. It was the Cross of St. Andrew, the banner of the Russian Navy.

Achmet poured on the speed, angling the smaller vessel toward the coast. Turkey was the nearest landmass and had a proper territorial right to the waters in which they were now traveling. Nevertheless, the Russians had made it abundantly clear that legal claims mattered little. The Black Sea was for all intents and purposes, a Russian domain. It was doubtful that the Turkish Navy would be willing to risk an international incident to protect them from the Russian destroyer. It was even less likely that Achmet's tiny boat would be able to outdistance the powerful warship.

Kismet and Irene remained astern, watching as the distance between the two craft diminished. Irene broke the tense silence. "So what do we do?"

Kismet managed a tight-lipped smile. "Why should we have to do anything? We've got as much right to be here as they do. All of our documents are in order. In short, there is no problem."

"Naiveté doesn't suit you, Nick. There is a *big* problem. At best they'll just bully us. At worst—well, it won't take them long to realize that I am Petr Chereneyev's only daughter."

"If it comes to that, just stick to the story. You're not the one they want."

The destroyer continued to close in on them, erasing any hopes that it merely shared their route through the passage. Achmet yelled for Kismet to join him, and asked what course of action they ought to pursue.

"Just keep going as you are. If they want us to heave to, they can damn well call us on the radio and ask nicely."

"Nick!"

Kismet looked away from the captain, and followed the direction of Irene's gesture. A lazy ring of smoke hovered like a halo above the destroyer. When he heard the shrieking whistle of incoming fire, Kismet dashed across the deck and threw Irene down, covering her with his body.

An instant later, the sea erupted as a 130 millimeter artillery shell exploded a stone's throw off the port bow of the small boat. The displacement of water and the shock wave tossed the little craft violently, pitching Kismet and Irene against the gunwale. Achmet tumbled from the wheelhouse and sprawled across the deck, striking his head.

As the tumult subsided, the small boat's screws continued turning, pushing it on a random heading out of the blast zone. Achmet rose unsteadily to his feet and staggered back to the helm to shut off the engine. Kismet held Irene a moment longer.

"I'm okay," she breathed, then added: "That was Russian for 'please,' in case you weren't paying attention."

He released his hold, and as she pulled herself erect, the Russian destroyer moved alongside their boat, looming over them like a skyscraper.

Kismet gazed up at the stony faces of Russian sailors perched high above on the main deck of the destroyer. He wondered if the shot had been an intentional near miss, or if it had been their purpose to blow them out of the water.

A launch was deployed off the stern of the destroyer with an armed company of sailors and officers aboard. The seamen on the deck of the warship continued watching, their fingers ready on the triggers of the stationary 30mm anti-aircraft gun emplacements. The motor launch cut a wide circle in the water as it came around to pull alongside Achmet's boat. The Turkish mariner sat alone in the wheelhouse, fidgeting as he watched the Russians draw near.

"So what do we do now?" Irene asked, a faint quaver betraying her anxiety.

"Keep smiling. We haven't done anything wrong. Like I said, just stick to the story."

The launch drew alongside Achmet's boat and Kismet strode casually toward it, signaling that he would tie their belay line if they threw it to him. The sailors disdained his gesture, waving with their firearms to indicate that he should back off.

The pilot of the launch idled close and one of the seamen clambered over the gunwale and moored the launch to the boat. As if directed by a single mind, the sailors spilled over into Achmet's vessel and without a word deployed throughout, searching every cabin, closet and locker. A man wearing a dark blue officer's winter uniform, with a single star and one wide gold stripe on each of his shoulder boards—the insignia for a Captain 1st Class—climbed from the launch and moved toward Kismet and Irene.

He was tall, with a prominent forward-thrust jaw and an extremely self-assured bearing. A smug grin crept over his face as he approached. "Good afternoon, Mr. Kismet."

Kismet hid his dismay, but the captain's words struck him like a fist. He could not believe that the Russians had learned of his identity and presence aboard the boat, and his mind raced to identify where and when the leak of information had occurred. If the Russians already knew about his plans, their mission was doomed. After an interminable pause, he returned the smile. "I don't believe we've had the pleasure, Captain—?"

"Captain Gregory Severin, commanding the destroyer *Boyevoy*." Although the Russian's English was thickly accented, with syllables that sounded as though they were being spoken through a mouthful of breadcrumbs, there was no disguising the man's satisfaction at having the upper hand. He said nothing more until one of the sailors stepped to his side.

Before the seaman could report, Kismet spoke up. "What's this all about, Captain Severin? Why did you fire on us?"

Severin ignored him and turned to the sailor. "*Report.*"

"*Nothing at all, sir. Everyone is accounted for.*"

On an impulse, Kismet feigned confusion at their conversation. "What are you guys talking about? I want some answers."

"As do I, Mr. Kismet," Severin barked. "I want to know why a notorious American espionage agent is trying to sneak into my country."

"Is that what you think?" Kismet affected offense. "You're wrong on so many counts I don't even know where to start. I'm not an espionage agent. I was in Army Intelligence a lifetime ago, but even you must realize that's not the same thing. And we're not going to 'your country,' we're going to Georgia. Furthermore, we aren't sneaking, captain. We are traveling openly and legally on United Nations' passports. The documents are completely valid."

"I'm sure they are," Severin answered with a sneer. "I will of course be looking at them in greater detail." His eyes fell upon Irene. "And this is your lady?"

The statement was guarded, and for the first time Kismet entertained a glimmer of hope that the Russian was in the dark. Maybe Severin had not yet identified Irene; didn't know of her true heritage, or her exile from the *Rodina*—the Motherland. Kismet squeezed her hand, hoping to impart to her the message 'volunteer nothing.'

As if to signal her comprehension, Irene gripped his hand tightly and took a step forward. "I am not his lady," she snapped in clear, unaccented English. "I am his fiancée. And I would also like to know why you were shooting at us. You could have killed us."

The captain chuckled mirthlessly. "You are too lovely a woman to be taking up with a rogue like Nikolai Kismet. I wonder what you see in him, Irina Chereneyeva."

Kismet's heart skipped a beat. So Severin was playing with them; teasing them with what he might or might not already know. Before he could stop her, Irene replied. "So you know my name. I'm not impressed. You have no right to accost us like this. We aren't even in Russian waters. You are nothing better than a pirate."

Kismet pulled on her arm, dragging her back a step and cutting her tirade short, before she could hurl further insults. They were in over their heads; there was no sense digging the grave any deeper.

Severin laughed toward the sky. "Pirate! Yes, I'm a buccaneer. Perhaps I should make you walk the plank." He guffawed again then fixed Kismet with his stare. "My question stands, Kismet. The Russian Navy is tasked with guarding our own shores and those of our confederates in Georgia. Why are you sneaking across the Black Sea on this decrepit vessel? The owner of this boat is a known smuggler, and you—a former spy who now 'protects' the art treasures of the world? A grave robber is what you are, I'll wager."

"Are you sure you don't have me confused with someone else?" Kismet replied in a casual tone, trying not to let the captain know just how rattled he was. "Anyway, you've got it all wrong. We're not here because of anything I want."

"Of course," Severin retorted sarcastically. "How foolish of me to think so."

"Look, if you know who Irene is, then you'll understand why we're here."

Severin's expression softened. He looked at Irene, searching her face for sincerity. "*What is the real reason for your return to your homeland?*"

Irene's forehead drew into a crease. "I'm sorry, it's been a while."

Severin repeated the question in his thick, but accurate English. Irene nodded, as if gradually remembering how to speak her language as he translated. Kismet felt like rewarding her performance with a kiss, but kept his emotional response in check.

"Why have I returned? I'm surprised that you have to ask. This is my homeland. I may be Russian, but I was raised on the Georgian coast. My mother is buried there. It's natural that I would want to revisit my heritage before Nick and I are married."

"Your argument is not convincing. Your father is an enemy of the state. I cannot believe you would be so brazen as to risk your own safety in returning to your homeland, placing yourself within our grasp. Surely you must fear that we will imprison you in order to extort your father's surrender."

"That would be difficult, since he's dead."

Severin raised an eyebrow and chewed on the revelation for a moment. "Then you have my sympathy. I understand now why you wish to make this pilgrimage to your old home." He turned to the assemblage of his sailors and barked for them to prepare for departure. As they hastened to obey, leaving an uncomprehending Achmet to tremble in the wheelhouse, Severin returned his attention to Kismet. "I apologize for having waylaid you. It was, I confess, a regrettable misunderstanding."

"No problem."

Severin shook his head. "You are too kind to dismiss this so easily. I must make amends." He snapped his fingers, as if suddenly inspired. "I know. There is no reason for you finish your journey in this unseaworthy craft. You must allow us to deliver you to your destination."

"Uh, that won't be necessary—"

"But it is. Admittedly, my ship is not a luxury cruise vessel, as you Americans are surely accustomed to, but it is far more accommodating than this Turk's boat." His hard edge resurfaced for a moment, just enough to let Kismet know that declining was not an option. "I insist."

Kismet looked over at Irene, then back at the Russian captain. "With an invitation like that, how can we refuse?"

Kismet gazed at the face framed in the worn mirror. The stubble on his chin was growing thick; it would be a full beard soon. He rubbed it thoughtfully and decided not to shave. The last thing he cared about was ingratiating himself to his host. He splashed a handful of tepid water onto his cheeks then toweled himself dry.

They had been on the destroyer for nearly three hours. Severin had shuffled Irene off to her quarters, and then insisted that Kismet accompany him on a tour of the ship. Kismet had affected disinterest as the captain led him through a circuit of the decks, but the intelligence officer he had once been couldn't resist taking mental notes. The *Boyevoy*, Russian for "militant" had been taken out of mothballs, retrofitted and added to the Black Sea fleet at the start of the South Ossetia conflict. Severin didn't go into great detail about the armaments, but seemed more interested in alternately boasting about his accomplishments and tossing out leading questions to probe the veracity of Kismet's claims. Finally, with the tour over, Kismet was directed to his berth and told to get ready for dinner.

The quarters were cramped, but according to Severin, the cabin Kismet would be using for the remainder of the voyage was the berth of the first officer, and was quite spacious by comparison to any others, save the captain's own. Irene had been installed elsewhere, and Kismet had not seen her since shortly after their coming aboard. He regretted that they had not been given the opportunity to further reconcile their cover stories. Doubtless, that was the very reason Severin had kept them apart.

A rapping at the door distracted him. He opened it to reveal a blonde, pale-skinned man wearing a star and two thin gold stripes on his sleeve, which identified him as a senior lieutenant; Kismet recognized him as Severin's executive officer, the man whose quarters he now occupied. The XO did not speak English, and Kismet wasn't about to reveal that he understood Russian. Instead he waved the officer away, indicating that he wasn't ready to be escorted to the captain's table.

As he began rummaging through his duffel, it was all too evident that the bag had been thoroughly searched in his absence. He kept his irritation in check, and with a nonchalant air began pulling out his clothes and laying them on the bed. His *kukri* lay sheathed in the deepest recesses of the duffel, but there was no sign of his pistol. He breathed a silent curse then repacked it, leaving out a fresh shirt and a rumpled sport coat, which he donned with exaggerated slowness. On the way out of the cabin he took a second look at himself in the mirror. What he saw nearly made him laugh aloud. He would be attending dinner at Severin's table looking like a skid row bum. The XO sniffed disdainfully, calling Kismet an uncivilized pig under his breath, then led the way to the officer's mess.

Irene was already seated at Severin's table, idly conversing with the captain. Severin rose to greet him then gestured for him to sit. The executive officer took a seat directly opposite Irene, leaving only one vacant setting, at the captain's left. As Kismet lowered himself into the heavy wooden chair, he was painfully conscious of the fact that the only person at the table he would be unable to see was Irene. This too, he knew, was no coincidence.

Two seamen dressed as waiters marched out of the galley. When they finished their ministrations, each guest at the table had before them a bowl of sour-milk *okroshka* and a crystal cordial snifter that was more than half-full of a clear liquid. Curious, Kismet lifted the glass and passed it under his nose. There was no smell, but a faint vapor stung his nostrils; the beverage was not water.

Severin took up his own glass and inclined it toward Kismet. "Are you familiar with the custom of the toast? Of course, you must be. I will begin. We drink to your impending marriage to the beautiful Irina Petrovna Chereneyeva." He quickly repeated the toast in Russian, for the benefit of his officers, then brought the snifter to his lips.

With one accord the officers raised their glasses and drained them. Kismet tilted his in the direction of the other guests then took a sip. The vodka burned cool on his tongue, leaving a frigid trail from the back of his throat all the way down his esophagus.

One of the officers pointed at Kismet and made a remark about his sincerity. Before he could pretend to have not understood, Severin began chiding him. "Ah, Nikolai. You barely tasted the vodka. Could it be that you are not looking forward to taking Irina as your bride?"

Kismet winced. "Forgive me. I guess I didn't understand the custom." He lifted the snifter a second time and poured its contents into his mouth. His stomach burned, as though he had swallowed a flaming snowball, and he immediately felt the warmth of the alcohol spreading to his extremities. The overall sensation was not entirely unpleasant. Before his glass was back on the table, the waiter was already decanting a second round.

"Tell me, Mr. Kismet. How did you meet your future bride?"

"I, ah—" Suddenly, Kismet drew a blank. It was as if the part of his brain where he stored their fictitious romance had been burned away by the liquor. He wasn't a lightweight by any means, but it had been several hours since he'd last eaten and there was nothing in his stomach to buffer the alcohol. "At work," he finally blurted.

"I see. An office romance. She was your subordinate...what's the word? Your intern?"

"No," countered Kismet, his manner measured and deliberate. He could hear his own voice and knew that his speech was unimpaired, but his body felt detached, and he was virtually certain that his words would be slurred and unintelligible. "Irene was working with the museum staff on a program for her students. We met in the lunchroom one day when she was visiting."

When not on the run from a gang of kidnappers, Irene Kerns spent her days teaching English to Russian immigrant children in Brighton Beach. The fabrication they had agreed upon seemed to adequately fit the facts without being needlessly complicated, but now as Kismet tried to put it into words, he found himself cringing at its implausibility.

"Forgive my error. When was it that you became romantically involved with each other?"

Kismet suspected Irene had already undergone an extensive, if polite interrogation and knew Severin would be comparing his answers with hers, hungry for telltale inconsistencies. He forced himself to relax, drawing several deep breaths in an effort to counteract the numbing effects of the liquor, and after a few seconds launched into the tale of his whirlwind romance with Irene Kerns.

The soup bowls were cleared away, and the waiters began shuttling out the main course; two platters of *zharkoye* roasted meat, carved into thin slices. It was blood red at the center and dripping with juices. The platters were placed on the table and the officers did not hesitate to load their plates with heaping portions. Kismet waited for his turn with the fork then speared two slabs of the meat. He noted that no one had begun eating, and waited silently for the signal to begin.

"We do not usually eat so well," Severin explained with mock humility. "But for guests, we hold back nothing. Irina, let us have your toast."

Kismet leaned forward slightly, and caught a glimpse of Irene as she reached for her glass. "To good food."

Severin repeated the toast in Russian, and all of the snifters were raised and emptied. Kismet watched as Irene tipped her head back, and then with a frown drank his own portion.

As another measure of strong spirits flowed into his bloodstream, Kismet had little doubt that Severin was trying to use the vodka to loosen his tongue. He knew, or at least had a rough idea, what his own tolerances were with respect to alcohol. But could Irene hold her liquor? He decided not to take that chance.

As he lowered his glass to the table, his let his elbow fall squarely in the middle of his plate. "Oops," he drawled. He tried to extract his arm, but only succeeded in knocking the glass over, and smearing gravy all over the tablecloth. "Looks like I've had a little too much to drink." His words were slow and sloppy, and as he spoke, he waved his hands in a series of uncoordinated gestures.

"*Nekulturny*," remarked one of the officers. *Uncultured.*

Severin affected a distasteful expression. "I wasn't aware that you Americans were such poor drinkers."

Kismet grinned foolishly. "Guess I'm a little tipsy. Don't mind me. Go on with your dinner."

The officers regarded Kismet as though he were a leper, but followed the lead of their captain and began eating. Kismet toyed with his food, occasionally fumbling his utensils to perpetuate his drunken act. Severin, however, did not relent in his search for answers. With Kismet seemingly out of the conversation, he focused his inquiries exclusively toward Irene.

"How did your father die?"

"I'd rather not speak of it," she mumbled. The liquor was clearly affecting her, but she seemed to retain a shred of good judgment.

"I understand. But it is important that I know the facts. Petr Ilyich had many enemies. Some might even wish to avenge themselves upon his heir. What will I tell them when they learn that his daughter sat at my table?"

"It was an accident. There was a fire."

Severin nodded slowly. "How sad for you." He waited silently, as if expecting her to reveal more, but Irene said nothing. The quiet hung in the air above the table like a pall, dissipating only when the waiters cleared away the platters.

Kismet contemplated yet another portion of vodka waiting in his glass as dessert--*bliny* topped with sour cream and honey--was served. The liquor was indeed potent. His intoxication was now no longer an act, but rather a measured relaxing of his usual self-control. Following yet another toast, he was all too aware of the difficulty he was having in discerning the difference.

"Mr. Kismet. Irina has told me of your latest endeavor. You should have been more forthcoming. You see, I have information that will be of great value to you."

Severin's speech was as smooth as the vodka. Kismet had to will up the last vestiges of his cognitive abilities even to comprehend what the Russian had said. "My latest endeavor?" he echoed stupidly.

"Yes Nikolai. I know all about it."

Kismet sat in a daze, trying to fathom the implications of Severin's statement. Surely Irene had not revealed anything. The captain was still probing, trying to trick him into giving up something. "I'm not sure I do," he replied. Leaning forward, he craned his head around to look over at Irene. "What's he talking about, dear?"

Irene's blank expression confirmed his suspicion that Severin's statement was indeed a ploy designed to trick Kismet into a self-incriminating admission. Rather than continue to profess his innocence, he tried a new tack.

With finesse apropos of a drunken fool, Kismet wrapped an arm around Severin's shoulder, hugging him in a buddy embrace. "Greg you sly dog," he slurred. "I'm not a kid anymore. There's nothing you can tell me that I don't already know."

It was Severin's turn to be confused. With an expression that hovered between disgust and befuddlement, the captain shrugged free of Kismet's grasp. "I am not sure we're talking about the same thing—"

"I don't know what either one of you is talking about," Irene proclaimed, now thoroughly in the dark.

Kismet continued to play the idiot. Raising a finger to his lips, he began whispering in a conspiratorial tone. "Bedroom secrets, darling. Captain Greg doesn't think I know how to please a Russian girl." He flashed a lascivious wink in her direction, purely for Severin's benefit.

The Russian captain looked stunned, but quickly recovered his composure. "How foolish of me. Of course, you are a man of the world, Mr. Kismet."

Irene seemed to take up the thread of Kismet's improvisation. "You men are disgusting," she sneered. "I sometimes wonder what I ever saw in you, Nick Kismet."

Her contempt was so palpable that Kismet found himself wondering if she was in fact sincere. Before he or Severin could answer, she stood up. "I'm afraid I'm not feeling very social tonight. I'd like to return to my room, if you please."

Severin nodded. "I apologize for any offense, Irina Petrovna." He gestured for the second officer to escort her, and the two of them left the officers' mess.

Kismet decided to stay in character. He playfully slugged Severin's shoulder. "Now look what you've done."

Severin whirled to face him. "You are drunk," he spat. "If you were one of my men, I would have you publicly disciplined for your foolish behavior."

Kismet folded his hands meekly in his lap. "Oops. Maybe I should go to my room, too."

"I think that would be the best thing for you to do."

Kismet rose, affecting unsteadiness, and staggered toward the exit, bumping repeatedly into the bulkhead. When he crossed the threshold however, leaving Severin's lion's den behind, he paused to breathe a sigh of relief. "That could have gone better," he muttered under his breath. "Then again, i suppose it could have gone a hell of a lot worse."

Kismet awoke the next day with a fuzzy mouth and a mild headache; a pleasant surprise inasmuch he had been expecting a hangover of epic proportions. He had slept soundly. According to his watch it was nearly noon, though it was possible that their journey had taken them across enough degrees of longitude to the next time zone, making it an hour later. Either way, he had overslept by a considerable margin. He swung his legs off the bed and struggled to rise. The deck was chilly beneath his bare feet and he hastily got dressed.

A taciturn sailor was posted at his door. Kismet pantomimed his desire to eat, and the seaman nodded, indicating that he should follow. He was led to the galley where a portion of leftover breakfast had been set aside for him, along with an urn of unpalatable coffee. With a grimace he swallowed some of the vile brew. The sailor, apparently his personal watchdog, remained at attention just inside the galley doorway.

As Kismet struggled through a mug of the coffee, he heard Severin's voice behind him. The captain dismissed the sailor, and then stalked over to where Kismet was sitting. "You have slept through the journey, Mr. Kismet."

"Guess I forgot to ask for a wake-up call."

"Indeed. No matter though. We turned north after crossing the fortieth meridian early this morning. We should be in sight of Poti within the hour."

Kismet grunted but said nothing. Severin helped himself to a mug of coffee and sipped it thoughtfully. "You know that I had your luggage searched when you came aboard."

"I noticed. You refolded my underwear all wrong."

Severin was not amused. "Among your belongings, we found a firearm. The Russian Navy does not take the matter of weapons smuggling lightly, even when it is simply a personal weapon for self-protection. We are charged with protecting the borders of Russia and her neighbors on the Black Sea. You have committed a grave offense, I'm afraid."

Kismet set his mug down. Severin had avoided mention of the issue on the previous night, but now the matter of the pistol represented the captain's final hole card. Kismet was ready to call his bluff. "Listen Greg. I've put up with enough of your crap. I wasn't sneaking into your country, and I wasn't trying to smuggle my gun in. I was in a boat showing the Turkish flag, in Turkish waters, with legal authorization to carry a pistol. It was you that violated the law by firing on that boat and by coercing Irene and I aboard your ship."

"You were not coerced," the captain replied defensively, startled at Kismet's vehemence.

"Like hell we weren't. Boarding of our boat was an act of piracy on the open sea. You pointed your guns at us and made it all too clear that we were your hostages. You seized our luggage, kept us under constant supervision, and probably tried to poison us with that godawful vodka. So don't give me any shit about my illegal gun."

Severin's face was growing red under the heat of Kismet's accusations. "I was only trying to educate you in the laws of the region. You are correct that I did not afford you the opportunity to declare your possession of the gun. That was an unfortunate oversight on my part. I merely seek now to explain to you why your weapon has been confiscated."

Kismet did not relent. "I think you're the one about to commit a grave offense. The United Nations has authorized me to carry that gun on my person at all times. Correct me if I'm wrong, but Russia is still part of the UN, right? Permanent membership on the security counsel, if I recall correctly. I'll have to report this of course, up my chain of command and down yours. That snowball is going to have a lot of momentum by the time it lands on your head."

Severin's eyelid twitched uncontrollably. "My apologies. You are correct of course. I will instruct the quartermaster to return your weapon as soon as we make landfall."

Kismet took another sip of the vile coffee but said nothing more, dismissing the captain with his body language. Severin bristled but before he could speak, a tinny voice scratched from the intercom, summoning him to the bridge.

"It seems we have arrived. I suggest you make ready to depart." He stood up and walked toward the exit. "One more thing, Mr. Kismet. Despite your impressive performance last evening, I am unconvinced that you have no ulterior motives. Your *official status*—" He filled the words with contempt-- "notwithstanding, if you attempt to perpetrate any crime or activity that poses a threat to Russia, her people or her interests, I will be there to stop you. Consider yourself warned."

Kismet matched Severin's smoldering stare without blinking until at last, the Russian took a backward step through the doorway and closed it between them.

"Same to you pal," Kismet muttered to the empty air.

Kismet gazed out across the water at the silhouette of the *Boyevoy*. The launch that had shuttled Irene and himself to the modestly industrialized harbor at Poti was a barely discernible speck racing back across the dark water to rejoin its mother ship.

Their arrival hadn't drawn much attention. During the South Ossetia conflict, Russia had destroyed the Georgian naval base in Poti and established a permanent and arguably illegal military facility of their own. The appearance of Russian warships offshore no longer struck anyone as out of the ordinary. A handful of swarthy, rugged locals paused briefly from their work to gaze at the tired couple that stood on the dock, but after a few exchanges amongst themselves they turned back to their errands, untroubled and unfazed by the presence of strangers.

Kismet looked over at Irene. She had been cool toward him all day, speaking only occasionally, and only then in reference to what a fool he'd made of himself the previous evening. Her statements were troubling, since it was beginning to look as though she had taken his coarse behavior seriously. Under Severin's watchful eye there had been no opportunity to rectify the situation.

Despite his earlier assurance, Severin reneged on his promise to return Kismet's Glock, claiming that the quartermaster had misplaced the firearm and would of course be disciplined. The captain had then bidden them farewell, assigning his executive officer the duty of shuttling them ashore.

Kismet had made a pretense of thanking Severin for speedy passage, and then climbed down into the launch. Irene had accepted his offer of assistance, but did not relent in her silence. Now that they were safely at their destination, away from Severin and his tricks, it was time to set matters straight.

"Listen Irene. About what happened last night—" He moved his head, trying to make eye contact with her. She dodged his stare at first, and then faced him squarely, cocking her jaw to one side, her dark eyes blazing with fury. The look pained him. "It was all an act. I was trying to—"

She looked away suddenly, unable to hold her expression. Uncontrollable laughter bubbled from her lips and she fell against him.

He caught her in a cautious embrace. "What the hell?"

Irene continued to laugh. Her rage had slipped away like a paper mask revealing a look of pure delight. "Sorry Nick, but as an actor, you make a hell of a good—well, whatever it is that you do."

Kismet rolled his eyes. "Christ, Irene. Don't ever do that to me again. I thought you were really mad at me."

"So did Captain Severin."

Kismet shook his head in disbelief. He hefted their luggage, one bag in either hand. "Next time give me some kind of signal so I'll know it's just an act."

"You were really concerned, weren't you?"

"Well, yes. What I said was pretty crude. I was afraid you'd taken me seriously. I don't want you thinking I'm that sort of guy."

Her humor subsided, and gave way to perplexity. "I don't understand you Nick. You treat me like a child, yet you claim to care about my feelings. Which is it?"

Kismet suddenly felt very foolish. He had intended only to apologize for the previous night's drunken act, but had instead opened an entirely different can of worms. "Can we discuss this later?"

"Why not?" She stalked off ahead of him, leaving him more troubled than at the start.

"Wait." He ran to catch her. "Where are you going?"

"My father's closest friend was a fisherman here. He kept his boat at this pier. I'm looking to see if it's... there it is."

"Irene, we need to keep a low profile. How do we know we can trust this guy?"

She dismissed his concern with a wave. "Anatoly's like an uncle. He would never betray us."

"Maybe not intentionally. But Severin let me know in no uncertain terms that we will be watched. I doubt he would have let us go so easily if he didn't have an informant keeping tabs on us. Maybe it isn't your friend, but you can bet they'll be watching him as well."

"Anatoly can keep a secret, Nick. I trust him, and you should trust me."

Kismet frowned. "Let's just tread carefully. Don't tell him everything all at once."

"I'm sure you'll see that he's trustworthy once you meet him." While they were talking, Irene had continued to lead the way toward a large wooden fishing boat. The craft looked to be about forty-five feet in length, considerably smaller than Achmet's vessel, and whereas the Turk's boat was for hauling cargo across open water, Anatoly's boat was clearly designed and equipped to harvest the sea's bounty closer to port. Heavy nets dangled from overhead booms and were spread out across the deck. A shaggy form was hunched down in their midst, performing some intricate operation on a section of netting.

"Anatoly Sergeievich!"

The wooly head swung in their direction, whereupon Anatoly rose to his full height and darted toward them. He moved so swiftly that Kismet was startled into dropping their luggage. He was reaching for his bag, intent upon brandishing his only remaining weapon, the *kukri*, when the bear of a man swooped Irene up in his arms.

"Irina!" he roared. "*My little Petrovna. You've come home to us.*"

It took Kismet only a moment to comprehend that he was witnessing a joyful reunion and not an attack, but his instinctive reaction was understandable. Built like an ox, the fisherman was half a head taller than Kismet and positively towered over the shorter Irene. A bushy black beard and an unruly mop of coarse hair shot through with some gray mostly hid his weathered, craggy face. He reminded Kismet of the pictures he had seen of Karl Marx, the German philosopher that had invented Communism, an image that triggered an admittedly irrational wariness toward the big fisherman.

Anatoly lowered Irene to the dock. "*You've grown up, little one. You are the very image of your beautiful mother.*"

"*And you seem to have grown even larger,*" she retorted. "*Anatoly, this is—*" She hesitated for an instant—"*My fiancé, Nikolai Kristanovich Kismet.* Nick, meet Anatoly Sergeievich Grishakov."

"*Greetings to you,*" the fisherman boomed in Russian.

Kismet frowned and scratched his head. "I'm sorry, but Irene's only taught me a few phrases of your language. Do you speak English?"

"Nick." Irene was frowning at him for the deception, but he remained unwilling to invest his trust in the big Russian.

Anatoly simply laughed. "I speak your tongue, like you speak mine, I think." His accent was heavier than Severin's and true to his claim, his pronunciation was very poor. "But, if it makes you happy, I try. I am pleased to know you, Nikolai Kristanovich."

Kismet offered a half-hearted smile, and stuck out his hand. Anatoly guffawed yet again, causing the pier to tremble, and then scooped Kismet up in his embrace. Before he could react, the fisherman had kissed him squarely on the mouth and set him back down.

Kismet resisted an impulse to wipe his lips. The fisherman had already turned back to Irene and launched a barrage of questions in their shared tongue. Before she could answer any of them, Kismet cleared his throat to get her attention. "Dearest, before we get carried away, shouldn't we find a place to settle down for the night?"

"You will stay with us of course," declared Anatoly.

"Great," Kismet replied, disingenuously.

Irene glared at him, but it was Anatoly that answered. "Da. Very good. It is very good to see you again, Irina. We have much catching up."

As he led the way up from the pier, Irene turned on Kismet, barely restraining her ire. "I thought we agreed to trust him."

"I didn't agree to any such thing."

"Then would you at least trust me?"

"I trust you." *But I don't necessarily trust your judgment*, he didn't add. "So tell me about Uncle Anatoly."

She sighed and gestured for him to follow her. "Anatoly is Russian. Back in the sixties a lot of Russian men—engineers like my father—came here to develop the area; they built railroads and conducted geological surveys and so forth. And like my father, Anatoly fell in love with a local woman and settled down. It's a whole different world out here."

Irene's statement about the Georgian community seemed true enough. Although the harbor had kept up with current industrial technology, the rest of the area appeared to have undergone its last period of urban renewal in the 1940's. The dominant structures at the heart of the city, including a spectacular Neo-Byzantine cathedral, built in 1907 as an homage to the Hagia Sophia in Istanbul, had more visual appeal than the products of Soviet central planning that made up the balance of the cityscape, but were themselves not much older. Poti might have had a long and storied history, but very little of it had been preserved through the ages.

Anatoly led them to a mongrelized pick-up truck. He shoved aside the haphazard scattering of fishing gear in the bed to make room for their luggage, and then he eased down onto the bench-style seat in the cab beside Irene. Kismet's sense of having surrendered all control of the situation was even more pronounced than when Severin had taken them aboard the *Boyevoy*, and in the absence of any real choice in the matter, he climbed inside and shut his door.

Their Russian host drove them away from the harbor and through the maze of city streets until they eventually passed into a rural area beyond the outskirts. The paved road soon gave way to what seemed like a deeply rutted trail through a forest of deciduous trees, denuded by the onset of winter, where they pulled over in front of a large house on an isolated piece of property. There, they were warmly greeted by Anatoly's wife, a hale Georgian woman whose head barely reached her husband's chest. It was only after what seemed like hours of reunion, during which Kismet sat patiently feeling like a third wheel, that he got a chance to speak to Irene in private.

"Anatoly was the one who found out my father was in danger," she explained, distilling the revelations her old friend had made in the earlier conversation. "He heard a rumor that the local political officer was going to have the KGB arrest father. He passed along the information, and we fled."

"Arrest him for what? Was your father outspoken about his political views?"

She shrugged. "I was a child. I don't remember and he never spoke of it."

"I wonder how Anatoly avoided trouble for having warned your father."

"Maybe no one ever realized that he is the one who warned us." Irene's answer was offhand, as if she found his line of questioning irrelevant. "Nick, I'm more concerned about what we're going to do next."

"We're going to do what we came to do: find your father. The longer we wait, the more likely we'll be exposed to whomever Severin sends to watch us."

"Where do we start looking?"

"You told me that your father did his surveying in the mountains," replied Kismet. "I'm betting that's where he'll take Harcourt. We need to narrow down the places where your father might have found those artifacts. I want to figure out exactly where they are before we launch our little rescue expedition."

"Nick, we can't just hike up into the mountains. They're covered in snow. We'd freeze to death before we even got started."

"I'm open to suggestions." When she didn't offer any, he continued. "I'm counting on you to help narrow the field."

She sighed resignedly. "Father kept extensive survey maps. One of them will likely pinpoint the site in the mountains where he found those artifacts. Anatoly put all our things in storage; that's where we should start looking."

Anatoly had indeed stored away all of Petr Chereneyev's belongings and equipment in a dim corner of his cellar. Armed with an old kerosene lamp, they commenced the search right away. As soon as Kismet pulled back the sloping wooden hatch, Irene stepped into the darkness.

Two indistinct shapes suddenly broke from the shadows and flapped soundlessly up at them. Startled, Irene fell back and lost her grasp on the lantern. Kismet reflexively thrust out his hand and caught the base of the lamp, but a splash of fuel suffocated the wick, plunging them into darkness. An instant later there followed the sound of glass shattering on the steps.

"Nick, I'm sorry." Irene was breathless from being startled. "Was that the lamp?"

"Just the chimney." A match flared in his hand and he relit the wick.

"Why don't you go first?" she suggested.

Without the glass flute, the lamp burned too rich, polluting the cellar's mildewy air with long tendrils of soot. They ignored this inconvenience and finished the descent without disturbing any other denizens—bats, rats or otherwise.

The cellar was a monument to one man's lifetime of clutter. There was no distinct pathway leading through it all. Rather, they had to pick their way across the heaps and place their feet on the sturdiest objects where the floor was completely obscured.

Although Kismet had witnessed the discovery of relics from the ancient world, mysterious devices the purpose of which had died with their creators, he found himself hard pressed to identify half of the objects strewn about on the cellar floor. There was an array of mechanical parts, gears and shafts—no two of which seemed to belong to the same machine. There were sheets of metal, flaky from oxidization and corrosion, and an assortment of heavy lead pipe-fittings. Two pieces of equipment in one corner looked vaguely familiar to Kismet; one was definitely an air compressor fitted with an enormous reservoir tank. The other, which also looked like a compressor, had been augmented with a series of mesh screens. Lying haphazardly atop the former was something resembling a folded up canvas tarpaulin, patched in several places and something else that looked vaguely a copper cooking pot, tinted with a patina of green corrosion. Kismet stared at the collection of items for a moment trying to ascertain what their function had been.

A makeshift workbench dominated the far wall of the cellar. It was there that Irene found her father's survey maps stored in long plastic tubes that had once been used to protect artillery shells. Kismet climbed over to join her, and together they unrolled the maps. Each one overlapped the next at the edges, piecing together to detail the topography of several thousand square kilometers from Sevastopol to the shores of the Caspian Sea, and south as far as the mountains of Ararat. Irene thumbed through them and selected the one pertinent to their search.

The map was divided by a grid, spaced approximately at five-centimeter intervals. Kismet reckoned that the reproduction was on the order of one grid equaling one square kilometer—a standard military scale. Irene pointed out their present location relative to the map. The port community did not actually appear on it, but Kismet recognized the sheltered inlet that formed its harbor. The scope of the map extended out into the sea and contour lines illustrated how the seafloor dropped from only about forty fathoms near the coast to almost a thousand fathoms only a few kilometers offshore. By contrast, the land surface went from sea level to over six thousand meters—the highest peak in the Caucasus and what had been designated the tallest mountain on the European continent, Mt. Elbrus in Russia. The latter was a tricky distinction; the border between Europe and Asia was more an intellectual concept than a physical one. The bottom line however, was that in a linear distance of only about a hundred miles, one could go from sea level to the highest point on the continent. Kerns' surveys evidently had not reached as far as Mt. Elbrus, but the maps showed that his explorations had taken him into the lesser peaks of the Caucasus.

Some of the squares were marked with numbers and Cyrillic letters; a private code detailing Petr Chereneyev's geological survey of the region. Irene pointed to one area marked by a broad circle near the eastern edge of the map,. A dotted line trailed away from it following a narrow gully that wound a vague course toward the coast.

"That's a dry riverbed, probably the original course of the Rioni River. My father discovered it shortly after we came here. One theory holds that the name Poti comes from an ancient word for 'gold river.' I'll bet that is where he found the artifacts."

Kismet leaned forward, placing his palms at the lower corners of the representation. He counted off the squares separating Poti from the site in the mountains. "The roads will get us most of the way, but it looks like we'll have to go about twenty-five miles overland."

"As the crow flies," Irene countered. "But you've got the change in elevation to contend with. And it's virtually impossible to travel in a straight line up there."

Kismet nodded. The contour lines illustrating relative elevation showed the site to be more than a thousand meters up—well above the snow line. "Well, I suppose it could be worse."

Before he could opine further on the trials that lay ahead, a booming sound rolled through the cellar. It was unmistakably the voice of Anatoly Grishakov, calling out to Irene. Kismet hastily gathered up the maps and rolled them into a tight tube, which he folded over and slipped into the side pocket of his jacket.

Irene frowned. "We need his help, Nick. To get up that mountain, if for no other reason."

"*Are you down there, Irina?*"

"All right," Kismet whispered. "But not a word about the Fleece. I still don't trust him."

The Russian's voice grew louder as he tramped down the steps. He poked his head out from the stairway, catching sight of them. "Did you find what you were looking for?"

Irene turned to face him. "Anatoly, old friend, we need your help."

Kismet pulled his heavy leather bomber jacket tight across his chest, trying in vain to shut out the permeating chill. While the landscape around him was blanketed in snow, it was the altitude that made the air so unbearably frigid. He found himself wishing that he had worn an extra shirt, but his duffel was back at Anatoly's house, now several kilometers away. His black waist pack held only his *kukri* and a few other utilitarian items, nothing that would fend off the cold.

Anatoly's assistance had proved to be more than worth the risk of trusting him. The big Russian had in fact closed his ears to the details of their quest, staunchly proclaiming that it was better for him not to know. As matters stood, Anatoly knew only that Irene and Kismet needed to trek into the mountains. To that end, he had supplied them first with a hearty meal and a good night's sleep; and secondly, with transportation into the foothills. At dawn, the big man had awakened them, stuffing yet another feast into them before loading them into his truck. Although the vehicle was lacking in creature comforts, the brief ride on the primitive roads that carved up toward the mountains cut their trip in half and Anatoly delivered them to a snow-covered farm at the base of the Caucasus in time for lunch.

The farmer, one of Anatoly's wife's many relatives, required even less convincing than Anatoly before volunteering his help. After dining, Kismet and Irene were taken to the barn where the farmer stabled his horses.

Kismet was duly impressed by the draft animals. Although he had done his share of riding as a youth, he had little experience with these enormous equines. Their hindquarters were nearly as tall as he was, supported on thick legs that rippled with muscle. Before he could inquire as to their purpose, the farmer selected two of the horses and led them to another part of the barn. It was there that Kismet finally began to understand.

Resting on a layer of straw, alongside a wheeled cart and various plowing implements was a sturdy sleigh. The horse drawn sled was almost exactly as Kismet had envisioned every time he heard Christmas carolers sing 'Jingle Bells.' While they watched, the old farmer strapped the horses into a yoke harness and hitched them to the sleigh.

"Can you drive this, Kristanovich?" Anatoly asked.

"I'll manage." Kismet climbed up into the bench seat and took the reins from the farmer. Irene hopped in beside him. Her colorful dress had been replaced by less elegant but more practical clothes; heavy trousers, a flannel shirt and a cable knit sweater. The farmer's wife appeared at the door, her arms piled high with hand-woven blankets of wool and even a few crudely sewn animal pelts. Kismet accepted these, grateful for the supplemental warmth.

Anatoly pulled Kismet aside for a final conference. "Kristanovich, the farmer tells me that three days ago, a group of men went up into the mountains."

Kismet forgot about the cold. "How many men?"

Anatoly repeated the question to the farmer in a tongue Kismet did not recognize. The farmer began to babble forth information, which Anatoly passed on to Kismet. "A dozen men. Six of them were soldiers—no, that's not right." His craggy brow furrowed, and then he shrugged. "He said 'sailors.' They wore naval uniforms. The others looked like laborers. He thinks they are prospecting for gold. Foolish of them to venture into the mountains in winter."

"Did he recognize any of the men?"

Anatoly gave Kismet an odd look, but passed the question along to the farmer and similarly relayed the answer. "No, but they were wearing heavy coats and mufflers."

"How were they traveling?"

"A truck. It is doubtful that they got very far. The snow is deep and hides much. There are many ravines and cliffs concealed by the drifts."

Kismet nodded. "That's very helpful. Thank you."

"I thought it might be. The farmer says you should watch out for them. He doesn't trust them. The search for gold makes men do wicked things." He looked Kismet in the eye. "Are you looking for gold also, Nikolai Kristanovich?"

"No, but if I see any, I'll definitely pick it up."

Anatoly laughed, stepping back and swatting the lead horse on the rump. The animal whinnied, then leaned into its yoke and strained to draw the sleigh forward. In minutes, the powerful team had pulled the sleigh out of the barn and into the snow. The farmer and his wife made a second trip out with supplies, this time in the form of dried foodstuffs, much more than Kismet anticipated needing. Nevertheless, he nodded his head to the farmer in gratitude.

They quickly found the tracks left by the vehicle the farmer had seen three days previously. The snow had partially filled in the ruts, but the long, perfectly parallel lines made them easily identifiable.

"Do you think my father is with them?" asked Irene.

"I'd say it's a good bet. Harcourt wouldn't attempt trying to find the site based on someone's directions alone. The fact that he took your father out of the United States in the first place suggests that he'll hold on to him until he has what he wants."

"It's been three days. Do you think they've found it already?"

Kismet sensed the unasked question in her voice. "I'm sure your father is fine. If the farmer was right, their progress will be slow. The trucks could only take them so far. They might have even had to finish the trek on foot. They may have reached the site, but I doubt they've excavated much. Harcourt is a fool to try doing this in the dead of winter. Either that, or he's desperate."

Kismet's words had been meant to reassure her, but he noted right away that they had the opposite effect. "Irene, we'll get him back. Don't worry."

The horses tirelessly drew the sleigh in the trail left by Harcourt's truck. Over the course of the afternoon, the grade increased from a slight incline to a slope of nearly thirty degrees. The tracks in the snow soon began to tell the story of the difficulties experienced by the group in the truck. Erratic variations led to massive drifts, evidence that the vehicle had on more than one occasion veered off track and become mired in deep snow. The laborers in Harcourt's party had probably been called upon to dig the truck out and carve a path back to the main road. Kismet estimated that there was an accumulation of ankle deep snow atop an icy hard pack of nearly five feet deep. With the use of traction chains, the heavy truck tires had penetrated down to the base, permitting them to make gradual progress up the mountain.

Soon, Kismet realized that their course was taking them laterally across the face of the mountain. Although there was no road marked on this portion of the survey map, he surmised that the primitive track they were following probably cut back and forth across the range in a series of switchbacks. Their own progress was apparently better than Harcourt's had been. The horses' hooves bit into the packed snow, but did not sink as deeply as the truck tires had, and the sleigh glided across the powdery surface with negligible resistance. As the incline grew steeper, the horses had to exert themselves more, but they required little more than a verbal command and a shake of the reins for motivation.

With the increased elevation, the chill factor grew more intolerable. Irene unfolded two of the blankets, wrapping them about both their shoulders, so that their shared body heat kept the cold at bay. Kismet found the arrangement especially pleasing, if a little distracting.

Night fell gradually as the sun dropped into the distant Black Sea horizon. With Irene pressed tightly against his chest and her arm around his waist, he realized absently that his vigilance was slipping. As they rounded a corner, the horses stopped abruptly, giving him a much needed wake-up call. Lying in the path, directly in front of them, was a body.

Irene's hold around him went slack, and Kismet immediately sensed her terror. He thrust the reins into her hands and shrugged free of the blanket. "Stay here," he directed, in a tone that brooked no refusal.

It had snowed at least once since the person had fallen in death. A layer of crystalline precipitation had accumulated on the corpse, partially melted, and then frozen into a translucent crust. Kismet hastened to examine the body and quickly realized that the dark spots on the ground around the motionless form were not shadows but bloodstains. The person had died within a few steps of whatever trauma he had suffered. He knelt beside the corpse and brushed away the shroud of snow.

A pair of blank eyes stared up at him, causing him to start. He took a deep breath to compensate for the surge of adrenaline that left his lips feeling numb, and then resumed his inspection.

The body was male, no more than twenty years of age. The young man's hair had been cut in a close, military style, but he was clothed in ill-fitting civilian garments. Kismet noted the eastern European facial characteristics, but there was nothing to indicate what he had been in life. It was far easier to determine how he had died.

The man's chest was a mess of ravaged flesh. Kismet immediately recognized the ragged tears as exit wounds. The tight grouping was unmistakably a burst from a sub-machine gun at close range. He had been shot in the back.

"Nick?"

Kismet looked up, reading Irene's concern. "It isn't your father," he answered, trying to comfort her. "I'm not sure who he was. Only that he was shot trying to run."

"Should we do something for him? Bury him?"

Kismet frowned. "Yeah. But we don't have the time." In the end, he settled for dragging the corpse off the track and covering the young man with heaps of snow. His efforts to close the young man's eyes were in vain; the flesh had frozen beyond any postmortem manipulation. Ten minutes after discovering the fallen man, he returned to the sleigh.

He silently cursed Severin for having confiscated his gun. All that remained in the way of defensive weaponry was his Gurkha knife. Although he was confident of his ability to use the heavy blade for self-defense, he doubted that it would help much if they were pinned down by foes armed with assault rifles.

Nevertheless, he positioned the haft of the *kukri* where he could reach it in a hurry. It wasn't his pistol, but it made him feel a little more secure. "The stakes just went up," he declared in a tight voice. "Harcourt and his men have killed. They won't hesitate to do it again."

Kismet checked his watch; it was after midnight. They had journeyed for nearly six hours after sundown to reach their destination. Now, perched behind a snowdrift, they gazed down at a loose collection of tents lit up by a chain of klieg lights and the lazy half moon overhead—Harcourt's mountain camp.

They had left the sleigh and horses some distance away in the woods to avoid detection. Harcourt's party had been blessed with extraordinary luck, driving their truck—a beat-up deuce-and-a-half—all the way to the site, in spite of the heavy snow. This had in turn worked favorably for Kismet and Irene, enabling them to travel on into the night. The trail was not without perils however. The track often skirted steep drop-offs, with overhanging shelves of ice and snow posing a constant threat of avalanche. Their caution and persistence paid off though, delivering them to their destination in one piece.

A single sentry patrolled the perimeter of Harcourt's camp, a limit that was delineated by a triple thickness of concertina wire. He had worn a path in the snow, the sharp tips of the crampons strapped to his mountaineering boots biting into the subsurface ice. Kismet could not make out the man's face, but his marching steps were rigid and uniform; he was not taking his duty lightly. His routine of moving from one edge of the camp to another was as regular as clockwork and that, Kismet surmised, was the weakness that would allow them to slip in unobserved.

Kismet carefully monitored his wristwatch as he watched the guard make three circuits; each round was within twenty seconds of ten minutes. He estimated that it would take four minutes for them to steal down to the edge of the camp, during which time they would be exposed to any watchful eyes. He saw no evidence of other lookouts, and thought it unlikely that Harcourt would be expecting intruders, but Kismet was nonetheless cautious.

The rolls of razor wire, which were stretched out to form a barrier around the camp, were merely an inconvenience. Because they were staked down to the snowpack, Kismet needed only to burrow out a crawlspace, which he did using his *kukri* like a shovel, during the moments when the sentry was out of view. With this one difficulty surmounted, he prepared to infiltrate the camp.

"I'll go first," he whispered. "Keep an eye on me. When I give the signal, you follow. But if I get caught, promise me that you'll go straight back to the sleigh and down the mountain."

She nodded, but he could tell that she wasn't committed to the idea of leaving him. He saw that it was pointless to argue the issue, and refrained from further exhortation. Instead, he waited until the sentry had turned his back on their position, and then started down the hill.

The descent went smoothly. In less time than anticipated, he reached the outermost tent and ducked behind it. He could hear the sound of the guard's boots crunching in the snow as the man marched his patrol route. Less distinct was the sound of a generator, humming as it produced the electricity to power the lights.

Kismet checked his watch again; five minutes until the sentry completed his round. He decided to use the time to reconnoiter the immediate area. He began by looking back for Irene. She was not visible, wrapped in the shadows where she hid, but something he did see started his heart racing.

Leading from the top of the snowdrift, directly to where he stood, was a succession of enormous black spots—his footprints. Each step he had taken had left a depression in the snow, which in turn cast a shadow in the harsh glow of the artificial lights.

I couldn't have been more obvious, he thought, *if I had come down blowing a trumpet.* It would be virtually impossible for the sentry not to see his tracks; the only question was how would he react? If he sent up an alarm, then Kismet was as good as dead.

Kismet's hand dropped to his belt, gripping the haft of the *kukri*, ready for the inevitable. The crunch of the watchman's boots grew louder. Kismet heard the drawn out sound of the man turning ninety degrees on his heel, and could almost visualize each step that brought him closer to where Kismet was hiding. He began counting the paces, dreading the instant when the steps would grind to a halt, the sentry suddenly aware of an intruder in the camp. His hand tightened on the wooden grip of the knife.

The guard marched by without breaking stride.

Kismet nearly collapsed in relief. The watchman had passed right by the telltale footprints without even stopping to scratch his head. Kismet wondered if the man had been miraculously struck blind. Rather than waste the reprieve, he kept listening until he heard the heel grind of a right turn, and then signaled for Irene to join him.

As she darted across the snowfield, creating a second set of incriminating prints, Kismet wondered again at the guard's failure to notice. The shadows were so glaringly evident from where he waited, standing out in stark contrast to the pale snow. After a moment's contemplation, he figured it out. From his position, staring up the hill with the klieg lights shining from behind him, the shadows were perfectly visible, but from the guard's perspective, walking perpendicular to the light source, the shadows would look irregular, masked by the uneven contours of the snow. The sentry's night vision was also likely diminished by the glare, making it even less probable that their intrusion would be detected. Once Irene reached his side, they remained motionless until the guard completed another pass without noticing their tracks.

The nearby tent was the largest of the camp. Its olive drab canvas clothed a surface area comparable to a circus big top or a backwoods revival tent. The overwhelming size of it piqued Kismet's curiosity. There was only one reason he could imagine for such an enormous covering. Using his folding Balisong knife, he sliced through the fabric and peeked inside.

His suspicions were confirmed. Beneath the great tent, Harcourt had begun an epic archaeological excavation. All of the snow had been cleared away and tons of dirt had been loosened and moved into heaps around the tent's perimeter. Near the north edge Harcourt had exposed a cave entrance, possibly where an underground river had issued from the mountainside. Kismet knew intuitively that this was the location marked on Kerns' survey map.

A handful of incandescent bulbs were strung throughout the tent, providing enough light for Kismet to conclude that no one was in the enclosure. "Let's go in."

"What about my father?"

"Once we find him, we're not going to have the luxury of time. I'd like to have some answers before I leave here. And I want to make sure that Harcourt doesn't get his hands on the Golden Fleece."

"I thought getting my father out was our first priority." The implicit accusation in her caustic tone stung.

He turned and took her shoulders in his hands. "It has always been my first priority. But the Fleece is something I can't ignore."

"Sure. If you find the Golden Fleece, you'll be rich and famous." She struggled free of his grasp. "I can't believe I ever thought you cared."

Fearful that she was going to blunder off in her rage and expose them to Harcourt's guards, he gripped her arm, causing her to wince. "Damn it, Irene, you've got it all wrong."

If the Fleece did exist—if it was composed of the strange reactive element that could be turned into a weapon—then it was more than just an important archaeological find. More importantly, it was exactly the sort of thing that might lure the agents of the Prometheus group into the light. But how was he to explain that to Irene before she betrayed their presence with an emotional outburst?

"It's not about fame or wealth," he continued. "It's about a relic of enormous historic value, and possibly incredible power, falling into the wrong hands. And I don't mean Harcourt. He's just a puppet, working for evil men who will use the Fleece in terrible ways. We can prevent that. We have to."

She shook her arm, trying to break his hold. "Let go of me. So help me, I'll scream."

"Five minutes," he pleaded, relaxing his grip, but unsure of how she would decide. "If we stick together, there's a chance we might pull this off. But if you go off on your own..."

Her eyes did not lose their hard edge but she relented. "All right. Five minutes."

He let go of her arm, nodded and commenced inserting himself through the rent in the canvas. Irene however, wasn't finished. "Nick. This changes everything."

He didn't know how to respond. Damn her for not understanding, for not realizing that his motives weren't selfish and for complicating his decision with emotional blackmail. But there was no way, given the urgency of the moment, to make her comprehend that his decision to find out the truth about the Golden Fleece in no way eclipsed his commitment to helping her. And valuable time was being lost as he wrestled with the problem. Unable to explain, he turned away and threaded himself into the tent.

After climbing over a heap of dirt, he found himself standing above a trench, six feet deep and terminating at the tunnel mouth. He squatted down at the edge then lowered himself in. A shadow fell over him and he looked up to see Irene, arms folded across her chest, watching him. He decided to ignore her.

Harcourt had been exceedingly professional in his excavation. Kismet could see the attention to detail; the careful laying out of reference grids with string lines and markers to indicate when and where something of importance was located. Chalk marks differentiated the soil horizons and rock strata on the trench walls, highlighting approximations of how the sediment had built up over the course of several millennia.

Kismet wished that he could have been more than just a hasty spy making a cursory inspection of the dig. Instead, he had to settle for making a few quick mental notes before hurrying toward the cave entrance.

Harcourt had been more successful there. A number of markers highlighted his discoveries: the petrified remains of a fire-pit, possibly used as a forge; animal bones in such a concentration as to indicate a refuse heap; even one wall of a wooden structure embedded in the embankment. Kismet pushed on and entered the tunnel.

It was darker here, and he paused to take the MagLite from his pack A red filter muted the intensity of the light, but provided enough illumination for him to survey the smooth rock walls, examining the marks left by the passage of time. The history of the place spoke to him. He lingered for only a moment, then shut off the light and hurried back to Irene.

When she saw him return empty-handed, she registered a puzzled expression. "Are you satisfied?"

"More than you can know." He scrambled up the side of the trench and brushed himself off. "Come on. Let's go find your father."

The next tent they looked into turned out to be a supply depot, piled with fuel cans, foodstuffs and other crates of unknown purpose. "They're being supplied by air drops," he deduced aloud. "There's no way they could have brought all this stuff up in a single truck."

"Supplied by whom?"

He raised his eyebrows knowingly, but did not answer her question. "I'd say they're planning on being here awhile. That could work to our advantage."

"What are you talking about?" He was intentionally evasive, more to annoy her than anything else. If she wasn't going to trust him, why should he be cooperative? He knew it was petty, but she had put him in a vindictive mood. He simply grinned and led her from the enclosure.

The next tent was the smallest of the camp. They did not go in, but Kismet cut a peephole, which revealed it to belong solely to Harcourt. Given the austere conditions, the interior was furnished like an upscale luxury hotel room, replete with a glowing space heater at its center. Repressing mischievous desires, Kismet led the way to the next structure.

"This is interesting," he whispered. "It looks like the main bivouac for the troops."

"Troops? Anatoly said there were only a few soldiers."

Kismet looked again. "Well, now there are a few dozen. Probably paratroopers who dropped in with the supplies."

Irene shook her head in confusion. "I don't get it. I thought this was just about Harcourt and Grimes trying to get the Fleece. Now they have an army on their side? Did they make a deal with the Russian government?"

"These aren't Russian soldiers. Could be mercenaries, or..." He thought about the computer file he had helped Lyse smuggle into the U.S. "Or KSK—German Special Forces."

Irene's stunned silence indicated that their earlier argument was all but forgotten. "German soldiers have invaded Georgia?"

"Hard to believe, isn't it? I suspected that Grimes was working with German intelligence agents when I found you in New York. One of the dominating tapestries in that underground hall belonged to an old papal order called the Teutonic Knights; that's what got me thinking there might be a connection. Then a few other things happened." He did not elaborate with mention of the file on the SD card or the spy that had accosted him at his brownstone. "But I really didn't expect them to make such a big production out of this. It looks like they're willing to risk an international incident, maybe even war with Russia, if that's what it takes to find the Fleece."

"Why didn't you tell me this earlier?"

"I wasn't sure. You didn't need to know. What difference does it make?"

"What difference?" Her stage whisper could barely contain the strident tone of her rising anxiety. "There's no way we can get my father out of here, much less the Fleece."

"Irene, I swear to you that we'll get your father out."

"And the Fleece?"

"Since when does that matter to you?"

"Since I found out that the people are willing to go to war over it."

"Fortunately, that won't happen." He eased away from the bivouac then walked over to the remaining tent.

"How do you know that?" Irene persisted, her whispers growing uncomfortably loud.

"Because the Fleece isn't here." He raised a finger to his lips to silence any further discussion, and then cut a tiny slit in the fabric wall of the shelter. After peering inside, he pulled her close and whispered into her ear. "Pay dirt. There's one guard, and I count five prisoners tied on the floor. One of them is your father."

Irene drew in a breath, suddenly overcome with emotion. "Is he all right?"

"They all look a little thin. My guess is that Harcourt's been using them for slave labor." He looked over and saw tears welling up in her eyes. Impulsively, he reached out to her, hugging her to offer consolation. "Hey, it's going to be all right. We'll have him out of there in no time."

Together they crept around to the opposite side of the tent, to the place Kismet approximated to be directly behind the guard. A second incision revealed his estimate to be correct, and he noiselessly sliced apart the canvas. The guard was standing at attention with his back to them, less than three feet away. After a moment of preparation, Kismet reached in and wrapped his arm around the man's neck.

Rather than raise an alarm by firing the rifle in his hands, the guard instinctively dropped his firearm and tried to pry loose the stranglehold. Kismet yanked him backward through the rent, maintaining constant pressure. After a brief struggle, the man went limp in Kismet's arms.

Like the sentry roaming the perimeter, this man also wore snow camouflage fatigues. The white nylon shell offered no indication that the man belonged to any nation's armed forces. Similarly, his weapon, the AK-47 Kalashnikov semi-automatic rifle—was an anonymous choice, easily obtained by anyone with the right connections and ready cash. That way, if anyone from the expedition was discovered or captured, the German government could simply claim that it was a mercenary force working for private interests. Kismet confirmed that the man was unconscious then dragged him through the hole, back into the tent.

The struggle had awakened some of the prisoners. Except for Kerns, who was still sleeping, the prisoners were all young men, dressed only in trousers and undershirts, with close-cropped hair. It was evident that the body they had found on the trail had once belonged to their number. Kismet gestured for silence and the young men nodded eagerly, understanding that liberation was near.

Irene pushed past him and rushed to her father's side. Kerns awoke gradually, and when his eyes focused and recognition dawned, grief twisted his countenance. "Oh my daughter, they have brought you here, too."

She laughed and pushed away the tears that had were beading at the corner of her eyes. "No, papa. Nick and I are here to rescue you."

Kerns' expression changed to confusion. He looked over to Kismet, who was busy cutting the young laborers free. "Nick?"

"Nick Kismet. It's true, sir. Your daughter and I are going to get you out of here." He extended his hand to the other prisoners. "All of you."

The other young men responded with looks of incomprehension. It was obvious that they did not speak English. "They are Russian sailors," supplied Kerns. "The Germans captured their patrol boat and took their uniforms. Then they forced them to dig."

Kismet nodded. He would have preferred to keep his knowledge of the Russian language a secret, but time did not allow him that luxury. "*Which of you is the leader?*"

One of the young men raised his hand and started to speak, but Kismet cut him off. "*Listen, I can set you free, but this place is crawling with soldiers. If you go to the supply tent, you can get enough food and clothing to make the trip down the mountains.*"

The young sailor nodded. "*Thank you.*"

"*Don't thank me yet. You'll have to go through hell to get out of here alive.*"

He bent over to Kerns, cutting his bonds and helping him to his feet. Kerns looked thinner than when Kismet had seen him in the hall of the Teutonic Knights. His face was bruised and cut, and when he stood he seemed frail, but after a moment he straightened, addressing Kismet in deeply accented English. "They've already been through hell. Getting off this mountain will be easy by comparison."

"I hope you're right." He saw one of the men stooping over the fallen guard, fishing in the man's jacket pocket. A moment later he drew out a silver flask stamped with the insignia of the old Soviet military, a five-pointed red star. The sailor took a long drink from the flask then passed it around to his comrades. A few moments later, the de facto leader of the group offered it to Kismet.

After taking an obligatory sip of the vodka, a somewhat superior distillation than what Severin had served aboard the *Boyevoy*, Kismet proffered the flask.

The Russian sailor shook his head, indicating that Kismet should keep the container, and then bent over the guard to commandeer his firearm. Kismet frowned. "*I recommend you shoot only as a last resort. The sound will awaken the camp.*"

The young man nodded, but nevertheless drew back the bolt partway to inspect the weapon, then let it go, leaving a round into the chamber. Kismet shook his head in resignation and turned back to Kerns and his daughter. "Are we ready?"

After receiving affirmative nods, Kismet led the way, exiting through the door flaps while watching out for the lone sentry. Once more, the marching soldier's bootsteps betrayed his location. They had only to wait until the footsteps grew softer to make their move. The Russian sailors waited for Kismet's signal then darted into the supply tent.

"They're on their own," Kismet declared. "Now it's our turn." The three of them crept from shadow to shadow until reaching the edge of the camp. The sentry marched past a few minutes later. Once he rounded the next corner, they started moving again. Kerns was slow, his limbs stiff from the cold, but with Kismet on one side and his daughter on the other, they made the top of the snowdrift with a minute to spare.

Irene was giddy with relief, as they reached the sleigh. "I can't believe we pulled that off."

"Wait until we're back home before you start celebrating," Kismet chided. "We've got a long trip ahead of us."

"Yeah, but it's all downhill from here. How long before they know we're gone?"

"It depends. If our Russian friends don't do anything foolish, we should be well on our way before anyone knows what happened. Hopefully, the

Germans will think that their prisoners escaped on their own. I don't want Harcourt knowing I'm here if I can help it."

Irene and her father got into the back of the sleigh and bundled up together in the blankets, while Kismet took the driver's seat and coaxed the team into motion. The horses effortlessly drew the sleigh in a wide circle until the iron rails slipped into the tracks they had earlier cut. From that point on, the ride was virtually self-guiding.

Kerns gradually revealed the events that had transpired since his separation from his daughter in New York. Harcourt and two of Grimes' agents had crossed the Atlantic with him, stopping in Germany long enough to assemble a team of *Bundeswehr Kommandos Spezialkrafte* elite soldiers. Together they infiltrated Russian controlled waters, captured a *Svetlyak* class patrol boat, the *Zmeya*, and used it to make a surreptitious landing at a remote point just south of Poti. Much of what Kismet had supposed was verified; the death of the fleeing sailor, the airdrops and the arrival of fresh troops parachuting in under cover of darkness.

Kerns had cooperated for fear of his daughter's life, taking Harcourt directly to the site of the ancient mining camp. Kismet did not comment, but continued to listen as Irene spun the tale of their own adventures. Soon thereafter, both father and daughter were lulled to sleep, while Kismet continued to tend the horses.

Traveling on the decline was more difficult than Kismet had anticipated. The sleigh naturally wanted to race downhill. The horses were no longer serving as a means of locomotion, but rather as a brake to prevent the sleigh from running away out of control. Since this was not the task for which nature had so perfectly endowed them, they were having difficulty in maintaining surefootedness on the icy slopes. Kismet's attention was totally focused on controlling the team.

The lights of dawn were beginning to shine over the crest of the Caucasus six hours after they left the mountain camp when Irene stirred from her sleep and crawled forward to sit beside Kismet. "What time is it?"

"After seven. It should be light soon."

"How much farther?"

"I'd say we're about halfway." Kismet relaxed his tense grip on the reins as the track leveled out briefly. The horses, sensing that their yoke was no longer pushing them from behind, also relaxed and began trotting forward as if grateful for the exercise. The track led into a narrow pass, with snowdrifts piled high on either side for several hundred yards. Kismet remembered that the defile curved around to the left, and began to gradually decline again before leading into the switchbacks. Nevertheless, he was happy for the brief respite.

"But they're probably awake up in the camp. They know my father is gone."

Kismet shrugged. "They've probably known that for hours. But even with the truck they can't make it down this path any faster than we can. We've got a good lead on them."

Irene cocked her head to one side. "What's that sound?"

Her hearing was sharper than his, but before he could enquire, he heard it too; the unmistakable sound of an engine. He turned his head sideways, trying to isolate the source. It wasn't coming from behind them, but rather from further down the trail. Suddenly, a massive vehicle rounded the corner, its headlamps blazing.

Reflexively, Kismet reined back the horses, halting them fifty yards from the turn. An enormous tracked snow-cat, the kind used to groom ski slopes at mountain resorts, rumbled toward them. Two more just like it followed close behind, their tracks digging deep parallel grooves in the snow pack. Painted white to blend in with the wintry background, each vehicle carried a complement of barely distinguishable figures, likewise camouflaged.

"Troop carriers," Kismet realized aloud.

As the driver of the lead vehicle caught sight of them, Kismet could hear gears whining as they were shifted down. The troop carrier ground to a halt less than twenty paces from the sleigh. Kismet's heart skipped a beat—not because of the standoff, but because of what he saw in the cab of the snow-cat.

He did not recognize the two men sitting in the front of the vehicle, but the identity of the third man, leaning over the back of the driver's seat, was beyond question. In a frozen moment, they recognized each other.

Through the frosty pane, he saw Halverson Grimes' lips slowly form a single word: "Kismet!"

Grimes' incredulous expression mirrored Kismet's own. Both sets of eyes narrowed into defensive slits as each man recognized the other's presence on this remote mountainside. Grimes broke the visual deadlock, turning to the driver beside him to bark an order.

Kismet also looked away, refocusing on the snow-cats and the terrain they dominated. The vehicles had turned the corner sharply, staying close to the right hand side of the track—Kismet's left. On the other side however, to his right, the gap between the snow bank and the sides of the vehicles was considerable, possibly even wide enough to....

Kismet did not hesitate. Grimes and his troops were already starting to move, beginning the process that would result in their capture or death. "Hold on!"

With a shout to the horses and a shake of the reins he urged the team into motion. Immediately as they began to move, he pulled them right, angling toward the gap between the drift and the leading snow-cat. The horses could not comprehend his urgency, but the ferocity of his manner sufficed to motivate them to a trot.

He heard Irene shouting in his ear, demanding an explanation but there was no time for him to give one. The side of the sleigh banged into the front corner of the first vehicle, sending a shock wave through the sled and jostling its passengers. The iron rails bounced out of the grooves in the snow, skipping sideways as the horses' forward motion pulled it into line.

The hop carried the sleigh into a snowdrift and dislodged a torrent of the frozen powder into the interior before it straightened out.

Kismet kept at the horses, shouting for them to go faster as they threaded the narrow gap. They shot past the first snow-cat and into the open space between it and the next vehicle in the convoy. The commandos clinging to the open platform on the rear of the transport stared in disbelief. Each one fingered his weapon nervously, but without orders from their commanding officer, chose to fire nothing except for harsh curses.

Abruptly, Kismet realized the fallacy of his thinking. The snow-cats were not in a perfect line. In fact, the second one was nearly two feet closer to the bank on Kismet's right side. He swore under his breath, unable to judge the distance between them and the gap or to tell if the space was wide enough to allow them to pass.

The problem solved itself. Ignoring the possibility of failure, Kismet adjusted the course of the horses so that the edge of the snowdrift was virtually brushing against the right horse's flank. The rest he left up to luck.

The horses balked, but Kismet shook the reins vigorously, snapping them like whips against the animals' hindquarters. Grudgingly, they responded and burst forward into the narrow pass.

Each horse tried to turn inward to avoid striking whatever lay alongside. The harness allowed for very little of this sort of movement, but somehow, the two mighty horses squeezed between the icy wall and the metal behemoth. The sleigh however was another matter.

The front end was too wide by a fraction of an inch, but that was enough for it to come to a dead stop, wedged between the unyielding fender of the second troop mover and the snowbank. The sudden halt confused the horses, causing them to slide and stumble in their rig.

"We're stuck!" Irene shrieked, once more stating the obvious to Kismet's continued chagrin. He ignored her. The horses were strong enough to get them through, even if it meant shaving off the side of the snowdrift with the sleigh. All that was required was the proper motivation. Shouting meaningless vocalizations at the pair, he repeatedly shook the reins, trying if nothing else to aggravate the horses into reacting. Eight hooves bit deep into the snow; massive legs that were nothing less than great pillars of muscle strained against the grip that held the sleigh in place.

"It's working," Kerns shouted, now completely awake. Kismet did not relent in his efforts, nor did he look to see if the assessment was correct. There was still a long way to go.

A towheaded man, about Kismet's age, looked down from the window of the vehicle directly above them. He shouted in German for them to surrender, and brandished a sidearm to enforce his command. In the reflection of the windscreen, Kismet saw the troops from the lead cat disgorging onto the snow and advancing on them with rifles at the ready.

The sleigh lurched forward nearly a few feet before binding up again. A second violent movement took it further, and this time it was not halted, but merely slowed as it scraped through. A burst of noise rattled the mountain pass as one of the Kalashnikovs discharged, and Kismet ducked reflexively. An instant later, the sleigh burst into the clear between the second and the last snow-cat in the convoy.

Troops from both vehicles were spilling out onto the snow, bent on impeding their escape. It seemed obvious that commandos were linked by radio and getting updates from the front. The men in the last vehicle had probably known about them almost from the start, and had formed a human wall in the narrow gap beside their cat.

The troops behind them had also closed the gap, the foremost attempting to manually seize control of the sleigh. Kerns roused himself to fight them off with his fists, and unprepared for foot pursuit in the icy conditions, the men slipped and fell against each other like dominos. Soon white clad commandos were piled up behind them in the narrow space.

Kismet leapt forward, onto the back of the left-hand steed, and used the reins like a whip against the soldiers directly in their path. The leather straps proved more intimidating to these well-trained warriors than a blazing muzzle flash from a machine gun. The thought of the rawhide burning into their exposed faces, tearing out their eyes or disfiguring them with long, painful cuts, caused even the toughest of them to recoil, and the human barrier crumbled.

The draft horses plowed forward. The troops ran from before them, knowing that a slip might find them crushed beneath the massive hooves or sliced apart by the iron rails of the sleigh. With Irene and her father successfully repelling the advances from their rear and sides, the sleigh passed the final snow-cat and burst into the open.

Right away Kismet found himself imperiled by a new threat. Beyond the mountain pass the trail began declining again. Moreover, a broad corner loomed ahead, with a precipice on one side. He immediately let the horses' pace slacken as to approach the curve at a less hectic clip.

As he clambered back to the bench seat of the sleigh, he risked a rearward look, confirming his belief that the pass was too narrow to allow the snow-cats to turn and pursue. Like the barbs on a fishhook, the vehicles were firmly inserted into the narrow passage. They might, with great difficulty, be able to back up, but the only viable way of using the caterpillar driven transports to pursue the sleigh would necessitate driving them forward until a space wide enough to come about could be found.

However, Kismet quickly realized the commandos would not need their vehicles to mount an effective pursuit. Dozens of the soldiers were breaking out long containers, from which they took narrow strips of carbon fiber, each as tall as a man, which curved like scimitars at one end.

"Skis," rasped Kismet, as if the word were an oath. The elite soldiers had brought along cross-country skis. In a matter of seconds, the first of the troops had secured his boots in the toe bindings and pushed off with his ski poles.

Kismet brought his focus back to the trail ahead. The snow-cats had stamped a broad path of packed snow leading back down the mountain. That was the good news. Their speed was gradually increasing as the slope began to drop away beneath the rails. Kismet felt the shift in their momentum as first, the horses altered direction, and then the sleigh, like a pendulum, swung into line.

Beyond the corner, the track led into a rapid descent across the face of the mountain. Sheer ice rose above on one side, while a drop-off opened up on the other. The side nearest to the edge of the precipice put them dangerously close to going over, but there was no way to effect a change. The only option was to once more put their fate in the slippery hands of luck.

Three fearless ski-troopers screamed toward them, leaning forward as the slope increased their own speed. The first tucked his poles under one arm and brought his rifle around. Using the web sling like a bracing arm, he fired the weapon one-handed into the air. They were only warnings shot, but nonetheless close enough to let the fugitives know where the next discharge would be aimed.

Kismet found the threat bitterly amusing. They were committed to a descent of the mountain; they could not stop now, even if they wanted to. Any attempt to slow the draft horses would end disastrously, with the sleigh jack-knifing and causing a lethal tumble down the trail, or shooting out over the edge. The commando dropped the smoking weapon, allowing it to dangle impotently from the strap and tucked in to increase his speed. As he maneuvered closer to the speeding sleigh, Kismet saw what he was up to.

Despite the urgency of the moment, gears were turning in Kismet's head. In the back of his mind, he was putting seemingly unrelated facts and observations together. It was glaringly apparent that Grimes and Harcourt still had a use for Peter Kerns. Perhaps Harcourt had begun to suspect what Kismet now knew; namely, that Peter Kerns had deliberately misdirected the British archaeologist, that he had not discovered the artifacts in the mountain camp, and that in all likelihood, the Russian engineer had already laid eyes on the Golden Fleece and probably concealed it somewhere far from the Caucasus. Irene was merely a pawn, useful alive, but no loss if killed. What was not so obvious was the value of his own life to Grimes. The pursuit in New York had seemed openly hostile, yet throughout Grimes had made a pretense of wanting Kismet's assistance. What was his value to the traitor now? Had Grimes ordered the soldiers to kill him, or to simply commandeer the sleigh and return all three to the mountain camp?

Because life or death odds gave him an adrenaline edge, Kismet chose to believe the worst. As the ski trooper drew alongside the sleigh and reached out to pull himself in, Kismet unleashed his *kukri*.

The wounded soldier cartwheeled away, his skis whirling like fan blades. His crash created an obstacle in the path of his confederates. The second commando's skis hit the motionless form of the fallen man, ripping his feet from the bindings to send him sailing through the air, over the cliff. The third skier turned hard, angling into the snow piled up along the wall. Rather than losing control, he skillfully negotiated the sheer wall and actually advanced upward as his skis cut a new path through the accumulated snow. Without slowing, he angled his skis down and skipped across the nearly vertical surface, directly ahead of the sleigh. As the horses passed beneath him he pushed out with his legs and launched himself at the sleigh.

Kismet had followed the soldier through his maneuvers, but the last move caught him by surprise. Unable to throw together a last-second response, he simply ducked his head as the skier slammed into him.

He felt a searing pain along his back as the sharp edge of one ski raked through his thick leather jacket, gouging a bloody trail from his shoulder blade to his waist. Before he could give voice to his pain, a second blow exploded like fireworks in his skull; the trooper's gun, swinging wildly from its sling, had chanced to clout him in the back of the head.

As he crashed down on top of Kismet, the soldier wrapped an arm around his neck. His head presented a perfect target for the German's blows. Flashes like lightning swam before his eyes while the dull hammering left his ears ringing. In desperation, he drove backward with his elbow. A grunt signaled that the blow had done some harm and was accompanied by a momentary respite in the assault.

Kismet became aware of two things in that instant. First, that Irene and her father were struggling to overpower the unwelcome visitor. This gave him the strength of will to muster his own retaliation, in spite of his indefensible position. The second observation, which lent urgency to the first, was that no one was driving the sleigh.

A second blow from Kismet's elbow elicited an outcry from the soldier. As his stranglehold weakened, Kismet changed his aim, driving downward into the man's genitals. The attack drew a primal response. Howling, the German's hands flew to protect his bruised groin. Kismet raised his head, and with a vicious grin, launched a cross-body left to the man's jaw. The commando rolled over, making a desperate effort to save himself with one hand, but was unable to resist the persuasive power of Kismet's boot in his back. He flipped over the side railing and tumbled into the snow as the sleigh raced away.

Through a haze of pain, Kismet looked with groping hands for the reins to the sleigh. Although several seconds had passed with no one to guide them, the horses had maintained reasonable control over the descent. Holding the reins loosely, he let them have their head and turned to scan the slopes behind for signs of other pursuit.

He quickly found it. Charging in loose formation down the trail were at least a dozen more skiing commandos. With their bodies crouched low and their weight forward over the curving tips of their Nordic skis, the soldiers were rapidly gaining on the sleigh.

Ahead, the trail was starting to level out. The merits of this fact were eclipsed by his realization that the short flat stretch was followed by a hairpin turn that led into a switchback. He had precious few seconds in which to slow almost to a complete stop, or their momentum would carry them past the turn and headlong into certain disaster.

Irene saw it too. She slid into the seat beside him and grabbed his arm. He shook his head and pulled free. "No time for that!" Thrusting the reins into her hands, he vaulted over the back of the bench and past Kerns.

With both hands fiercely gripping the backboard, he hurtled out over the snow. Like a crazed gymnast, he dangled behind the sleigh, thrusting forward with his legs. His feet hit the snow heels first. He kept his knees locked and ankles rigid so that the thick boot soles would dig into the icy surface. For a moment his plan seemed to work. Then his feet hit an unyielding bump and his legs were driven backward under his torso to flop uselessly behind him.

Seeing his peril, Peter Kerns leaned out over the back end of the sleigh and grasped Kismet's forearms. At the same time Irene began to haul back on the reins, attempting to convince the horses to arrest their downhill charge, but her efforts were futile. The horses had too much momentum and not enough room to stop.

Kerns' timely assistance roused Kismet for a second try. Swinging his legs forward, he once more attempted to slow their descent. The friction of his heels in the snow, coupled with the leveling of the trail and, in some part, Irene's efforts to control the team, accomplished the impossible. The horses came to a complete stop a few lengths from the hairpin curve.

Kismet let go and dropped back into the snow. Icy shavings had filled his trouser legs up to his knees, but there was no time to shake the cold powder away from his clothes.

The skiers were visible but still a ways off, but in the time it took Irene to maneuver the horses around to face the next leg of the descent, they halved the intervening distance.

"Go!" Kismet urged as he scrambled aboard. He made no effort to take the reins; her control of the draft horses was far superior to her performance behind the wheel of the garbage truck in New York. As they began descending once more, he retrieved his *kukri* from the splinters of broken skis and poles and slid it into its leather scabbard.

His assumption that his foes would have to slow down before making the hard turn was only partially correct. Several of the more confident among their number elected to cut out the switchback altogether by turning prematurely and charging down the vertical face of the cliff.

"They're crazy." whispered Kismet. "And they're about the best damn skiers I've ever seen. We've got to try something else, and fast."

Irene took his final word literally. With a shout, she urged the team into a full run. Their path took them directly under the skiers and just past them before they could complete their descent. Nevertheless, as soon as they touched down on the slope, the commandos were in close pursuit. Less than a hundred yards separated the sleigh from a pack of four soldiers. The rest of the group had already rounded the hairpin curve and was not far behind.

The trail they followed soon opened up into a broad powder valley. The passage of the tracked vehicles had carved a pathway through the soft accumulation, allowing them to proceed without slowing, and soon they were once more following a gradual decline. They were no longer on the trail that they had originally followed up from the foothills. Instead, they were now on the path Grimes' snow-cats had blazed, a route that would bring them east along the southern flank of the range.

"We can't keep running like this," he announced. "Eventually we're going to get chased over a cliff, or worse."

"So what have you got in mind?"

"Change the rules," he replied, understanding even as he said it, what that would mean. "Go on the offensive."

"How?" wheezed the Kerns. "We haven't any guns. And as good as you are with it, I don't think that knife of yours is any match for an automatic rifle."

"You might be surprised," he muttered, then in a more commanding voice added: "Get down this mountain any way you can. Then go to Anatoly's house. I'll catch up to you as soon as I can."

"What?" Irene gaped at him and let her hold on the reins momentarily go slack. The concern in her eyes hit him like physical blow. "Nick, you can't leave me."

Her tone said more than her words. Without even realizing it, she had fallen for him, and the thought that he might vanish forever from her life was too horrible to contemplate. This unspoken revelation filled him with apprehension. He didn't want to leave her behind, didn't want to face the prospect of death or capture alone. More than anything, he wanted her to get away safely. But there was the Fleece....

The Golden Fleece. That was what it was really all about. Men and women would continue to fall in and out of love for the rest of eternity. Once in a millennium such a love might actually shape the course of history, but more often than not, even the greatest lovers faded into obscurity. Not so with power. Power, used or abused, left a mark for generations. Just as it was impossible for mankind to unremember the atomic bomb, so too the Fleece and whatever diabolical machination Grimes and his allies had planned for it, would surely haunt the planet for the rest of its existence. He alone was in a position to prevent that—to stand between that relic of uncertain power and the forces of evil. Nothing else really mattered.

Peter Kerns knew where it was, of that Kismet was certain. He could not allow Grimes to recapture the old man or his daughter.

"If I don't make it back by midnight tonight, I want you both to head two miles north of the city. Wait on the shore for an hour. Lyse—a friend of mine—will rendezvous there and get you back home. As for you, sir, I want you to promise to tell my friend the truth."

Kerns looked back at him with a stupefied expression, but Kismet wasn't buying. "I mean it. Grimes must not be allowed to get it. I think you know that."

The old engineer tried to maintain his poker face, but finally relented, sagging as if the acknowledgment left him drained. Irene was not so quick to accept his decision. "Nick, stop talking like this. We've got to stick together."

"No. That's just it. We've got to split up. I have to slow those soldiers down, or misdirect them somehow." He saw emotion welling up in her eyes, but willfully ignored it. Instead, he rose and crawled out onto the back of the left-hand horse.

It took him less than a minute to loose the steed from the yoke that held it in thrall. Although it continued to trot apace with the other animal, it no longer contributed its power to pulling the sleigh.

Kismet quickly realized how awkward it would be to ride the creature. Its back was virtually twice as broad as any horse he had ever ridden; his legs were spread painfully apart as he straddled its bare torso. He was confident with most horses and had ridden camels and even an elephant, but rarely faster than a brisk walk. There was simply no way to ride the draft horse in the conventional manner. He was unable to exert any pressure with his inner thighs, so instead he leaned forward against its neck, gripped either side of its bridle with his hands and shouted into its ear: "Giddyap!"

Instantly, the great steed pulled away from its shackled cousin. Kismet ran the horse out ahead of the sleigh, and then tugged its bridle to swing it around. As the sleigh drew close, his gaze met Irene's.

"Nick."

He could see it in her eyes; the declaration that she had not quite been able put into words. "Don't say it. You'll only make this harder."

She shook her head, blinking back the tears. "Just be careful."

He knew those weren't the words that were poised on her lips, but was grateful that she had held back. With a nod, he coaxed his mount back up the trail, letting the thump of hoof-beats refocus his attention. After a few moments, he looked back, but the sleigh had already diminished to a dark speck in the snowfield. When he returned his gaze forward, half a score of white-clothed skiers had appeared directly ahead of him, and suddenly there was no more time for emotional turmoil.

Grimacing, he urged his mount onward, racing toward the pack like a runaway boulder down a mountainside. Hugging the horse's neck with one arm, he drew the Gurkha knife and raised it in the air over his head. A moment later, he was plowing through the midst of the loose formation. The knife slashed down repeatedly, causing confusion and not a few superficial wounds. Half of the group, in their haste to get out of the way, went down, crashing into each other or veering off course into the mire of the powder valley. The few left standing after his passage snowplowed to a halt and turned to face him.

Kismet also came about for another pass. One skier raised a pole to block the downward stroke of the blade, only to have it shorn clean in two. A kick from Kismet sent him flailing. A soldier on Kismet's left stood his ground, raising his rifle, but before he could fix his sight picture, Kismet twisted his body in order to launch a vicious slashing attack. The knife quivered in his grip as it struck flesh and smashed through the man's collarbone and stuck there.

He urged his mount ahead with another shouted vocalization. The horse charged ahead and the soldier was dragged along, in shock and unable to resist. Kismet kept his hold on the hilt of the *kukri*, twisting it until the blade slipped free and the wounded man fell away.

Behind him, the commandos hastened to close ranks and get back on their skis. It was time, Kismet decided, to lure the hunters away from his friends. The trail ahead was marked by the very obvious passage of the sleigh—deep parallel lines cut by the steel rails and enormous craters stomped by the massive hooves of the draft horses. Kismet sheathed the knife and urged the horse forward, all too aware that his back was now a target.

He followed the path of the sleigh for several hundred yards, passing the point where he had separated from Irene and her father. He stayed on that course a while longer, occasionally looking back to check on the pursuit and was dismayed to see that more troops had arrived to supplement the ranks of the fallen.

Riding full out across the flats, the horse was superior in speed to the skiers. Kismet held back however, at all times keeping himself in view of the German troopers. He didn't want them splitting up to follow the sleigh; beyond that, he wasn't really sure what he hoped to accomplish.

The treetops alongside him exploded in a spray of noise and ice. The skiers were shooting after him in a wasteful and futile attempt to slow him down. Because they were in a flat snowfield, the soldiers could not advance and fire at the same time, giving him a chance to widen the gap if he successfully dodged their fusillade. Kismet urged the horse forward, angling right and ducking behind a snowdrift that was twice as high as the horse's head.

The grade of the terrain abruptly began to fall away beneath him. The snow was much softer and deeper here, slowing the draft horse, bogging it down as each step sunk knee-deep. The landscape ahead was clear—a sloping plain with only a few treetops barely visible. The Germans would have the advantage here. They would be able to utilize the slope for locomotion while focusing their attention and their weapons on him. The distant treetops would be his only cover. With renewed urgency, he began coaxing speed from the horse.

At a point midway down the hill, he risked a rearward glance. The commandos were rounding the corner, poling and stepping vigorously to close the gap. Though unable to get a head count, Kismet had the sickening feeling that at least a few of the elite soldiers had veered off in pursuit of Irene and Peter Kerns. The narrow cross-country skis buoyed the commandos atop the powder, and in a matter of moments, his lead was erased. Three of their number blazed a trail down the hillside, compressing the grainy snow deep beneath the curved tips. The tracks they left behind provided an effortless path for their comrades to utilize.

The trees Kismet sought for cover remained frustratingly distant. Only the tops were visible, as if the entire system of trunks and branches had been buried beneath deep snow. The slope remained consistent though and Kismet was plagued by the vague notion that he was failing to see something obvious.

In one heart-stopping instant Kismet saw that the hillside ended at a plunging embankment—the edge of a deep ravine—where the draft horse abruptly halted. As it planted its forelegs, hooves biting into the snow for stopping traction, it also lowered its tremendous head, removing the only obstacle between Kismet and the ravine. He shot forward, hitting the slope six feet ahead in the snow.

As he tumbled toward the edge he frantically plunged his hands into the deep powder, searching for some way to arrest his fall. The snow compressed into a tentative barrier, but his momentum caused his lower body to whip around, his legs sticking out into empty space. He could feel the snow beneath him crumbling and compacting as his weight settled. He drove his hands deeper, desperate to find something solid, aware with each heartbeat that he was slipping away toward the ravine.

A cloud of white sprayed into his face as the leading soldier realized too late that he was racing to his doom. A hasty attempt to turn parallel to the edge threw up a dusting of powder, but failed to stop the skier's doomed plunge. He shot past Kismet, screaming as his skis lost contact. The man made a last-ditch attempt to assume the position for a Nordic ski jump, but his skis and his body were turned irrecoverably sideways. His curses were cut off as he crashed into a web of tree branches.

Kismet was only peripherally aware of the commando's demise. His own situation was growing more precarious by the moment as the snow-bank against his belly eroded. A second wave of snow splashed over him as another skier plowed to a stop right above him. Kismet raised his head enough to clearly see the soldier slowly working his way back up the slope.

As he stepped sideways away from the edge of danger, the commando flashed broad grin of triumph, directed solely at his dangling prey. Kismet saw the taunting smile and grimaced in return as he slipped another inch. With casual slowness, the soldier unlimbered his rifle and flipped off the safety, preparing to blow Kismet into oblivion.

Sacrificing his failing grasp on safety, Kismet drove forward, making a mad grab for his foe. He immediately began to slide into the ravine but before gravity could fully claim him, his right hand found the tip of the man's ski. His fingers wrapped around the carbon fiber, clutching it tightly as he started to fall. Unprepared for the desperate move, the soldier fell back as his leg was yanked from beneath him. The rifle fell from his grip as he began sliding toward the precipice.

Kismet gripped the ski with both hands but was still descending into the ravine as his weight drew the soldier toward him. He stuck his feet out, trying to brace them against the sheer cliff but his boot soles slipped ineffectively on the ice, making it appear as though he was running in place on the vertical wall. An instant later, his downward journey halted and he slammed against the ice encrusted sheer face.

Shaking off the daze of the impact, he looked up and saw a foot, bound to the ski, protruding over the edge above him. Without hesitating, he began pulling himself up. His muscles screamed with the exertion but the adrenaline in his bloodstream provided a surge of nearly superhuman strength. He seized hold of the soldier's ankle and hauled himself above the level of the precipice.

The commando had stabbed one of his poles deep into the snow and was holding on for dear life; it was the only thing preventing him from being pulled over the edge. But when he saw Kismet attempting to climb up his leg to safety, he released one hand and fumbled for his weapon.

Kismet saw the black barrel swing his way and instinctively ducked. On an impulse, he grasped the ski and twisted savagely. Bones and tendons snapped apart and the soldier screamed, forgetting about everything except the pain his foe was inflicting.

The move bought Kismet the time he needed. Grabbing first the soldier's trouser leg, then his belt, he heaved himself onto the slope, away from the deadly drop-off. The German commando faced him, seething with primal rage, but before he could give voice to his wrath, Kismet's right fist battered him senseless.

Escape from the edge of death fueled the fire of Kismet's will to survive. He plucked the fallen soldier's weapon from the snow and ripped the sling free of the man's shoulder. He knew how to operate the weapon, even realized in a distant corner of his mind that it was cocked and ready to fire. He rolled away from the unconscious German and without even picking a target, sprayed the hillside with a storm of lead.

The snow blossomed red as the commandos fell, wounded and dead, in the sweeping volley. Kismet immediately released the trigger, conscientious of the need to conserve ammunition, and scanned the slope for signs of enemies still standing.

His grim satisfaction turned to horror as the crimson-splotched hillside was rent by a jagged, horizontal shadow. The entire snowfield and the hard ice beneath, loosened by the impact of bullets and the percussive explosions of gunfire, split apart. The lower portion fell lazily away in massive chunks, which in turn dislodged everything below.

In the space of a heartbeat, the hillside above him became a tremendous wave of rolling snow, an avalanche that would sweep away everything in its path, including Nick Kismet.

10

As she had done every few seconds since he'd left, Irene glanced over her shoulder to see if Kismet had caught up. Once again, there was no sign of him.

Deprived of half its impetus, the sleigh made slow progress across the flats and tended to veer off course in the direction of the remaining draft horse. She had to keep a constant rein on the animal to correct this leaning. Not long after Kismet's departure, the trail took them into a gently sloping pass, following the course of what was likely a snowed-in ravine. The rising walls of snow on either side offered cover from any pursuing forces, and the distinctive pattern left by the snow-cats pointed the way off the mountain.

Peter Kerns crawled over the back of the bench seat and sat beside his daughter. "A brave man," he commented wistfully. "He reminds me of myself."

Irene raised an eyebrow. "Is that supposed to mean something?"

Kerns laughed. "Well, look where it got me; always in trouble and on the run. You should find someone with a little more stability in his life."

Although she had already decided not to have this conversation with her father, she couldn't hold back her riposte. "Someone more pedestrian, maybe? How about a lawyer?"

He shrugged.

She shook her head disparagingly and corrected the horse's path again. She was too confused by her feelings to even attempt to argue them with her father. Her intended but unspoken declaration of uncertain emotion now haunted her with its potential for insincerity. Her thoughts were punctuated by a burst of noise through the trees; the staccato beat of automatic weapons in the distance. The sound hit her like a physical blow. The shots were surely aimed at Kismet.

A wave of nausea clenched her gut, then rose into her throat; a sour mixture of concern, guilt and certainty that he was dead. With a shudder, she fought back the premonition and regained her composure, but there was no stopping the tears.

A fatherly response moved Kerns to place a consoling hand upon his daughter's neck. A second volley of gunfire echoed across the mountainside, shorter bursts at sporadic intervals. "You see?" Kerns whispered. "They haven't got him yet. He'll get away. The horse is faster."

She nodded, blinking at the tears and wiping their trails with the back of one hand. She was distracted momentarily by a sudden cloud of snow that arose for no apparent reason alongside the path of the sleigh. An instant later, another short burst of machine gun discharge split the air, but this time closer. Much closer.

In disbelief, both Irene and her father turned their heads to look. Four shapes, nearly indistinguishable because of their white camouflage clothing, were speeding along their trail, fifty yards back but rapidly closing. Irene swung her attention to the horse and began shaking the reins and shouting for it to move faster. Another burst from the lead soldier's weapon kicked up an eruption of snow to their right.

"Here!" She thrust the reins into her father's hands. His jaw dropped in incomprehension, but his fists tightened on the leather straps. Irene rolled over the back of the seat and stayed low on the floor of the sleigh.

"Be careful, Irina!" Kerns shouted, knowing it was fruitless to ask what she was up to. He was correct in this assumption; Irene herself had no idea what to do next. She glanced around for inspiration, trying to imagine what Kismet would do.

The floor of the sleigh was littered with the broken remains of a pair of skis left behind from the earlier invasion by one of the daring troopers. She gathered the fragments into her arms and hurled them off the back of the sleigh. The lightweight pieces of carbon fiber didn't seem like much, but to a speeding skier any obstacle might prove hazardous, and a sudden turn to avoid such a hurdle might likewise cause a crash. Soon other pieces of detritus were scattered out behind them. Irene even sacrificed a few of their warm blankets.

The jetsam worked exactly as she had planned. The leading soldier was forced to slow and carve a wide turn around the wreckage. A piece of ski pole, all but buried in the snow, caught the left ski of the rearmost trooper, stopping it dead. The soldier flew headlong and went cartwheeling down the slope, his gear flying in every direction.

"One down," Irene muttered under her breath, unable to suppress a self-satisfied grin. The remaining skiers picked their way carefully through the debris field, impeded but only briefly. The delaying tactic had earned Kerns and Irene a few precious seconds of lead time, but in her heart, she knew more desperate measures would be necessary to guarantee their escape.

"Irina!" Kerns shouted. "Listen!"

Climbing into the front seat, she cocked her head to the side. "What?"

"It's stopped. The shooting. A moment ago, there was a long burst. I heard faint screams and a strange noise, almost like distant thunder. What-ever has happened, I fear the worst for our friend."

Irene bit her lip. Somehow, the immediacy of their plight insulated her from a physical reaction to her emotions. She dissociated from her feelings, put them in a distant corner of her mind, and focused on their flight from the commandos. If and when they reached safety, there would be time to grieve.

The pursuing soldiers had retreated to mere specks in the distance. They did not attempt to fire their weapons, yet it was clear that they were once more on the move and gaining ground.

For several long minutes the sleigh held its lead, winding through a needle's eye pass and onto a shallow grade, which cut across the face of a mountain. Kerns had coaxed the horse up to a trot, but controlling the sleigh still proved difficult. It kept veering to the right, toward the edge of the trail and a precipice overlooking a sheer drop. He had to focus all his attention on steering it. Irene, on the other hand, continued to monitor the progress of the pursuit. The three remaining soldiers had lost their advantage temporarily, unable to close the gap because of the shallow gradient. There was no sign whatsoever of the fourth, fallen skier. If he had regained his equipment and joined the chase, he was too far behind to be of consequence.

"Irina!" Kerns' voice was filled with trepidation. Irene had witnessed her father's flight from the Soviet secret police, his captivity to Grimes, and other terrifying events, but had never heard the tone of desperation that now trembled in his words. "Look ahead."

As she turned her gaze forward, she felt the sting of her father's infectious dread. At first, all she saw was the radical increase of the slope. The angle of descent changed from a mere ten percent to nearly forty-five degrees. It continued like this for only a few hundred yards however. After that, it appeared to end altogether.

"A switchback," she gasped.

Kerns nodded. "We'll never make it. We can't slow down. We have to jump."

"No." She didn't have to look back to verify her next statement. "They'll have us for sure if we do."

"We're dead if we don't."

"There's another way." Tearing her eyes away from their doomed course, she began looking for the miracle that would save them. To her surprise, she found it. "Nick had the right idea!"

"I don't understand!" Kerns shouted, his tone more insistent. "And we're running out of time."

"The horse. If we can get onto it, and cut the sleigh loose—"

He nodded, brightening at the suggestion. "Yes. It will be much easier to control the horse. And we'll be able to outrun them."

"You climb out. I'll steer until we're ready."

"No," he protested. "You should go first."

"Not a chance. You're still pretty beat up. It will be easier for me to make the jump at the last second. Go!"

Kerns handed over the reins and leaned forward onto the rigging. At that instant, Irene felt the forward shift of the decline and the subsequent increase in speed. The sleigh began pushing against the horse, causing the animal to behave skittishly. She pulled back on the straps, forcing its head up, but failed to slow their inevitable race toward the edge.

Kerns reached the hindquarters of the massive draft horse without losing his tentative grip. From there it was a simple thing to pull himself onto its broad back. Knotting his fingers in its mane, he dragged himself forward until he was leaning against its neck. The bony fingers of his right hand were white from the intensity of his grip on the coarse mop of horsehair. He cautiously leaned sideways, reaching out with his left to free the animal from its harness.

The yoke was held only by a simple pin and came away in an instant, but the harness strap was more cumbersome. The farmer who had rigged the team had knotted the leather to prevent it from slipping. Subsequently, melting snow had caused the leather to swell and stiffen, and Kerns' cold fingers seemed unable to loosen it. He cursed aloud for not having a knife in his pocket to cut it with. From as early as he could remember, he had always carried a folding knife, and had used its blade for every conceivable purpose, but his captors had taken his knife, and now in his moment of greatest need he was without it. Gritting his teeth, he attacked the knot until the leather yielded and the strap came free. Only the grip of his two hands held the horse in thrall to the sleigh. Fearful that his fingers might slip at any moment, he shouted for his daughter to join him.

His success buoyed Irene's spirits. This was actually going to work. She knotted the reins together, bunched them into a ball, and tossed them out to her father who awkwardly pinned the bundle between his torso and the horse's neck.

Kerns could feel the harness strap sliding through his fingers. "Jump now, Irina! Quickly!"

Irene eased forward and reached out for the horse, but was suddenly pulled back. Confused, she turned and found herself staring into a pair of blue eyes. A young soldier, a mere boy, had managed to board the sleigh and had wrapped his arms around her torso, pinning her arms to her body. She felt the shift of his weight as he attempted to launch them both away from the doomed vehicle.

She heard her father cry out frantically, a single word: "No!" The strap slipped from Peter Kerns' old, cold fingers and the rigging tackle, no longer connected to anything, fell into the snow.

Irene's stomach dropped. Her mind could not keep up with what was happening, but she was aware that the sleigh had become airborne and the she and the young soldier were still its passengers. Her captor let go in a survival reflex, and both of them clawed at the air, knowing that it was already too late.

Nearly two thousand cubic yards of snow and ice had been displaced by the avalanche. The movement had scraped away a layer of accumulation to a depth of nearly six feet, revealing a glistening ice pack that remembered none of the crimson stains left by Kismet's counterattack. It was as if the slide had erased the violence done upon the mountain. In the chaos below, where shifting snow had all but filled the ravine, there was no indication that any living thing had survived. The snow had broken away in great fractures, piled up in thick sheets, like the walls of a collapsed house of cards, and buried everything. It was inconceivable that any man, even having survived the impact of the avalanche, would be able to free himself from the crushing snow.

Remarkably however, mere minutes after the turmoil had ceased, restoring quiet to the mountainside, something began to move beneath the frozen covering. Massive pieces of ice rose and slid away near the edge of the ravine, as something larger fought its way to the surface. Snorts and grunts of exertion heralded the rebirth of a survivor from the dark, icy womb. A regal head broke through the frozen scree, followed by a pair of equine forelegs.

The draft horse, with power that dwarfed the reserves of the strongest man, and hooves capable of digging into the hardest ice, wrestled itself free from a prison of cold nearly a fathom deep. Had the covering been any greater, perhaps even the animal's prodigious strength would have been insufficient to save it, and therefore, though the horse could not comprehend such things, it owed its survival, more than anything, to simple luck. After a few more minutes of thrashing and pulling, the great beast slipped free of the ice and stood on all fours upon the surface.

Yet it remained anchored to the snow; the long reins attached to its bridle were still buried deep in the avalanche. Planting its hooves firmly, the animal struggled against the final impediment to its freedom. The muscular legs, capable of drawing a heavy plow or pulling large trees from the forest, strained and pulsated with each backward step, and once more the ice yielded to its might.

It was not the leather straps that prevented the animal from getting loose, but rather something larger; the motionless figure of a man. With a final heave the horse pulled the body from the grip of the snow and was free at last. The man remained prone upon the surface of the snow. The beast tried to move away from him, but succeeded only in dragging the man along behind. Its reins were wrapped around his waist and tied in a hasty knot. The animal relented, choosing instead to satisfy its instinctive curiosity. Lowering its head, it began prodding at the man, exhaling hot steam onto an ice-encrusted face.

From the depths of a great darkness, like the frozen grave from which he had been liberated, Nick Kismet struggled to the surface of consciousness. He could not feel any of his extremities, nor could he make sense out of the lights and sounds flooding into his brain. The breath of the horse, a strange sour vapor, evoked nothing, even when he was able to bring into focus the bestial muzzle, with its gaping nostrils and liquid eyes.

His cognitive abilities gradually returned, commencing with a sense of grim satisfaction. He had survived. Slowly, his memories began to fall into a logical chain, allowing him to reconstruct everything leading up to the slide. At the same time, he began to regain the use of his body. The first message his nerves sent him was brief and to the point: cold! Snow had penetrated his clothing and was leeching away his body heat. It was a wonder that hypothermia and frostbite had not already claimed him. He knew that he had to get moving right away if he wanted to live.

Concentrating on a single effort, he swung his hand up and grasped the horse's bridle. Immediately the animal pulled away, but Kismet kept his grip. The result was that he was lifted erect. He quickly flung his arms around the animal's neck, clinging to it because he couldn't trust his legs to hold him up. His recovery culminated when he hauled his cold, tired body onto the back of the draft animal, and gathered its reins into his hands.

Although the horse was damp from melted snow, its warmth penetrated Kismet, stirring him to do what he knew must be done. Irene and her father were still out there, still fleeing from Grimes and the commandos. He had to go to find them.

At his urging, the horse scaled the remaining few steps onto the newly uncovered ice field. It then negotiated the slippery ascent, roughly thirty feet of hard ice, and plowed into the deeper snow above the fracture line.

At some point in the ascent, Kismet became aware of the rifle, clogged with snow, but still containing half a magazine of ammunition, dangling from a web strap slung over his shoulder. His *kukri* was also still with him, shoved into the sheath at his belt.

He had a vague memory of the preparations he had taken, just before diving onto the loose reins of the horse. As the great sheets of ice had begun to tumble down, he had spied the horse, already attempting to dance its way over the crashing wave of snow. Inspired, he had lashed himself to the beast in the final moments before it was overwhelmed. Nevertheless, those few seconds where the draft animal had evaded the slide had placed both it and Kismet, near the surface, making possible their eventual liberation.

He ceased reflecting on the past, and focused on the immediate situation. He brushed the snow from the assault weapon, checking its barrel and internal mechanisms, and popped out the magazine. Ice crystals that had accumulated around the 7.62-millimeter cartridges and a sheen of *verglas* now laminated the inner working of the assault rifle. When the hot metal had been immersed in snow, melted ice had seeped into every cavity and then frozen again. There was a good chance the gun would misfire or even blow up in his face if he attempted to use it.

He contemplated throwing it away, but decided it might still have value as, if nothing else, an instrument for intimidation. Besides, escaping from the mountain wouldn't necessarily mean the end of his battle with Grimes. In fact, with the information he expected to get from Peter Kerns, a future confrontation with his nemesis and the soldiers the portly traitor commanded was almost a certainty. Twenty rounds from the AK might not count for much, but it was a difference he could ill-afford to dismiss.

Once above the line of the fracture, Kismet easily distinguished the pattern of hoof prints and ski trails that had brought them all to that fateful last stand. From there he needed only to backtrack. He urged the horse to a trot then coaxed it to a full gallop across the snowfield.

As his body grew warmer, he began receiving urgent messages from every quarter thereof. He envisioned himself now as a living mass of bruises, and the pounding motion of the horse's gait did nothing to assuage his discomfort. Just as quickly, he realized that his mount had been buried in the slide as well, and was likely in just as much pain. Without being conscious of it, he reached out and stroked the mane of his savior.

It took only a short time for Kismet to reach the place where he had separated from his friends, and what he saw hit like a physical blow. The signs were all too easy to read. The sleigh pulled by the remaining horse had gone off in the path of the vehicles that had ascended earlier in the night. Four deep ruts, interspersed with numerous small holes, followed the same path. Kismet quickly surmised that at least two pairs of skiers had pursued the sleigh. Because they had traveled in only two columns, it was conceivable that many more soldiers had gone after the sleigh. Kismet turned his mount and charged off after them.

A few hundred yards down the road, he spied evidence of the Kerns' countermeasures against their pursuers. A large depression in the snow showed that one of the commandos had crashed after striking a piece of debris. Apparently, the soldier had picked himself up and rejoined the pursuit.

He caught up to the straggler a few minutes later. The young skier was huffing through the flats, making too much noise to hear the muffled thumping of hoof-beats in the snow. Kismet pulled alongside him, and as the soldier became aware of his presence and looked up at him, Kismet planted his boot in the man's face. For a second time, the unlucky ski trooper went tumbling, this time to lie in a senseless heap. Kismet pulled back on the reins, causing the massive animal to rear up. When its hooves came down, they smashed one of the soldier's skis, snapping it in two.

Only moments later Kismet caught a glimpse of the sleigh, and the three soldiers chasing it. The trail led out onto the face of the mountain, gradually descending at first, but an ominous hairpin turn lay directly ahead. Kicking the horse's sides with his heels, he charged after them. As he neared the rearmost skier, he saw Peter Kerns climbing out onto the draft animal, and knew what they were attempting. A desperate measure, he reflected, but possibly their only chance at evading the commandos and surviving the switchback in the path ahead. Swinging the rifle by the barrel, he clouted the skier in the back of the head with the rifle butt and hurried onward.

As he pulled within striking distance of the second soldier, Kismet saw the leader of the pack make a courageous attempt to thwart the Kerns' escape. With an all out effort, the commando caught the back end of the sleigh and pulled himself aboard unnoticed by Irene. He kicked his skis off, and leaped forward to wrap his arms around the young woman.

Swinging the rifle like a club, Kismet downed another skier and charged after the doomed sleigh.

At that instant, Peter Kerns lost his hold on the harness. The rig slipped down, burrowing into the snow like a vaulting pole, and the entire sleigh jack-knifed, catapulting into the air and flipping over in a deadly arc. The bench seat struck the horse's hindquarters, knocking it and Kerns to the ground. Irene and her captor separated in mid-air and flew out ahead of the sleigh, which in turn hit the snow behind them and bounced up and over the edge of the trail. Irene and the soldier rolled uncontrollably toward the precipice, and then vanished from sight. Kismet reached the edge in an instant that seemed to stretch out into an eternity, a sickening certainty forming in his throat.

Miraculously, the falling soldier had found a tenuous handhold; the ice shelf was solid enough—for the moment at least—to bear his weight. His gloved fingers dug in with almost superhuman determination. As he depended from the precipice, Kismet saw another shape directly below him.

With equal tenacity, Irene clung to the soldier's boot. Kismet felt weak-kneed with relief. Peter Kerns was at his side a moment later, hesitant to look over, knowing that his daughter was surely dead three hundred feet below.

Though Irene's grip was unbreakable, Kismet knew that the soldier's hold on the ice might fail at any moment. He drew his *kukri* and sliced off a long section of leather from the reins of his horse, then looped the stiff line around his fist and knelt at the edge to lower it down. Kerns saw what he was attempting, and moved to secure Kismet's legs, allowing him to extend his reach out over the precipice.

The soldier chattered in German, begging for Kismet to simply pull them both to safety, but he ignored the young man. Irene's safety was the priority; saving the commando would depend upon how charitable he was feeling afterward.

"Irene. Grab it."

She looked up, into his eyes, and was magically transformed. Her fear vanished, melted by the revealed glow of his appearance. Kismet had survived, against all odds, and charged in like the prince in a fairy tale to rescue her from the jaws of the dragon. Without hesitation she released one of her clinging hands and grasped the strap. Wrapping the leather around her palm, she hugged it to her breast, and then grabbed hold with the other hand. As she swung away from the soldier's feet, Kismet began pulling on the line, reeling her in. With Kerns' help, Irene was drawn to safety in a matter of seconds.

Almost as an afterthought, Kismet reached down and grabbed the soldier by the back of his collar. "What the hell," he muttered through clenched teeth, pulling the man to safety. "I'm feeling generous."

Irene appeared in front of him and wrapped her arms around him. He grimaced involuntarily as her embrace aggravated bruises on his torso too numerous to count, but it was only when the soldier was lying face down in the snow, hands behind his head, that Kismet relaxed and allowed himself a contented sigh of relief.

PART THREE
INTO THE BLACK

11

Kismet contemplated the burning match in his fingers for a moment then waved it in the air until its flame was extinguished. Although there were yet a few hours of daylight remaining, the mildewed confines of Anatoly Grishakov's cellar saw none of it, forcing Kismet to once more make use of the old kerosene lamp with the missing chimney.

The lamp was actually the second flame he had lit; the first was in the dusty hearth, where a fire now crackled, warming the exhausted pair, father and daughter, that were stretched out before it on a bed of blankets.

Their journey down the mountain had taken several more hours, and the path they followed had brought them to the coastline a couple miles north of the city. None of them had really slept in over twenty-four hours, and exhaustion was beginning to take a toll, especially on the Kerns. Practically sleepwalking, Irene and her father had allowed Kismet to tuck them in front of the fireplace in Irene's room. Kismet too had fought a battle with heavy eyelids and muscle aches for much of the descent, but as they neared the city, his mind came fully awake. His fatigue evaporated as he began to contemplate the next step in the quest for the Fleece.

He already had a notion of where he would find it; it would fall to Kerns to supply the details that would make searching unnecessary. He spread one of Kerns' old survey maps out on the tabletop, and studied it in the flickering glow of the lamp. The paper had gotten damp during the course of their adventure on the mountain, but it was intact and the ink markings had not blurred.

His forefinger moved lightly across the paper, first settling on the site of the mountain camp where Harcourt was conducting his futile search. He then followed the line identifying the old riverbed that cut a meandering path down to the sea, a couple miles north of the inlet. There were no further markings along that line, but Kismet didn't need any. The map showed him where to find the Fleece, as effectively as if Kerns had engraved it with the traditional "X" to mark the spot.

He checked his watch; dusk would soon arrive. He knew he should force himself to get some sleep, but his mind would not turn off. His new knowledge had created an entirely different set of problems; getting to the Fleece would require specialized skills that he did not have. Moreover, the equipment he would have to use was antiquated and there was no guarantee that it would work. He would literally be staking his life on its reliability.

Because he could not sleep, he chose instead to search for something to eat or drink. Anatoly and his wife were nowhere to be found, but in their pantry, he found a supply of coffee, and set about brewing a pot. As he savored the first cup, he became conscious of the darkening sky. It would soon be time for his rendezvous with Lyse. Before that, he needed to ask the old man a few questions; tough inquiries of which Irene might disapprove. He decided not to awaken her as he knelt down and shook the engineer.

Peter Kerns was practically stove-up from the ordeal of his imprisonment and the brutal trip down the mountain. Kismet nevertheless roused him with a mug full of coffee and planted him at the table in front of the map. Kerns stopped in mid-sip, suddenly aware of the paper spread before him. "Ah."

Kismet sat across from him. "You found the Golden Fleece," he stated plainly. "But it wasn't up in the mountains."

Kerns sighed. "How did you know?"

"There were too many pieces to the puzzle that didn't fit. The first was when Harcourt showed me a golden helmet fragment that you had found.

The metal had a trace of salt scale on it. Of course I really didn't believe there was a Golden Fleece to be found at that point." He paused to take a sip of his coffee. "The equipment down in your cellar was another clue, but I still wasn't sure; not until I got a look at the mountain dig site."

"How did that help?"

Kismet smiled patiently. "Although Harcourt hasn't figured it out yet, I immediately saw what you did all those years ago when you first discovered that old mining camp. The settlement had been abandoned. The Greeks, or whoever, had mined the ore until the vein was dry. Then they packed up everything but the trash and left. If they found the Golden Fleece, they certainly wouldn't have left it behind."

"No. I suppose they would not."

Kerns remained evasive, unwilling to be forthcoming with the answers Kismet needed. Kismet decided not to press him just yet. "They must have followed the old river down to the coast, loaded their ships, or more likely built a new ship to ferry their wealth back home. But something terrible happened. Their treasure ship sank, not too far from the shore, and the Fleece was lost to the ages."

"How do you know that they did not make it safely home? The Jason legend says that he did return with the Fleece."

"I'm not talking about the legend," Kismet snapped, tiring of Kerns' feigned ignorance. "I'm talking about reality and we both know it. So cut the crap and tell me the truth about what you found."

Kerns sagged in defeat. "I should not tell you. Better that the secret remains lost. This world is no place for such powers."

"I understand your concerns. But the Fleece will be recovered. If not by us, then by Grimes and his gang, or by the Russians. Who would you prefer possess it?"

"You are right, of course." He drew in a breath, steeling himself for the confession. "You are wrong in one respect. I did not find the Golden Fleece; only a few artifacts scattered on the sea floor. I dove to retrieve them—"

"SCUBA?"

"No. All I had available was an old Russian Navy-issue three-bolt rig, with compressed air pumped down from the surface. I had to install a second petrol tank on the compressor in order to work alone. I told no one of my discovery; not my daughter, nor my best friend Anatoly."

"I thought we were finished with this little game, Kerns. You found more than just a few old relics."

The old man sighed, sinking back into his memories. "It took me weeks of secret diving, in a careful search pattern, to find the pieces. But when I began discovering fragments of gold and temple stones of marble, it was as if my feet were set upon the path. As I moved from one discovery to another, I drew closer to something strange.

"I first began to notice the fish. It was as if they stood guard around a certain place. I remembered hearing talk--superstition really--from the fishermen in the village. They spoke of a place that was haunted, where the ocean glowed with a yellow light during the night. Nets lowered there would always come up filled, but no one lingered in that place, fearful of tempting whatever powers lurked below. I, of course, dismissed the stories, trusting the assurance of my intellect that no such haunting was possible. But as I stood on the ocean floor, surrounded by some increasingly aggressive fish, I became a believer."

"Just because of some fish?"

"Not just the fish. I saw something else. A wreck, I think, though I cannot to this day be certain. It was the axis around which the sentry fish orbited. Whatever they protected was concealed there. I know, for the whole place was alive with a golden light."

Despite his willingness to believe, Kismet was momentarily plagued with skepticism. "You never went any closer? Why do you believe the Fleece is there?"

"I did not. In fact, upon returning to the surface, I stored my equipment and never dove again. I had already taken enough relics to pay for my flight from the USSR. It did not occur to me that the Golden Fleece might be there until I was captured by those men and interrogated concerning it. Only then did I realize what it was I had seen."

"But you didn't tell them anything. And when they pressed you, you led them to the old mountain camp. You took a hell of a chance with your daughter's life."

Kerns returned his gaze with an earnest expression. "I believe you would have done the same thing, Mr. Kismet. We both know that one life here or there is of little consequence against something as potentially dangerous as that Fleece. Power like that could reshape the world.

"However, my efforts to mislead them might have proved successful. The site is genuine. Harcourt verified that from the beginning. They would have searched for a while and, finding nothing, given up, believing that I had cooperated fully. It was the only thing I could think of doing."

Kismet sat back, unconsciously stroking the stubble on his chin. "You probably made the right decision. Your cooperation would not have made a difference though. Grimes ordered Irene's death the minute they had you out the door."

"I feared as much. Still, I had hoped they would honor their word."

"All of which leaves us with the question of how to proceed. Despite our escape, I believe Harcourt will continue to dig up there, at least for a while. I want you to do two things for me. First, show me on the chart exactly where you found the wreck. And second, teach me how to use the diving equipment."

Kerns hesitated only a moment then stabbed at the map with a finger. He was pointing to a shelf, roughly twenty fathoms below the surface, after which the sea floor dropped dramatically. Anything lost beyond that point would be gone forever from the world of mankind; sunk to depths where the pressure would crush any diver or submarine. Kismet studied the location carefully, committing it to memory. He had no intention of leaving a paper trail for his foes to follow.

"My equipment ought to function, despite the years," Kerns offered. "But it will take me a while to show you how it works."

Kismet checked his watch. "You've got three hours."

Three hours and fifteen minutes later, Nick Kismet swung down from the broad back of the draft horse and scanned the inky waters of the Black Sea for signs of motion. He saw nothing, but the moon was still low in the sky and the sea revealed little about itself. Still, he was where he was supposed to be, and even a few minutes early. He dug into his waist pack, took out his MagLite and removed the red lens cover. After a quick compass reading, he positioned himself facing due west, after which he flashed the naked light three times out across the black water. A moment later three pulses of light, like echoes of his own signal, flickered in the distant darkness.

"This is it," he declared, offering his hand to Irene. With some difficulty, due to fatigue and soreness, she and her father dismounted from the other horse.

They waited in silence for fifteen minutes. Before that time had passed, Kismet was sure that he heard the distinct whine of an outboard motor, but the noise ended abruptly before his eyes could distinguish the source. Shortly thereafter, he glimpsed a shadowy spot that didn't reflect starlight. The form drew closer, but it wasn't until the small craft was drawn onto the beach that Kismet and the others could correctly identify it as a large inflatable rubber boat.

Two large men dressed entirely in black, with faces stained by dark greasepaint, stowed their oars in the raft, then jumped out into the gentle surf and pulled the boat onto dry ground. A third person, smaller than the others, but similarly decked out, remained seated in the craft until it was secure. Kismet went down to meet them.

"Hey, Lyse."

The smallest member of the shore party looked up, her grin a white crescent in an otherwise darkened face. "Nick. Son of a gun, you're still alive."

Eschewing what he expected to be the protocol of clandestine meetings, Lysette Lyon threw her arms around him. Somewhere behind him, he thought he heard Irene clearing her throat.

"You sound surprised."

She withdrew after a moment. "Pleasantly so. We've been monitoring all kinds of radio traffic. You've definitely stirred up a hornet's nest or two."

"I was only aware of one. Germans."

"The Russians are talking about you too, both military and something else. A code we haven't been able to break yet. Face it; everyone knows you're here. The sooner we get out of here, the better." She gazed past Kismet at Irene and her father as they moved to join the reunion. "I see you got what you came for."

"Not quite. But I'll have the Golden Fleece in two days. What I need right now is for you to get them—" He jerked a thumb casually in the direction of his companions, speaking softly so that they would not over-hear—"somewhere out of the way until I can get it."

"What's going on, Nick?" Irene touched him on the shoulder as she came to a standstill beside him. Kismet couldn't tell if she was harboring jealousy toward Lyse's unexpected presence or merely curious.

"I'm entrusting you and your father into the care of my friend Lyse. She works for the--"

Lyse quickly cut him off. "Ah-ah, Nick." She then addressed Irene. "We're just some concerned folks, looking out for our fellow citizens abroad."

"Right. Anyway Irene, I want you and your father to stay with Lyse while I go after the Fleece."

"My father should go with you," Irene agreed, addressing Lyse. "He's suffering from fatigue, and God only knows what else those bastards did to him. Is one of you a medic?"

"I'll get him some medical attention," promised Lyse.

Irene nodded. "However, Nick, I am staying with you."

"Absolutely not."

"Think about it. Everyone knows we're together. You said you were afraid that someone in the village might be an informant. You're bound to raise suspicions if you show up without me."

"She makes a valid point," Lyse intoned.

"Stay out of this." He turned to Irene, but she was already forestalling him. "Face it, Nick. As long as we're together, no one will be any wiser."

His retort fell silent. He knew that her logic was sound, yet the thought of exposing her to further risk filled him with dread. "All right," he relented. "It will only be for a couple days. Lyse, we'll be back here in exactly forty-eight hours. If all goes as planned, we'll have the Golden Fleece. Then you can get us all out of here."

"I think it would probably be better for you to plan on exfiltrating through normal channels," Lyse opined. "You've got the documentation. If you two vanished from here then popped up back in the States, people would notice and it might cause an embarrassing situation."

"I would personally find it a lot more embarrassing if I got killed trying to smuggle the Fleece across the border."

"I thought you were in the business of protecting sovereign claims to these relics?"

Her question was rhetorical, but still gave him a pang. It was true; he was doing the very thing he sought to prevent as part of the UN Global Heritage Commission. It had been easy enough to justify, at least to his own conscience; the Fleece wasn't simply a valuable relic, it was potentially very dangerous. It might also be just the thing he needed to gain the upper hand on the Prometheus group.

Lyse did not wait for him to answer. "All I'm saying is you should plan on leaving through the front door, whether or not you find the Fleece."

"I'll find it."

"Fine. When you do, we'll go from there. Deal?"

Kismet narrowed his eyes, suddenly suspicious. "You're up to something, Lyse. I can tell."

She raised her hands in a gesture of innocence. "*Moi?*"

Kismet nodded, waiting for the other shoe to drop. Lyse didn't disappoint.

"Well, there is one thing, but it's nothing you're not already aware of."

"Go on."

"It's just that things are heating up here, Nick. Even you'd agree that you're working under somewhat dangerous conditions."

"I've had a busy couple of days," he said equivocally.

"It might be a good idea for you to tell me what you did with the information from the statue, right now. If anything were to happen to you, that data might be lost forever."

Although he had been expecting the request, it triggered an unexpected realization that caught him by surprise. "I don't believe it," he whispered hoarsely, more to himself than to the CIA operative. "You're giving up on me."

"Nick, please. We need that information. There is a new kind of arms race heating up, and we need to know what the other side is up to."

Kismet barely heard her. "You don't think I'll find it," he accused, then amended: "Your people—CIA, or whoever you work for—they don't believe me. You're just humoring me until you get the information. Then what? Leave me out here on my own? Or just turn me over to the Russians and let them quietly dispose of me?"

Lyse started to protest, but closed her mouth without speaking. She glanced at Irene and her father who looked on, uncomprehending, then looked back at her two accomplices who waited apprehensively by the raft. "Walk with me."

They stepped a few paces away from their companions. Lyse then moved close to Kismet and began speaking in an urgent whisper that was barely audible over the lapping of the sea. "Damn it Nick, this has gone far enough. I've jumped through too many hoops for you. What you're doing by withholding that information is treason."

"Treason," he echoed, loud enough for the others to hear. "You don't get it, do you? If you let Grimes get the Golden Fleece by not helping me, you're the one who will have sold out our country."

"You said it yourself. The Fleece is a fairy tale."

"Grimes doesn't think so."

Lyse shook her head and rubbed her eyes, like a weary parent unable to reason with a wayward son. "We think this whole affair with the Golden

Fleece is a smokescreen designed to distract attention from the real reasons Grimes has defected. He probably wanted your help to lend more authenticity to the illusion."

"Bullshit."

She ignored him. "Grimes doesn't care about fairy tales. He's pissed off at the Pentagon for giving him the boot, not to mention for backing down from Iran and North Korea...Hell, he'd like to pave all of Asia. He hates the President with a passion. And it turns out he's been getting chummy with a German defense contractor, who also happens to be a leading figure in their Nationalist Party. This is all about money and revenge, Nick."

"Ans I'm just a pawn in some political game?" Kismet accused. "His pawn and yours. Believe it or not, that doesn't surprise me. What I don't get is why you've gone along with me so far. Why not just arrest me for withholding the information you need? It would have been a lot easier."

"No kidding. If you had any idea how much the President has authorized for this little jaunt of ours—well let's just say that if it ever got out, he could kiss his Presidential library good-bye."

"Then I repeat: Why go along with it until now?"

"Because you still have something we need," she explained, her voice growing taut, as if tiring of the argument. "And you have to give it to me now."

"You would go to all this trouble just to get the information on that memory card?" Kismet shook his head. "I find that hard to believe."

"You shouldn't. People died to get that information out of Germany. You said you thought it was research for some kind of bomb, right? Well it is. It's a formula for a super EMP bomb. I don't really understand the details, but I know that whoever can make a weapon like that could rule the whole planet. We, meaning everyone from the President down to me, think that getting it before the Germans, or anyone else, is worth any expense or risk."

Kismet was unimpressed. "So why not try to buy me off? Or threaten me? Hell, you might have appealed to my patriotic fervor; waved the flag and told me I'd be a hero."

"Actually, it was my idea to go along with you," Lyse stated with unexpected sobriety. "I certainly haven't forgotten how you served your country during the first Gulf War; it's what inspired me to talk to a Company recruiter in the first place. More than that, you know how to keep a secret. I thought you deserved a little better treatment, especially after I scammed you into helping me get the information back to America."

"You should have been up front with me Lyse," he accused. "I'd have rather known the score going into this."

"You know how this business works, Nick. Need to know."

He sighed. "What about Grimes?"

"That's the other reason for all of this. My team has another assignment besides babysitting you. We're going into Germany to grab Grimes and take him back to the States to stand trial."

Kismet chuckled. "Grimes isn't in Germany. He's here with an entire company of commandos, trying to recover the Golden Fleece. Right now, they're camped up in the mountains about thirty miles from here, because they believe that the Golden Fleece is real and that it is worth any effort to recover. So do I, but apparently I'm the only one on our side who does."

Lyse began shaking her head. "I don't get it. It's just a myth, and not a particularly interesting one, at that. Our researchers looked into it. The Fleece has no real value as an occult object or weapon; even in the legends it was mostly a curiosity piece."

"Since when did you become an expert?" Kismet snorted derisively. "Look, as things stand now, Grimes will never find the Fleece. But I know where it is and I can get it inside of two days. I just need you to keep the status quo until then."

Lyse pressed her hands together under her chin, deep in thought. Kismet knew he had failed to convince the intelligence officer of the Fleece's importance, and so he was mildly surprised by her next statement. "All right. This is too important to be overlooked. You can have your two days. Hell, take a week if you can do it without arousing anyone's suspicion. No more than that though."

"I won't need it," he replied confidently. "What's the catch?"

"The catch—and this is not open to debate—is that you will immediately tell me where you hid the information."

"Sure. And that will be the last time I ever see you."

"You have my promise of support, Nick."

"From Lysette Lyon, my old college crush that would actually be enough. But from you, now, secret agent and patriot, I just don't know."

"Then you have my word as an American." Her grin was not insincere. "How's that?"

"Better. I would prefer the truth. Why are you really doing this? No bullshit."

"Grimes. I want him, Nick. If he's as close as you say, we can sneak in and nab him. It's perfect. Trying to get him out of Germany would have been tough, but this will be a cakewalk."

Kismet scratched his head. "I don't know. There are an awful lot of them up there. If you try anything, it might bring them down, and that will make my job harder."

"I've got reinforcements of my own. Don't worry. By the time you have the Fleece, you won't have to worry about Halverson Grimes."

"So why can't you wait the extra two days for the information?"

"I said no arguments, Nick. If you want my help, cough it up now."

Kismet grinned, ready at last to spring his own mean surprise. "Actually, you already have it. I emailed it to you."

Lyse stopped moving and began speaking very slowly. "You did what?"

"I compressed the file, and uploaded it to the UN server. And then I sent you a link. I guess you haven't checked your email in a while."

"Oh, my God. I can't believe you did that. Do you realize how irresponsible that was?"

"About as irresponsible as the stunt you pulled in Morocco. No, strike that. What I did was a lot safer and smarter. The servers are as secure as anything the CIA has, and the file is encrypted and booby-trapped. Any attempt to access it without the link I sent you will not only erase the file but seek out the person who tried to hack in."

Lyse did not seem greatly relieved by his assurance. "And the original?"

"Like I told you before. It's with a trusted friend. Don't worry. You will get the original as soon as we get back. And you've already got the information, so if something happens to me, you're covered that way, too. Take it or leave it."

She ground her palms into her eyes as if the exchange had given her a headache. Kismet knew he had won. "Okay," she relented. "That will have to do for now, but you will give me that original copy as soon as this is over."

He nodded, but then she did something unexpected. He looked down to find her gripping the lapels of his jacket and staring up into his eyes. "Nick, I mean it. You will give it to me personally. That means you'd better not get yourself dead."

"Understood," he replied solemnly, feeling suddenly very uncomfortable.

Lyse stepped back and faced the shore party. "Gentlemen, let's get out of here."

As the two men made ready to shove the raft back into the surf, Irene and her father exchanged a tearful but brief farewell. Then Peter Kerns climbed into the rubber boat and vanished into the sea.

Kismet placed a consoling arm around Irene. Tears had left their tracks on her cheeks, but her emotional state seemed otherwise healthy. "We'll be with him again before you know it," he promised.

Irene nodded, but said nothing. Kismet could sense her fatigue; she was nearly asleep on her feet. With gentle firmness he maneuvered her away from the water's edge and assisted her up the trail to where the horses were tethered. He helped her to mount one, and then led both animals on foot back toward town.

The safe delivery of Peter Kerns left Kismet with a feeling of accomplishment. He had rescued an innocent man from Grimes' machinations and prevented the traitor from capturing the prize. Yet he was anxious about the remainder of mission. Despite his confident poise while verbally sparring with Lyse, there remained untold potential for things to go dreadfully wrong; knowing that Irene would share the risk added to his fears. Grudgingly, he acknowledged that he was going to have to extend a degree of trust toward someone he instinctively doubted in order to ensure success.

They arrived back at their host's residence about forty minutes later. Kismet led Irene through the darkened house to the second floor guest bedroom. He tucked her into bed and as he turned from her closed door, found himself facing the burly, scowling form of Anatoly Grishakov.

Kismet took a step back, bumping into the wall. "Uh, sorry. Did I wake you?"

Anatoly's hard edge suddenly vanished as his bearded face was split by an enormous smile. "Of course you did!" he roared. "Never mind. Come to the table and we will have something to drink."

Kismet breathed a sigh of relief and followed the big man through the house. Anatoly left the electric lights off, using a kerosene lamp for illumination. He placed it at the center of the table, but the perimeter of the room remained cloaked in shadows. "Sit," he beckoned. "My wife sleeps, so we will not sing too loudly."

Kismet smiled in spite of himself and went to take a seat. As he passed the Russian, he found the man staring at his shoulders. Looking down, he realized that the AK 47 he had confiscated on the mountainside was still slung diagonally across his back. He had taken it along for the seaside rendezvous and gradually forgotten about it.

"Did you find what you sought on the mountain?" Anatoly asked, tearing his gaze away from the firearm.

Kismet sat down, putting the gun on his lap, out of view. "I think so. Let's say I'm off to a good start."

Anatoly set the lamp down and disappeared from the room. He returned with a bottle, and two glass jars into which he decanted a fair amount of the bottle's contents. "Irina sleeps?"

Kismet nodded. "It was a long day." The clear spirits burned cool on his tongue. The anonymity of the bottle led him to believe that the vodka originated locally, possibly distilled by Anatoly himself.

"And why are you not also asleep?"

He drew in a deep breath. "I need your help."

Anatoly broke into another grin. "And I was beginning to think you didn't trust me. Of course, Nikolai Kristanovich. In whatever way I can help, I will..."

The Russian's voice trailed off and he turned his head to one side as if distracted by a noise in the distance. Kismet listened too, but heard only the faraway sound of barking dogs. Before he could frame a question, there was a rapping on the front door. Kismet dropped his hand to the firearm beneath the tabletop, and watched cautiously as Anatoly opened the door.

The portly figure of Halverson Grimes filled the doorframe. Dressed in a heavy gray greatcoat and fur cap, the traitor carried only one item in his gloved hands: a stick with a white handkerchief attached to one end. Grimes proffered the makeshift truce flag, waving it to get Kismet's attention.

Before Anatoly could say a word, Kismet snarled: "Grimes. What the hell are you doing here?"

"Easy," Grimes soothed. "I wish only to parlay. Will you hear me out?"

"There's nothing you have to say that I want to hear."

"Are you so sure? I beg you, fifteen minutes of your time. If I have not convinced you, I will go my way honorably and trouble you no more."

Kismet was curious in spite of his reservations. "Why not? Have a seat, but keep your hands on the table." He turned to Anatoly and addressed him in Russian. "*Let's give him some vodka.*"

Both Grimes and Anatoly registered mild surprise that Kismet was speaking in that tongue. The latter quickly recovered his composure, and went grinning in search of another jelly jar.

"What I have to say is meant only for your ears," Grimes continued. "This country is rife with informants and mobsters—"

Anatoly returned a moment later with a glass, filling it to the rim with vodka and setting it in front of the newcomer. Kismet waited until he had taken a seat to answer Grimes. "Anatoly doesn't speak English," he explained. "He may as well not be in the room, for all he will understand."

Growing wise to the deception, Anatoly feigned bewilderment then turned to Kismet and asked him in Russian to translate.

"I did not know that you spoke his language, Mr. Kismet." Grimes chuckled theatrically. "Ah, but of course you traveled extensively in your youth. In how many languages are you fluent?"

"I'm sure that's not what you came here to talk about." Kismet picked up his glass and tilted it toward the other men. "Salud. Bottoms up, Grimes."

With a distasteful look, Grimes drank from the glass, wheezing a moment later as the neutral spirits burned down his throat and into his belly. "No," he said, coughing. "I didn't come to discuss your prowess with foreign tongues. It is your knowledge of antiquities that interests me."

"I thought that Andy was your resident expert."

"Sir Andrew has been most helpful, but he is a visionary, while you are a man of action. The chaos on the mountain has provided me with overwhelming evidence to that effect."

Kismet ignored the jibe, brusquely seizing the vodka bottle and splashing some of its contents into each of the glasses. "I guess I gave you too much credit, Grimes. I would have thought it was obvious that I'm not interested in helping you."

"What are you interested in, Kismet? Saving Petr Chereneyev from my wicked schemes? I think we both know better." Grimes took the glass and raised it to Kismet before downing it in a gulp. This time, the vodka did not produce so much as a grimace.

"That's where you're wrong," Kismet countered. "The safety of Peter Kerns, whom I might add is an American citizen, is very important to me; especially when creeps like you think you can snatch him right out of the States to play your little spy games."

Grimes folded his hands on the table. "Spare me the rhetoric, Kismet. It ill becomes you. The truth of the matter is that you and I have both been victims of our government's treachery."

Kismet was, for the first time, genuinely puzzled. "What in the hell are you talking about?"

"I think you know exactly to what I am referring," hissed Grimes. "You risked your life on a mission that led you to one of the most sought after treasures on the planet. But someone else knew about your mission. A second team was sent, your prize was snatched away and you were left to die in the desert. Who do you think sent that second team?"

Kismet heart skipped a beat as Grimes spoke. Was it possible that this man, who had become his sworn enemy, possessed the answer to the riddle that had haunted him for most of his adult life? Out of the corner of his eye, he saw a perplexed look flicker across Anatoly's mien. Struggling to maintain his poker face, he sneered: "I really don't know what you're talking about."

"I was head of joint military intelligence. We were very troubled by Samir al Azir's request, naming you personally as the only man he would meet with to negotiate the disposition of that sacred relic. How was it possible that this Iraqi engineer had knowledge of you, a mere second lieutenant? We could not simply sit by and entrust such an important matter to a junior officer and a platoon of disposable Gurkhas. I received orders from the desk of the President himself, to send another team to secure the relic and leave no witnesses. Your escape across the desert was nothing short of miraculous.

"I'm sure that in the years since, you have imagined a scenario exactly like the one I have just described. I think deep in your heart you have always believed that it was your own country that betrayed you, leaving you to die."

Kismet threw a sidelong glance at Anatoly. The Russian was doing a good job of concealing his ability to understand the conversation—no mean feat considering Grimes' revelations. He was beginning to wonder if he had erred by encouraging Anatoly to stay, but there was nothing he could do about it now. For his own part, there was just enough truth in what Grimes was saying to plant a seed of doubt. "Assuming any of this is actually true, why tell me? If you really did what you said, then I should kill you right now."

Grimes smiled coyly. "Like you, I was a soldier, following orders. But those orders, and many that have followed, were troubling to me. I was shut out of the after-action review. The final fate of the recovery team and the disposition of the relic were kept secret from me, as were too many other things. I began to suspect the existence of a secret coterie within our own government; a cabal following an agenda that has nothing to do with the interests of the American people."

"Ah, the diabolical conspiracy." Kismet tried to inject sarcasm into his tone, but his mind was racing to assimilate the Grimes' suspicions. "A secret society—the Freemasons or the Tri-Lateral Commission perhaps. Or the Teutonic Knights?"

Grimes smiled humorlessly at the last statement. "So you know something of my quest for answers. Yes, I accepted membership into the Teutonic Order of Saint Mary. And when I was forced to resign from the Defense Department, that affiliation opened doors for me overseas. It was not possible to fight the enemy from within his own castle, so I sought willing allies where I could find them."

"Look, Grimes, I think you're too smart to be drinking the conspiracy Kool-aid, but if that's what you want to believe, fine. Why are you so bent on getting me to believe it?"

"As you have also surely surmised, the shadow government has a vested interest in the secrets of the ancient world. Even I do not fully grasp the extent to which they have hidden the true history of mankind, but my new allies are aware of many such discoveries, secreted away in the name of protecting mankind from itself. The Golden Fleece is just such a secret, and you can be sure that even now the shadow government is preparing to strike to prevent its power from coming into the light. I would think you of all people would appreciate that this must not be allowed to happen. We must find it first and take it to a place of safety."

Kismet's eyes darted toward Anatoly at the mention of the Fleece, but the Russian had chosen that moment to drain his vodka glass, hiding his reaction behind a mouthful of liquor. Grimes appeared not to notice and continued speaking. "Sir Andrew is capable enough, but you—when you decide to find something, nothing can prevent you. I want you working for me, Mr. Kismet. And I want you to receive the recognition you deserve. I can't change what was done during the war, but the Golden Fleece is another matter. The German government won't hide it away. The man who finds that treasure will be greatly honored. More importantly, I believe that the discovery will draw our mutual enemies into the light."

Kismet weighed Grimes' arguments quickly, trusting his gut reaction as a litmus test. The man he now thought of as a traitor had once been a flag officer in the US Navy and an expert in espionage. Intelligence operations weren't just about gaining information, but also had the goal of winning hearts and minds, using whatever means—and whatever lies—necessary. But why was Grimes trying so hard to convince him? He splashed more liquor into the glasses. "Nice try. But I'm not interested in proving Harcourt's pet theories. If the Golden Fleece really does exist, you're welcome to it. I'm going home."

Grimes disdained the final toast, pushing away from the table in preparation to depart. "Then may I at least have your assurance that you will not continue to interfere?"

"If you stay out of my way, I'll stay out of yours."

Grimes inclined his head and pushed away from the table. "Please thank our host for his courtesy. I wish that you and I could have been allies."

Alarm bells were going off in Kismet's head. After making such an impassioned plea to swing his loyalty, why had the traitor capitulated so quickly? Something was wrong—dreadfully wrong. As Grimes grasped the door handle, Kismet sprang erect and brandished the rifle. "I think you forgot something."

Grimes stared at the firearm as if he did not understand its purpose. "Already breaking the terms of our truce, Kismet?"

He wouldn't just give up. That's not his way. Kismet's mind flashed through what he did know about the way Grimes operated. He suddenly realized he had given Grimes too much credit; the portly spy had shown a preference for brute force over subtlety and sophistication. A sick feeling began to creep across his gut; the certainty that Grimes' call for a truce had merely been a diversion to conceal something more treacherous. *Irene!*

He hid his anxiety behind a fierce mask. "What's your hurry? The night is young."

"This has grown tiresome, Kismet. Stay out of my way, or you'll regret it." Grimes turned again to the door.

Kismet answered by pulling the bolt on the weapon, advancing a round into the firing chamber.

Grimes stopped dead in his tracks. "All right, Kismet. What now?"

"Come back to the table. There's one more thing we need to discuss. It's simple really. You can leave here alive, when your men release Irene."

"What on earth are you ranting about?"

Kismet jabbed the gun toward Grimes. "Nothing's ever what it seems with you. Sure, you want my help looking for the Fleece. Peter Kerns might have told me something that he didn't tell you. Or he might have told his daughter. This meeting was just a diversion, so that you could try to kidnap her again."

"You're paranoid, Kismet."

"And you're dead if Irene Kerns isn't standing here in front of me in five minutes. Shall we go up to her room and take a look? Or will you save yourself a few precious minutes and make the call?"

Grimes stared defiantly, impassively blinking in the face of Kismet's threat. Anatoly stood mutely to one side, still feigning incomprehension, but clearly ready for action should the need arise. Finally, Grimes relented, reaching slowly into the folds of his coat. Kismet stepped closer, ready to take action in the event that Grimes was drawing a weapon, but the traitor produced only a small walkie-talkie.

Kismet darted across the room, taking a station directly behind Grimes as the latter spoke to his unseen comrades. Grimes spoke in English, and received only a curt affirmative in reply. A few minutes later, the door opened to reveal a haggard looking Irene, who ran into Kismet's embrace.

"Satisfied, Kismet?" growled Grimes. "I could have my soldiers burn this house to the ground with all of you inside, but what would that accomplish? There is no need for us to continue as enemies."

"Go to hell, Grimes."

The large man inclined his head. "Pray that our paths never again cross."

With that, he ducked through the door and escaped into the night. As soon as he was gone, Irene poured out the story of her abduction by the commandos, told how they had scaled the outer wall of the residence, stealthily gaining entry and taking her hostage while Kismet and Grimes talked.

Kismet tried to listen but found that his nerves were too jangled to make sense of her tale. Part of him was still wondering if he had made the correct decision in shutting Grimes out; what if the man truly did have insight into the events that had changed his life that night in the desert? With almost trembling hands, he set the rifle on the table and downed another shot of vodka.

Anatoly joined him, gulping down a similarly copious dose of the spirit. "Kristanovich. Was there something you wanted to ask of me tonight?"

Kismet laughed in spite of himself. "I honestly don't remember."

12

Despite his fatigue, Kismet's sleep was troubled. His mind would not let go of the things Grimes had revealed, but continued churning them over and over, looking for some bit of information he might have missed that would supply the necessary confirmation. It would have been almost too easy to accept the traitor's statements as fact; indeed, Grimes' assertions fit perfectly in many respects. And if Grimes was telling the truth, then he was standing on the brink of a replay of those events. Even now, Lysette Lyon was poised with a team of CIA operatives, ostensibly to capture Grimes, but what if they were receiving orders from the so-called 'shadow government' to seize the Golden Fleece as soon as Kismet located it? Had he unwittingly played, once again, into the hands of that conspiracy by trusting Lyse?

On the other hand, Grimes could just as easily have cooked up a deception after reading Kismet's own after-action report from that doomed mission into the desert. If Hauser and his team had indeed been American Special Forces soldiers, then why had they conversed in a language that, more than a decade later, Kismet still could not identify? Furthermore, why had Hauser spoken of Kismet's mother as though he knew her personally?

In the end, he could not make Grimes' statements gel with the facts as he saw them. Grimes remained the enemy, and one of the most basic rules of warfare was to ignore enemy propaganda, even when it sounded plausible.

Anatoly kept watch throughout the night, an old shotgun resting on his lap. Over breakfast the following morning, the big Russian listened patiently as Kismet attempted to explain the events of the preceding night.

"There is much that I do not understand," intoned the Russian. "You tell me that my old friend Petr is alive, but was a prisoner of these spies? And that they have brought him back here?"

"Until we rescued him yesterday," Irene supplied.

"Foreign agents—soldiers--moving illegally through my country. Very bad. Worse that they have threatened my friends in my own house. Why have they done this?"

Kismet sublimated a nagging urge to withhold the full explanation from Anatoly. It was time to show a little trust. "Grimes—the unpleasant fellow you met last night—believes that there is treasure hidden up on the mountain."

"Ah, yes. The Golden Fleece. He spoke of it to you. And do you also believe?"

"It's not where he thinks it is. Peter—Petr—knows where it is. He told me where to find it, and how to get to it. That's where you come in."

Anatoly raised a hand. "A moment, please. If you have rescued Petr Ilyich, then where is he now?"

"Safe. And probably already on his way home."

"And how was this accomplished?"

Kismet abruptly realized there were still a few things he wasn't ready to give up. Before Irene could reply, he answered in a decisive tone: "Petr Chereneyev is a problem solver. He escaped once before. It's probably better that we don't know where he is, or how he plans to get out."

Anatoly nodded slowly. "Of course. A pity though that I could not see my old friend."

"After we recover the Fleece, you could leave with us," Irene suggested. "You could start a new life for yourself in America."

Anatoly chuckled at the idea, but offered no comment. Instead, he turned his attention back to Kismet. "So, where do I, as you say, come in?"

"The artifacts that Petr Ilyich discovered weren't up on the mountain. There was an old camp up there, probably a mining camp, but it was abandoned. The relics came from the sea. Petr showed me where he found them."

"I do not understand. From the sea? Did he drag the bottom with hooks and nets?"

"No. He used an old diving apparatus and walked on the bottom of the Black Sea."

Anatoly registered disbelief. "It would appear that my old friend had more talents than even I was aware of."

"The suit and compressor are in the cellar. He told me how to use the equipment, but I need a boat to operate from. That is where, as I say, you come in."

The big Russian stroked his shaggy beard thoughtfully. "Well then. We should get started."

Had anyone paused to notice, they would have observed their neighbor Anatoly, along with his two visitors, shuttling between the dock and his home. By midday the equipment was loaded and tested, and Kismet announced his readiness to commence. Anatoly cast off the moorings, coaxed his trawler out of its slip and headed for open water.

The fisherman navigated according to the chart Kismet had given him, while the latter remained in the bow, fastening air lines to the compressor. Despite their age, both the suit and the compressor proved to be in remarkably good repair. Chereneyev might have been a daredevil in his own way, but he took pride in his work and apparently valued safety. The suit was a little tight, but not uncomfortably so, and Kismet donned it with help from Irene.

The journey to the dive site was brief. The weather was clear and the sea calm when Anatoly went aft to drop anchor. Kismet scanned in all directions, assuring himself that no one was watching. The shoreline and the towering mountains stretched across the eastern horizon, but the village was an indistinct speck. No other boats were visible, although Kismet knew that the fishing fleet had departed from the harbor hours before.

To give the illusion that they were simply fishing in the remote area, Anatoly lowered his nets into the water. Meanwhile, Kismet made the final step in putting on his aquatic suit of armor: the helmet. Cast of solid copper, the critical piece of headgear was typical of the hard-hat dive rigs that had been in use before the invention of the Aqualung and self-contained breathing apparatus. Its creators had simply called it *tryokhboltovoye snaryazheniye*, literally "three-bolt equipment" because of the fact that the helmet was secured to the chest piece by three bolts spaced evenly around the apparatus at roughly chin level. The helmet and chest plate together weighed nearly eighty pounds. It looked like something Jules Verne might have dreamed up, and in fact an earlier version of it had been in use during Verne's lifetime. Nevertheless, for extended dives with long decompression periods, the old hardhat system was superior to SCUBA, and the three-bolt suits had served the Russian Navy's purposes well into the twentieth century.

As soon as the metal globe enveloped his head, Kismet experienced a wave of trepidation. The helmet was a tangible manifestation of the fact that he was about to plunge into a wholly foreign and potentially fatal environment. His only means of communicating with the surface took the form of three small orange floats, which he would release to signal either his need for a gradual ascent, or an emergency withdrawal from the depths. The words Kerns had uttered the night before now echoed in his head with ominous finality. The thought of being trapped below and suffocating, or being forced to make an ascent too rapidly and suffering the painful effects of the bends, or of losing his cognitive abilities to nitrogen narcosis, now seemed not simply to be requisite risks, but unavoidable certainties.

Kismet had SCUBA dived before and would have preferred the independence of carrying his own supply of air, relying only on himself to survive the unpredictable variables of a descent, but that just wasn't practical. Not only was there the obvious problem of acquiring the equipment, but the depth to which he would be diving was at the limit of what was termed recreational diving. At the depth Peter Kerns had indicated, bottom time for a SCUBA diver using compressed air was measured in mere minutes; in fact, with decompression stops, the dive would more than exceed the capacity of what he could bring along in two tanks. Most deep diving of this sort was now done with helium-oxygen mixtures, which were much safer but required even more in the way of specialized equipment and topside support. Like it or not, Peter Kerns' old school diving technique, despite the inherent risks, was simply the only option under the circumstances.

A tapping on the left porthole distracted him from his rising apprehension. It was Irene. "Are you going to be alright?"

Kismet turned his head to face her. The barrier between them muffled her voice. Her concern was evident, yet Kismet could see that she really had no idea of the dangers he was about to confront. He wanted to scream, to tear the metal and rubber from his body. Instead, he forced a smile and nodded. Anatoly started up the compressor and a rush of oily smelling air filled the helmet.

"Great," he murmured to himself. Without further delay, he ambled across the deck to the nets and lowered himself into the water.

As soon as he was beneath the surface, he felt better. Though the dampness from the water could not penetrate his suit, its cold quickly seeped in, calming his nerves.

Underwater, everything was different. The compressor was still audible, chugging and hissing to provide him with breathable air, but the undersea world was a place of perpetual green twilight and serenity. He released his hold on the net and allowed himself to sink. Anatoly was controlling his descent from the boat. A cable attached to a winch was gradually played out to provide him with a measured rate of descent, as well as a lifeline back to the surface. Even so, the bottom quickly rushed up to greet him.

At this depth, darkness reigned; very little light from the surface could penetrate. When he looked up, Kismet had no difficulty seeing the keel of Anatoly's trawler, with its nets spread out behind it like drably colored plumage. But that light could not pierce to the shadows around him. When his booted feet touched down, sinking several inches into the sediment and kicking up a tremendous cloud of silt, he discovered even greater respect for Petr Chereneyev, who had made this same journey without support from allies on the surface. When the cloud finally settled, Kismet looked around at the alien landscape where he was the intruder.

Faint silhouettes of the rocky outcropping surrounded him, a veritable labyrinth of obstacles. After a few moments, Kismet became conscious of fish swimming through the maze. Even in this inhospitable place he was surrounded by life.

As he surveyed the submarine environment, he gradually became aware of an unusual light source off to the west. The quality of the illumination was negligible, but Kismet knew that nothing in the natural world could account for it. Kerns' comment about golden light shining from beneath the sea echoed in his head. He hadn't really expected to witness any such manifestation, but if the Golden Fleece was indeed the source of the light he was now seeing, then he would have little difficulty locating it.

A step in that direction created yet another obscuring silt cloud. Rather than wait for it to subside, he proceeded more cautiously, taking long, deliberate steps. By this method he was able to keep silting to a minimum while making good progress toward the light source.

In terms of actual distance, the light was very close. Kerns' coordinates had been right on the mark. Nevertheless, distances in the underwater realm were exaggerated. It took Kismet almost half an hour to cross a few hundred yards. From time to time he would gaze upward toward the idle trawler, and was amazed to find that its position in relation to his seemed unchanged. The cable connecting him to the boat was still being played out as needed, but he was beginning to wonder if he had actually gone anywhere.

The amount of time he was spending below was beginning to concern him. Kerns had outlined decompression recovery times for him on the previous night. Kismet knew that minutes spent under the influence of the sea's tremendous pressure might require hours of gradual ascent to avoid the bends—bubbles of gas in the bloodstream that caused painful cramps or even death. In spite of the risk of further obfuscation due to the silt clouds, Kismet strove to pick up his pace.

He was quickly rewarded. The glow soon became a ray of golden brilliance guiding him through the underwater labyrinth. He passed from behind a large outcropping and got his first look at the place where Petr Chereneyev had discovered the relics of a forgotten age.

The rocky maze gave way to a broad plain, broken up by a scattering of small rocky nubs that barely poked out of the soft mud. Chereneyev's footprints were still visible, as were the depressions in the sediment where he had removed artifacts. As Kismet's eyes roved across the plain, he made out dozens of holes, and realized that the artifacts Harcourt had showed him were merely the tip of the iceberg.

As he continued west, his gaze began to focus on the source of the golden illumination, directly ahead. Another of Kerns' caveats occurred to him as he crossed the expanse. The old Russian had warned him of unusual activity from the fish; he had used the word "aggressive." Kismet was now seeing exactly that kind of behavior. The area before him was thick with schools of fish. Smaller fish from the herring family formed a virtual curtain, sparkling in the unnatural golden light, while larger fish—dogfish, rays and even enormous sturgeon, all of which should have been devouring the smaller prey creatures—cut harmlessly through the traffic, content to patrol the region without feasting. Kismet realized that he was becoming the object of their interest when a large stingray seemed to erupt from the silted seafloor. The creature's barb hovered dangerously close as it circled his chest, and Kismet decided it was time to bare the blade of his *kukri*. The ray's flanks rippled menacingly and then it retreated into the silt cloud.

A few more steps brought him close enough to discern the outlines of a sunken wreck laying on its side, half buried in silt, in the midst of the yellow brilliance. The lack of distinctive features led Kismet to believe that he was looking at the underside of the vessel. He noted also that the sediment, which had built up around the craft, did not significantly eclipse the golden light; it seemed to shine evenly from the hull of the wreck, passing through the silt as through a veil of gauze.

Suddenly something struck him from behind and sent him stumbling. He struggled to recover his balance, but the weight of the helmet took him over and he ended up face down in the muck. He pushed himself up, but saw only a dark shadow pass over him and faint eddies in the swirling murk. With one glove he smeared away the algae that clung to the front view port of the helmet.

When he got to his feet, he realized that the crowd of bottom dwellers had moved away from the wreck and begun orbiting a new axis: him. Like a squadron of fighter planes, the larger fish seemed to be circling, preparing to dive-bomb their target. Before he could raise the knife in his own defense, an enormous sturgeon, like some prehistoric monster from the fossil record, veered toward him.

Instinctively, he tried to dodge the creature. The fish smacked into his shoulder, but did not succeed in knocking him down. As it flashed past, he slapped at it with his empty hand, striking it in the gills. Enraged, and possibly injured, the sturgeon retreated hastily toward the wreck. With its flight, the attack ended. Kismet remained ready to slash at the next assault, but the schools held their distance. He took a tentative step toward the wreck, then another.

His earlier assumption about the vessel lying on its side was soon confirmed. As he drew closer, he could discern the outline of the keel just above the mud line. Kismet was not an archaeologist by trade, and certainly not an expert on maritime history, but he had studied Jason and the Argonauts during his classical education and knew enough about ships of the era from various contemporary sources to recognize a Greek galley about fifty feet long and twenty feet broad of beam—more a big boat than a ship in the modern sense. But no galley in myth or history looked quite like this one, ablaze with golden brilliance. The illumination was indeed shining from the skin of the craft, which to Kismet's surprise, did not appear to be wood.

A few more steps brought him close enough to place a gloved hand against the ship. As he pressed experimentally against the surface he could feel a tingling in his fingertips but no heat. When he moved his hand away, he saw the indentations left behind, as though he had pushed into stiff clay.

Pondering this observation, he started walking toward what he presumed to be the stern of the craft.

The coating on the hull was uniform, like a layer of paint. The natural world was filled with luminescent fungi, plants, insects and fish, but Kismet was certain that some other phenomenon was at work. The overlay on the ship was smooth and consistent, whereas lichen growth would adhere to a more chaotic pattern and would certainly have rubbed off when touched. There was only one explanation: the ship was coated in luminous gold.

Kismet was also not a metallurgist, but he did know a thing or two about the corrosive power of salt water. Even in the Black Sea, where the salinity was about half that of the world's oceans, time and oxidation would have corroded any other substance, leaving a wooden ship to decay into pulp. Only gold could resist ravages of the sea for so many centuries. The vessel had evidently been overlaid with gold in a manner similar to the helmet fragment Harcourt had displayed in Kismet's office. What he could not fathom, as he rounded the stern and got his first look at the topside of the ship, was why the ancients had covered their sea-going craft in one of the heaviest substances known to man, and why that normally inert element was glowing like an incandescent light bulb.

The galley held yet another surprise. Situated aft, but extending forward to dominate roughly a third of the craft, was an enclosed superstructure. He had been expecting an open craft; essentially a big rowboat. The ancient Greeks, despite their mythic reputation for adventurous wanderings, had never perfected the art of sailing on the open sea. They had preferred to row, assisted by a single square sail, within sight of the shore by day, and would beach their vessels at the onset of night. Their ships, much like Viking longboats, had little in the way of creature comforts. Even the description of the Argo in legend suggested an open craft, not a ship with a superstructure. Kismet found himself wondering if Kerns' discovery perhaps had nothing do with the legend of Jason and the Golden Fleece. The answer, he reasoned, must lie within the enclosure.

The open decks of the ship were empty. Nothing of the crew or their belongings remained. The oarlocks held only water, even the rudder oars were gone, and the stump of a mast protruded from the center of the craft, just aft of the enclosure. Likely, the event that had sent the ship to the bottom had also washed overboard anything that wasn't secured. Kismet did not pause to inspect the gilt beams or the benches where the oarsmen had labored centuries before, but continued purposefully toward his goal.

The enclosure had been designed for more than just shelter. A colonnade of ornamental pillars, suggesting that it might have been used for worship, ringed the solid walls. The columns were spaced far enough apart to allow for easy passage, and Kismet could see that something had been erected between the colonnade and the interior structure. He moved closer to get a better look.

As he peered through the pillars, leaning sideways, he immediately recognized the foundation of a small altar. The base, set into the floor of the shrine, was overlaid in glowing metal. Kismet glanced down and saw one of the altar stones resting on a pillar. Behind his glass porthole, his brows drew together in contemplation. The displaced stone was also gilt, whereas the altar stone recovered by Kerns and shown in the photographs Harcourt had displayed was of white marble.

Curious, Kismet reached down and shifted the stone. Where the relic had been in contact with the pillar, idle for millennia, the underlying white marble was visible in a thin stripe. The clean stone seemed dark against the luminescent metal. Likewise on the pillar, a smudge of shadow revealed the resting-place of the stone. He could draw but one impossible conclusion: the gold that covered nearly every inch of the ship had accreted after the wreck, after the craft had rolled over onto the bottom.

Kismet released the stone and returned his attention to the enclosure just behind the base of the altar. A thin seam revealed the presence of a door, sealed for ages by the accumulated coating of shining gold. He traced along the seam with the tip of his knife. The plating was thinner than beaten foil and split apart without resistance. Minute bubbles of trapped gas trickled out of the cut. Kismet sheathed the knife then placed both hands on the featureless portal and pushed.

The door opened a couple inches and released a gasp of bubbles that momentarily obscured his view. Then the tingling in his palms suddenly blossomed into a pulse of pain that jolted up his arms and through his torso. He jerked back in surprise and looked at his hands.

Dark shapes swarmed over his arms; moving shapes that he could not shake loose. Kismet did not know their taxonomic nomenclature—*Torpedindae torpedo*—but he recognized them easily nevertheless. Electric rays.

More of the flat speckled fish wriggled out of the colonnade to join in the assault. Kismet staggered back, brushing at the creatures, which continued to send surges of pain up his arms.

In an instant, the torpedo rays enveloped him; a cloud of writhing forms blanketed his head and chest. He flailed at them blindly, his muscles seizing every time they released their potent charges.

He knew that the rubber of his diving suit should have insulated him from the shock, but the electricity seemed to pass right through. Gritting his teeth, he took hold of a ray in either hand and started pulling them away from his helmet.

Blinded, he took another step back...and fell into nothingness.

Irene was in a state of panic.

Her anxiety had begun the moment Kismet disappeared into the still water. It was inconceivable to her that her own father had made repeated forays into the underwater realm, utilizing his antiquated equipment, without her ever knowing. Stranger still that he had used the gains of that enterprise to finance a venture of even greater risk, namely their flight to the United States. But her father's success did not necessarily translate into confidence in Kismet's ability to survive the peril into which he had so willingly plunged.

She had looked to Anatoly for encouragement, but the big Russian had simply shrugged. "He'll make it," he had assured her, in a less than inspirational tone. "You watch the compressor. Make sure it doesn't run out of fuel. I'll radio for a weather report. Storms on the Black—well, you know how quickly they can rise. We might be out here a long time."

The comment, delivered in Russian, was a veritable oration from Anatoly, who was not generally loquacious. He had turned away however, leaving her to watch the chugging compressor, the slow unspooling of the cable and the calm surface of the water.

Her uneasiness did not abate during his long absence. When he returned, some fifteen minutes later, he inquired briefly about Kismet's status. Irene had nothing to report; Kismet could be dead for all she knew.

Ten minutes later, the panic set in.

Irene saw it first, a barely perceptible speck creeping over the western horizon and trailing a plume of white vapor. She knew instantly what it was. "That's the *Boyevoy*. It's the ship that brought Nick and I here."

Anatoly did not seem concerned. "I'm sure it's a coincidence."

"You don't understand. Captain Severin doesn't trust us. He thinks Nick's a grave robber, trying to steal national treasures."

Anatoly's bushy eyebrows went up. "Is he not?"

"That's not the point. It won't take him long to figure out that Nick is down there. Once he does..." She couldn't put her fears into words that conveyed the panic she felt.

"What should we do?" asked Anatoly.

Irene wanted to scream at the big Russian; to tell him to think of something, but it was evident that he did not share her urgency. She would have to be the one to come up with a solution.

Severin's destroyer was chugging steadily toward them, grinding out its maximum speed of thirty-two knots. "He'll be here in a few minutes," grated Irene. "We've got to do something."

She ran to the edge of the boat and started pulling at the fishing nets, trying to camouflage Kismet's air hose and lifeline beneath the old twine webs. Anatoly helped her complete the illusion, but it was obvious to both of them that, if they were boarded, even a casual search would pierce their veil of deception. One thing they could not hide was the compressor; its motor chugged loudly, exhaling a cloud of blue exhaust smoke. Irene stared at the rickety machine, well aware that Kismet's life depended on its continued operation.

"We could shut it off," suggested Anatoly, as if reading her mind. "He probably has a few minutes of air in his helmet."

She cringed at the thought. "Only if it becomes obvious that we're going to be boarded. And we don't turn it off until we absolutely have to."

Anatoly nodded gravely. "If we are boarded, it may not matter. We cannot hide this."

Irene turned away, unable to answer him. She didn't know what else to do.

All too soon, the *Boyevoy* grew large with its approach. There could be no questioning its intention to intercept the trawler. The *Sovremenny* class warship cut a path straight toward them, reversing its screws only when it seemed that a collision with the idle boat was unavoidable, and even as the ship was still coasting forward, the efficient crew lowered the motor launch into the water.

Suddenly, a whirring noise caught Irene's attention. The cable that connected Kismet to the boat was spinning out of control. Thirty yards of twisted wire snaked out in a matter of seconds. Similarly, the rubber air hose was jumping out of its coil on the deck at an alarming rate. While the lifeline had over a hundred yards of reserve, the air hose was about to run out. Panicked, she rushed to the winch and engaged the ratchet. The cable seized instantly and snapped taut. The remainder of the air hose lay in a loop on the deck; a mere six feet in length.

Something disastrous had occurred below; something had happened to him and there was nothing she could do about it. She raised her eyes to the approaching launch and knew that she had one more task to perform; a duty that might well spell the end for Kismet. Gathering her courage, she stepped to the compressor and pulled the choke lever. The engine roared for a moment, then sputtered into silence.

Anatoly placed a protective hand on her shoulder, offering no assistance to the Russian seamen that swarmed onto the deck of his boat. For Irene, it was like a replay of the events a few days previously, when Severin had accosted them aboard the boat of the Turkish smuggler. The cocky Russian captain addressed her with the overly familiar patronymic.

"Greetings, Petrovna. How pleasant to see you again."

"What do you want?" she croaked, surprised to find her voice thick with fear and anger. She blinked away tears, trying to keep the emotion off her face.

Severin ignored her question as he gazed curiously around the boat. "Where are you hiding the dubious Nick Kismet?"

Irene sensed that he was toying with her. "He stayed behind. He wasn't feeling well."

"Ah! But you thought you would help your father's old friend with his fishing. How kind of you." He swiveled his gaze to face the unbowed fisherman. "I am curious, Anatoly Sergeievich Grishakov. How will your nets catch any fish if you are at anchor? Is this some new technique?"

"Why are you bothering us?" Anatoly snapped. "We aren't doing anything wrong. Go pester someone else."

Severin spat out derisive laugh. "State security has not forgotten you, Sergeievich. Your name is on a list of known troublemakers. You would do yourself a favor by cooperating."

"I am cooperating, fool. I've let you come aboard my boat, even though your warship has driven all the fish away and ruined my catch."

Severin smiled and turned away, walking to the stern gunwale and peering into the water. "Apparently you are the only fisher in your city who believes there are fish to be caught here." He faced Anatoly once more. "There is an FSB informant in the city who overheard your call for a weather report. He thought it curious that you would fish here, where no one ever goes. He also told me how you and Kismet spent the morning loading equipment onto your boat. So you will understand if I tell you that your answers thus far have not impressed me."

He took a step closer, his smile drawing into a menacing sneer. "You will cooperate."

"I have grown weary of threats," sighed Anatoly, unmoved. "If you wish to torture me, do so. I have nothing to say that I have not already said."

"Perhaps I will—torture?—ha! Perhaps Irina Petrovna will be more co-operative. Or perhaps, for her sake, you will leave off your posturing, and tell me where I can find Nick Kismet."

As he spoke, Severin moved closer, increasing his pitch and volume. His last words were shouted, though he was less than a hand's breadth from her face. She tried to shrink deeper into Anatoly's embrace.

"She told you!" the fisherman roared, equally stentorian. "Kismet isn't here."

The Russian captain turned away once more, walking in a slow circle around them. "Indeed. My men have searched your vessel and Kismet quite obviously is not here. But that does not answer the question of why you are here, in these waters where no one ever fishes."

He paused, standing directly behind Irene and Anatoly so that they could not see him. "What is this?" Severin's tone was mockingly inquisitive. "It looks like an engine, but there is hose of some sort that goes into the water. Is this also part of your unusual fishing technique?"

The Russian naval officer did not wait for an answer. He barked an order to one of the seamen, who strode forward and started reeling in the cable with the winch. At least seventy-five yards of the twisted metal line had been played out and it took the burly sailor almost five minutes to wind it in. Severin leaned over the stern, eyeing the cable hungrily, eager to see what he had caught.

Abruptly, without any disturbance of the surface, the end of the cable popped up. A gated carabiner was secured to a loop at its end, but nothing was connected to that hook.

"*Nyet!*" raged Severin. He pushed the sailor away and snatched the air line off the deck. Furious, he began pulling it in. As the rubber hose piled up around his knees, two of the sailors, acting on a cue from the XO, stepped in and took over for their superior.

Irene gazed at the empty carabiner in mute terror. That cable was Kismet's only lifeline. The hose connection wasn't strong enough to lift Kismet and his heavy suit off the bottom. The rubber tubing might with-stand the strain, but the brass fittings of the helmet would surely crack before he could be brought up. Even if they didn't break off altogether, the rupture would certainly fill the protective suit with seawater, drowning him before he could be lifted to the surface. In his rage Severin either failed to conceive this possibility, or simply didn't care.

Then the sailors stopped pulling in the hose, and Irene turned to see why. She couldn't hold back a low cry when she saw the ragged end of the hose in their hands. Severin's face twisted with rage, then slowly relaxed. After a long silence, he began laughing.

Kismet was in a cold, dark place.

Immediately after his fall, the torpedo rays had relented. Perhaps satisfied with having repelled the intruder, they retreated to their defensive perimeter. It was also possible that the colder water and harsher extreme of pressure at the depth where Kismet now found himself was disagreeable to the electric fish.

He couldn't see anything. The golden illumination from the wreck was gone. Gone also was the ground beneath his feet. He was hanging in the water suspended by the cable leading to the surface. Why that line had suddenly gone taut was a mystery, but he knew that the interruption had probably saved him. He had no idea how far he had descended, but was certain that the atmospheres weighing upon him had more than doubled. He sucked greedily at the air that was being pumped down from the surface, trying to calm his racing heart.

He fumbled in the dark to find the net bag tied to his belt, intent on sending up one of the orange floats. One ball was the signal to begin the gradual ascent, allowing for decompression at certain intervals. Releasing all three of the floats would indicate an extreme emergency, dire enough to supersede the risk of the bends. Terrifying though it had been, he didn't think his encounter with the electric rays or the subsequent tumble into darkness justified such a drastic measure.

It was clear now what had happened. Blinded by the attack, he had wandered off of the submerged shelf that formed a perimeter along the coast of the Black Sea. The Caucasus didn't really stop at the water's edge, but plunged more than a mile below sea level. No diving or exploration, at least not with the antiquated equipment he was using, was possible in that dark beyond where the combined mass of water would crush his diving helmet like an eggshell. That the ancient ship had sunk so close to that shelf without going over was a coincidence that verged on miraculous; had it gone down just fifty yards further to the west, the secret of the Golden Fleece would have been lost forever.

His fingers closed around one of the floats, but before he could withdraw it, he found himself unable to draw breath; the air refused to enter his lungs. Concentrating on his chest, he tried again to inhale. He could feel the resistance, like trying to suck the air out of a bottle and a breath was grudgingly granted. Intuitively, he realized his air supply had been cut off; the compressor was no longer pumping air down to him.

Kismet immediately tried to reassure himself; the mechanism had simply stalled. He envisioned his companions on the boat frantically trying to restart the motor, and was confident that they would succeed and that at any moment precious air would resume flowing into his helmet. But thirty seconds passed, then a minute, and his ability to restrain the growing panic was diminishing with every heartbeat. Every inhalation was an effort. Each strained breath was using up his precious reserve of good air, and each exhalation further poisoned his environment with useless carbon dioxide. He closed his eyes, willing himself calm, and drew another shallow, labored breath. His hands once more sought out the floats in the net bag. He debated sending up all three, but thought better of it. Anatoly and Irene certainly must have recognized that restarting the compressor was an emergency. There was no need to compound his peril by signaling for a hasty extraction from the depths. But why were they taking so long?

Before he could release a float however, he felt a tugging across his back. A tremor vibrated along the length of cable connecting him to the boat and he slowly began to ascend out of the pit. The flow of fresh air, however, did not resume.

Instantly, the panic returned. Had the compressor failed, breaking down beyond Anatoly's ability to repair? If so, was there sufficient air remaining in his helmet to make the ascent? Even without the requisite decompression stops, the upward journey would take several minutes.

He arched his back, tilting his enclosed head to get a look at the surface. Very little illumination could penetrate the thickness of the water, but he was able to pick out the oblong shape of the trawler. He squinted at the keel, trying to estimate the depth to which he had plunged and how long it would take for his friends to draw him up. As he stared at the boat, steeling himself against the inevitable moment when he would feel the painful cramps of the bends, he became aware of a smaller boat, orbiting the trawler like a satellite.

No, he realized. *The second shape is the trawler.*

There was another vessel right next to Anatoly's boat; a craft much larger than the tiny fishing vessel. With equal parts intuition and dread, Kismet realized that it was not another fishing boat but a ship. It could only be the *Boyevoy*. The Russian captain and his armed sailors were undoubtedly already aboard the trawler and probably knew that Kismet was in the water. They had likely cut off his air supply, intending to bring his lifeless body up as evidence against Irene and Anatoly. Kismet imagined the delight they would take in watching his agonizing struggle to readjust to topside pressurization, provided he did not suffocate during the ascent.

Neither fate was one he could accept. The secret of the Golden Fleece was so tantalizingly close he could not die without knowing the truth.

A few seconds later, feeling the faint delirium of hypoxia, Kismet rose to the level of the shelf where the golden ship rested on its side ablaze in supernatural glory. As he swung toward it, he knew what he had to do.

He twisted around until he could reach the clip that secured his harness to the cable and popped the hook free. As soon as he let go the cable shot away, continuing the ascent without him, while he plummeted to the sea floor.

His sudden reappearance startled the mass of briny creatures surrounding the wreck. They immediately shifted, circling close to drive him off once again. He did not balk; too little time remaining to be slowed down now.

Heedless of the silt cloud he was stirring up, he raced toward the sunken vessel. His helmet suddenly resounded with a loud noise; the sound of an unseen fish striking at him. At almost the same moment he felt a blow to his abdomen, but neither collision was sufficient to slow his charge. Yet, despite expending all his energy, he could barely move through the fluid environment faster than a jog. He began swinging his arms to ward off the aggressive marine life but his movements were hampered by the thickness of the water.

Larger fish descended on him; bulky sturgeon, moving fast enough to knock him off balance and spiny dogfish, nearly as large as Kismet himself, flashing their menacing teeth.

He ignored them all.

The nest of electric rays reawakened as he approached the sunken shrine and the doorway behind the colonnade. Their shocks stung, but he blindly pushed them aside, refusing to be driven from the precipice a second time.

Seizing the threshold of the portal, he pushed the gilt door open and threw himself inside. Gasping for a breath that would not come, he fell against the door, shutting out the sea and the defenders of the golden ship.

13

The door refused to close. Kismet struggled with it for a moment before realizing that his air hose was the obstruction. He stared at the rubber tube, wondering what to do, vaguely aware of how stupid the predicament made him feel. The lack of fresh oxygen was clouding his ability to think.

He finally gave up trying to secure the door. The attack by the sentry fish had ceased as soon as he had gained the safety of the structure, making his efforts to shut them out unnecessary. He turned away and surveyed the enclosure. Though the ornate exterior had suggested a ritual significance, the interior appeared to be nothing more than a cargo hold. Rope webs held chests in place in two long rows, one on either side of a center aisle, the entire length of the enclosure.

Although the ship now rested on its side, creating a top and bottom aspect to the cargo arrangement, the ropes remained secure. The cargo had barely shifted in spite of the wreck. It took Kismet a moment to realize that, as with the exterior, the interior of the hold as well as the rope nets and the cargo casks were covered in a layer of brilliant gold, preserving everything intact despite centuries of exposure to salt water. He had no difficulty discerning any of the details in his surroundings because the covering of gold in the cargo bay of the wreck was brilliantly aglow.

There were more than three feet of clearance between the cargo above and below, plenty of room for a man to walk through, even carrying a heavy load in his arms, when the ship was in an upright position. But with the ship keeled over ninety degrees, Kismet was forced to crawl on his hands and knees along the crates resting on the starboard wall of the enclosure.

With so many casks to choose from, he simply selected one at random. He slashed his *kukri* at the gilt ropes, slicing through metal and ancient fibers with relative ease, releasing the first crate on the port wall. It tumbled down, sinking through the water like an anchor, and landed on its side. When he tried to maneuver the oblong case, he found it impossibly heavy. Though he was unable to lift it, he managed instead to push it over. He pierced the gold overlay with the edge of his blade. It separated easily from the wood, allowing him to peel it away like the soft lead on a bottle of wine. Beneath was unfinished white wood.

There appeared to be no hinges or latches securing the lid, leaving him to wonder the was box upside down. Rather than attempt to turn it over, he chose instead to cut through the wood with the knife. Working along the edge, he found the seam where the rough-hewn boards were joined and began prying them apart. Immediately upon breaking the internal sanctity of the cask, a flood of air bubbles rose up, tickling at the faceplate of the helmet before gathering above him in a small air pocket. Golden rays also shone from the gap he had created, stimulating him to work faster. Once the board was loose, he laid his knife aside, wedging his fingers under the wood and wrenching at it until it broke free. Through the hole he could see gold.

Bubbles of gas continued to trickle up through his fingers, obscuring his view of the prize within. He yawned, vaguely aware that the periphery of his vision was starting to go dark, and went to work breaking another of the boards free. The panels had been assembled without fasteners, utilizing a tongue-and-groove method, and after he had loosened one segment, the rest popped free with very little effort. In a matter of seconds, the contents of the box were plainly visible.

Kismet yawned again, struggling to keep his eyes open. He felt extraordinarily drowsy and found the trail of bubbles ascending from the cask to be almost hypnotic. "Got to stay awake," he muttered to himself, hoping that the sound of his own voice would do the trick. Hypoxia was taking him to the brink of consciousness. If he could not hold on for just a few more minutes, he would die without seeing the object of his quest, the reason for his sacrifice. Blinking away the somnolence, staying awake by a sheer act of will, he took the golden artifact into his arms.

It was much heavier than he expected, but he succeeded in raising it out of the cloud of air bubbles and into full view. Despite the fog that clouded his mind, he felt a shudder of excitement and incredulity as he held aloft the Golden Fleece.

It appeared as nothing more than a lambskin, heavy with gold. The wool was indistinguishable, matted with glowing metal flakes of varying size. Kismet estimated that it probably weighed at least a hundred pounds. Curiously, the Fleece continued to issue bubbles of gas, no larger than the effervescence in a glass of soda water. Though tiny, the bubbles, which seemed to trickle from every surface of the golden artifact, formed a veritable swarm. Kismet tilted backwards to get a look at the starboard side of the hold, where the globules were collecting into a great mass.

Inspiration crashed over him like a wave.

Hovering over his head was a pocket of gas, growing larger by the second. He could not explain how that atmosphere had been stored, or perhaps generated within the Golden Fleece. Nor did he pause to consider whether the gas was poisonous, or whether he would be able to survive a pressure change if he attempted to breathe it in. In the fugue of carbon dioxide poisoning, he was unable to conceive of such notions.

Casting aside what vestiges of caution remained, he dropped the Fleece into its cask and seized his air hose. He kinked it in his left hand, and then sliced it in two with the razor sharp edge of his *kukri*. The long end, still connected to the compressor, trailed impotently away like a decapitated python. Kismet took the remaining end, still bent double in his hand, and thrust it up into the growing air pocket. As he did, he relaxed his hold, which allowed the hose to open and the gas pocket to flow into and mix with the stale air in his helmet. He detected no immediate change. His tunnel vision did not brighten, yet neither did his delirium increase. He didn't smell anything noxious in the confines of his helmet, but then he knew that most gases, even the poisonous ones, were odorless and tasteless. In the absence of any other alternative, he continued to take deep breaths, hoping against hope that the gas pocket held breathable air.

He glanced back down at the Golden Fleece. The fizz of bubbles continued to trickle from it without interruption. Kismet knew that what he was witnessing could not be the result of trapped air; the volume of gas that had ascended exceeded the total volume of the crate. The only other explanation was that the Fleece was somehow producing the atmosphere he now breathed.

He vaguely recalled Harcourt's words that fateful day in his office; that the gold—or rather *ubergold*—layer on the helmet shard could pull electrons out of the air. He knew that water was simply a combination of hydrogen and oxygen atoms, both of which existed separately in a gaseous state, but bonded together in a liquid molecule that could be broken by the application of an electrical current The Fleece was evidently doing exactly that, electrically breaking the molecular bond of the water and separating its gaseous constituents.

Kismet gazed once more at the air pocket over his head, amazed that he was breathing in atmosphere produced by a talisman of ancient legend. Hydrogen, the lightest of all elements, occupied the uppermost reaches of the air pocket, leaving him with a layer of almost pure oxygen, which was even now mixing and diluting with the carbon dioxide he had exhaled.

That he was able to put this chain of reasoning together was evidence enough that he was recovering. How exactly the ancient object was able to perform that miracle remained a mystery, which even under the best of circumstances he feared he would be unable to resolve.

Though the Fleece had given him a second chance, he still felt like a man living under a death sentence. He could breathe again, and probably had a virtually inexhaustible air supply, but he was trapped on the sea floor. If he left the safety of the enclosure, he would at best have a few minutes of breathable air in his helmet, hardly long enough to make a free ascent. Moreover, the suit was too heavy to permit him to swim free, and even if he could, such a journey would carry the risk of decompression sickness. He could not remain here indefinitely, yet there was no way for him to reach the surface. Marooned in the wreck of the golden ship, Nick Kismet gazed at the object of his quest and began to despair.

Captain Severin tossed the severed and useless hose to the deck. Anatoly tightened his embrace on Irene, fearful that she might further endanger them by lashing out against their tormentor, but she did not move or say anything. She merely choked back her sobs and kept her head down, denying the Russian sailors a look at her tears.

"A most unusual way to catch fish," repeated Severin, mockingly. "I hope you have better success in the future. However, I must now order you to raise your anchors and leave this area. Whatever activity you were truly engaged in is finished, and tragically it would seem."

"We'll go," rasped Anatoly. "Now get off my boat."

Severin nodded, gesturing for his first officer to begin the egress. "*Do svidania*, Petrovna," he sneered, boarding the launch. "Give my regards to your poor, sick fiancé."

Anatoly watched them go, aware that his boat would remain under the shadow of the destroyer's artillery emplacements until he obeyed the Russian captain. He tenderly released Irene, turning her so that he could see her face.

"He's gone," she whispered.

"There's nothing we can do for him. He took a great risk; he knew this might happen. We must save ourselves."

Fifty yards away, as the captain of the *Boyevoy* was heralded back onto the deck of his ship, a great splash signaled the deployment of a marker buoy.

"We must leave here," urged Anatoly. "Can you help me?"

She nodded.

"I need you to bring up the forward anchor." He brought her to the motorized capstan and briefly showed her how to operate the device. "I must haul in the nets and start the engine. Can you do this?"

In a haze of grief, Irene nodded again. Kismet was gone; nothing else mattered.

Kismet bent the remnant of his air hose in his fist. He had no intention of giving up. He had been prepared for that eventuality before entering the enclosure, but discovering the Fleece had changed everything. If he was not going to suffocate quickly, then neither was he about to settle for a protracted death by thirst or starvation. There had to be a way for him to reach the surface and he was going to find it.

With the hose blocked and only a few minutes of air in his helmet, Kismet approached the door and pulled it open. There was no sign of the rest of his air line and he could only surmise that Severin had pulled it up after finding nothing attached to the cable. When the cut hose reached the surface, everyone would assume that he had suffered some tragedy below. The Russians had surely guessed that he had dived on the site, but had Severin been able to extract from Irene or Anatoly the reason for his descent?

Beyond the opening, the sentry fish had resumed their defense perimeter. Kismet wondered if they would attack him if he was moving away from the wreck; it was a sure bet that they would do their best to prevent him from regaining the safety of the hold. He decided not to take that risk, venturing out only with his head and shoulders. The fish did not move. He looked up and could see the activity on the surface as the motor launch shuttled back to the massive destroyer. A chain of ripples spread out from the point where the Russians dropped the marker buoy, and he could just make out the steel float bobbing on the surface, held in place by an anchor which plummeted through the water to bury itself on the sea floor less than a hundred yards from the wreck of the golden ship. A cloud of sediment rose up around the impact but did not obscure Kismet's view of the cable connecting the buoy to the anchor.

It was enough to give him hope. If only there was a way for him to climb up that cable....

He realized right away how impossible that would be. But time was running out. The two vessels on the surface would not remain in the vicinity much longer. Once they left, he would be stranded.

He considered releasing one of the signal floats, but quickly discarded the idea. Irene and Anatoly would never believe that he could still be alive, while Severin might interpret the signal as a reason to linger in the area.

The deployment of the marker buoy suggested that the Russian captain planned to return to the site. He would probably put into port at Sevastopol, take on a salvage crew and divers of his own, then return to discover what fate had befallen Kismet at the bottom of the sea. It would likely be days before the *Boyevoy* returned. Even with an inexhaustible source of oxygen, he could not hope to stay alive that long, and in the unlikely event that he did, he would most certainly face a much worse fate at Severin's hands.

Kismet ducked back into the hold and refreshed his air supply. There was a solution to this—there had to be—but loitering in the interior of the golden ship wasn't going to get him back to the surface. The Fleece remained in its box, giving him a plentiful supply of air, but offering no other insight. He realized with a defeated grimace that he would have to leave the Fleece behind. It was much too heavy for him to carry across the ocean floor.

Even as he considered this, a plan began to take shape; all of the pieces of the puzzle came together in an astonishing moment of clarity. He took several more deep breaths, trying to super-oxygenate his blood, then kinked his hose again tightly in his left hand.

This time he did not linger in the hatchway, but hastened though the portal as if escaping a burning building. The ring of fish immediately shifted toward him but he was not attacked. Moving with the greatest possible speed he bounded along the floor of the shelf toward the anchor that secured the buoy. As he had feared, there was no way he could ever ascend the heavily greased metal cable, but that was no longer his intention.

He was standing almost directly under the *Boyevoy*. It loomed above him like a great black cloud. He gazed up at it, but could not see what he was looking for. A churning of the water off her stern signaled that the destroyer's screws were now turning; she was about to get underway. Kismet abandoned his first plan, leaving the buoy anchor behind, and charged out across the sea floor yet again.

He tried to place himself directly beneath the shadow of Anatoly's fishing trawler. It was a much smaller area to locate, made more difficult by the vertical distance and the distorting effects of the water. A moment later however, he spied his goal.

It was the movement that caught his eye. Thirty yards away, well to the left of where he had positioned himself, the small anchor from Anatoly's boat was being reeled up. Rather than rising vertically, the anchor and the boat were performing a sort of tug-of-war. The slack in the anchor line had allowed the boat to drift a ways, but now both the boat and the anchor were swinging toward each other.

As soon as the bow of the trawler came directly over the weight at the other end of the line, the anchor would rapidly disappear toward the surface.

Kismet hastened toward it, watching as the anchor was dragged along the bottom, plowing a furrow of silt. Suddenly the cross-shaped hook of iron swung like a pendulum and began to rise. It seemed to jump towards the surface, moving in sudden bursts. Kismet, three steps away, found himself staring at the crosspiece, which was now at eye-level. He took two more steps toward it, but it jumped again, almost out of the reach of his fingertips. He bent his legs, then leaped straight up. His hand caught the upright, just above the flukes. It was enough. When the anchor rose again, he rose with it.

Kismet held on with all his might, unable to lift himself any higher or to improve his tentative hold on the anchor. He did not try; doing so might result in his sinking back to the bottom and there would be no second chance at this.

Kerns' warning about decompression sickness was ringing like a siren in his head, but there was simply no other option. The possibility of suffering from the bends was preferable to the certainty of a slow death beneath the Black Sea.

The ascent seemed to take forever. As the surface became more distinct, he imagined that he was getting heavier; that his grip would eventually fail. He stared at the crimped hose in his left hand and thought about releasing it, in order to use that hand also to secure himself to the anchor. He resisted the impulse.

Soon, he felt the pressure increasing inside the helmet. The relief valve began hissing, equalizing the pressure inside by venting out some of the air. This surprised him at first, but he quickly realized it was a normal function of the helmet's regulator. As he rose from the depths, the gas molecules would naturally expand, increasing the volume of air. Kerns had warned him not to hold his breath at any time, especially when coming up; the air in his lungs would also expand, causing the delicate tissues to rupture if he did not maintain steady respiration. Kismet reminded himself to keep breathing, wondering as he did if there was sufficient oxygen remaining in the helmet to keep him conscious until he reached the surface.

The *Boyevoy* lurched into motion, plowing up a frothy wake as it angled away from the trawler. The destroyer suddenly cut sharply to port, crossing the trawler's bow in an unmistakable display of force. The threat was apparently understood, for the reeling in of the anchor line seemed to take on a frenetic urgency. Kismet could feel the change in temperature as he rose up into the warmer layer of water near the surface.

The last few feet took an eternity. He kept expecting to break through at any moment, but some trick of the water—an optical illusion caused by light refraction—made the surface appear within reach while still he rose. He endured the agonizing passage of that remaining distance, confident that he had escaped death at the bottom of the sea, and that he would, in a second or two, be hoisted up onto the deck of the trawler.

The journey finally came to an end when the anchor broke the surface in a splash of white spray. As the flukes emerged from the sea, sliding through the gap in the gunwale, his extended arm came out of the water as far as his elbow. The crown of his helmet broke the surface ever so slightly...and then Kismet stopped moving.

The anchor was completely drawn in, yet Kismet remained there, clinging with one hand to the metal crosspiece, almost completely submerged. He stared up at the peeling paint on the hull of Anatoly's boat and cursed his ill fortune.

He tried to pull himself up, flexing his right arm, but relented when he felt his grip start to fail. A rushing noise, muffled by the insulation of his helmet, signaled that the engine was turning over. The water around him started to move then he realized that it was not the water, but rather he and the boat moving through the sea.

Anatoly wasted no time driving the boat's engine to maximum thrust. Soon, the trawler was churning toward shore at fifteen knots. The drag of water flowing past Kismet was not as great as if the trawler had been a speedboat or even a craft like the Russian destroyer which still shadowed the fishing vessel, but it was taking its toll. He threw his left hand up, seizing the anchor but losing the remnant of the air hose in the process. The severed rubber line trailed along behind him, partially filling with water.

With his left arm now added to the struggle, he was able to heave himself nearly two feet above the surface. He released the hold of his fatigued right hand and thrust it up to grip the gunwale. With a second stretch and reach of his left arm, he managed to pull his head and shoulders above the agitated surface.

Immediately, he began screaming for Irene or Anatoly to help him up, but his words merely bounced back at him, trapped in the metal globe. He tried to pull himself up farther, but there was nothing else to grab onto, and the weight of the dive suit was too great. He even attempted kicking the side of the trawler with his heavy boots, but nothing could get the attention of the two persons on board.

Even though he had reached the surface, he was still in danger of suffocating. The hose was blocked, and the air supply he had stored from the hold of the golden ship was already stale. The helmet, his salvation against drowning while beneath the sea, now prevented him from breathing the life-giving atmosphere above the water. He could not hope to manipulate the clamps and nuts, which locked the portholes shut, not while hanging from the moving trawler.

His right arm was burning from the ordeal of hanging onto the anchor and Kismet knew he couldn't trust that solitary limb to keep him from slipping back into the sea. Instead, he put his faith in the grip of his left hand and released the right. The boat's forward motion caused him to twist, straining his good arm, and banging his back against the hull, but he ignored the pain and focused his attention on seizing the air line with his free hand. After a moment of fumbling, he fished it from the water and held it upright to restore the flow of air.

A splash of cold seawater drained into his suit as the hose cleared, then cool salty air filled the helmet and subsequently his lungs. With the rubber tube tucked between his thumb and hand, he twisted back around and reached for the gunwale. There was nothing to do but hang on. For almost an hour he remained suspended there, unable to move. His arms began to ache with fatigue, but letting go would mean certain death.

The *Boyevoy* had broken off and headed west shortly after Anatoly had gotten underway. Not long after the destroyer disappeared over the horizon, the sun began to follow. Anatoly piloted the trawler into the harbor in the gray of twilight. No one at the dock seemed to notice the strange figure clinging to the bow of the craft. Even when a young dockhand cinched the belays, firmly mooring the boat in its berth, Kismet went unseen.

He watched in impotent frustration as his companions disembarked, Anatoly sheltering the younger woman in an avuncular embrace, both of them deaf to his cries, then sagged in defeat as the pair vanished into the growing darkness.

There was nothing left for him to do. He knew he couldn't hang on forever, certainly not until morning, when someone might happen to notice him. With no other options available, Kismet decided to simply let go. He slipped from the bow of the trawler and vanished into the water without a splash.

Irene drank from the glass Anatoly set before her—vodka—but its fire could not cauterize the wound in her heart. The big Russian and his wife looked on, unsure of how to comfort the girl. Finally, Anatoly spoke. "Irina, I know how you must grieve. But think. Your father is safe. You must join him. Go back to your life."

Irene coughed, trying to choke back a sob. "I don't even know how to find him. Nick...I don't know where my father went."

"Kismet said he would make his way home, did he not?"

She shook her head. "Nick met with someone, a friend of his, a woman. My father went with her. But I don't know how to reach them. I'm stuck here. And Nick's gone. What difference does it make?"

Anatoly tried to speak again, but his wife forestalled him, touching her husband's forearm in a gesture that said: 'Leave her be.' The Russian nodded to his spouse and they left Irene alone with her tears.

"A bad day," said Anatoly, when they were out of Irene's earshot. "Kismet did something that was either very brave, or very foolish. He did not come back—"

A loud knock interrupted him. After the events of the previous night, Anatoly was apprehensive about opening the door. "Go to the girl. Hide her."

Irene was numb. The trepidation that gripped Anatoly and his wife ought to have triggered in her a sympathetic release of adrenaline, but she felt nothing at all as she was pushed toward the hearth. They thrust her into a shadowy niche behind the firewood bin. Sealed into a dark, claustrophobic space, still she felt no fear. Through her hollow grief, she had heard the disturbance at the door, and knew that either Severin or Grimes—it didn't matter which—was waiting on the threshold to take her away and subject her to unimaginable torments in order to learn the truth about Kismet's fate, but the realization was meaningless.

There was a metallic click as Anatoly breached his shotgun, and another as he snapped it closed on two loaded barrels. In her mind's eye, Irene saw him warily approach the door, opening it with one hand, while the other remained poised on the triggers. She waited for the sound of a shot, but instead heard only a long silence, broken by the impossible.

"It's about time," complained a familiar voice. "Now can you help me get out of this thing?"

Irene exploded out of her hiding place and gracelessly tripped over the scattering of cordwood in her haste to reach him. She knew, even as she ran, that she must have fallen asleep and was dreaming this moment. Fearful that the ghostly figure might evaporate if she lingered too long with her incredulity, she threw her arms around him and held on with all her might.

Nick Kismet had returned.

14

"So the Golden Fleece is real? It saved your life?"

Kismet smiled. It was not the first time he had heard the incredulous questions. Irene's joy at seeing him had left her virtually paralyzed for several minutes. After being relieved of the burden of the bulky diving suit, Kismet found himself once more submerged, only this time it was a sea of difficult questions in which he foundered.

"Yeah, I guess you could say that. It created a supply of oxygen which I was able to breathe after the compressor was shut off."

Irene looked chastened, as if she were to blame for that act, which at the time she had believed to be a deadly one. Anatoly now spoke. "Then the Fleece is a... a magical thing?"

Kismet shrugged. "In the legend, it has supernatural origins."

He had looked up some of the details of the myth prior to their departure, but those defied credibility even more than the events of the Argonauts' adventures. The Golden Fleece was said to be the skin of the winged ram Chrysomallus, sent by the god Hermes to rescue Phrixus and Helle, the heirs of King Athamas, who had been targeted for death by their ambitious stepmother. Their literal flight took them east across the Black Sea, though Helle fell along the way, and according to the myth, her death created the strait known in ancient times as the Hellespont--since renamed the Dardanelles. Her twin, Phrixus survived the journey and eventually came to the kingdom of Colchis where he sacrificed Chrysomallus out of gratitude to the gods, and gave the Fleece to the king of that land. In many respects, the elaborate nature of the myth had been part of what had led Kismet to give some credence to its actual existence, albeit not in a strictly literal sense. Myths often ascribed supernatural origins to geological formations—and that was certainly the case with the death of Helle. There was a certain logic to the idea that the Golden Fleece might have been as real as the Hellespont, though formed in an equally mundane fashion.

He briefly pointed out some of the more salient facts. "Some of the later Jason stories do speak of his using it to end a drought, but it is usually thought of as a trophy, not a talisman."

"But it saved your life. It turned water into air; what other explanation is there?"

Kismet equivocated. "It may have something to do with electrical fields—"

"Electrical fields," Irene scoffed. "You think that electrical fields could encase an entire ship in gold, turn sea water into breathable air, and cause fish to defend the Fleece with their lives?"

"It's not so farfetched," he replied, choosing his words carefully so as not to sound foolish. "It's a known fact that electricity can split the water molecule into hydrogen and oxygen atoms. And the ancient Greeks knew how to electroplate bronze. Sea water is loaded with dissolved metal particles; over the course of three thousand years, an electrical field generated by the Fleece could draw quite a bit of gold out of the water."

"That might also explain the light you described," offered Anatoly. "And the fish would naturally be drawn toward the oxygen rich waters of the wreck site."

"Even if I accept that theory," Irene retorted, "it doesn't explain what causes the Fleece to generate an electrical field in the first place."

"Some kind of galvanic reaction with the sea water," Kismet speculated, withholding the information Harcourt had earlier entrusted to him. "I don't know; I'm not a chemist. But I can see why Grimes is interested."

As Kismet attempted to change the subject, Irene realized that she did not care one whit about learning the source of the Fleece's power. She was arguing with Kismet simply to hear the sound of his voice. The sea had given him back to her and she was overjoyed.

After losing his hold on the anchor, Kismet had immediately sunk to the bottom of the harbor. However, the sea floor beneath the trawler's moorage was only about five fathoms deep; cold and dark, but not an especially dangerous depth to Kismet in his diving gear. All he had to do was walk up onto the shore beneath the dock pilings. Once on dry land, he was able to force open the faceplate of the helmet before cautiously making his way to Anatoly's house. Thus far, he had experienced none of the symptoms associated with the bends.

"I thought you dead," Anatoly confessed. "It was impossible that you could have survived, yet you were clinging to my boat all the time. I am such a fool."

"You couldn't have known. But maybe next time we can figure out a better way to communicate—"

"Next time?" Irene gasped. "You almost died. You can't go back."

"I have to. Now, more than ever. Severin marked the site; if he gets there first, he'll have the Fleece and that will be the last anyone ever sees of it." *Unless the Russians learn about the EMP weapon, and then we're really in trouble.* "But if we act quickly, we'll be long gone before he returns."

"I can't believe I'm hearing this."

"Irene, this is something I have to do. Now listen, I know what I'm going to be up against. And I know what the dangers are. I've got a plan."

She threw up her hands and headed for the door. "I'm done shedding tears for you, Nick. Go on, get yourself killed. Leave me out of it."

Kismet stopped her with a firm hand on one shoulder. "Irene, I need you."

She refused to face him, but dug the heels of her hands into her eyes, ashamed that she still did have tears to shed for him. "Damn you, Nick."

"Irene. I will come back. I promise you that. And you know that I keep my promises."

She slowly turned toward him, still refusing to look him in the eye. Her hands came up to his chest, her fingers knotting in the fabric of his shirt. "That's not good enough," she rasped, her voice thick with emotion.

"What else can I give you?"

She looked up, biting her lip, as if afraid to answer the question. But Kismet knew the answer, and let her draw him down against her body.

Anatoly gaped in disbelief as the kiss grew more passionate, but his wife quickly took his hand and led him from the room, giving the couple a measure of privacy. Kismet and Irene were too lost in each other's arms to notice or care.

Almost twenty-four hours later, Kismet, Irene and Anatoly stole quietly through the city and boarded the trawler. It had taken most of that day for Kismet to make all the preparations for his second attempt to gain the Golden Fleece. One of the technically complex jobs had been rigging a telephone line, which would link him to the surface. Many of the other details had been time consuming and given the threat of surveillance from enemies on two fronts, somewhat dangerous. Other aspects of the preparations seemed like a scavenger hunt. Anatoly's mechanical skills had been invaluable, and Irene had proved quite capable, apparently having inherited her father's talent for engineering.

Leaving under cover of darkness had been essential to Kismet's plan for several reasons. Primarily, he hoped that it would spare them from the spying eyes of informants in the village. Whether or not they were successful in this regard was difficult to ascertain. Kismet was confident that his return from the sea had gone unnoticed by the locals, but there could be no disguising the sound of Anatoly's trawler chugging out of the harbor and out to sea after dark.

The night was astonishingly clear, the stars and moon shining down with alarming brilliance. The still waters of the Black Sea reflected the myriad points of light, giving the journey a surreal aspect, as though they were sailing on a sea of stars. Kismet found himself wondering if Jason and the heroes of the Argo had experienced such a sight on their voyage.

He knew better. The story of Jason and the Argonauts was just a fairy tale. That the Fleece, or rather *a* golden fleece did exist, proved nothing. Likely, the very real object that he had discovered in the wrecked ship had merely served to inspire the legend.

As his thoughts wandered, Irene joined him. She had not voiced any misgivings since their coming to an understanding on the previous night. Remarkably, she had maintained her good mood throughout the day, evincing confidence not only in Kismet's plan, but also in his promise.

After a full day, Kismet was convinced that he had dodged the bullet of decompression sickness. He had always understood that the bends were by no means inevitable. Nevertheless, the incautious nature of his escape from the depths had left him feeling like another character of Grecian myth: Damocles, who was forced to sit beneath the point of a sword which was suspended by a single hair. But twenty-four hours later, with no signs or symptoms of the bends, Kismet dared to believe that the danger had passed. Returning to the pressurized environment of the deep would actually alleviate the risk by breaking up any pockets of nitrogen gas lurking in his muscle tissue, and Kismet was determined, upon his next descent into the sea, to religiously observe decompression times.

"Is that it?" whispered Irene.

He followed the line she was pointing, expecting to see the buoy left by Severin. But Irene was calling attention to something else; a faint gleam in the depths, which might have been reflected moonlight, except for its golden hue.

Kismet nodded. The luminescence from beneath the sea underscored the second reason for his attempting another dive on the golden ship after nightfall. Because the ship was a superior source of light, it would be much easier to find in the dark. He had gambled on being able to visually pinpoint the exact location of the ship from the surface, and that risk had paid off.

Irene helped Kismet don the completely repaired diving suit. Anatoly dropped the bow anchor, although the seas were calm enough to prevent the boat from drifting without its help. That was about to change. Still positioned in the bow, Anatoly pitched two small packages, both wrapped in several layers of plastic sheeting and taped watertight, into the water.

The packages vanished toward the bottom, leaving concentric ripples that disrupted the reflected star field. "Get ready!"

Fifteen seconds later, the improvised depth charges erupted silently in close succession. Two enormous bubbles of gas raced upward, heralding a tremendous shock wave. When the bubbles broke the surface, they released not only the smoke and noise of the underwater explosions, but also the destructive force. The trawler pitched back and forth in the center of the detonations.

The tumult subsided after a moment however, with no injury to any of its occupants. A few seconds later, other shapes broke the surface; dozens of fish, stunned or killed by the explosions. The way to the golden ship was now clear.

Anatoly dropped another parcel into the water. This package was substantially larger than the homemade depth charges and did not destroy itself in the course of its downward passage. Two magnesium flares tied to the bundle blazed with solar intensity as it spiraled toward the sea floor.

Irene placed the helmet over Kismet's head and locked it in place. She then lifted the telephone handset they had rigged, and spoke into it. "Can you hear me, Nick?"

"Loud and clear," was the tinny reply. "I just hope we insulated that cable well enough."

"Are you ready?"

"Ready or not, let's go."

Anatoly joined them. "The equipment is down."

"Start the compressor."

As soon as air started flowing into the helmet, Kismet made his way to the stern and lowered himself into the dark waters. This time however, he would not be descending in lonely silence.

"I'm drifting away from the wreck," he called into his microphone. "There must be a current here."

Irene stopped the unreeling of the cable, while Anatoly jockeyed the boat's engines to give Kismet a better shot at landing precisely on the site. "That's good," he called. The downward journey resumed, and a few minutes later Kismet was standing once more on the bottom, facing the wreck of the golden ship.

Its light was brilliant against the ebony expanse above. He could not see the stars, much less the keel of the trawler. The perimeter of sentry fish was gone; the depth charges had removed that barrier to the wreck, but he had no idea how extensive the shockwave had been, or how long it would take for other marine creatures to investigate and replace their decimated ranks. He knew only that time was in critically short supply.

His greatest concern in utilizing the depth charges had been a fear of smashing the golden ship flat. Not only had the blast left the ship undamaged, at least so far as he could discern, but it had served to scour away several layers of sediment, exposing even more of the vessel's hull.

He did not immediately approach the wreck. His first task was to locate the equipment package that had preceded him. He saw its flares blazing a hundred yards from the ship, and hustled toward it. "I'm going after the gear," he reported. "I'd say it got caught in the same current that I did. Probably some kind of upwelling from the depths beyond the shelf."

He was speaking primarily to maintain contact with his friends above. As long as he kept talking, Irene would know that he was in no danger.

"Everything looks fine up here," she answered. "I think Severin is going to leave us alone tonight."

"Let me know if anything changes up there." A few minutes later he reached the bundle and quickly cut away the magnesium torches; they had served their purpose. The parcel was wrapped in canvas tarpaulins and tied with ordinary ropes.

He gripped one of those ropes and commenced dragging the package along the sea floor, toward the golden ship. This labor took several more minutes, and Irene could hear him grunting across the telephone line, though he said nothing until he had accomplished the task.

After untying the package, he began shuttling the different articles within to various points around the golden ship. When only the canvas tarps remained, he picked these up also, draping them over the decks, both fore and aft.

"I'm going into the hold now."

He approached the colonnaded superstructure cautiously, as if expecting the electric torpedo rays to materialize at any moment and assault him, but nothing happened. When he pushed the hatchway open, only a rush of air bubbles greeted him.

Nearly a third of the enclosure, everything above the level of the sideways doorpost, was clear of water. During the twenty-four hour period since his opening of the Fleece's cask, a great quantity of seawater had been converted into its constituent atomic components. Kismet smiled and backed away from the enclosure, pulling the door shut as he went. So far, everything was going according to plan.

He spent nearly an hour moving around the wreck, securing the tarpaulins in place with lengths of rope. Doing so required him to dig underneath the hull, which he did using an old entrenching shovel that had come down with the equipment package for just such a purpose. But that was not the strangest article in the bundle. Large eye-hook screws, truck tire inner-tubes, fishing nets cut to resemble enormous hammocks, and pieces of air hose, spliced together like enormous arteries--all of these came out of the bundled tarps, and were secured to the hull of the golden ship. The eye-hooks he screwed directly into the metal and wood, while ropes attached the rest of the items.

"I think I'm just about done down here. Get ready to bring me up."

He made a final survey of the wreck, convinced that everything was in place, and then signaled Irene to take him to the first decompression stop. He would make several more stops, using up most of the night in the process of evacuating excess nitrogen from his bloodstream. Finally, at about four a.m. Anatoly and Irene pulled him onto the trawler and helped him out of the diving suit. Irene threw her arms around him before he could wrestle free of the heavy boots, almost knocking him off his feet. He didn't mind.

"I hope I never have to lay eyes on that thing again," he said, gazing at the helmet. His clothes were damp with sweat, leaving him at the mercy of the night air, but zipping into his heavy leather jacket helped ward off the chill. He carefully dried the *kukri* and returned its sheath to his waistpack. Then, he ran down his mental checklist, wondering what he had forgotten. He could think of nothing.

"Let's do it."

The golden ship on the sea floor was connected to the trawler by two different lines, set in place by Kismet and brought back to the surface. One was a heavy cable, of the same gauge as the one used to lower him into depths. The other line however was hollow and incapable of lifting any weight. It was an air hose—actually it was several short lengths of hose, cannibalized from numerous sources and spliced together. The line from the diving suit was removed from the compressor, and the second, piecemeal line was clamped to the fitting.

Kismet screwed the regulator valve down several notches before nodding to Anatoly. The big Russian switched on the compressor, and immediately air from the surface began trickling down to the golden ship.

"How do we know if this is working?" Irene inquired.

Kismet shrugged. "I don't know. I've never done this before."

Anatoly raised a sincere eyebrow. "I have difficulty believing there is anything you have not done, Nikolai Kristanovich."

Kismet laughed. "Thank you, I think."

He twisted the valve half a turn, and watched the needle on the gauge slowly creep. He let it build for several minutes, and then tightened the valve. The compressor immediately began to bleed off the excess, and he shut it off to avoid wasting fuel. "Anything?"

Irene stared into the inky depths. The golden light was less visible because of the tarpaulins Kismet had secured over its exposed decks, but she located it without difficulty. "I don't think so."

"Okay, let's try something else. Anatoly, fire up the engine. We'll give her a little tug."

As the Russian throttled forward, Kismet switched on the air a second time. Irene continued her vigil at the stern. The trawler glided forward a ways, and then stopped, as if caught on something. The engines roared louder, churning up a spray of foam, but no further movement was evident.

"I see bubbles!" Irene squealed.

Kismet immediately turned off the compressor and yelled for Anatoly to back off the engines. He then joined Irene. Large eruptions were indeed rising from the depths; bubbles of air from the submerged ship. He placed a hand on the cable, stretched tight between the two vessels, and could feel a tremor in the metal. "Something's happening."

Indeed, the boiling on the surface grew more intense, while the taut cable fell slack. A close examination unquestionably revealed that the source of the golden light was moving, getting closer.

An enormous bubble broke the surface, and Kismet intuitively guessed that one of the inner-tubes had burst. He had attempted to regulate the airflow to the enormous rubber bladders, trying to fill them only partway, so that the reduction of pressure caused by the ascent would not rupture them, but apparently one of them had failed. Nevertheless, the shape beneath the waves did not recede. The surface continued to churn as the air he had pumped down into the golden ship expanded and overflowed.

Suddenly, the surface erupted in a foaming mass that dwarfed even the explosive depth charges. A wave lifted the trawler, heaving Kismet and Irene across the deck, where they remained prone until the turbulence calmed. Kismet heard the engines shut down, but did not attempt to rise until Anatoly appeared and beckoned. The big Russian seemed unable to speak; he gazed astern, gesturing weakly for the two of them to look. Kismet got to his feet and went to see what had so amazed the fisherman.

"I don't believe it," gasped Irene, gazing at the spectacle, which bobbed in their wake. "Nick, you actually did it."

Kismet was inclined to echo the former sentiment, but instead chose to grin and bask in a moment of pride. Rocking gently in the becalmed waters of the Black Sea, attached to huge, bloated inner-tubes and covered by bulging, inflated canvas tarpaulins, was the golden ship, sailing once more after untold millennia below the waves.

PART FOUR
THE GOLDEN VOYAGE

15

Using the winch, they drew the two boats closer together. Kismet leapt over to the deck of the golden ship, tying a second line in place so that trawler was fixed firmly to the galley, which rode slightly higher in the water than Anatoly's trawler. As he turned, surveying the golden ship for the first time under normal circumstances, he was overcome by the knowledge of where he was. Bold adventurers, kindred spirits who lived thousands of years before his birth, had stood aboard this vessel. There was nothing to compare with what he was feeling.

Science had no real knowledge about the design of ancient, pre-Hellenistic sailing vessels. It was all conjecture, really. Even the seafaring Phoenician culture had not been survived by as much as a single ship. Only a few incomplete wall murals and the words of ancient historians, who had given little thought to the fact that those ships would someday crumble to dust, remained to reveal how the ancients had roamed the seas.

While it would have been far simpler to just enter the enclosure and grab the Fleece, that would have meant abandoning the galley and all its other secrets to Severin. And since the galley was completely intact and relatively small, raising it in its entirety was only a matter of hard work, not technical know-how. The fact that it now bobbed a few feet away seemed to bear witness to his abilities as an amateur marine salvager.

The canvas blankets concealed much of the ship from his view, but he immediately began comparing the suppositions of contemporary scholars with what he was seeing. The colonnaded superstructure was inconsistent with theory, but other features were right on the mark. A girdle of ropes, now gilded, encircled the hull like a net. Kismet recalled that the purpose of this arrangement was to add strength to the overall structure, especially when battle conditions required the sailors to ram another vessel.

The bow of the ship--a galley, and not an early Bronze Age explorer scout as the Argo would have been--rose high above the gangway, even above the roof of the enclosure. Kismet could make out a gilt ladder ascending to the bowsprit and the carved foremast. The latter, an ornate spar that protruded out over the water ahead of the vessel, had been crafted to resemble a woman both delicate and fear-inspiring. Remembering the altar stone he had first viewed in Harcourt's photograph, Kismet wondered if he wasn't looking at a likeness of Medea herself. Directly below the bowsprit, the hull swept ahead at the waterline and continued forward beneath the surface to form the galley's ram.

Irene crossed over to stand beside him. "I'm really very impressed, Nick."

"You're not the only one. Come on; let's clear some of this stuff away."

As they started removing the three remaining makeshift float bladders from the net slings, Irene noticed something that Kismet had missed. "It's not glowing anymore."

Kismet stood up and scanned the golden surface. He could see the impressions of their footprints, stamped in the soft metal overlay, but there was no hint of the illumination that had pierced the undersea darkness. A sudden wind came up, blowing against the tarps and causing them to flap noisily. "That's strange." His words were lost in the clamor.

Anatoly crossed over to join them. "May I see it?"

Kismet nodded and led the way back to the entrance to the hold. The interior was dark, no longer illuminated by the glowing metal. "I guess we'll need a light or something. Wait here."

Before either of them could protest, Kismet had ducked out of the hold and jumped back over to the trawler. Anatoly quickly followed, but Kismet waved him off.

"I'll just be a minute. Stay there."

He knew exactly where his flashlight was; tucked in his waist pack, the batteries still relatively fresh. But he had another purpose for returning to the fishing boat; a detail which had been nagging at the back of his mind ever since the failure of his previous attempt to recover the Golden Fleece. It was a matter that he had not been able to resolve, primarily for lack of an opportunity, but now a chance had presented itself.

The instruments were basic; the trawler was almost as much an antique as the golden galley. He quickly located the bulky marine band radio transmitter and laid a hand on the case; it was still warm. The radio had been used recently. He drew back his hand and stared at the metal box, as though it had confirmed his suspicions. There was nothing he could do about it now.

A glance over his shoulder confirmed that the others had not left the golden ship. He raised the headphones to one ear and switched on the radio, making a note of the frequency to which it was tuned. He then adjusted that knob to another position and sent out a brief message, nothing more than a greeting, but using code words in the Russian language. He continued to do this, nudging the tuner until he received a reply. He then rattled off several sentences, all of which would have seemed harmless and not especially noteworthy to any eavesdroppers. He waited for a confirmation then switched the set off, after which he quickly loosened the antenna wire. He had almost passed from the wheelhouse before remembering to return the tuner to its original frequency. As he departed the wheelhouse a second time, his gaze fell on a battered electric lantern, powered by a large dry cell battery. Deciding that the lamp was better suited than his MagLite to the pretense upon which he had made his exit, he scooped it up then raced back to the golden ship, painfully aware that he had been gone for nearly five minutes.

"Here it is," he called, waving the light like a trophy. He pushed past them into the hold and switched the lamp on. Its beam shot through the darkness, glinting off of the now dormant metal and was reflected throughout the structure.

"It's beautiful," gasped Irene.

The cargo had not shifted dramatically during the ascent. The ship had rolled over almost right away, guided to an upright position by the air bladders strategically positioned on the hull. The cask which had contained the Golden Fleece itself had tipped over, and was now lying in the aisle at the center of the hold. "Give me a hand here."

With Anatoly's help, he turned it over so that the opening he had made was facing up. He then set the lantern down, and thrust both hands into the crate. "It's still here," he said, grinning.

It felt profoundly heavier as he lifted it from the confines of the box. Anatoly and Irene reached out to help him lay it out flat on the empty crate.

"So that's the Golden Fleece," Irene remarked.

Spread out before them, Kismet had to admit that it seemed rather ordinary; an animal skin, maybe large enough to be worn as a shawl over the shoulders but for the prodigious weight of the gold. He brushed a hand through the gilt wool, and then inspected his fingertips in the lamplight. Tiny particles of metal dust glinted in the whorls of his fingerprints. Impelled by curiosity, he flipped back one corner of the Fleece, revealing sodden leather.

"Not what you were expecting?" Anatoly inquired.

"I'm not sure what I was expecting," confessed Kismet. He played the beam of the flashlight around the hold once more, inspecting the dozens of almost identical cargo crates that lined the walls.

"Shall we open them?"

"Maybe in a minute. First, I want to test a theory." He set his flashlight down beside the Fleece and switched it off, plunging them into darkness. Irene's sigh of irritation was audible in the sudden blackness that filled the hold.

"Scientific method," he muttered. His fumbling fingers unscrewed the wire leads from the battery terminals. He then brought the wires in contact with the Fleece and was instantly rewarded with illumination. "Aha! I think we can safely say that it is an electrical phenomenon at work here, not a magical..."

The light at his fingertips suddenly flared with blinding intensity. Before he could even think about letting go, the bulb imploded with a pop that startled all of them and returned them once more into darkness.

"Was that part of the experiment?" remarked Irene.

"As a matter of fact, it was," he replied, matching her sarcastic tone. "Anyway, there's not much more we can do in here now. We'll wait until we're safely ashore to find out what other secrets this ship is hiding."

"I agree," rumbled Anatoly, breaking his long silence. "I don't like the feel of this wind. I don't want to have to navigate the harbor, towing this ship, in the middle of a storm." The big Russian turned to leave the hold, but Kismet forestalled him.

"Wait. We can't go back there."

The fisherman faced him, his features growing stern. "We must. There's nowhere else to go."

"We've got to get this ship away from Russian waters. Severin's jurisdiction extends to the Georgian Coast. If we go back, he'll just kill us and tow the ship back to Sevastopol."

"I don't believe that would happen," Anatoly replied in a grave voice. "But it does not matter. This discovery belongs to my people, Nikolai Kristanovich. Surely you must respect that."

"I'm afraid I agree with him," Irene intoned. "If you take the ship away from Georgia, then you'll be no better than Grimes and his thugs."

"Under normal circumstances, I would agree. But these aren't normal circumstances. Listen, I don't care who claims ownership of this galley. But if we don't let the world know what we've found, then no one will ever learn of it. This is a secret that the Russians would kill to protect."

"You're being paranoid."

"I don't think I am. Severin tried to do away with me once already. Not only that, if we take this ship back to harbor, do you think Grimes won't notice? Our only hope is to get into Turkish waters. Then, when I've announced the discovery to the world under the aegis of my office, we can worry about whose property it is."

As he spoke, Kismet became increasingly aware of the ship's undulations. The sea was no longer the calm surface it had been during the salvage. Anatoly had been correct about one thing: a storm was rising.

"We must put into port," Anatoly urged. "I understand your concerns, but the sea is not a safe place for us to be right now. As long as my boat tows this ship, both vessels are in danger of being battered against each other."

Kismet couldn't argue with the immediacy of the threat posed by nature's fury. "You're right. You take Irene back to Poti. I'll ride the storm out aboard the galley."

Irene jumped forward, shouting into his face. "Are you out of your mind? You'd never survive."

"It's either that, or we sail for Turkey. You decide."

Anatoly's eyes drew into narrow slits. "You risk all our lives with this foolishness, but I will do as you ask."

"Great. You go back to the trawler and let out the tow cable. Irene and I have some work to do here."

Both the Russian and Irene asked simultaneously. "What?"

"An ancient Greek galley, overlaid in gold is a bit obvious, don't you think? We'll try to rearrange the tarps to camouflage it. Make it look more like an ordinary boat. We'll float over on the inner-tubes as soon as we're done."

As they moved out onto the gangway, it became apparent that the weather was changing more rapidly than Kismet would have thought possible. "Storms rise quickly on the Black," Anatoly shouted over the roaring wind. Nevertheless, Kismet could not believe that the clear night had so quickly become filled with thunderheads. Distant lightning licked at the water, and the rolling detonations of thunder, followed quickly. The storm was not far off.

Anatoly loosened the ropes binding the two vessels and the galley immediately began to drift away. Larger and heavier than the trawler, the golden vessel seemed a perfect target for the tempest; the wind and swells quickly pushed it away to the full length of the towrope. The cable snapped out of the water, springing taut, and then the galley, driven by the persistent wind, started pulling the fishing boat along backwards through the water. Anatoly corrected this problem by revving the engine, but the strain on the tow cable was audible over the howl of the storm.

Kismet and Irene worked quickly, first stowing the inner-tubes between the columns and the hold, then draping tarpaulins and nets along the hull. The gusting wind made this task all but impossible. At one point, a sustained blast tore a canvas blanket from their combined grip. It sailed away into the night, skimming along the waves like a magic carpet.

"This is crazy!" Kismet admitted, shouting to be heard, as fat raindrops began pelting them at a forty-five degree angle. He took Irene's hand and led her back to the hold. The sound of the storm was muted, but when the rain changed to hail, it banged on the gold-covered enclosure like an enormous snare drum.

"I agree," replied Irene, when they were sheltered. "Why didn't you just let Anatoly tow us back to port?"

"Because Anatoly is an FSB agent, or at least an informant."

"That's ridiculous. You weren't there when Captain Severin questioned us. He hates Anatoly. He thinks he's a traitor for helping my father escape."

"All an act. Ask yourself this; how did Severin find us out here?"

"An informant in the city. Severin admitted as much."

Kismet shook his head. "An informant might have seen us leave, but he wouldn't have known where we were going. Only Anatoly could have supplied that information."

"Severin said that he found us when Anatoly radioed for a weather report."

"Well, I think that he called for another weather report just after we raised this galley. Funny that he didn't mention that a storm was rising. I'd say the forecast calls for trouble."

The slopes on the eastern face of the Caucasus were calm. No wind stirred the dusting of snow that had fallen earlier in the day; no breeze caused the bare limbs of the trees to sway. But something was passing through the woods, something unseen like the wind, but with a greater potential for destruction.

The men were by no means invisible, but the white camouflage shells that covered their winter parkas blended in with the snowscape and made them almost impossible to see. Their stealthy progress through the forests and up the slopes would not have attracted the notice of a casual observer.

After hours of hiking and climbing, their destination was nearly in site. As they crested a hill, getting a good look at the German encampment, they paused briefly to go over the plan and make a few last minute modifications, and then fanned out, encircling the small tent city.

Lysette Lyon took the opportunity to review her objectives: recover the plans for the EMP bomb, capture or terminate Halverson Grimes, and if possible, bring back the Golden Fleece. This raid, if successful, would accomplish the second of the three.

So far, Kismet had mostly outmaneuvered her efforts to recover the data, smuggled from Germany to the United States via Morocco. She had received a severe dressing-down for having involved her former lover in the first place, a civilian in the employ of the United Nations, though to Lyse it had seemed like a perfect plan. However, that indiscretion was quickly forgotten when she had delivered the spy, captured at Kismet's apartment, as well as the news that Halverson Grimes was a traitor, to her section leader.

The confirmation of Grimes' treachery was important, but what mystified her was the response of her superiors to the news of Kismet's search for the Golden Fleece. Though she was given explicit instructions that Kismet should not know of their interest, she was left with no illusions about the intention of the United States government to gain sole possession of the legendary relic. Lyse was awarded an unexpected commendation, and given command of a Crisis Operation Liaison Team—the CIA equivalent of the German Special Forces team they would be facing—in order to secure her objectives. Little had Kismet realized when demanding her help that he was playing right into their hands.

Nevertheless, she still did not comprehend everyone's interest in the Golden Fleece; she had seen a movie about it and it hadn't struck her as being especially useful. When she had convinced Kismet to give up a copy of the plans at the shore side rendezvous, she had believed one of those directives to be more or less satisfied. But the news that Grimes was in the mountains and not in Germany as everyone had assumed was welcome beyond words. With luck, she and her team would be able to snatch the traitor out of the Caucasus without having to risk an international incident with Germany.

Their penetration of the camp went unnoticed by the bored sentries who patrolled the perimeter under the glare of klieg lights. Lyse and the COLT squad leader went from tent to tent, listening and observing for any clue that might direct them to their target. Finally, they reached the edge of the big tent concealing the dig site. Lyse lifted the heavy canvas and peeked inside.

Soldiers milled about, some standing guard and others laboring in the pit. She ignored them, focusing on a table near the edge of the dig where three men were conversing in heated tones. She recognized Grimes instantly. The tall blond man with whom he was arguing she identified as Sir Andrew Harcourt, Kismet's nemesis. The third man she did not know, but took him for a German commando. His impudence in conversing with the other men suggested he was more than just an aide-de-camp. Lyse cupped one hand over her ear, to make out the argument.

"...failure, Harcourt," Grimes roared. "Kismet would have found it days ago."

"Kismet is an amateur," retorted the seething British archaeologist. "He is a cowboy. Like the rest of you Americans, if he can't find something in a few days, he gives up. Archaeology is about patience and persistence...."

"Spare me your lectures," the commando officer interjected tersely. "I am here for results."

"I beg your forgiveness Colonel," Grimes remarked, as though he found the man's ire merely inconvenient. "My 'expert' was apparently vastly overrated."

"If you think Kismet is so vital to the success of this endeavor," snapped Harcourt, "then you ought to have kidnapped him, as you did Chereneyev. That seems to be the way you fellows operate."

"That's not a bad idea," observed the colonel.

"As a prisoner, Kismet would accomplish nothing. I had believed that he would undertake a search on his own that would prove more successful than our excavation here. But my observers report that he has not left the city. Perhaps the artifact does not exist, as Mr. Kismet has repeatedly asserted."

"It does exist." Harcourt was insistent. "Chereneyev verified its existence by bringing us here. Your scientists verified it when they analyzed the metal fragments."

"Nothing has been 'verified.' A rare metal was discovered. It was you that made the connection to the Golden Fleece. And a tenuous connection it has proven to be."

"Then our work here is in vain." Lyse had difficulty understanding the German officer's heavily accented English; she could not tell if it was a question or a statement. "We risk war with the Russians so that you, Herr Harcourt, can chase a wild goose? Or to find your magic metal, Herr Grimes? This madness must end. This operation is over."

"I agree," intoned Grimes.

"Well then," Harcourt huffed. "When I find the Golden Fleece, we shall see who has the last laugh."

From her vantage point, Lyse resisted the urge to chuckle at the stuffy Brit's indignation. Before the three men could go their separate ways however, a soldier in blank white fatigues approached the colonel, snapping to attention. The officer addressed the soldier in German then took a brief report.

"What is it?" Grimes inquired. "Kismet?"

Lyse's heart skipped a beat. Had her team been detected?

"There is an unusual storm on the sea," the German explained. "If we do not make haste, we will be trapped up here."

"Give the order."

"In what respect is the storm unusual?" Harcourt asked.

"What?"

"You said that the storm was 'unusual.' What makes this storm different than any other?"

The German turned to the soldier and snapped off a question. As the young trooper answered, the colonel translated. "The storm rose out of nowhere, just a few kilometers offshore. It has grown quite intense; lightning and wind. At present, it is hanging out over the sea."

"Why do you ask, Sir Andrew?" Grimes' tone suddenly grew deferential.

"I think we need to find out what caused that storm."

"'What caused the storm?'" echoed the German. "God caused the storm. Storms simply happen."

Grimes, however, was more thoughtful. "I think Sir Andrew may be right. Oversee the dismantling of the camp, Colonel. Sir Andrew and I will be leaving presently."

Lyse pulled away from the tent as the three men started moving. *Snafu*, she thought bitterly. There was no way they would be able to grab Grimes now. The traitor would soon be heading down the mountain, and she and her men would be left behind, far from their support base.

She shadowed Grimes and a group of others through the maze of tents. A detachment of troopers, along with a few people that Lyse recognized from the church basement in New York City, climbed onto the rear of a snow cat while Grimes, Harcourt and another soldier got in the cab. Within minutes, the tracked troop mover was plowing up snow on its way down the mountain.

Lyse and the COLT leader slipped back to the perimeter of the camp and called the rest of the unit in for a huddle. It was clear what they would have to do. Lyse outlined her new plan, and after a brief weapons check, the men dispersed again.

Five minutes later, the stillness of the mountain camp was shattered by gunfire.

The hail passed after a few moments and returned to heavy rain punctuated by flashes of lightning spaced at intervals that were becoming shorter by the minute. Realizing that the fury of the storm was still building, Kismet led Irene back onto the deck. They lashed themselves to one of the inner-tubes and lowered it into the churning sea. The swells instantly drove the inflated rubber circle into the side of the ship. He ignored the violent pounding and gripped the tow cable with gloved hands. Little by little, he pulled them away from the galley and across the open expanse between the two vessels. They were both soaked through and shivering by the time Kismet heaved the inner-tube, with Irene still tied fast, onto the trawler's deck. He quickly loosened the knot, and they both hastened to find Anatoly.

The Russian was almost frantic. He had one shoulder braced against the rudder wheel, while his right hand feathered the throttle controls. His eyes flashed between the compass, which was spinning wildly, and the engine gauges.

"We're being driven away from shore!" he shouted when he saw them. "It's the damnedest thing I've ever seen! Take the wheel."

Uncomprehending, Kismet took Anatoly's place at the controls, while the Russian seated himself at the radio and began frantically shouting out a distress message. The urgent call was repeated several times before the fisherman threw the headset down in disgust. "There's no reply. I must know where the storm is coming from or we might sail into the worst of it."

A weather report, thought Kismet gritting his teeth. Anatoly was right. Even though it would potentially reveal their location and purpose to the Russian Navy, it might also get them through the night alive. "Maybe there's a short in the transmitter," he offered. "Or a loose antenna wire."

Anatoly turned the unit around. "*Da.* That is it." He quickly reconnected the wire Kismet had disabled, and resumed sending the message. This time he smiled as he heard a reply in the headphones. He continued sending and receiving for several minutes, then tore the headset off.

"They do not know where the storm came from. But we seem to be in the heart of it. None of the weather stations were reporting any storm activity. Not even a drop in the barometer. It is most unusual."

"So what are we supposed to do?"

"We cannot push through it, and it is between us and the shore. If we are to survive, we must ride with the storm."

Kismet immediately cranked the wheel, steering the trawler toward the east. He felt an instant surge of forward movement as the power of the engine aligned with the thrust of the gale. "Irene, go check on the galley. I don't want the wind to blow her past us. Or into us."

She nodded and ventured out onto the deck, returning less than a minute later. "It's gaining on us, but not too quickly."

"Which way? Will she ram us?"

"No. It will pass on the right."

Kismet immediately cut hard to starboard, then let the wheel straighten itself. "Now where is she?"

"Swinging to our left," Irene reported after another quick trip aft.

"Perfect." He turned to Anatoly. "I think we'll be fine, as long as this storm doesn't change directions."

The Russian nodded, but his expression was troubled. "This storm...it is not natural." He shook his head, as if his thoughts had crossed into a forbidden area.

"What? Do you mean to say it's supernatural?"

The big fisherman raised his hands. "You spoke of the Fleece creating electrical fields, did you not? Perhaps, when we salvaged the ship, those fields began to influence the weather."

"The storm started right after the galley came up," Irene agreed. "Maybe the Fleece *is* causing the storm. Or the storm is nature's way of protecting it, the same way the fish tried to keep you from approaching it when it was underwater."

"Do you realize how crazy that sounds?" Kismet knew in his heart that his skepticism was insincere. Something extraordinary was happening; he had no doubt of that.

"Is the Fleece's causing a storm any crazier than it creating air underwater or making the whole ship glow?" retorted Irene.

"It was you who suggested the theory of electrical fields from the Fleece, Kismet. And what is lightning but electricity from the sky?"

"If that's true, then we'll never be able to ride out the storm. It will stay on top of us indefinitely."

"Maybe that's what sunk the galley in the first place," suggested Irene. "Didn't Jason use the Fleece to end a drought in his kingdom? Maybe this is how; weather control."

"So what should we do? Cut the galley loose and make a run for it? Not after all we've been through to bring it up."

"I agree," voiced Anatoly. "That should only be a last resort, if conditions get worse."

Kismet nodded. "Why don't you two try to get some rest? I can handle the wheel for now. We can trade off after a few hours. Maybe the storm will blow itself out."

Neither Irene nor Anatoly seemed eager to leave, but there was little they could do to assist him. After they left to go below decks, Kismet turned his eyes forward, gazing through the water that poured across the windscreen as he held the wheel steady.

He contemplated trying to make a second covert radio contact but decided against it. There wasn't anything to report and it wasn't worth risking discovery if his suspicions about Anatoly were true. He was troubled by the possibility that the fisherman was working for the Russian intelligence service, primarily because the big man had been so helpful in their efforts to recover the Golden Fleece.

Irene reappeared after nearly half an hour, carrying a soggy sandwich and a half-filled cup of coffee. "This was full a minute ago," she complained, passing it to him. "It's a good thing I don't get seasick."

"Thanks. I thought you were going to get some rest?"

"With the boat pitching like this?" She shook he head. "I thought I'd try to make myself useful. Anatoly helped me get the stove going. I left him holding the coffee pot so that it doesn't end up getting spilled."

Kismet took a bite of the sandwich. Tucked between the two slices of bread were several fillets of oily sprat--a fish from the herring family. He managed to hide his lack of enthusiasm for the repast behind a more or less sincere smile.

Irene leaned against the bulkhead. "Well, you've brought us this far. What's next?"

"The compass is pretty much useless with this much electrical activity, so it's tough to say exactly where we are right now. But the coast of Turkey occupies all points to the south. If the storm breaks even a little, we'll turn and make a beeline in that direction."

"That's not exactly what I meant."

He raised an eyebrow. "Then I don't follow you."

"I have no doubt that you'll be able to get us safely to Turkey. For you, the impossible is routine."

"Thanks. Or was that not a compliment?"

"I mean, what will you do once you've succeeded? Once you've told the world about the Fleece?"

"If things work out as they usually do, the ship and everything on it will become a political bargaining chip. I might get a little credit for discovering it, but it will eventually be taken away from me. Since it was discovered off the coast of Georgia, they will have the most binding claim. But if it can be authenticated as a Greek artifact, then the Greek government will want it."

"And of course, if you take it to Turkey, they will want a piece of the action."

He laughed. "I think you're beginning to understand how the game of international antiquities is played."

"So why do you do it? Why chase all over the world for things that you'll never get to keep, or even get credit for?"

"I could give you my standard answer; insatiable curiosity and a thirst for knowledge of the ancient past."

"But we both know that's not really it."

"No." He unconsciously chewed his lip. The purpose that fired him, linked to that fateful night in the desert so many years before, was something he rarely revealed to anyone. He was not oblivious to the overtures Irene had made—not simply the mutual physical attraction, but something much deeper. Along with the kind of commitment she yearned for, there was a degree of trust, which he remained unwilling to share.

His personal quest was a jealous mistress, yielding precious little space in his heart for romance and even less time to pursue it. It had destroyed his relationship with Lyse, and God only knew how many other opportunities had been missed through the years. Yet, Irene deserved some kind of answer. "This is just something I have to do."

Even as he said it, the foolishness, not only of his words but of the very argument that generated them, rang in his head. Why indeed did he remain on a path he had chosen more than a decade previously, when years of searching had failed to yield a single clue? How many chances for happiness had he passed up because of his vendetta against an unknown and perhaps unknowable enemy? How many more chances would he get? He tried to meet her eyes; to make some small token to indicate that perhaps with just a little more coaxing, he might be persuaded to accept her implicit offer.

"Sounds like a lonely way to live." Her tone was solemn.

He couldn't match her stare. Deep down, he knew that, were he to attempt to lay aside his quest, the hunger for answers would consume him. There could be no rest, no ordinary life, not while those questions remained unresolved. He might not find those answers in the Golden Fleece, but recovering that mythic artifact was simply a facet of what he had become. As a tangible link to events shrouded in mystery, that gilt lambskin held answers to a different set of questions, but answers nonetheless. His eyes quickly returned to the rain-drenched windscreen. "I guess I've gotten used to it."

Somehow Irene must have sensed that she had lost him, for she made no further inquiries. After a few moments of silence, Kismet tried again to look at her, but discovered that she had already gone.

Dawn soon broke but the sky did not brighten noticeably. The thunder and lightning stayed with them, as did the wind, rain and occasional outpourings of hail. Kismet had not been able to turn south as hoped. Rather, the storm had chosen the next course change, and it was due north.

Though it flew in the face of reason, Kismet was beginning to accept that the storm and the salvage of the golden ship were indeed linked. He would not go so far as to accept that a supernatural intelligence was behind the weather—it was not mighty Zeus hurling thunderbolts down at them—but several undeniable facts were pointing to a similarly improbable conclusion. The weather system had definitely risen as soon as the galley and its spectacular cargo had been lifted from the depths, and the center of the storm had been chasing them for hours. An ordinary tempest would have eventually passed them by, but this phenomenal front seemed to match their pace, driving them ahead even as it tried to close the gap, not unlike a donkey chasing a carrot held out by its rider. He further surmised that the cyclic nature of the disturbance, due to the Coriolis effect, was responsible for what was pushing them in a gradual curve that would eventually bring them full circle. It was like being caught in a whirlpool. If the Golden Fleece was the shackle that bound them to the vortex, their only hope of survival might be to surrender their prize once more to the depths. It was a decision that would have to be made soon. Trying to ride out the storm was like playing Russian roulette; every wave that crashed over the bow might be the one that would capsize or crush the trawler.

Anatoly came up to the wheelhouse, confessing to them that he had finally nodded off for a while. Kismet turned the wheel over to the Russian, but did not leave the cabin. He was too keyed up to even think about sleep. The rational man that he was kept telling him to hang on just a little longer; that the weather would eventually pass and the Golden Fleece, as well as he and Irene, would be safe. However, his travels had taught him that there were a great many things that science and rationale could not explain. It was getting harder to deny that the events they were experiencing fell into that category.

"I'm going to go out on the deck and check the tow line!" He had to shout to be heard over the howling wind, but Anatoly did hear and nodded affirmatively. Kismet stole a glance at the radio, wondering if he should trust the Russian, but his momentary suspicion passed; there were more pressing matters to attend to.

Irene followed him out into the storm. If the hours under cover had allowed their clothes to dry out a little, the torrential downpour quickly reversed that condition. The driving wind tore at his jacket, dumping rivers of chilly water down his collar. He pulled the lapels of the jacket tight at his neck, but the damage was already done.

A night spent enduring the constant pitching had given him sea legs and he was able to make the traverse to the stern without falling. A quick inspection of the tow winch showed some wear, but he felt confident that the cable would hold at least a little while longer. He then peered through the rain and spray to see how the golden ship was holding up.

The galley had not been designed for prolonged journeys under harsh conditions; it had been built by seafarers who never sailed beyond sight of the shore. When seas were rough, they drove their ship onto the beach rather than attempt to ride out the storms. Notwithstanding the intentions of her shipwrights, the vessel was holding up remarkably well. It was both light enough to ride over the swells and broad enough to avoid being rolled over.

"Nick!" He turned to see what she wanted and found her pointing urgently in the general direction of the galley. He tried to follow the line of her finger, but for a moment saw nothing.

"What is it?"

"Just watch. There it is again."

This time he too saw the flash of orange light; not lightning, but something artificial. "There's someone else out here. But no one in their right mind would be out in this storm. That means they must be looking for us."

"Do you think Anatoly called the *Boyevoy*?"

That Irene voiced the suspicion only reinforced Kismet's distrust. If she was no longer confident of her old friend's fidelity, how could he believe that the fisherman was not a spy? "Let's go ask him."

He half expected to catch Anatoly in the act of transmitting a signal to the destroyer, but the Russian had his hands full trying to wrestle control of the rudder from the storm.

"Do you have a pair of binoculars?" Kismet asked. "There's another boat following us."

Anatoly looked genuinely surprised. He reached into a cabinet and withdrew a pair of binoculars. Kismet thanked him and went back out into the tempest.

The lenses became smeared with rain as soon as he attempted to peer through them. He wiped it away, but was unable to keep them clear for more than a few seconds. Nevertheless, through the distorting rivulets of water, he could make out the silhouette of the other vessel as it crested a swell.

"Is it Severin?" Irene shouted.

"No. It's too small. But it's military all right. Probably a patrol boat." He motioned for her to join him below decks.

"Then maybe they aren't after us," she suggested, once they were out of the storm. She futilely tried to squeeze the water from her hair then gave up in disgust.

"No. They know we're here. But maybe they haven't been in contact with Severin. We might be able to bluff our way past them."

"And if not?"

Kismet contemplated returning to the wheelhouse, where he had left the captured AK-47 with a half-full magazine of ammunition. "The odds will be a lot better than if we were taking on the *Boyevoy.*"

Irene swallowed, but said nothing more. A moment later, Anatoly stepped onto the deck and moved close enough to speak without shouting. "I've tied the wheel down. It's useless to try to navigate in this storm anyway. Well, is there another ship out there?"

"Yes. It's looks like a patrol boat though, not Severin's destroyer."

Shock registered on the Russian's face. "*Not possible,*" he whispered in Russian, then abruptly turned and hastily fled the cabin.

"What the hell do you suppose that was about?"

Irene shrugged. "He must know something we don't. Should we clue him in on your plan?"

"As soon as I figure out what it is, I'll tell you, then him. Any ideas?"

"We could tell them we were taking a cruise in our Greek galley when the storm came up. And that Anatoly found us, and was trying to tow us back to port."

Though she spoke half in jest, Kismet suddenly brightened at the idea. "It might work." He raced once more out into the storm and stared across the water at the valiant golden ship.

"Mind sharing that with me?" Irene yelled, her dark hair once more plastered to her head by the driving rain.

"Okay, try this!" The wind seemed to steal the enthusiasm from his voice, and his words came out in terse blocks of speech. "World renowned adventurer Nick Kismet and his lovely assistant attempt to recreate the historic voyage of Jason and the Argonauts by building a replica of the Argo and sailing it across the Black Sea. My dad used to do things like that all the time."

"That's crazy." She drew closer so that her argument would not be lost in the tempest. "They'll never buy it."

"It suits the situation. A gunboat isn't going to be crewed by suspicious officers like Severin. We'll probably end up talking to some poor lieutenant who'd give his left testicle to be back on dry land. We can pull this off. We just have to speak with authority."

Irene gazed through the sheeting rain at the approaching patrol vessel. It was no longer a flashing light in the distance. The patrol boat's more powerful engine was stabbing through the tumultuous seas, gaining on them with every passing second. "Speak with authority? That doesn't seem like your style."

"That will be the easy part. Remember, I'm a lawyer. Besides, these guys probably won't understand English. You can translate for me."

"Wonderful." She made no attempt to hide her sarcasm. "Shall we at least let Anatoly in on this little scheme?"

When they entered the wheelhouse, the big Russian was hunched over the radio, listening intently. Somehow, Kismet wasn't surprised. "Who are you calling?"

"Silence!" His outburst caused him to lose his concentration and he pounded the counter in frustration. Composing himself, he fired off a message that Kismet found impossible to decipher. They watched in mute confusion as he continued this way for several minutes. He then tore the headset off, and started out of the wheelhouse.

"Anatoly!" Irene shouted. "We've got a plan!"

The Russian either did not hear or chose to ignore her. Kismet chased after him. "Just a damn minute—"

Anatoly stood at the stern, staring intently at the approaching gunboat. It was now close enough that they could easily discern the radio mast, as well as the forward mounted machine gun emplacement. Just above that, a light was flickering on and off.

"Listen Anatoly," Kismet began, trying to calm the fisherman. "We've got a plan that just might work."

"Are you still ignorant?" ranted the Russian. "Or just a fool? Look!"

He was pointing to the flashing light, and Kismet realized that it was a signal being sent in Morse code. He had learned the antiquated method of communication as a Boy Scout, and despite a few mental cobwebs, began to piece together the sequence of long and short flashes into a comprehensible message. Though he had missed the first half, he got the gist of it just from the last few letters.

"What are they saying?" demanded the Russian.

"'Heave to and prepare to be boarded.' Or they'll open fire. I thought all mariners knew Morse code." Even as he said it, he knew the answer. "They're sending in English."

"Those are not Russians!" Anatoly spun on his heel and vanished below decks.

Kismet's mind raced for another explanation. If the Russian sailors knew he was aboard, it would make sense that they would communicate in English. But whom had Anatoly been talking to, and why was he so upset? Frustrated, he made his way back to the wheelhouse where Irene was waiting.

"What was that about?"

"I'm not sure." Kismet checked the engine speed indicator, and then shifted the throttle to idle position. "But I don't think we can count on Anatoly for help."

"So what do we do?"

"Stick to Plan A for now. Let's go out on deck and prepare to be boarded."

"Is that like waiting for the axe to fall?" she asked, dismally.

"Let's hope not." He took her hand and guided her outside. With the screws no longer turning in the water, the trawler was completely at the mercy of the storm. The golden ship appeared to be moving closer, but it was the approaching gunboat that held Kismet's attention. It had closed to within hailing distance and another minute would bring it alongside the trawler. Despite what Anatoly had implied, the Russian tri-color flag and the Navy jack snapped in the wind on the bow line. Kismet threw an insincere wave to the crewmen on its deck, but received only steely stares by way of reply; the sailors had no intention of moving their hands away from the triggers of their guns to be polite.

Two of the sailors on the opposing craft lofted grapples across the distance. Kismet took no action as the hooks bit into the gunwale and the trawler was pulled in like a prize catch. Though the gunboat rode higher in the water, the crew of the naval vessel had no difficulty jumping down onto the smaller boat. Kismet raised his hands to indicate that he was not armed.

"Is that how you project authority, counselor?" Irene observed, imitating his posture.

Before he could answer her sarcastic quip, another group of men appeared on the deck of the patrol boat and one by one lowered themselves onto the trawler. Kismet groaned aloud as he recognized two of them, Halverson Grimes and Sir Andrew Harcourt. "So much for Plan A."

16

As torrential rain continued to hammer down from the heavens, the boarders herded them toward the stern where all had a clear view of the vessel in tow. Despite the dark clouds and curtain of precipitation, the ancient outline of the galley was unmistakable.

Harcourt gaped in breathless amazement. "You've done it, Kismet! You've actually found the Argo!"

Kismet laughed in spite of the situation. "You're doing it again Andy; confusing mythology with archaeology. This is exactly what got you into trouble with the Beowulf fiasco."

Harcourt whirled on him, his tone strident as he shouted to be heard over the wind. "Do you dare to deny that the Golden Fleece is on that ship? We've followed the storm all night, and the storm has followed you. You've found it! I know you have!"

"Be silent," Grimes barked. "I am sick of your prattle."

Harcourt glared at the portly traitor, nursing his wounded pride, but said nothing more.

"Nice boat," Kismet remarked. "I had almost forgotten that the first thing you did after getting here was capture a Russian patrol boat and enslave its crew."

"I am not interested in discussing trivial matters with you Kismet." Grimes motioned for two of his soldiers to man the winch. They immediately complied and began reeling in the towline. "I gave you every opportunity to join me in this historic endeavor. Now, thanks to you, I have what I want, but Sir Andrew will get to take all the credit. There's nothing left to say."

Kismet glanced at the British archaeologist. "If he's going to take all the credit, then he should at least get his facts straight."

"And what facts are those?" snapped Harcourt.

"When you go on TV to tell the world that you've found the ship of Jason, you'll end up looking like a rank amateur. If you're going to use mythology as a basis for identifying your discoveries, then you really need to review the legend. The Argo, the ship built by Argus and sailed by Jason and the heroes, returned to the Greek Isles. With, I might add, the Golden Fleece. Why on earth would he sail her back here with the Fleece? That makes no sense. Besides, according to the legend, the Argo was beached and fell apart. If I remember correctly, Jason was killed when a timber from the Argo fell on him."

"Then pray tell us," Grimes interjected. "What is it that you have found here, Mr. Kismet?"

The distance between the galley and the trawler was closing rapidly. Despite the ragged tarpaulins and nets that Kismet and Irene had tied along its hull, the gleaming gold overlaying every square inch of the ancient craft seemed to shine in the stormy gray dawn.

"Would you believe that we built this ship ourselves? We're re-enacting the voyage of the Argo." He turned his head to Irene. "What the hell. It's worth a shot."

"Expensive paint you've chosen," remarked Grimes as the bowsprit of the galley loomed over the trawler, nearly at arm's length.

"Why, it's made of gold." Harcourt reached out to touch the galley, but was restrained by one of the soldiers. The ferocity of the storm had not abated and the danger of being crushed between the boats was very real. Harcourt acknowledged the need for caution. "Try to secure it. I want to go aboard." He turned to Grimes. "It's just like the helmet fragment; a thin layer of gold."

"But it isn't really gold, is it." Kismet directed his words at Grimes. "You told me as much that day in my office, Andy. You called it 'ubergold.' It's not an ordinary metal. I'm right, aren't I?"

"What difference does it make?" retorted Harcourt. "It takes nothing away from the significance of this discovery."

"I don't think you understand the significance of this discovery, Andy..."

"Stop calling me that." Harcourt sounded petulant. "And just what do you think *is* the true importance of finding the Golden Fleece?"

"Do you want to tell him, Grimes? Or shall I?" The traitor ignored him. Kismet continued, "It's not the Fleece he's after. It's the ubergold, or whatever you want to call it. And you're right about it having unusual properties."

"It caused the storm somehow, didn't it?" Harcourt speculated.

"Sir Andrew," Grimes cautioned. "I'll thank you to remember that Kismet is our enemy."

"The storm," Kismet confirmed, ignoring the threat. "But that's only the tip of the iceberg. Your partner here wants to turn it into a superbomb."

"Preposterous."

"I've seen the plans."

Grimes now took an interest. "If such plans existed, how would you of all people, know about them?"

Kismet grinned at the tacit admission, but refused to let Grimes take control of the conversation. "That's not really the issue here. We are discussing the future of the Fleece. It took me a while to figure out what your interest was, Hal. All your talk of shadow governments rang hollow. You're a military man, and it makes a lot more sense that you're looking for a way to turn this into a weapon."

Harcourt's lips formed an unspoken question. "Weapon?"

Kismet pressed his point. "You don't give a damn about science or history, Grimes. There had to be some other reason for you to go to all this trouble; you could start a war with Russia, for God's sake. Or is that what you really wanted all along?" He swung his attention back to Harcourt. "Grimes and his buddies at Alb-Werk believe that the ubergold is the key element to an electromagnetic pulse bomb. Not just one that would knock out computer circuits. No, this little gem will microwave you where you stand." He made a gesture with his hands like a magician. "Poof. Vaporized just like that. What do you think of that, Sir Andrew? Do you want to be responsible for helping them create the ultimate weapon?"

Harcourt broke in. "A clever argument, Nick. But I'm onto your game. The quest for the Golden Fleece was always my project. I brought it to Alb-Werk, not the other way 'round. The fact that you were actually the one to find it is nothing more than a fluke. I deserve the credit, and I'm going to get it."

"But I'm telling you that you've become part of something terrible," said Kismet. "If you stand by and do nothing, you'll share a corner in hell with him."

"You've said quite enough, Kismet." Grimes interrupted the conversation, ordering his soldiers to hold Kismet and Irene at gunpoint. Others from the boarding party began stringing rope ladders from the trawler to the bow of the galley, just aft of the bowsprit.

"Nick?" Irene spoke in a barely audible whisper, as Grimes and Harcourt were helped to board the ancient vessel. "Where's Anatoly?"

"Are you coming, Kismet?" Grimes stood nearly six feet above him, gazing down from the deck of the golden ship. His tone was triumphant, mocking; He knew he had won, and wanted to rub Kismet's nose in the victory.

But with Anatoly missing, there was still hope. "Why not? You guys need at least one voice of reason."

As the commandos hustled them onto the galley, Kismet got a look at what the storm had done to the ancient vessel. It had held up well, but eighteen inches of water was sloshing about in the bilges. "Looks like you'd better start bailing," he suggested. "Unless you're prepared to salvage this ship a second time. And if my knowledge of the Black Sea serves me correctly, it's about four hundred fathoms to the bottom."

"Excellent observation," Grimes commented. He turned to one of his subordinates and ordered the man to fetch a pump, then returned his attention to Kismet. "Are you reconsidering your loyalties?"

"I'm not a traitor, if that's what you mean."

If the words stung, Grimes did not let it show. "I believe we've already discussed that matter, Kismet, and it has grown tiresome. Now, if you would please be so kind, show us the Golden Fleece."

"It's in there." He gestured toward the colonnade encircling the hold. The portal, which led into it, was on the opposite side. "Look for yourself."

Grimes nodded to one of his men. Kismet realized it was Rudy the behemoth from the hall of the Teutonic Knights in New York. The hulking figure moved toward him with surprising swiftness, but before Kismet could so much as take a step back, Rudy took hold of Irene and yanked her away.

"I want you to show me," Grimes clarified. "I think Miss Chereneyev has already demonstrated her usefulness as leverage in getting what I want. I have no compunction about letting Rudy toss her overboard—" He looked at the giant and shrugged—"or whatever else he feels like doing. He can be a little vindictive, you know."

"Save your threats, Grimes. I'll open it for you." He stalked aft, followed by the others, then circled around to the sternward end of the enclosure and pulled open the hatch, revealing the darkness that lay beyond the golden columns. He then looked back to Grimes, who nodded for him to step inside. With a shrug, he complied.

"No booby traps? I'm almost disappointed."

"I wasn't expecting you," replied Kismet. "Good idea, though. Wish I'd thought of it.". He stared straight ahead into the darkness of the enclosure, wondering if the Fleece would be able to save him this time.

"Kismet?" The whisper from the shadows startled him.

"Anatoly?"

"You must distract them. I have a plan, but there is no other way for me to get out of here."

"Kismet?" Grimes called, sticking his head through the opening. "Who are you talking to?"

SEAN ELLIS

"Just praying to Zeus for a miracle." He reached out to the Fleece and lifted it in his arms, and then muttered under his breath: "I think he might have been listening this time."

Harcourt pushed past the stout traitor and attempted to snatched the gold-laden sheepskin from Kismet. He was unprepared for its heaviness; the transfer threw him off balance and he teetered backwards. Only Kismet was near enough to prevent the British archaeologist from toppling over, but he merely watched his rival fall with a grin.

The indignity of his clumsiness did not seem to register with Harcourt. He struggled to his knees on the deck, gripping the Fleece with both hands. "I can feel its power," he crooned. "Tingling in my fingertips. This truly is the Golden Fleece."

"Yeah? Well, congratulations Sir Andrew. It's another feather in your cap. I'm sure Oxford will be buzzing with talk of your triumphant act of piracy. You'll finally get the respect you really deserve."

"My goodness," Grimes clucked. "Kismet, you sound like a child who's lost his toy."

Kismet grinned again. "As for you, Grimes, I'm surprised you can be so calm, when there's an FSB agent hiding just inside the hold."

Grimes' expression instantly turned severe. "Explain."

"The owner of the fishing boat, Anatoly Grishakov, works for Russian intelligence. He's probably already informed his superiors that we're out here. I expect they'll be showing up any time."

"You're bluffing," Harcourt spouted, struggling to lift the Fleece off the deck.

Kismet shrugged. "Ask him yourself."

Grimes nodded to his subordinates and two of the soldiers swung their rifles around, and advanced on the dark hold. Before they could enter, a muffled voice issued from beyond the colonnade. "Don't shoot. I will come out."

Anatoly stepped through the hatchway, hands raised, flashing a betrayed look toward Kismet, who spread his hands in an apologetic gesture.

"Are you a spy?" Grimes demanded.

"Of course not. Kismet is lying, though I can't imagine what he hopes to gain."

A faint grin crossed Grimes' expression. "You are speaking English. But the other night, you pretended not to understand. Isn't learning English a requirement of the FSB?"

"I told you," Anatoly spluttered, his accent noticeably thickening. "I do not work for that agency."

"I know that he's sent several messages," supplied Kismet. "He sent one as soon as he saw you guys." He glanced over to Irene. She was listening intently, but he could not tell if she approved of what he was doing. "He's been in contact with a Russian destroyer. Two days ago, he tried to kill me to keep the discovery of Fleece secret. If you think he's going to let you just sail away with it, you're in for a big disappointment."

Anatoly glowered. "This is the act of a coward, Nikolai Kristanovich. I expected better of you."

Kismet faced the big fisherman. "You were pretty convincing. What I can't figure out is why you let Petr escape in the first place. That must have gotten you in hot water."

The big fisherman continued to glare, but his frown changed from a look of betrayal to one of contempt. "You understand nothing. Petr Ilyich Chereneyev was—is—my friend. Always. I would die myself, before allowing harm to come to him. Or his daughter. Even from them."

"Anatoly?" Irene's tone was soft, almost inaudible in the fury of the storm, and full of confused sympathy. "Is it true? Are you FSB? Were you, even then, with the KGB?"

"If he defied the order to have your father killed," Kismet suggested, "and didn't end up dead himself, I'd say he must be pretty important in the organization."

"There are those who are in my debt." The Russian's statement indicated that his denials were finished. "In turn, I owe a debt to my country. Thieves and grave robbers must not be allowed to steal a great treasure."

"I am afraid you can do little to prevent that," intoned Grimes. "You've lost."

"I do not need to act. This storm will sink the galley before you can loot its gold. If we do not leave this ship quickly, we will all sail it to the bottom."

"Perhaps you are right about that. Sir Andrew, please get up off the deck. It's unbecoming of you to grovel like that." Harcourt did manage to stand, with the Fleece weighing heavily over his left shoulder. Grimes began passing along orders to his men. He ordered them to continue pumping the bilge water, while another group made fast a second tow line; this one leading to the gun ship. "With two boats towing, we can beat this storm."

"Aren't you listening?" Anatoly hissed. "If we do not leave, right now, we will all die!"

The urgency in the Russian's voice seemed out of place. He had spent the night towing the ship through the storm and Kismet couldn't understand why he was suddenly so eager to get off the galley. He gazed at the fisherman, looking for an explanation, and saw in Anatoly's eyes a desperation that frightened him. Acting on an impulse, he moved closer to Irene. Rudy-- Grimes' pet behemoth--still held her in his grip, and threw Kismet a threatening stare.

"What's the rush, Anatoly?" Kismet spoke in order to distract both the giant and the Russian. He managed another step toward Irene, almost close enough to touch her. "She's not going to sink, not after riding out the storm all night."

Anatoly seemed to draw into himself, like a snake coiling before a strike. "*If the storm does not sink her, then my bomb will.*"

Irene mouthed the word "bomb" as if unable to comprehend, but Kismet understood all too well. Anatoly suddenly launched into motion, pushing away from the soldiers who guarded him.

In a heartbeat, chaos broke out. Kismet hurled himself at Rudy, gouging at the giant's eyes. In the same instant, Anatoly dove from the galley, leaping out into the storm tossed sea. His escape commanded the attention of the soldiers who, as one, rushed to the gunwale.

Rudy's reflexes proved faster than Kismet would have believed. He swatted Kismet's hands away, delivering a follow-through punch that dumped Kismet onto the gangway, sending him sliding backwards on his tail bone.

Four semi-automatic rifles spoke, splitting the howl of the wind with their deafening report. Bullets sprayed the water where Anatoly had splashed a moment before, but he did not resurface. The commandos stopped firing and waited to see if he ever would.

Kismet looked up from where Rudy had knocked him. Grimes and Harcourt were staring down with amused expressions. The giant was positively gleeful, taking a step forward, balling his enormous fists in preparation to take Kismet apart, limb-by-limb. Kismet scrambled backward without rising, and scooted along the deck to put some distance between himself and the enormous fighter. His escape was abruptly blocked. He turned his head and saw that he had backed into the column that stood to the right of the hatchway. Somewhere in the blackness of the hold, the explosive device Anatoly had planted was ticking inexorably toward zero. About five seconds had passed since the big Russian's flight. Rudy took another step toward Kismet, towering over him.

Suddenly, a brilliant flash of light burst at the far end of the cargo compartment. A tongue of flame and a wave of compressed air as hard as concrete raced through the structure, driving gold covered cargo crates and debris ahead of it.

Anatoly's bomb had detonated.

17

The explosive device, placed near the far end of the enclosure, was relatively small; it was the same design as the depth charges Kismet had employed to eliminate the threat posed by the sentry fish near the wreck site. Anatoly, realizing that Grimes and his men were about to seize the galley, had rigged a timer to one of the bombs and planted it in the rear of the cargo area, then waited for his chance to escape. But Kismet had stalled him too long, and forced him to take a desperate plunge into the sea.

In the hyper-awareness of adrenaline, Kismet could see the ball of flame rolling through the hold toward the opening. He was directly in its path.

Unlike Rudy, Kismet was expecting the bomb to go off and did not require a split-second in which to decide what to do. As the blast hurtled toward him, he rolled forward at an angle that took him a hair's breadth from Rudy's size sixteen boots.

The former boxer may have had lightning-fast reflexes when it came to blocking a punch, but he was totally unprepared for the detonation of an improvised explosive device. His eyes widened slightly as a pillar of fire erupted from the portal and erased him from existence.

The entire superstructure swelled like a balloon about to burst. The columns bowed outward as the enclosure changed from a roughly cubic shape to something more closely resembling a sphere. However, that seemed to be the extent of the damage caused by the explosion. The blast did not rip apart the hold as Kismet had expected; it was as if the enclosure had almost completely absorbed the violent release of energy. Almost. Though barely perceptible to the naked eye, under the skin of gold, the wooden frame of boat had been smashed into splinters, and those splinters had been driven outward, through the foil-thin layer, allowing water to begin seeping in.

The flames that had vomited from the hatchway ceased immediately. Kismet felt the blast beating against his back, but was unhurt. Grimes and Harcourt had likewise passed through the explosion unscathed, although the British archaeologist was having difficulty keeping his balance.

"Back to the gunboat!" Grimes shouted. "Quickly, before it sinks!"

Harcourt protested. "We can't just abandon ship. This discovery is too important."

Kismet ignored them and searched for Irene. He found her on hands and knees, thankfully untouched by the blast. "Stay there!" he shouted at her, but stopped motionless after only a step.

Something else was happening. At first, it was nothing more than an unsettling sensation, but that premonition quickly manifested into something more profound, if no more tangible. An invisible crackle of energy passed through the length of the ship. Kismet felt it tingling on his skin; a spider web of static electricity that tickled his face and caused his hair to stand on end.

The phenomenon was not limited to the ship. As if harmonizing with the vessel's energetic discharge, the pitch of the storm changed abruptly. The sky directly above the galley began to swirl like a vortex of shadow, and the golden ship was now the nexus of the tempest.

Grimes prevailed in his argument. A loud, eerie groan shivered through the ship, and Kismet felt the galley begin slowly rolling to starboard. Though no leaks were evident, the vessel was nonetheless taking on water and beginning to list. The time remaining before the golden ship began her final voyage, the one that would take her to the unreachable depths of the Black Sea, would be measured in mere minutes.

The soldiers stumbled over one another in their haste to flee. Harcourt watched them in mute amazement, as if he were merely a spectator. Grimes too, hastened to the edge of the galley and lowered himself to the deck of the trawler.

No one seemed to care any longer about Kismet or Irene. He crossed to her and embraced her as if they had all the time in the world. "Are you all right?"

She nodded into his chest. "Anatoly?"

"I don't know. But Grimes was right about one thing: this ship is going to sink." He glanced down at the trawler. The commandos had already cast off the belaying lines that secured the Anatoly's vessel to the gunboat. Grimes stood at the rail of the patrol craft, gazing over at the prize that had been denied him, while his men pushed away from the doomed galley and the smaller boat that would inevitably be dragged down when the golden ship went under. As if to punctuate their peril, a blinding tongue of lightning licked across the water, less than a stone's throw from the port side of the galley. The ear-splitting concussion of thunder that followed made the explosion in the hold seem insignificant by comparison.

"That was too close," Kismet muttered. He wasn't sure if he had actually spoken; his ears were ringing and no other sound was audible. He looked at Irene to see if she had heard him but found her gaping in amazement at something behind him. She spoke but her words were indistinct. He turned to look, expecting to find Rudy, back from the dead and seeking vengeance.

Instead, he saw something wonderful. Golden light was pouring from the passageway that opened into the hold, the same hue he had witnessed when first discovering the ancient ship on the coastal shelf off the Georgian shore. That light had fallen when their salvage efforts brought the galley to surface, but now it was back.

The radiance was momentarily limited to the interior of the hold, but as he watched, luminescence pooled on the exterior surface, spreading like puddles of fire, connecting and redoubling until the columns glowed incandescent.

Another flash of lightning, more distant than the first, overwhelmed the glory of the golden ship and underscored the need for a hasty departure. It seemed a shame to abandon their discovery, especially with its power suddenly waking, but that power would be of little help when the ship slid beneath the waves. Kismet turned back to Irene. "We've got to get to the trawler!" he yelled.

The list of the galley was already at twenty degrees. The bilge pump on the port deck began to whine as the slope carried the water away from its intake, causing it to suck air, while the starboard pump was completely flooded and stalled. In that instant however, before they could take a single step, the radiance of the gold began to shine beneath their feet.

Kismet gripped Irene's hand as they made their way down the length of the tilted deck toward the rope ladder that led to the trawler. The list of the larger, ancient vessel was causing the fishing boat, still lashed to its bowsprit, to twist dangerously in the water. As they looked down from the galley they saw Harcourt, standing alone in the stern of the trawler with the Golden Fleece still weighing on his shoulder. The archaeologist was fumbling with the belays, trying to free the smaller craft from the galley's death grip.

"Harcourt! Help us!"

The Englishman looked up, as if surprised that Kismet was still alive. "Sorry, old boy!" he shouted over the din. "Not going to let you take this one away from me."

"For Christ's sake—" Before Kismet could complete the invective, a dark shape appeared in the air right in front of him. He jerked back instinctively, but not before being struck in the jaw.

He turned as he fell, landing face down on the pitching deck, and slid toward the starboard gunwale, which was just dipping under the surface. He was unable to arrest his fall in time to keep from splashing into the swirling waters, but as he went in, he heard Irene gasp the name of his assailant:

"Anatoly!"

The Russian fisherman looked like the walking dead. Blood streamed from his forehead and from ragged wounds in his torso; the gunshots of the soldiers had found their mark but had failed to kill the Russian agent. He had survived by diving deep beneath the galley and clinging to the nets which had earlier been draped over its sides for camouflage, waiting for a chance to exact his retribution on the man he held most responsible for the situation: Nick Kismet.

Hurtling over the side of the galley, Anatoly plunged past Irene. Kismet raised his head from beneath the water in time to see the Russian's boots moving on a collision course with his face. He tried to twist away, but was too late. The tread on Anatoly's boot sole glanced along his cheek and smashed into his right shoulder, burying him once more in the turbulent water. Gritting his teeth against the pain, Kismet braced himself against the side of the ship and stood up underneath Anatoly, catapulting him away. As the Russian splashed down, Kismet waded toward him.

Anatoly recovered quickly, whirling in the knee-deep accumulation, with one foot on the sloping deck and the other against the gunwale. A bitter smile creased his bearded visage as he raised his hands. Kismet took a step toward him, brandishing his own fists. When Anatoly's gaze seemed to lock onto his hands however, Kismet lashed out with his foot, planting it in the larger man's crotch.

The big Russian grunted and his intimidating smile fell. He cupped a hand to his bruised groin and staggered backward a step, but that was the limit of his reaction. He recovered quickly and advanced to deliver a round-house punch that split Kismet's cheek open. The force of the blow spun him around again, dropping him to his hands and knees.

"Why doesn't that ever work?" he muttered under his breath, shaking his head to clear away the fireworks. Then his head went underwater as Anatoly landed on his back. Kismet thrashed, but Anatoly's knees were on his shoulder blades and his arms were pinned so that he could do little more than turn his head.

After a few seconds of futile struggle, Kismet felt the burden on his back grow even heavier, forcing the last gasp from his lungs. Then the weight suddenly vanished. He squirmed free and hastily crawled forward, sucking fresh air in desperate gasps, then turned to face his assailant.

Irene was on Anatoly's back, clawing at his eyes. Despite his professed fondness for her, the Russian grabbed her wrists, lifted her over his head and hurled her toward Kismet. She crashed into him, driving both of them into the water. Kismet felt Irene bounce off of him, then saw her splash into the open sea. She flailed in the water, her soaked clothing weighing her down.

Forgetting Anatoly, Kismet reached out to her, but she was too far away. He quickly shed his leather jacket, holding onto one sleeve while flinging the other toward her. She caught it, but then vanished beneath a wave. When he hauled her in, she came up choking on seawater but tenaciously clinging to the jacket sleeve. Another pull brought her close enough to grasp the inundated starboard gunwale.

The big Russian chose that moment to renew his attack. Another stunning roundhouse blasted Kismet toward the bow. There was no way he could hope to overpower the fisherman. Anatoly not only outweighed him by a good fifty pounds, but was also in the grip of a primal anger that Kismet's own desperation could never equal. He would have to outwit the Russian, not outfight him—a difficult prospect since Anatoly was knocking his wits out with each blow.

Anatoly stalked past the still submerged form of his best friend's daughter, ignoring her life and death struggle. Without his help she managed to pull herself from the sea and got to her feet, sagging against the deck, which now rose to a forty-five degree angle beside her.

Kismet did not attempt to make a stand against the Russian. Instead, he retreated along the bow, climbing onto the tilted bowsprit. Anatoly was literally at his heels, grasping at his boots in an effort to trip him as he attempted to climb up to the spar protruding from the bow.

Below him, Harcourt had succeeded in cutting the mooring lines that had tightly secured the trawler to the ancient sailing vessel. The fishing boat popped upright with a suddenness that surprised the archaeologist, causing him to topple over. The trawler then bobbed away from the galley, taking with it Kismet's best plan for escape.

Anatoly's fingers snared the cuff of Kismet's right trouser leg. He was yanked back, stretched between the Russian's grip on his leg and his own desperate hold on the ladder to the bowsprit. He slipped his left foot off of the rung and drove it repeatedly toward Anatoly's face.

At first, the Russian seemed impervious to the blows, but the insistent pounding of Kismet's boot savaged his face, tearing skin and smashing cartilage and bone. Kismet felt the grip on his leg weakening and yanked himself away, scrambling to the top of the spar.

Normally, the bowsprit would have been the highest point on the galley, save for its mast when the ship was whole. But now the deck leaned over drunkenly, borne down by the weight of the water that was inundating the galley. Kismet crawled out onto the exterior of the bowsprit, along the port side edge that now faced skyward, clinging to the foremast. Anatoly's bloodied face rose alongside him.

Kismet took a swing at the Russian, hoping to knock his foe into the sea, but the impact of the blow rebounded, causing him to lose his own grip. He slid along the smooth surface of the hull, his feet flopping out into empty space. He managed to grasp the foremast, his fingers finding a purchase in the intricate whorls of the design. The carved hair of the image, layered with gold, was the only thing that prevented him from tumbling into the storm tossed waves. It was as if Medea had once more intervened to rescue her champion.

Anatoly now pulled himself erect and loomed over Kismet like an executioner. He stood with his feet apart, bracing himself against the inexorable roll of the galley. Blood streamed from his shattered nose and dripped down onto the shining gold, where the rain and spray washed it away. "We die together, Nikolai Kristanovich Kismet." The trauma to his face distorted his words even more than his accent, but Kismet understood all too well. "You will not steal this treasure from my people."

"What about Irene?"

His remark had the desired effect of causing Anatoly to hesitate, but the pause benefited him little. He was stuck, dangling from the bowsprit, unable to pull himself up or to get a foothold. The big Russian looked away, staring down at the place where Irene now struggled to get above the rising water. "Forgive me, Petr Ilyich," he whispered apologetically then returned his attention to Kismet. "I cannot save those who join with the enemies of the *Rodina*."

Kismet started to reply, but was overcome by an unusual sensation. A preternatural stillness enshrouded the bow of the galley, a faint hum and tingle pervading the void in the fury of the storm. Later, he would swear that everything began to glow with blue light in the moment before he let go. Heeding the premonition, he surrendered himself to gravity. He opened his hands, released the foremast, and dropped two stories into the frothing Black Sea. When he hit the water, he stabbed nearly as deep into it, before his own buoyancy arrested his plunge. He did not bob back to the surface however, but was bogged down by his sodden clothing and boots.

Suddenly, the world above was filled with light. Though it lasted for only a heartbeat, Kismet knew what it was—his prescient moment had saved him from a deadly bolt of lightning.

Rather than struggling to swim impeded by the weight of his boots, he doubled over and began unlacing his footwear. The knots were swollen with water and resisted for a moment, but in his desperation he succeeded in breaking the heavy strings. He kicked the boots off, and stroked toward the surface.

Medea was gone. The lightning blast had sheared off the top of the bowsprit, sending the carved image of the sorceress into the depths. Black scorch marks obscured the glowing metal along the point of severance. There was no sign of Anatoly.

Kismet swam toward the nearly vertical deck and sighed in relief when he spied Irene clinging to the distended columns around the hold. She was sobbing when he reached her, but he did not press for an explanation. She had just witnessed her oldest friend burned to a cinder by lightning. Whether it was Anatoly's death, or his treachery, she had good reason to be upset. He silently enfolded her in his embrace and waited for the end.

Grimes stood on the deck of the captured gunboat, calmly watching the demise of the golden ship. To lose such a great prize was tragic, but that failure was mitigated by the primary success of the entire endeavor. They had recovered the Golden Fleece. From his vantage, he could see his hired archaeologist likewise watching Kismet's final journey with the mythic sheepskin still adorning his shoulder.

Grimes cared not for the legendary—purportedly supernatural—origins attributed to the Fleece. A nominal Christian, he was quite certain that the gods and heroes of Greek mythology had never really walked the Earth, so there could only be a mundane explanation for the astonishing properties of the ubergold, and that was for the scientists to unravel.

Despite Kismet's casual accusations, the decision to alienate himself from the country of his birth had not come easily. In his heart, he remained a patriot, sworn to defend the Constitution of the United States from enemies both foreign and domestic. The problem was that America's true enemies had risen from inside her very leadership. After years of trying to right those wrongs from the within, he had come to realize that the mechanism of American government could not be adjusted incrementally; something more dynamic would be needed to put not only America, but all the nations aligned under the North Atlantic Treaty back on the track to global military and economic supremacy. The weapon proposed by his new acquaintances at Alb-Werk had the potential to do just that.

It was a terrible device, to be sure. It had to be. No one feared or respected a threat that did not promise extremes of destruction. Its very existence would send a message to the insurgents and extremists buried in the civilian populations of developing countries around the world: resist and you will be obliterated. Not merely blown apart or burned beyond recognition, but atomized; not even ashes would remain to inspire the next generation of terrorists.

The menace of such a device would no doubt have been adequate to force the hand of the Iraqi dictator without necessitating the war that had fractured years of diplomatic progress in Europe and inflamed the Arab world. Alb-Werk's scientists had promised a working prototype within two years and Grimes had lobbied the President to exercise patience, but his arguments had been in vain. The timetable was unrealistic and the Commander in Chief did not like the idea of waiting on a former enemy nation—Germany—to develop and ultimately exercise control over a strategic weapon. An ultimatum had followed and Grimes had made a hard choice, but not one that he had cause to regret. When Germany added the EMP weapon to NATO's arsenal, subjugating the last of the free world's enemies, the wisdom of his decision would become manifest.

The ubergold in the Fleece alone was adequate to supply a dozen warheads, but Grimes had full confidence in the ability of Alb-Werk's scientists to crack the atomic code of the strange metal in order to synthesize an endless supply. The loss of the golden vessel was merely inconvenient.

He turned to the leader of the small commando unit. The German Special Forces officer had been champing at the bit to return to the Georgian coast in order to link up with his superior and the bulk of the contingent. Since their hasty departure the night before, they had been unable to establish radio communications with the main force that had remained behind to sterilize the mountain camp. The squad leader was justifiably concerned, and with success so near at hand, eager to get his men back home with the prize.

"Bring us around to the Russian's boat," Grimes ordered. "We'll pick up Sir Andrew and then proceed to the rendezvous."

Before the officer could turn to execute the command, a shrieking whistle cut through the dull roar of the wind, causing both men to freeze where they stood. The sound grew louder and lower in pitch, then abruptly fell silent.

Grimes knew the sound: the unique whistle caused by the fins of an artillery round as it descended toward its target. It was a noise every soldier knew and dreaded. But the screech had not reached its lowest note—the precursor to impact and detonation. There could be but one explanation for the sudden quiet. As he looked up and around, he heard the German colonel cry in alarm; a harsh sounding German phrase which he both understood and echoed.

Like the eye of a hurricane, the one place where the shriek of an incoming round could not be heard was at ground zero. Somewhere high overhead, the projectile—fired from God only knew where—had completed its parabolic arc and was descending directly onto the target.

"*Scheisse*, indeed," Halverson Grimes muttered, repeating the commando's oath.

Then he vanished in a spray of smoke and tissue.

In the distance, beyond the exploding gunboat, Kismet could make out the broadside silhouette of the *Boyevoy*, materializing wraith-like from the veil of storm clouds on the horizon, arriving too late to rescue the agent that had summoned her, but not so tardily as to let the rest of her prey escape. Her guns were lobbing anti-ship mortars with startling accuracy toward the renegade patrol craft.

The first shell—the one that had blown Grimes out of existence—landed amidships to port, knocking a sizeable chunk out of the hull. That shot alone was fatal to the gunboat, but Severin's artillery men did not relent. The patrol vessel never got a chance to sink; shells from the destroyer blasted its flaming wreckage across the water.

The commandos that survived the initial blast quickly abandoned the doomed vessel, hurling themselves into the storm-tossed water. Random discharges of lightning illuminated them as they struggled in the driving rain amidst oil slicks and debris. Some were trying to reach the galley, though that seemed akin to leaving the safety of the frying pan for the fire; the golden ship would likely sink before any of them could get there.

The *Boyevoy* came around, plowing through the tempest toward the wreckage. Although her big guns had fallen silent, the destroyer continued to visit death upon her enemies. Sniper fire was picking off the derelict survivors. Kismet wondered idly if Severin would bother to take him and Irene prisoner, or just machine-gun them and leave them to sink with the golden ship.

All of a sudden, the galley lurched forward. At first, he thought it was a final shift, angling toward the bottom, but then he realized that the golden ship was starting to move. "What the hell?" He loosened his hold on Irene. "Wait here."

Grasping the port gunwale, he traversed the length of the deck like a rock climber, hand over hand, with his stocking feet braced against the sloping deck. As he moved forward, he saw that his first assumption was partially correct; the bow was indeed shifting downward, and would precede the rest of the vessel in the journey to the bottom. But the movement was caused by something altogether different.

"Harcourt!" he shouted. "You bloody fool!"

He could not see the British archaeologist aboard the trawler, but it was evident that Harcourt had succeeded in engaging the idling motor. The trawler had started forward, but moved only a short distance before hitting the end of the tow cable. In his ignorance, Harcourt had failed to disconnect the line when cutting the mooring ropes. The trawler's small engine was still capable of tugging the ancient vessel, but when the galley went under, the fishing boat would sink with it.

The Englishman now appeared on the deck. Harcourt apparently realized his peril, and was investigating the umbilical attachment. Kismet noted that his rival still had the Golden Fleece draped over one shoulder. Its weight caused him to stagger as he crossed to the stern and inspected the winch assembly. He fumbled with it for a moment and managed to release the ratchet, allowing the cable to unspool. The trawler immediately shot forward leaving the golden ship behind, but his efforts only temporarily forestalled disaster. The winch continued turning until the line was played out. After only a few seconds, the tow cable snapped taut, rising out of the water with a thrumming vibration, and the fishing vessel stopped dead.

Harcourt stumbled and fell onto his back, but managed to crawl over to the winch. Though he was now almost a hundred yards away, Kismet could see the archaeologist beating out his frustration on the capstan housing, like a child throwing a tantrum. There was no way for him to release the cable.

Heavy bolts secured the last loop in the winch; the towline could only be cast off from the galley.

Kismet lost interest in Harcourt's struggle as the sea rushed up to meet him. The bow of the galley was plunging downward rapidly. Before he could even begin moving, the water was up to his waist.

"Irene! Get to the hold—"

His words were cut off as the sea washed over his head. The stern of the galley suddenly rose out of the water, and then the entire vessel, like a golden needle, pierced the darkness below and vanished.

Once the galley, overlaid in one of the heaviest elements known to man, committed to its downward plunge, it sank rapidly. Kismet could feel the rush of water passing him by. At the same time, his inner ear throbbed painfully with the rapid changes in pressure. He tried to compensate by working his jaw to pop his ears, but could not equalize fast enough. Howling the last air from his lungs, he released his hold on the ship and clamped his hands ineffectually against the sides of his head.

An instant later he was struck from above and borne down once more. He opened his eyes, and through the blur of seawater, saw that he had become entangled in the colonnade around the superstructure. The golden columns were blazing with magical illumination, like beacons of false hope. Then Kismet remembered what he had shouted to Irene, and why.

He snaked through pillars distorted by the blast of Anatoly's bomb, letting them fall past, one by one. In moments he reached the open portal to the hold. Bubbles were streaming from the enclosure as the air in the structure was displaced by water. Without hesitation, he plunged into the torrent.

Whether because of his shouted admonition, or because there was nowhere else to go, Irene had sought refuge within. Lost in the agony caused by the increasing pressure inside her head, she struggled in the rising water, floating at arm's length from where Kismet treaded.

He tried to close the hatch, but was repelled by the blast of water flooding into the hold. Then the last of the air vanished and the hatch slipped into place, sealing them in—a golden coffin for their burial at sea.

18

Harcourt felt no satisfaction as the galley vanished. His joy at having found the prize and proving superior to his old foil had been supplanted by a more immediate concern: survival. The Golden Fleece, his trophy, hampered his movement, but never for a moment did he even think about laying it aside. Unable to release the tow cable, he had impotently pounded the winch with his fists. When the golden ship went under, he knew that he wound soon face a similar fate.

He tried to think logically; he was a scientist after all. The cable, a mere three-quarters of an inch thickness of braided metal wires, was the chain that bound him to disaster. It was anchored to the motorized winch that was bolted to the wooden deck in four places. The solution was obvious: cut the cable, knock the winch free...either would do. He raced to the cabin in search of an axe, a hammer, or any heavy implement that he might use to bludgeon his way to safety.

He got about halfway before the trawler shifted beneath his feet. The sinking galley had been steadily pulling the fishing boat backward, against the thrust of its engine. Now, the ancient ship was directly below the fishing boat, exerting its full weight on the cable. The bow of the trawler rose up suddenly, its stern buried in the water. The abrupt rise of the deck catapulted Harcourt out over the roiling sea.

In that instant, the full weight of the submerged ship tore the winch mechanism away from the deck of the trawler. The boat bobbed on its stern for a moment, then toppled forward, splashing heavily into the water. Because her screws were still turning, the fishing vessel immediately chugged forward, turning a lazy circle that would eventually bring it back to where the archaeologist had splashed down.

Salvation was offered, but for Harcourt, the price was too high. The weight of the Golden Fleece quickly bore him into the depths. His pulse pounded loudly inside his head, a clock by which to measure the seconds remaining in his life. The pressure between his ears grew with each thump of his heart until he felt his head would implode.

At no point during the final thirty seconds of his conscious awareness did it occur to him that he could save himself by letting go of the Golden Fleece. That was unthinkable. Nick Kismet would never let something like dying stand in the way of victory. Kismet would find some other way to survive, emerging with both his life and the treasure.

But Sir Andrew Harcourt did not find that answer. Clinging to the Golden Fleece, he sank into the darkness. His descent to the bottom of the Black Sea would take several more minutes, but for Harcourt, the golden voyage was already finished.

In the sudden stillness that permeated the hold, Kismet felt an over-whelming sense of finality. Completely immersed in water, he realized that he had not taken a breath in what seemed like ages. The stale air in his lungs demanded to be replaced. His diaphragm convulsed in an unsuccessful attempt to inhale. It seemed that his only choice was to open his mouth and take that final liquid breath.

Irene floated face down beside him, air trickling from her nostrils. She had ceased struggling. The sight wrenched at his heart, impassioning him to continue fighting the inevitable. He swam toward her, clamping a hand over her mouth in a futile effort to prevent more water from flooding her deluged lungs.

Misshapen lumps crowded the space near the door; the remains of cargo casks battered out of symmetry by the force of Anatoly's bomb. It took him a moment to comprehend that the crates were floating.

Inspiration dawned more brightly than the luminescent metal surrounding him. The casks could only be buoyant because they were full of air. He released Irene and tore at the nearest crate with his fingers. The metal overlay shredded under his nails, releasing a shower of effervescence, after which the cask came apart and disgorged a single enormous bubble, which spread out across the bulkhead to form a pocket of air a fraction of an inch thick. A lumpy yellow shape, emitting a trail of gas globules, fell from the broken wooden fragments and sank through the hold.

It was a second Golden Fleece.

Ignoring this revelation, Kismet kicked up to the air pocket, pressed his lips to the bulkhead, and greedily sucked in the air. The fire in his lungs instantly abated, but he did not pause to savor the respite.

He snatched hold of Irene, pinched her nose shut and exhaled into her mouth. She reflexively gagged on the breath, but her eyes fluttered open. Despite her violent reaction, Kismet turned her over, so that the air at the top of her lungs could force out the water. She immediately began coughing and thrashing spasmodically, but his firm grip compelled her into the tiny gap where water became breathable atmosphere. He caught her eye, making sure that she understood, and then seized another of the battered crates.

More air bubbled up to the pocket as the crate came apart. Then, yet another sheepskin heavy with gold, settled through the enclosure.

Kismet muttered an oath into the water. How many Golden Fleeces were there?

In the next moment, as he tore apart another cask to reveal a fourth Golden Fleece, he realized how terribly close Grimes had come to unleashing a Pandora's Box of evil upon the world. The traitor had sought a single Fleece to help his new allies build an EMP bomb. What would have resulted if they had gained control of the golden ship's true cargo—not one, but perhaps dozens of Golden Fleeces?

As Kismet liberated the air and cargo from one crate after another, the pocket of gas against the bulkhead grew. It was not just air from the crates that filled the growing space however; the Fleeces piled up beneath them were rapidly breaking the water apart at the molecular level, converting it into its gaseous components. With six of the crates opened, Kismet swam up to take another breath.

"Nick," Irene gasped, when his head broke the surface. "What are you doing?"

"Getting us out of here. Don't go away. I'll be right back."

He plunged once more into the water, and dived into the aisle between the cargo rows. Near the doorway, the casks had been spared the impact of the explosion. The nets that had secured the containers for centuries were still intact and the crates themselves showed no sign of damage. It seemed as if the gold had absorbed most of the energy from the violent eruption. He wondered if the blast had somehow acted as a catalyst to the metal's unusual properties—properties he was counting on to save them once more.

A glowing crate came free with a little prying, and then rose gently toward the bulkhead. Kismet followed it up, but did not tear it open as he had done with the others. Instead, after returning to the top for a deep breath, he dove down to find the bottom of the cask and peeled away the gold to reveal bare wood.

It required more force to pry apart the slats on the underside of the cask, and he did so carefully so as not to allow the container to rotate and fill up with water. When the first board came away, he could see another sheepskin, matted with gold. He pushed it back and loosened the next board. The Fleece slid toward the opening and broke through the thin wood.

He caught the Fleece with the crooks of his elbows, both hands still gripping the box to prevent it from flipping over. He was surprised that the buoyancy of the boxes was not offset by the heaviness of the gold; it certainly felt like dead weight in his arms, tugging against his handholds in an effort to tear him loose from the crate. He brought his knees up to brace the sheepskin, and then cautiously moved his hands until he felt he could safely hold the container upright with one hand. Now fully immersed, this new Golden Fleece immediately began to trickle bubbles of gas up into the cavity.

When Irene felt the gentle pull on her ankle, and looked down to find Kismet with his head inside one of the golden crates, she immediately understood what to do. A moment later she popped up inside the cask with him.

"Irene, I need you to hold this thing steady."

She nodded, grasping his plan, insane though it seemed. When her hands were firmly in place, he let go.

The Fleece instantly tried to sink him. He wrestled the shapeless mass away from the well created by the aisle, and laid it on another of the cargo crates. He was determined to find a way to bring it to the surface, but that was not his most immediate concern. He swam up to the doorway and inspected the hatch cover. Although it opened inward, the cover resisted him. It was as if the door had fused to the bulkhead.

His eyes flashed around the hold, looking for some object rigid enough to be used as a pry bar, but everything he laid eyes on was made of soft gold. Then he saw the one thing in the hold that was not left over from its original owners: the remains of Anatoly's electric lantern.

He had not gone back for the lamp after the electrical discharge from the first Golden Fleece had melted the bulb into a lump of metal and glass. The housing and battery were still intact, but seemed useless without a bulb. Nevertheless, he scooped it up and made a quick adjustment to the remains of the filament wires, then reattached the power source. He prayed that the dry cell had not shorted out upon being immersed.

Before executing his plan, he returned to the Fleece and lifted it over his shoulder. He then braced his legs against the secured cargo and jumped, kicking furiously to compensate for the added weight of the Fleece. At the apex of his underwater leap, he thrust the light into the uppermost recesses of the hold and flipped the switch.

Because he had shortened the distance between the filament posts, the flow of electricity was able to momentarily bridge that gap in a single unrestrained blue spark before the short completely discharged the battery. That lone spark however, was all he needed.

From the moment he had begun exposing the many Golden Fleeces to seawater, the process of electrolysis had been stripping apart the fluid molecule into its atomic gaseous components—two atoms of hydrogen and a single atom of oxygen. The latter element had the potential to be both poisonous in pure concentrations and a highly flammable accelerant when exposed to fire, yet at the same time remained essential to the existence of life. Hydrogen, the lightest of all elements, was simply reactive, and when the insignificant blue arc of electricity sizzled through a nearly pure pocket of the gas, it ignited.

Kismet was not able to snatch his hand away in time to avoid a flash burn, nor could he do anything to prevent being pummeled by the force of the explosion. The shockwave felt like being hit by a bus. Yet, the second explosion to occur within the small enclosure, like the first, was muted by the strange properties of the ubergold. The destructive energy triggered a sympathetic display of light, but caused no real damage to the vessel. It was just enough however, to blow the door open.

In the relative safety of the container, Irene began to ascend, buoyed by the air trapped in the box. As she slid through the portal, Kismet snared her foot, and then managed to pull himself up until his head was above the water line. They pressed their bodies together, legs entwined, and kept a fierce grip on the cask as they rose toward the surface.

The golden ship vanished quickly beneath them, shrinking to a pinpoint of light in the black beyond, and then disappeared forever.

Captain Gregory Severin of the Russian Naval destroyer *Boyevoy*, Sovremenny class out of Sevastopol, stood at the prow of his ship and gazed down at the oil slicks and smoldering debris—all that remained of the

Svetlyak class patrol vessel *Zmeya*. His keen eyes picked out yet another straggler clinging to a ship timber.

"Twenty degrees off starboard," he called. The message was passed back to the sailor manning the aft deck gun. Although the 30-millimeter battery was intended to blast attacking planes and incoming cruise missiles from the sky, Severin derived a perverse satisfaction from watching bullets as thick as his fingers, tear apart the flesh of his enemies. The AA gun released only a short burst, but it was enough to shred the struggling commando.

The call from FSB informant Anatoly Grishakov had almost come too late. Severin had prematurely congratulated himself on disposing of Kismet and was halfway to port before the alert was sounded. Anatoly should have reported the American's resurrection immediately, but for some reason, the agent had not made contact until late the previous evening, some ten hours ago. The destroyer's chief engineer had to push the boilers into the red to catch up to the fishing trawler and the vessel it towed. Even at that, they had not arrived in time to save the prize for the *Rodina*. An urgent message from the undercover operative had revealed that foreign infiltrators were about to seize the golden ship. Severin had personally given the order for Anatoly to scuttle the galley. *Boyevoy* had arrived just in time to see the ancient wonder vanish once again into the Black Sea.

At least the fate of poor *Zmeya* was now apparent. No word had been received of her crew, but obviously the invading foreigners had captured or killed the young, inexperienced sailors, and commenced using the patrol craft for clandestine acts of war. Severin had not hesitated to give the order to blow her out of the water.

The FSB agent's fishing boat was still turning lazy circles in the sea. Severin noted absently that the ferocity of the storm, which had repelled them throughout the night, now seemed to be abating. He scanned the trawler with a pair of binoculars to see if Anatoly had somehow reached its relative safety. The boat appeared to be deserted. One of the lookouts had reported seeing someone that matched Grishakov description being struck by lightning during a struggle aboard the doomed galley. If it was the Russian agent, it seemed unlikely that he could have survived.

"Our enemies, if any still live, might try to escape in that boat," he said, thinking aloud. "Remove it."

The order was passed down, and Severin knew that when the shell was finally fired it would unfailingly strike its target; his gunnery officer was a prodigy. The *Boyevoy*'s artillery had pounded the patrol craft when it was nothing but a spot in the distance. A deafening noise roared from behind him and a moment later the trawler vanished in a cloud of smoke and spray. One less thing to worry about.

"A good day," he said, still speaking mostly to himself. "Our enemies are dead. The treasure they tried to steal is safe from them forever. Even that American meddler has gone to the depths. And with Grishakov dead, perhaps we can finally deal with the traitor Chereneyev."

The destroyer cut a straight line through the wreckage, and then came about for a second pass, along the outer edge of the flotsam. They had dispatched half a dozen surviving commandos, and administered the coup de grace to a handful of other motionless, face down corpses just to be sure. Severin was satisfied that his work was done.

"Captain, we have a new sighting. Distance, five hundred yards. Ninety degrees astern, moving to starboard."

"What the devil...?" Severin stalked along the length of his ship, to make a personal identification of the new visual contact. The position given was on the other side of the ship. It was inconceivable that any of the stragglers could have drifted so far from the wreckage. Severin reached the observer's station and demanded more information.

"They just surfaced a moment ago," answered the sailor, passing his binoculars to the captain. The ship's speed had carried them even farther past the bobbing shape.

Severin swiveled his head slightly and adjusted the focus until he locked onto the floating shape. "It is only a crate. Wait...I'll be damned." He handed the glasses back to the sailor. "Keep an eye on them. Bring us about, and then cut to one-quarter ahead."

As the ship carved a tight one hundred and eighty-degree turn, its captain raced to the bow, his hand on the butt of the Glock automatic pistol he had taken from Nick Kismet. The destroyer's new heading would bring it within shouting distance of the target. After about a minute, he could, with the naked eye, discern the bedraggled pair that treaded water furiously in the open sea.

"All stop."

Severin heard the message passed down, and then returned: "Answering all stop." He leaned out over the rail to gaze helpless pair in the water now almost directly below and sighted down the barrel of the Glock.

"It is better this way!" he shouted. "I should be the one to kill you, Nikolai Kismet."

19

The water they had passed through immediately after escaping the galley was bone chilling. Irene's teeth still chattered uncontrollably. Nevertheless, both of them could feel it growing warmer as they ascended.

Their rate of travel seemed to increase the higher they rose. The air trapped in the container expanded, nearly doubling in volume to spill out past their fingers. As they moved through the water, Kismet could not tell if the Golden Fleece was continuing to supply them with air to breathe, but that was irrelevant; there was enough air trapped in the box to last for several minutes.

"Don't hold your breath," Kismet cautioned, as soon as he felt the air pressure increasing. "The air will expand as the atmospheric pressure diminishes. If you're holding your breath, you might burst your lungs."

She nodded, making a visible effort to breathe regularly. "Will we get the bends?"

"There's no reason we should. They're caused by prolonged breathing of pressurized air at depth. We haven't been under long enough."

When the crate broke the rough plane of the surface, its momentum tore it from their grasp and shot it into the air. Kismet and Irene scrambled to keep the box from crashing down on their heads, and then to prevent it from filling with water and sinking. Only when they were clinging to its smooth sides did they become aware that *Boyevoy* was still on the prowl.

A roar and a plume of smoke signaled that the ship's guns had fired. Kismet was unable to follow the shell, but an explosion on the far side of the ship revealed the target. "They just blew up Anatoly's boat," he observed. "I guess Harcourt didn't make it."

Irene stared in horror at the destroyer. "Maybe they won't see us."

He scanned the horizon in all directions. Swells occasionally brought pieces of debris into view, but there were no other vessels. The shores of the Black Sea, in any of the countries that bordered it, lay well beyond the horizon. "It might be better if they do. Otherwise, we'll die of exposure out here."

"Better that than to give Severin the satisfaction of gunning us down."

"Maybe they'll fish us out and send us to Siberia." His tone was not hopeful.

The destroyer suddenly turned hard in their direction.

"Well, I guess we won't die of exposure" Kismet observed darkly.

"Come on, Nick. You're Mr. Lucky, remember. You've gotten us out of every scrape so far. Tell me you've got one more trick up your sleeve."

Before he could even begin to formulate a plan, the swells from the wake of *Boyevoy*'s first pass washed over them. Kismet's hold on the crate slipped for a moment. The golden cask flipped onto its side and was instantly inundated. Irene cried out, but was forced to let go as it sank into the sea.

"Where's that plan, Nick?" Irene shouted as she thrashed to stay afloat.

"Sorry. It just went under."

The destroyer slowed as it came abreast of them. The eager faces of the crew looked down from high overhead and Kismet recognized many of the sailors from their earlier ride aboard the warship. The rugged features of Captain Gregory Severin loomed largest. The hungry look in his eye and the set of his jaw, advertised his intentions. Kismet held his breath as the Russian naval officer extended his gun arm and took aim.

He made one last desperate play. "Irene! Dive under and swim closer to the ship."

"Closer?"

"Now!" He placed a hand on her head and forced her beneath the surface as he himself dove. There was a report of a shot and Kismet saw something strike the water at an angle not far from where he had been a moment before. A diagonal line, the path of the bullet in the water, extended a few feet below the surface. If Severin's aim improved, the water would not save him.

They were still a few yards from the ship when burning lungs forced both of them to resurface. Kismet looked up at the destroyer, satisfied that they were now out of the line of sight for an observer standing on the deck. However, the Russian captain had climbed over the rail and was leaning out over the water to get a clear shot.

"Quick, Irene. If we can get to the ship, we might stand a chance."

She did not question his statement, but nodded tersely, took a deep breath and plunged below of her own volition. Kismet felt like a hypocrite. Her confidence was badly misplaced; even if they could get closer, there was virtually no way to board the ship, much less evade the crew or survive until the ship put into port.

He surfaced too close to the ship and banged his head on the steel armor plating. Muttering a curse, he then pushed away to get a look from this new vantage point. The dull gray hull sloped outward above him, an immense steel wall over a football field in length. They were close to the bow, but Kismet's best plan—to climb the anchor chain—was quickly thwarted; the anchor was secured to the hull twelve feet above the waterline, well out of reach.

"Nowhere to go, Kismet," said an all too familiar voice. "Nowhere but down."

He looked up at the Russian captain. "Then get it over with. I won't feed your ego by begging."

Severin laughed. "In a moment. But I think you have something that belongs to mother Russia. I don't want your lifeless body to sink to the bottom with such an important treasure. I will regret passing up this opportunity to kill you, but if you are willing to cooperate and let my men bring you aboard, I will let you live."

Kismet glanced at the Fleece still clinging to his shoulder. He had almost forgotten about it. Why hadn't its weight dragged him under? It looked different somehow....

"That doesn't sound like you, Greg. You're not that generous."

"Oh, you misunderstand. As a criminal and enemy of the State, you will certainly spend the rest of your days in prison. But I will be a hero for returning you alive to stand trial, as well as saving the treasure. You at least would live to die a more pleasant death." He leveled the pistol. He was too close to miss. "Or I can shoot you now?"

"Not good enough." He shrugged out from under the Golden Fleece, holding it at arm's length with one hand. It seemed impossibly light. "You're welcome to the Fleece. But you have to guarantee our safety, especially hers."

"Nick," Irene whispered. "Are you sure this is a good idea?"

Severin tilted his head sideways, considering Kismet's counter-proposal. He then snapped upright, his arm stiffening as he verified his aim. "No deal."

20

Suddenly the air was filled with shouting and a claxon began to wail aboard the ship. Severin lowered his arm, but before he could refocus his attention, the deck lurched. A vibration traveled the length of the vessel, and Kismet saw a cloud of smoke bellow from the stern. Severin flung his arms around the rail, losing his grip on the Glock. The automatic pistol bounced off the deck and dropped over the side, vanishing into the water.

Kismet could hear the Russian cursing, demanding both an explanation and assistance. Though he could not make out the reply, Severin's subsequent orders revealed that the destroyer was under attack. The captain ordered evasive action, but the answer he got left him frustrated. After several seconds of clinging to the rail, a sailor rushed to help him back over onto the deck. Then the cries of alarm were renewed.

Kismet drew the Fleece back to his body, and looked around for some sign of the attacker. He saw no other ship, but something much smaller was burrowing through the sea just below the surface on a collision course with the hull of the destroyer.

"It's a torpedo!" Kismet swam closer to Irene, unable to hide his elation. "Here's that miracle we needed."

The torpedo finished its deadly journey by impacting the *Boyevoy* about twenty yards forward of the stern. The explosion ripped upward and tore a hole in the side of the warship. The aft end, where three of her four gun emplacements were situated, as well as the 30-millimeter anti-aircraft battery, was ravaged by the detonation and the subsequent fire. The destroyer was now a sitting duck, unable to maneuver or defend herself, and taking on water through two wounds.

"Oh, my God," Irene gasped. "Nick, what's that?"

Something was breaking through the surface, a pillar of dark metal, as tall as a man. The object was indistinct because they were looking at it head on, but it looked like a small boat with its deck below the surface. Men appeared on the exterior of the newly risen craft. Two of them deployed an enormous inflatable raft, while others hastened to affix a bulky shape to a pedestal in front of the upright column.

Before he could answer, the newly assembled gun on the deck of the surfaced craft spewed a burst of cover fire. The bullets raked the destroyer's bow gun, forcing the Russian sailors away from their last line of defense.

The inflatable raft, driven by an outboard motor, sped across the water directly toward them, bouncing as it hit each swell. Small arms fire from the destroyer imperiled the men in the rubber boat, but the submarine's deck gun swiveled to meet this challenge, sweeping the deck. In a lull between bursts, Kismet could hear the howling of wounded sailors high above him.

The men on the inflatable cut their engine at the last minute, turning so that the raft bumped against the hull of the ship. They wore the distinctive uniforms of Russian submariners, but did not speak as they reached out to Kismet and Irene. As she was lifted over the bulging rubber, Irene saw numbers and Cyrillic letters stamped on the vulcanized hull next to a five-pointed red star; the designation of the parent craft, a Russian *Akula* class submarine.

Kismet was helped aboard as well, sagging into the recesses of the raft in an effort to stay out of the way of their rescuers. One of the men waved toward the submarine, and his signal was answered when another hundred rounds of machine gun fire splashed the deck of the destroyer. Beneath that deadly curtain, the outboard engine roared to life and hastened them back to the mother vessel.

The impact of hitting the swells was ferocious. Kismet felt like he was taking repeated blows from a prizefighter. He had to cling to the rope strung along the sides of the boat like a rail, to avoid being catapulted into the sea. Slowing the craft could have minimized the turbulence, but the sailors had other reasons for haste.

Kismet heard a hissing near his head. He glanced up and saw a ragged hole in the rubber bladder. The sailor at the rudder also saw it, but could only shrug as he lowered his head. Despite the cover fire from the submarine, someone aboard *Boyevoy* was not going to let them go without a fight.

The leak in the raft posed no immediate danger. The inflatable hull was divided into several independent cells; the loss of pressure in a single one would not cause the craft to sink. But as the air escaped, the boat began to lose rigidity and allowed seawater to splash onto the passengers.

It took about two minutes for them to reach the sub. The sailor at the helm drove the rubber boat up onto the deck of the vessel, just aft of the sail. Through the salt spray in her eyes, she could barely distinguish the shapes of two men waiting near the sail, but there was no mistaking their uniforms: Russian naval officers. Her blood ran cold when she heard one of the men speak in heavily accented English. "So Kismet. *Vee haf* you, at last."

Kismet sounded merely irritated as he replied: "Cut it out, Lyse. Those Russians are shooting at us."

His tone confused Irene. She couldn't reconcile what she was seeing and hearing with what she thought she knew. Why was Kismet's friend Lyse an officer on a Russian submarine? Irene looked at both figures, and then faced the remaining officer.

"Hello, Irina." The man took off his hat, revealing the smiling face of her father.

Irene was paralyzed. Nothing made sense any more. Kismet took her elbow and guided her to the ladder that ascended to the top of the tower. Below, the sailors manning the forward gun fired off the last of their ammunition then abandoned the gun and joined the retreat to below decks. The men that had piloted the raft drew long knives and slashed the remaining cells, then pushed the shapeless mass into the sea and joined their comrades in boarding the submarine.

As they passed through the narrow hatch, a bottleneck that permitted only one person to descend into the submersible vessel, a siren blasted from the interior of the vessel.

"That's the dive warning," Lyse explained. "We have to hurry."

Irene was still confused. "We're going underwater?"

"It's already started," Lyse said, sliding off the ladder and stepping away. "We've all got to be inside and get that hatch shut. Move it, people!"

Kismet was next. The interior of the submarine was dark and claustrophobic. The electric lights were spaced far apart, offering minimal illumination, especially after daylight on the surface. Nevertheless, this metal cave beneath the waters was their salvation.

The top hatch clanked shut and was sealed. The sailor atop the ladder shouted the 'all clear' message, and then made his descent. Kismet thanked each of the men for risking their lives to rescue Irene and himself, but the sailors seemed uncomfortable with his gratitude. "Just doing our duty sir," one of them shrugged.

"Would someone please tell me what's going on?" Irene finally complained. "Father, why are you wearing that uniform? And what are you doing on a Russian submarine?"

Kismet's friend laughed at her confusion. "Let's go meet the captain. Then we'll explain everything."

A distant explosion rocked the sub as they moved through the cramped corridor toward the control room. "That was close," Lyse remarked.

An upright column dominated the center of the room. One man, a tall figure with wavy black hair, lightly peppered with gray, stood with his face pressed against the periscope viewport, slowly turning in a complete circle. Finally, he straightened and addressed the newcomers. "Not really," he said, contradicting Lyse's observation. "They're shooting in the dark. They have no idea where we went, and they're in no shape to pursue. Our first fish took out their screws, and I think the second might have knocked out the whole engine room."

Kismet was struck by the tall man's green eyes, which were oddly contrasted with the bright orange face of his diver's wrist chronometer. He had the unmistakable feeling that he had seen him before. "I guess we have you to thank for getting us out of that mess."

"No more than I have you to thank for giving me this little job. A fishing trip to get me out of the office was just what the doctor ordered."

Irene was still looking around in confusion, turning first to Kismet then to the rugged looking captain. The latter shook her hand. "My goodness, you're shivering."

He shrugged out of his jacket and draped it around her shoulders. Kismet felt an almost adolescent twinge of jealousy at the man's act of kindness toward Irene, but Lyse distracted him. "I see you found it. The Golden Fleece."

He glanced down to the sheepskin on his shoulder, and then slipped it off to examine it more closely.

"One of them," Irene intoned. "Nick, would you please tell me what happened down there? How many Golden Fleeces are there?"

He knelt and spread the Fleece out on the metal deck. His fingers brushed through the damp wool, revealing an occasional auric glimmer, but that was all. Most of the metal had been rinsed away during the ascent from the galley. What gold remained neither glowed nor tingled with any discernible electric current. He estimated that the sodden sheepskin now weighed less than ten pounds.

A steward brought them steaming mugs of coffee and Kismet drank deeply before attempting to explain. "Here's what I think happened:

"Three thousand years ago, after the story of Jason and the Argonauts was already a legend, a group of adventurers, probably Greeks, decided to seek out the land of Colchis. Perhaps they knew something about the true nature of the Fleece, or maybe they were just crazy treasure hunters. In any event, they certainly believed in the legend, because they sought the protection of the witch Medea, Jason's lover in the myth, by erecting a shrine to her on their galley. When they arrived at the kingdom of Colchis, they headed up into the mountains. They weren't looking for the Golden Fleece; they were just looking for gold.

"An ancient Greek geographer, Strabo, speculated that the gold on the Fleece was the result of a mining technique called 'gold washing.' Ancient prospectors would lay a sheepskin in a gold bearing stream, and when the silt passed through the wool, the heavier gold particles stayed in the fleece. Well, that's what these adventurers did. They set out dozens of fleeces, and harvested a lot of gold dust.

"But it wasn't ordinary gold. For some reason, this gold could store, or under the right circumstances release, electricity."

"How is that possible?" inquired Lyse. "Gold is just gold."

"Maybe it came from somewhere else," Kismet speculated. "According to the legend, the Golden Fleece was the skin of the flying ram Chrysomallus. Maybe instead of a flying ram, Chrysomallus was a gold meteorite that crashed in the Caucuses."

Lyse raised an eyebrow. "Sounds like something from a comic book."

Kismet shrugged. "Regardless of where it came from, those ancient explorers harvested a bunch of it. Then they abandoned their mining camp and prepared to sail home with their treasure, but the electrical field created by the huge quantity of this extraordinary gold caused an atmospheric disturbance. A storm arose that sunk the galley, taking its cargo to the bottom, only a few miles from shore.

"Over the centuries, the electrical field stayed active underwater, drawing more solvent gold particles out of the water. I know that sounds far-fetched, but the sea is full of dissolved metals and minerals. I think atoms of gold were pulled out of the water and gradually accumulated on the surface of the ship. Maybe the water itself perpetuated the reaction; I'm not a chemist, but there seems to be a connection."

"So when we raised the ship," Irene observed, "The electricity stopped."

"Not entirely. It was still powerful enough to blow out the lamp. I think what really happened was that it changed its manifestation. I think it created that storm with a massive electrical field." He took another sip of coffee. "When Anatoly's bomb went off, the kinetic energy was absorbed, recharging the gold."

"We can test your theory on this Fleece," suggested Lyse.

Kismet looked down at the gray wool on the deck. "I doubt you'll get any kind of reaction. Most of the gold has washed out of it." He had mixed feelings about that. No ubergold meant no EMP bomb, and on balance, that seemed like a good thing. "But maybe what we learned about the ancient wanderings of the Greek adventurers is more valuable to the scientific world than this Fleece would have been. There are enough witnesses to document the existence of the galley and its cargo."

"Ah, Nick, I don't think you'll be able to tell anyone about this."

"And why not? This has nothing to do with your military secrets, Lyse. This is about history and culture."

"I think what the lovely Ms. Lyon means," the captain supplied, "is that your presence here, and for that matter our actions today, are illegal. We did just shoot up a Russian destroyer, you realize."

"But as far as they know, that action was carried out by a Russian submarine. There will be no contesting that identification. And since the Russians have sold off several of their older subs, there'll be no shortage of possible suspects."

The captain shook his head. "If you were to go public with your discovery, their government might be more scrupulous in demanding an accounting, both of the attack on the destroyer, and your presence in Georgia to begin with."

"You can't tell the world Nick," Lyse stated. "Not yet, at least. We can't afford to have Russia pissed off at us right now."

Kismet sighed. He knew she was right, but it irritated him to have worked so hard for nothing.

"Nick, there is yet one thing I do not understand." Kismet turned to hear out Peter Kerns. "I can accept your theory of the gold being drawn out of sea water, and accumulating on the ship. But the relics I found were not on the ship itself, but in the silt nearby, unaffected by the electrical field. The altar stone, for example, must have broken off when the ship went down. It did not have any gold on it. But the helmet fragment did. How is that possible?"

He reflected on the day Harcourt had brought the bronze and gold fragment to his office, nearly two weeks before; a dented and torn shard of a helmet that had been forged for a smaller head than his own..."It must have been plated prior to the sinking of the galley."

"Maybe the helmet really did belong to Jason," Irene suggested, unknowingly voicing Kismet's own wild speculation. "Remember that Medea used her magic to protect him when he slew the serpent that guarded the Fleece. And when he sowed the serpent's teeth, and fought the champions that grew out of the ground, her magic guarded him. If the gold was the source of her magic, perhaps she used it on his armor somehow. I seem to recall that at one point, Jason threw his helmet into the midst of the champions, causing them to turn on each other and kill each other in the confusion."

Kismet couldn't remember if the last part of her recollection was really part of the Argo legend, but he didn't contradict her. Her hypothesis was no more elaborate than his own.

"Then the helmet shard you spoke of was something the Greeks brought back with them," offered the captain. "Perhaps it was hidden beneath that altar stone; a sacred relic from the time of the real Jason."

"I guess we'll never know," Kismet concluded.

"Okay, I understand all of that." Irene faced her father again. "Now, why are we on a Russian submarine?"

"That was my idea," Kismet hastily supplied, trying to prevent the captain from grabbing any more glory. "When I first decided to go after Harcourt, both to rescue Peter and maybe find the Fleece, I made a deal with Lyse. She would back us up secretly, from a submarine, so that when we succeeded, we could sneak out unobserved."

"Almost sinking the *Boyevoy* isn't exactly my idea of stealth."

"It sure beats the alternative."

"You may have suggested using a sub, Nick, but it was the Colonel here—" Lyse nodded to the sub's pilot—"that gave us the K-322."

"Air Force, retired," explained the captain. "Nowadays I earn my pay with a certain maritime agency that disavows any knowledge of this little jaunt. After the end of the Cold War, the Russians sold off a few of their older boats, and this one found it's way into the hands of a drug cartel. The Navy sank it in about four miles of water, and then the CIA asked my agency to help salvage it so they could use it for...well, for days like today."

"They'll be wise to the deception now," Kismet intoned. "What's next?"

"Well, now the fun really begins. The captain of that destroyer will have already sounded the alarm, so the entire Black Sea fleet will be after us. Unfortunately, there's only one way out the Black, through the Bosporus."

"Can we get there before they blockade the strait?"

"Officially, they can't blockade it. But that won't stop them. And the answer is: probably not. In any event, we won't be trying. We're now heading south, toward the Turkish coast. Once we get there we'll scuttle this boat, and make landfall. Then we'll break up into smaller groups and make our way home."

"They'll be looking for Irene and me."

"It would probably be best for you two to split up." Lyse supplied. "Eventually, when you've made it back to the States, you can concoct some story about escaping from a rogue Russian military group with their own submarine."

"Wonderful," said Irene, sarcastically. "I thought all this insanity was finally over."

The captain smiled. "Well, I can promise you a few hours of peace. No one's using the officers' quarters. Why don't you grab some shut-eye? You look like you could use it." He proffered a hand, which, after a quick glance in Kismet's direction, she accepted. Kerns raised an eyebrow, and then moved to follow them.

Lyse threw a wry grin at Kismet. "Better watch out, Nick. He moves pretty fast with the ladies. Speaking as one, there is something...irresistible about him."

Kismet hefted the Fleece, avoiding her eyes. "Lyse, what makes you think that I would even give a damn?"

"Uh, oh. Things not working out between you and Svetlana?"

He considered matching her barb for barb, but thought better of it. "No. I guess there's not much room in my life for romance."

"Hell, I could have told you that. I figured that out years ago."

He chuckled, but there was no humor. "Yeah, I guess you did." He tossed the Fleece onto his shoulder and turned in the direction the others had gone, eager to find a quiet place to relax.

"Nick, wait."

"I'm keeping the Fleece, Lyse. You owe me that much."

"Sure, whatever. But there's something you owe me. The memory card? Remember? You told me you gave them to a friend. I need to know who that is."

Kismet almost laughed. It had all started with those plans; plans to build a super weapon using the mystery element contained in the Golden Fleece. Now that the ubergold was beyond reach, at the bottom of the Black Sea, Kismet wondered if the plans would do anyone any good.

"Why not?" He reached for his waist pack. The nylon bag, which had somehow survived the assault by Grimes and the final descent of the golden ship, was bloated with seawater. He turned it over, and the contents splashed on the deck, drenching Lyse's shoes. He laughed as she jumped back self-consciously, and then drew out the sheath of his *kukri*. The scabbard of carved wood, overlaid with black leather was probably ruined but it was replaceable. Using the blade of the big knife, he cut apart the seams that held the leather together along the backside of the sheath. The dyed covering spread apart, revealing the plastic bag with the SD card inside. He pulled it loose and tossed it to her.

Lyse was livid. "You told me you gave it to a friend."

He held the *kukri* up, inspecting it in the subdued light, and remembering a fateful night many years before when he had been given the blade as an almost sacred trust between warriors. "One of my oldest and dearest. And might I add, the only one I trust implicitly."

"What if you had gone down with that ship? Then it would have been lost forever."

"That probably would have been better. The world would be a better place without your superbombs."

She wagged her head in despair, and then went to work unwrapping the package, as if still convinced that he would again try to swindle her. Leaving her to inspect the SD card, he continued down the companionway, into the heart of the submarine. A narrow portal in the bulkhead opened into a cramped room with two vacant bunks. As he entered, he heard his name called yet again, but this time it was not Lyse.

"Irene?" He was mildly surprised to find her at his door. "Was this your room?"

"No." Her smile was coy and eager.

"Irene..." He tried to find the words that would make her understand that 'happily ever after' was something he could never offer, but something about her expression weakened his resolve. He shook his head and tried a different tack. "You forgot to give the captain his jacket."

"My goodness. Are you jealous?"

"Of course not." He tossed the now gold-less Fleece onto the upper bunk. "You're an adult. You can...."

Before he could finish, she darted forward and shook her hand in the air above his head. A dusting of glitter drifted down from her fingertips, and Kismet felt as though he had walked through a cobweb. He brushed reflexively at his face and found specks of gold clinging to his fingertips. "What's this?"

"Magic dust," she replied, with a straight face. "I found it in my pocket. It must have brushed off when we were down there."

"Well why did you throw it at me?"

She shrugged. "Medea used it to make Jason fall in love her."

"No she didn't. Besides, that whole story is just a myth anyway."

She stopped him with a sultry look, moving closer. "Maybe she did," she continued, threading her arms around him and gazing up into his eyes. "Maybe it's more than just a story."

If he had a counter to her statement, it was restrained as her lips met his; her tongue silenced his own. He savored the kiss for a moment. "Magic dust," he whispered close to her ear. "So did it work?"

"Hmm?"

"When Medea used it on Jason—did it work? Did it make him love her?"

She drew back far enough to look him in the eyes. "What are you worried about? I didn't think you believed in the magic of the Fleece."

"Maybe I'm starting to."

He did not resist as she pulled him into the small space between the bunks. "Good," she said, her voice low and intent. "Because it works."

EPILOGUE
THE ARGO DESTINY

EPILOGUE

Langley, Virginia—Two months later

Lysette Lyon hastened from the chilly interior of her car to the airlock-like foyer of the reception building. The bulletproof glass doors slid shut behind her, locking out the frigid air of a Virginia winter, but the cold lingered in her extremities for several minutes as she moved through the final security checkpoint and into the heart of the Central Intelligence Agency headquarters building.

She had not been back to the Langley facility since receiving the orders that had sent her to the Black Sea, two months earlier. In fact, she had only set foot on American soil six hours earlier, just enough time to shower and eat before delivering the bad news. The dread that had robbed her of her appetite during her brief visit to her apartment now loomed heavily as she exited the elevator and traversed the remaining distance to the section chief's office. The secretary admitted her without question.

Her immediate superior was not alone. She instantly recognized most of the other faces sitting around his desk; it was as if the entire upper echelon of Central Intelligence had decided to conduct a top-level meeting in the small room. She closed the door firmly and strode toward the desk and into the monster's lair.

"Field Officer Lyon." The section chief rose to greet her, his face unreadable. "I hope you don't mind if the Director sits in on your debriefing."

It wasn't a question, so she withheld a verbal response. The DCI (Director of Central Intelligence) nevertheless rose, and inclined his head politely.

She answered with her trademark smile and was pleased to see a faint rush of color in the old bureaucrat's cheeks. The department directors and their deputies followed his example but one man, who stood facing the large window behind the desk, did not even turn to acknowledge her. His face was barely visible in the reflection.

Once the pleasantries were exchanged, everyone but the man at the window returned to their seats. Lyse was acutely aware that she too would have to stand. Evidently the DCI's chivalry did not extend to offering his chair to a lady if that lady happened to be in his employ. Perhaps it was for the best; she might need to make a hasty retreat from the room if they took the news the way she feared they might. Her lips drew into a tight grimace, and then she commenced her report.

She started from the beginning, not so much because she felt the need to brief those men who might not have actually been privy to the details of the mission, but because she was stalling. Maybe, after telling the whole sordid affair in its entirety, her failure would seem less important. She recalled the efforts to gather the intelligence on the EMP weapon from Germany, and the unfortunate decision that had brought Nick Kismet into the loop.

Her first mention of her former paramour's name had elicited a fidgety response from the DCI, who unthinkingly glanced at the man near the window; the latter did not react in any way. She filed their reaction away as something to look into, and then continued with her tale. Much of what she told them from that point onward was gleaned from her interviews with Kismet and Irene and Peter Kerns, the only surviving witnesses to Halverson Grimes' treachery and ultimate demise. Despite a great deal of evidence to support the charge of treason, Lysette had already heard rumors that Grimes' death would be attributed to a boating accident, and that no mention of his traitorous leanings would ever see the light of public scrutiny. He would be remembered only as an American hero.

She nevertheless reported what she had seen with her own eyes: Grimes and Harcourt conversing with the leader of the German KSK unit. Grimes had evaded capture that night, slipping away with the British archaeologist and a handful of commandos moments before Lyse and the COLT operators raided the mountain camp, leaving no survivors. From there, they had raced back down to the shore in a captured snow-cat and returned to the submarine. From beneath the storm tossed sea, they had managed to follow Kismet's progress across the sea using sonar, and intercept the *Boyevoy* in time to save him and Irene from a brutal death.

The DDO (Deputy Director, Operations) seemed especially pleased with the success of the COLT team against the German commandos. They had completely overwhelmed the larger force, sustaining no casualties among their own ranks, and completely sterilized the area, right down to the last brass shell casing. No one would ever know that anyone had established a camp in the Caucasus or that a battle had raged there.

The minor naval skirmish on the Black Sea was a slightly different story. Back-channeled information indicated that the Russians knew all too well who was behind the torpedo attack that had crippled one of their destroyers, but as there was no proof, the incident was being reported as an accidental explosion. Lyse had also heard that representatives of the UN had casually mentioned that further exploration of the matter might reveal that a certain Captain Severin had committed a number of international crimes, not the least of which was the attempted murder of a UNESCO representative. Despite that part of the affair being swept under the carpet along with the rest, DDO was understandably concerned at the level of exposure.

With Kismet and the two Russian émigrés safely on their way back to the States, Lyse and the retired USAF Colonel who had skippered the K-322 on its last mission, returned to the Black Sea, this time with an upgrade. Using a state of the art deep sea submersible, they scoured the lowest reaches of the Black Sea in hopes of locating the golden ship for further study and possibly retrieval.

She took a deep breath. "On January 21, we located the wreckage of the fishing vessel Kismet used in his initial survey and recovery. The debris was scattered in an area roughly one kilometer in diameter and only three kilometers from the GPS coordinates of the boat's last known location, indicating only a slight degree of subsurface drift. Using these figures, we were able to create a computer model of where our target vessel might have settled.

"Unfortunately, a thorough search of the area did not lead us to the target. For two weeks thereafter, we continued to broaden the search, but without success."

"You found nothing?" It was the section chief that spoke, but she sensed the question was being asked collectively.

"Actually, we found thirteen wrecks dating back as far as the seventeenth century. The comparatively low salinity of the Black Sea and the cold at those depths preserved—"

"You know that's not what I meant," he snapped.

Lyse bit her lip. The other faces in the room remained unreadable. "We were unable to locate the target vessel."

"Maybe we should get someone else to look for it," suggested the Deputy Director, Intelligence. "From what I understand, this fellow—" He named the former US Air Force Colonel with a derisive snort, as if referring to a hole in the ground. "—is something of a maverick."

"Nonsense," retorted DDO. "I've worked with him in the past. If he can't find it, it can't be found."

Lyse saw her opening. "On that subject..." She took another breath, gathering her courage to drop the other shoe. "We think we may have been too late. He...We believe that someone got there first."

The uproar that followed was about what she expected. DDI was the loudest voice. "Preposterous. The Russians don't have the resources for that kind of work. Hell, they couldn't even bring up the Kursk from four hundred feet, and they knew exactly where it was. And they sure as hell couldn't have pulled it off without our birds snapping their picture."

"We have satellites tasked to monitor the Black Sea?" inquired DCI skeptically.

"Well...."

"Ms. Lyon?" The voice was strangely familiar and though spoken in a low tone, it instantly silenced everyone else. Lyse glanced around to identify the speaker; it was the man at the window.

"Ms. Lyon," he repeated, still gazing through the glass. "Did you at any time see this supposed Greek galley with your own eyes?"

She frowned. "No, but Nick—"

"I understand why you would want to put implicit trust in Mr. Kismet's word, both for professional and personal reasons, but leaving that aside, can you or anyone else corroborate his claim?"

"Irene Kerns was with him." She sensed that he was chuckling, but his face remained indistinct in the reflection. "No. When we surfaced to rescue them, it had already gone down. We did however track the vessels on sonar. There was a larger craft being towed by the fishing boat."

"But there is no way to verify its origins or any of the other qualities Mr. Kismet attributed to it. Would you agree with that characterization?"

Lyse's heart began to pound. She had anticipated a degree of reproof for having failed to recover the golden ship, but nothing like this. She cursed herself for not having seen it coming. This sort of scapegoating was common practice in the political environment that pervaded the Company; they even had an acronym for it: CYA—Cover Your Ass.

"Christ," scowled the section chief. "What a circus. We're a hundred million in the red on this and absolutely nothing to show for it."

"Oh, it's not all bad." The man at the window slowly turned as he spoke, affording Lyse a chance to glimpse her accuser. She barely held back an audible gasp; it was him—the man that had recruited her all those years ago. His appearance had changed little, save for one distinct feature; where his left eye ought to have been, there was only a square of black cloth.

"Hindsight is rarely perfect," he continued. "Mr. Kismet seemed a credible source, and Ms. Lyon cannot be faulted for acting on the information he provided. It was after all his tip that helped you expose Admiral Grimes as an agent of foreign influence. Perhaps this business with the Greek galley was merely a practical joke on his part; payback for your having involved him in the espionage business."

Lyse opened her mouth to defend Kismet, but thought better of it. The man was giving her an exit.

"A damned expensive joke," muttered the DCI. "Someone is going to have to pay for this screw-up."

His declaration seemed to signal the end of the meeting. The section chief shifted in his chair, but did not rise. "Field Officer Lyon, pending the outcome of an internal investigation into this matter, you are suspended." Then, as if to soften the blow, he added: "Paid, of course. Go home, get some rest."

She could barely hear him through the rushing noise in her ears, and it required an effort of will for her not to run from the room. As she closed the door and crossed the reception area, she had to fight back tears. Without being consciously aware of her movements, she walked to the elevator and summoned the car. It was only when a hand slipped into the gap between the closing doors and arresting their movement, that she looked up to acknowledge her surroundings.

The doors slid silently back to reveal the man with the eye patch. He stepped inside the small enclosure and turned his back so that he was standing beside her, facing the doors. As they slid into place a second time, he spoke: "I'm sorry I had to do that Lyse."

"Sorry?" she echoed.

"I've followed your career with great interest. You've exceeded my expectations. But this latest matter… Perhaps your feelings for him got in the way of the mission. It's understandable really; after all, that's where all of this began."

"I was telling the truth in there and you know it. You threw me under the bus."

The man sighed. "I may have been hasty in debunking the premise upon which your recent efforts were based, so I thought it only fair to give you an opportunity to acquit yourself."

She glanced sidelong at him and noted that he was still staring straight ahead. Because she was on his left, it was impossible for him to see her at all, but she nevertheless felt his scrutiny.

"It occurred to me," he continued, "that there might be some physical evidence to support Kismet's claims; some sort of object or artifact that would validate his assertion that he had recovered an authentic Bronze Age sailing vessel. Something he may have kept as a souvenir, perhaps. "

Lyse's heart leaped into her throat. *He knows.*

It was such a small thing that she had thought nothing of the omission. And Kismet *had* deserved something for his troubles. At the time, she hadn't been able to think of a single reason to deny his request—no, his demand—that he be allowed to keep the soggy sheep's hide he claimed to have recovered from the doomed galley. Yet, to avoid possible recriminations, she had elected not to include any reference to that Fleece in her reports. Now, she would have to expose Kismet and admit the indiscretion in order to save herself.

Except it wasn't really a big deal. She didn't owe Kismet that much after all, and since the Company was more concerned about validating the expense of the search effort, she wasn't likely to be in too much hot water for having let Kismet keep his Fleece. She turned completely to look at the man who still faced straight ahead.

Although the admission was on her lips, something forestalled her. She pursed her lips and looked away. "I'm sorry," she began, choosing her words carefully. "I know that you must be cleared for this since you were in that conference room, but we're not there anymore and to be frank, I have no idea who you really are."

A dry chuckle shook the other man's chest as he at last turned to face her. "It's no secret, Ms. Lyon. I'm Rich Houseman. I work under the President's national security advisor."

Lyse had no reason to doubt his statement and no inclination to ask for credentials, but something about his expression made her instinctively distrustful. She had an urge to look away from his monocular stare, but sublimated it as best she could. "Well, Mr. Houseman, let me just say that I remain convinced that Nick Kismet was telling the truth about the existence of the galley—"

You know it too, don't you?

"—and I'm likewise certain that somebody beat us to it. Maybe it wasn't the Russians, but somebody with a lot of money or a lot of influence, or both, got down there ahead of us and recovered that galley."

"I'm curious in spite of myself, Ms. Lyon. Who, if not the Russians, do you suppose might have done this? Who else indeed even knew of its existence?"

"I don't know. Kind of a scary thought, isn't it?" She became increasingly convinced that he already knew the answer. There was only one nation on Earth with the resources to recover a sunken vessel from the extreme depths of the Black Sea; a nation whose leaders had made a study of deception and denial. She wondered if a similar disaffection with America's clandestine oligarchy had led to Grimes' defection.

"Scary," he echoed.

The elevator car settled to a stop and a chime announced its arrival as the doors slid apart. Lyse needed no other cue. She immediately stepped forward, eager to be away, but Houseman was not done. "Lyse, you haven't answered my question."

She faced him steadily, maintaining eye contact so that he would have no reason to doubt her veracity. "If Nick did take a souvenir, I didn't see it. Maybe you should ask him."

There was another chime, and as the doors began sliding shut Lyse saw the man's lips draw back in a feral, wolf-like grin. His words chilled her more than the bitter winter air outside.

"Oh, I will. When I see Kismet again, be sure that I will."

ABOUT THE AUTHOR

SEAN ELLIS is the author of several novels. He is a veteran of Operation Enduring Freedom, and has a Bachelor of Science degree in Natural Resources Policy from Oregon State University. He presently lives in Arizona where he divides his time between writing, fatherhood, adventure sports, and trying to figure out how to save the world.

Visit him online at www.seanellisthrillers.webs.com.